MISSIONS

To Annie...
My OLD & long-suffering
friend. **

Glenn

** Whom ... Gawd Help Me! ...
I actually do quite like.

MISSIONS

Glenn Hamilton

TREWELLARD,
CORNWALL
November 2003

To order additional copies of this book, contact:
Xlibris Corporation
1-888-795-4274
www.Xlibris.com
Orders@Xlibris.com
18564

'For G.J.B.'

By the same Author:
'CHARLIE'S MOUNTAIN' (1998)

PRE-MISSION . . .

With daybreak, the wild geese would fly low across the airbase, heading down to the nearby river marshes. Betrayed overhead by the rushing beat of their wings, and by their companionable honking.

It was odd, the way they honked like that. The young men on the base, lying awake and waiting before the coming mission, would speculate upon why it was that, in flight, the geese beat their gums at one another so, all the time yackety-yak. Whereas, down on the water, paddling about, they were silent. Like mute swans.

Once airborne, though, off they went, gab, gab, gab; no radio discipline at all. Wild geese in flight were every bit as bad as the worst prattling crews of any Marauder squadron sharing an open frequency.

The cheerful sounds of geese would penetrate the warm, fusty blackness of the British-built Quonset huts—the British called them Nissens—to beat at the tense, wide-awake brains of crews scheduled to fly that day. Waiting for the un-needed wake-up call, the shower and shave, the fumble-fingered dressing for battle; the indigestible breakfast to order of scrambled eggs, soggy toast and coffee. Before preflight mission briefing, then the truck ride to the armed, laden aircraft parked out on their lollipop hardstands.

Listening to the geese, the airmen would hear, too, the high, muttering drone of the night shift clocking off; Royal Air Force Lancasters and Halifaxes stumbling home from dark Germany.

Gearing reluctant bodies and minds for the full extent, immediately measurable in too-brief hours, of their foreseeable futures, the crews would pay envious attention to the geese sounds as they came in to beat up the base, flying for fun, for the hell of it, the whole stringy Vee of them triumphant above the silent, cold-metal medium bombers standing out with dew beading on their surfaces. Dew that, later on, would coalesce into rivulets, streaming under the shock-wind of turning propellers.

The geese would buzz with impunity the control tower and hangars, the admin block and mess-hall and weather shack and motor pool and living quarters. Cocky as a sneak flight of Kraut Ju. 88s creeping in under the radar screen to catch the *verdammt Amerikaner* airfield wide open to the sucker punch. Some of the wakeful men would make that comparison in their minds, and be glad then that they were, indeed, geese, and smile a little, and forgive them their small, passing trespass.

While, for others, it would seem that the geese called down to offer comfort: 'we're airborne, and you're not. But it's okay. We see what you won't for hours yet; skies free of hazard, the way ahead clear . . .'

Each man listening knowing that message to be a bare-faced lie, yet able still to feel some re-assurance under their drab U.S.Q.M.C. blankets as they waited for the wake-up corporal to appear, snapping on the lights. Although what the geese were telling you was bullshit, at least there was no malice in it.

Their honking, deceitful message came through the curving roofs and the dawn-pale windows, mingling with the rhythmic creak of wing pinions as the stragglers dropped toward the welcoming marshes. Fading then, leaving the men with all their returning thoughts of . . . the mission. Of destinations yet to be disclosed.

ONE

"Gentlemen, the object of our affection on this day is Cherbourg. And now your en-route and target weather."

There stands Major Ambruster, boss meteorologist, beaming down from the platform like a benevolent master of ceremonies. Always happy to be there with his maps marked with contoured pressure gradients measured in inches and millibars, the wind speed and direction arrows and clever symbols denoting cloud cover suspended over hostile Europe: scattered, broken, overcast, obscured.

He is a good forecaster, and well-liked for his caring and precise work on our behalf. Although, how anyone gets to be a major on the strength of a piece of dried seaweed and a tin cup anemometer beggars all understanding for the men of the bombardment crews to whom he makes his address. Who are, variously, sergeants, lieutenants, at best captains. But still, he is good, and, in our line of business, good forecasters are treasured for their rarity.

So I am thinking then as, with calm certainty, Major Ambruster informs us that, "Cherbourg this morning, gentlemen, will be scattered. No more there to trouble you than a little fair weather cumulus."

He gazes down benignly upon us; pilots, bombardiers, navigators, each feigning bored indifference, gum-chewing in our leather jackets and 'chute harnesses and 'fifty mission' hats. The crews for that morning's target briefing. For me, and my crew, the first such for-real briefing: we are here to learn, dry-mouthed and with fluttering hearts, of destinations, objectives, flight plans and assembly points. Of fronts, winds en route and over the target, of turbulence, precipitation and icing levels. Of altitudes assigned and elapsed times estimated, and the pinpoint rendezvous where we will meet our escorting P-47 and P-51 fighters. Merely a token force of these because—reliably, it is claimed—all of Jerry's 109s and deadly Focke-Wulfs are being held back over Germany to counter the deep-penetrating B-17s and B-24s. It is said that Jerry has hardly any fighters left in France. Where we are heading for today in our fast, twin-engined B-26 Marauders.

There will, however, be flak: wherever two or more Germans foregather, there is always flak. Although, our experts predict, we will be able to handle that with ease. Experts who will not accompany us. They are much of a muchness, these experts. Who, like us, affect seasoned 'fifty mission' hats. Who, unlike us, fly no missions.

The Thunderbolts and Mustangs, the experts advise, will be along simply for the ride; put there to boost our confidence and morale, to be admired and envied for their swift, graceful selves. Cruising off our wingtips, giving us the finger, showing off the immeasurable superiority of their purebred mounts over our burdened draft horses. A token force . . . in case. Yawning their boredom as we bomb. Snide on the radio, picking holes in our marksmanship.

All to take place, we now know, at Cherbourg, a port city at the tip of a peninsular called the Cotentin. To which I, the pilot of B-26, serial number 43 (for the year of manufacture) 2693, 'Big Apples', will fly my crew and our load of high explosive and incendiary ordnance. The first time today for us all, bar one. First mission of a scheduled thirty five which will comprise one full tour in the European Theater of Operations.

Cherbourg, we are joshingly assured by the Colonel, our C.O., will be a 'milk-run'. "So easy it shouldn't count as a mission at all. More of a trip to Coney Island . . ." Which is fine for the Colonel to say. He, like the other experts, will not be flying. Although, to give him his due, the Colonel does, from time to time, fly missions.

It is to be a three-pronged milk-run: B-26s to Brest, B-25 Mitchells to Le Havre, our Group of B-26s to Cherbourg. We, the Squadron, flying out of Tiverell Lacey, Essex, England, a former R.A.F. Bomber Command station, now re-designated U.S.A.A.F. Base 909.

Each but one of our number in 'Big Apples' is fresh out of training, and as green as grass. That exception being O'Connor, the bombardier, who has done it before; twenty five missions on Fortresses with the Eighth Air Force. Back now for more with the Ninth. For a run of thirty five.

This, our first together, is to be, they say, a milk-run. And spoil it then with this talk of flak. Which, for me, makes Cherbourg, two hundred and twenty five air miles—one hour's flying time—distant, sound anything but easy.

Sixty minutes en route, then two minutes—if there are no snafus—over the target, then sixty minutes back again. On the deck once more to debrief, have lunch, stand down. Hitch a ride down to the village to drink warm brown English beer. Definition in depth of a milk-run.

We, new to the job, know nothing of milk-runs; what the British flyers call 'a piece of cake'. On milk-runs is it usual to predict heavy, accurate anti-aircraft fire, or the possibility, albeit remote, of mixing it with unfriendly black-crossed fighters; that possibility strengthened in our minds by the knowledge of a fighter *escort*: forget about 'token', and boosting our morale. If there is to be no fighter opposition, then why? That sounds to me like no milk-run I ever heard of.

At least—a small advantage, one supposes—there should be no grief with the weather as Major Ambruster deals slickly with the pressure gradients and ambient temperatures, wind vectors and cloud types: " . . . scattered cumulus with bases reported at fifteen hundred feet Mike-Sugar-Love. Thin cirrostratus overcast above twenty thousand. Nothing to complicate your navigation, or obscure the target zone."

We listen and jot down our notes, crowded together on wooden forms in the operations shack, scratching and farting, grinning inanely, rolling our eyes: fiddling nervously with whatever lies at hand; map cases, pistols, navigation slide rules. With the snap hooks of parachute harnesses, the cords and jack-plugs of radio headsets. Twiddling the over-elaborate aviators' chronometers that we all love and simply cannot live without. Each with his secret thoughts well-concealed behind expressions of contrived boredom; no doubts or fears . . . ha! Never asking the frightening, unanswerable questions that plague us before departure.

In no real mood, not then, for the carefully-prepared quip with which Major Ambruster terminates the weather briefing . . .

"Following your imminent visit, gentlemen, one would envision Cherbourg as even more scattered than before!"

TWO

The start-up flare rises from the control tower balcony.

I hit the buttons as the starter motors reach their highest pitch, first left, then right; the big, grumbling radials flowing smoothly to life, blue oil smoke swirling from exhaust stacks and thinning in the cool slipstream. Instrument needles slipping into place, duplicating and supporting each other: oil pressures, temperatures, fuel flow, hydraulics, amperage, cylinder heads, carburetor air. All 'in the green'.

Rolling off the hardstand, waved out by the crew chief into our ordered place in the traffic stream, the machines bowing and bobbing on their nosewheel oleos as if in polite morning greeting; early morning commuters on their way to the train station.

Marauder 43-2693 is ninth in line.

Running over the checklists, the roll call: everything and everyone present, correct and buttoned down. As ready as we'll ever be.

Magneto check . . . a small but acceptable drop in revolutions on both engines, within tolerated limits.

Both propellers fully responsive from high to low R.P.M., and all the way back again.

Manifold pressures okay. Stabilizers set for take-off on elevators, rudder and ailerons. All control surfaces free-moving, external locks removed. Pitot cover removed. Flaps, pre-select fifteen degrees. Generators charging. Pitot heat operative. Cowl flaps open. Fuel boosters on. Take-off fuel tanks selected. All gyros uncaged. Altimeter set to field elevation and double-checked against the known barometric pressure. Park brake released . . .

'Big Apples' swinging her head into wind on runway two-seven, shuddering in the lingering slipstream from previous departures. Align the nose on the runway's center line, and set the directional gyro at two seven three degrees, the runway's precise heading, then compare that against the reading of the magnetic compass card swimming in its liquid bath.

Hold both engines at half-power with the throttles, feeling the strain of the airframe against the brakes as it seeks release. Waiting for the signal. And . . . there it is, the control tower flashing me green for Go! Brakes off . . . throttles advanced all the way to the stops, and the blood tingle induced as thirty seven hundred horses begin their romp under my hand on the twin levers. Throttles 'to the firewall', engines answering with their howling thunder of power, the mesmeric snap and drone of four-bladed props turning at maximum R.P.M . . .

And yet . . . as we roll forward, something is not right: it is not now as it has been at other times, on training flights and dummy missions. Now, we gain speed only draggingly, and, suddenly, alarmingly, there is the need for some quick answers as the too-short runway streams by. What can be going haywire at the start of this first of all combat missions? Why these unresponsive control surfaces, no perceptible tightening of lifting airflow? Where now the vital hardening of air needed to grip tons of airframe, engines, equipment, men, fuel, bomb-load and ammunition, and bear them up and keep them up? For Christ's sake . . . what IS this?

I simply do not know . . . I haven't the experience; a raw beginner with a few hundred hours total flying time logged. Not, after all, the wise guy I had imagined myself to be . . .

Until the belated, nick-of-time realization: of *course*, the first honest-to-God combat mission, and thus, the first experience of a Marauder absolutely and fully loaded, and then a little more so. There is nothing wrong with the airplane; it is willing to get up and go, but is woefully over-burdened; so much more leaden inertia for the engines to overcome and rise above.

And, yes, we *are* accelerating, but it is not enough as I squander the barely-adequate length of the airstrip with its small overshoot area bounded by a row of tall poplars, and the inevitable powerline beyond those. Getting close, closer, *too* close.

A try, fearful and tentative . . . easing back on the control column. The nosewheel responds, lifting, as at last airflow begins to stiffen over the elevators. Still too cumbersome, though, by far. Like a fat man with a creaky heart and laden shopping bags. Doubting that he will make it to the top of the stairs . . .

A fresh worrying thought nags the mind: should an engine decide to quit now, it will be the end for us all, curtains. Before an honest beginning has been made. In a laden B-26, a streamlined bomb all primed to blow. And is that why some people have named the Marauder 'The Widowmaker'?

Sweating, scared silly, feeling horribly alone, I scrabble for alternatives . . . and what alternatives *are* there? Should I abort the take-off, maybe, bang-smack in the middle of a full Squadron maneuver? Yank the throttles closed, hit the brakes, and too bad if they burn out and the tires shred under us. Just get us stopped and turned around to limp back with my sheepish explanation. That I, the pilot, trained to do so at the cost of many thousands of dollars of taxpayers' money, could not make the airplane fly.

There is just enough in that shameful option to re-kindle fading resolve . . . keep *going*. Committed, anyway, because there is insufficient runway remaining in which to bring us to a halt. We have to go, even though we hit the trees, the wicked, waiting powerline. With full tanks, H.E., incendiary, fifty-caliber ammunition for eleven guns. Game over . . . TILT! Written across the sky in letters of fire.

Keep the throttles forward, the nosewheel off . . . keep your nerve somehow. Hold to the centerline and sweat and pray. Until there comes that first but definite hint of blessed tautening air, control surfaces soaking up its life-giving flow. Feeling the tremor through the feet as the rudder begins to respond. The breathless thought then that she might just go?

Only one way to find out.

Easing back further on the column . . . and feeling response. Risking a quick glance at the A.S.I., and—according to the flight manual—enough airspeed showing there to make us fly. Enough, though, for all that extra deadweight? Let's see. More back pressure, and the wheels' dragging rumble ceases to leave a sensation less of flight than of suspension. *In the air, yet not borne by it.* We are hanging on the propellers with absolute full power applied, not a drop left in reserve. Should 'Big Apples' elect to stall now—and she has every right to do so—a wing will drop, plowing into the ground at more than a hundred knots, cartwheeling us to destruction. Nothing left that cannot be swept up with brooms, hauled away in buckets.

She sinks once more, and takes my heart with her, the wheels crunching back into asphalt . . . a rolling, booming bounce . . . and we stagger back into the air. Where, this time, the airplane chooses to stay.

Risking another glance at the airspeed indicator where the needle is now creeping up into regions where, according to the manufacturers' estimates, the B-26—even one so mishandled—will, for a while, defy gravity.

Swift movement below, viewed from a corner of the eye; the tree barrier falling behind, then clearing the powerline with feet to spare. Climbing now . . . the way a rock climbs. 'I said it to Orville, and I said it to Wilbur . . . that thing will never *fly!*'

Still shaking, I trip up the landing gear, easing back on the throttles and propeller controls to the less-taxing climb settings; then, at a hard-won five hundred feet, milk up the flaps, re-set the trims, and begin the slow, climbing turn on to the heading to bring 'Big Apples', the Squadron, the Bomb Group, to the rendezvous over Hampshire.

*

"Have to tell you, son, it's sure nice to be alive."

Captain 'Buzz' O'Connor, our salty lead bombardier, is grinning tightly up at me from the nose compartment crawlway. His irony is evident, even on the metallic, de-personalizing intercom.

I look down at him, and become defensive. "You getting at me?"

"At *you?*" He affects bafflement. "*Would* I?"

"I expect so," I tell him, and picture all the others in the crew listening in to this exchange.

At twenty nine, O'Connor is the sad old man of 'Big Apples" crew, with a tour on B-17s behind him already, and an Air Medal to show for that. Which makes him, in the nicest possible way, a little disdainful of the rest of us. He derives evident enjoyment from reminding us frequently of our newness, our greenness, our abysmal ignorance in all matters martial, emphasizing each telling point with playful accusatory stabs of his corncob pipe. He relishes calling each of us 'kid' or 'son'. The vast difference in age and rank allows him to get away with that.

We had reached our assigned altitude, holding position in the swarm of accompanying medium bombers. At my side, strip map and slide rule in hand, stood Andy Devine, aged twenty, second lieutenant, indifferent navigator. Who preferred to be called by his given name of Steve, and who, in this tightly-shared life of ours, had no hope of that. Not with a name like Devine. From the moment of meeting he had been 'Andy'. His Oklahoma accents only strengthened the ties we forged for him with his Western movie star namesake.

I saw how Andy's gaze switched in delighted anticipation from O'Connor to me, and back to O'Connor. Following every word; absorbing O'Connor's firmly-expressed opinions of my God-awful take-off.

At least, I could counter O'Connor weakly by getting in the first shot. "I know . . . you didn't like the take-off." Him and me, and everyone else!

"Who said that?" O'Connor's dark, heavy brows wig-wagged quizzically. "Did I say that?"

"You hated it," I amended.

"Ah . . ." He grew pensive. "Now, hate's a different thing. A whole lot more positive. You can get your teeth into hating something." He gave a nod. "Tell you frankly, kid, that-there split-ass departure of yours scared the piss right out of me. It also set me to thinkin' . . ." His languid Virginia drawl was very pronounced. "If yon's how things are shapin' in these parts, then it's gonna be a very long war . . . or a very short one. Either which way . . ." He speared me with a glance. "It'll *seem* long."

Strong warning lay beneath the banter. All in 'Big Apples' were airmen: not only pilots knew how airplanes flew, and should be flown. Every man on board would be aware when the man on the stick did a good job, and also, for a brief while before the final curtain, when he screwed up. I had come close—too close for all of them—to screwing up.

Quite simply, I had not finished my homework, assuming instead, unforgivably, a performance level from a complex, finite machine supposedly under my control which could not be forthcoming. The B-26, when flown within its strict limits, was a good airplane. It was never, though, one in which anything was assumed, and it seldom forgave lapses.

I thought then, crushed and contrite, forget about the Germans. As I imagined my crew viewing *me* now as the real enemy. If we were to get through our tour together, then I had to know my business from A to Z. Not just part-way, and take a chance on the rest.

*

From over the Stockbridge assembly point, we crossed the English coast on the heading to carry us to Cherbourg.

A perfect flying day; Major Ambruster had called it right on the nail; now his friendly fair weather cumulus floated below dutifully, casting indigo shadows on the dark sea.

Ahead, behind and out to the sides, above, below and at matching levels, cruised the B-26s of our Squadron and others, plexiglas noses pointed straight at France. Close enough, maybe, for the Kraut radar to pick us up . . . a thought to tweak a beginner's nerves.

Everywhere, it seemed, dozens of dully-painted bombers rising and dipping in the mild air currents, borne aloft by wide, tapering wings, by the thrust of great engines in barrel-shaped nacelles.

Fighters, the 'Little Friends', had waited for us, orbiting

Southampton, attaching themselves smoothly to the diverging bomber streams. The sortie for Brest had turned away, heading out past Portland, taking their drop-tank laden P-47s with them, dwindling together into the bright, white sky.

Away to our left the Mitchells for Le Havre were still in sight, their courses almost parallel to our own, graceful machines with gull wings and twin rudders.

We had scored a Mustang escort, slim, beautiful P-51Ds with teardrop canopies, their wings laden with fifty-caliber machine guns and hundreds of belted rounds. Riding along with us as shotgun. Fighters which, with their disposable auxiliary fuel tanks, would fly all the way to Berlin and back. Cherbourg, for them, was a mere local hop. There would be no enemy fighters, and little for the escorts to do but *be* there. We were still happy to have them, a big stick for Cherbourg. Although it may never be needed, for 'Big Apples' and her raw, uncertain crew, it was fine to have around . . .

*

When our new aircraft was allotted, O'Connor—who knew about such things—informed us, "we must give the beast a name, ladies." He looked around, explaining gently to the novices, "new crew, new flying machine . . . it's the natural order of affairs."

43-2693 had come to us fresh from the aircraft pool with only a few hours total time on the airframe and engines, everything gleaming, smelling new, no scuff marks on the metal heel plates beneath the rudder pedals. The seats were clean, and the handgrips of the control yoke remained unworn, not yet darkened by the sweaty hands of scared, harassed pilots.

A complex and very expensive Martin Model 179, designated B-26C by the U.S.A.A.F. A high-performance medium bomber powered by two Pratt & Whitney R-2800 air-cooled Double Wasp radial engines of eighteen hundred and fifty horsepower each. Turning Curtiss four-bladed, automatic, fully-feathering propellers.

She had protective armor, self-sealing fuel tanks, and plenty of guns to fight back with: four forward-firing fifty calibers in fuselage blisters, a single fifty in the nose compartment to provide diversion for the bombardier when he was not busy dropping bombs. A dorsal power turret carried two more, and there were side positions in the rear fuselage with a gun apiece, plus the sting of a final pair in the tail.

Seven men comprised her crew: pilot, navigator, bombardier and four gunners. All that she lacked at that moment was a name.

"The way things are," O'Connor declared. "She's anonymous, a nonentity. Which makes of *us* likewise anonymous nonentities." He held up an admonishing finger. "Which simply will not do. So, friends and neighbors, we need us a suitable name, and lickety-split. To bind us as one until the magic figure of thirty five missions in the bag do us part."

No mention made of other, more drastic, possibilities that might serve to sunder this fresh partnership; there was the unwritten and inviolable rule that *that* was never discussed knowingly or thought of aloud.

We had assembled unbidden, drawn to the hardstand to check out our airplane. O'Connor, Andy Devine, Smithson, Deeks, Cohn, Patecki . . . and me. One captain, O'Connor. Two lieutenants, Devine and myself. Smithson, Deeks, Cohn and Patecki were all sergeants. Standing now in the shade of a wing as O'Connor sounded off.

"There is on the base one gifted in the naming and decorating of airplanes. A wizard of the paint brush, a dilly at design. Who, for the right small consideration, could be prevailed upon to raise our bird phoenix-like from the ashes of obscurity, and make of her . . . a star." He gestured melodramatically and beamed around, pleased by his eloquence.

"He some relative of yours?" Andy Devine wanted to know. "You gettin' a rake-off?"

"For shame, sirrah!" O'Connor looked wounded. "I am above all thoughts of personal gain. I covet not my neighbor's wife, nor her ass."

I enquired, "who is this Michelangelo?"

"Technical Corporal Flaherty of the base motor pool,"

O'Connor replied. "A name in itself to instill confidence. No one named Flaherty could be all bad."

*

Technical Corporal Flaherty was gifted in his ability to reproduce in paint those types of the female human form much sought-after by aircrews. To order he would create them in differing positions, standing, leaning, lolling or reclining, belly up or belly down, full frontal or end on.

He painted the nudes which were most in demand, and girls in bathing suits, in nightgowns, negligées, panties and bra, panties and no bra. They could wear ball gowns or, as in the case of the oddly-named 'Welcome Wagon', be dressed as brides. The girl figure was the foundation upon which Technical Corporal Flaherty spun his magic, devised his special effects, making real in paint the fondest fantasies of men who flew.

He painted also the bomb symbols under cockpit window which denoted the numbers of missions completed. Likewise— although rare in these days for short-range bombers—the swastikas that testified to German planes destroyed . . .

"Way I always see it, sirs . . ." He bobbed his head at O'Connor, Andy Devine and me. "Guys . . ." He grinned more familiarly at the sergeants. "Youse'll be lookin' for somethin' of a particul-iarity."

"That ought to do it, son," O'Connor agreed.

"Just a female." Andy Devine looked away into dreamy distances. "A hot little body scantily clad, or better."

"Nothin' to it." Technical Corporal Flaherty nodded. "I can give ya bareass anytime."

"What's with particuliarity?" I asked him.

"Somethin' particular that goes wit' all of youse, Lieutenant. Which is, of course, up to youse to decide," Technical Corporal Flaherty explained in the accents of deepest Flatbush. "Mos' popular I always find is to do wit' where guys comes from. Like . . . uh . . . 'Millinocket Joy-Girl', one o' my best." He preened before us. "Lieutenant Redvers which flies the airplane, he's from Millinocket, Maine, get it?" Technical Corporal Flaherty was shaking his head in seeming puzzlement. "Although, for me, it sounds like a piss-stop on the road to Hell."

"How about 'Welcome Wagon'?" O'Connor wanted to know. "That one of yours?"

"They all mine, Captain." Technical Corporal Flaherty was patient with him. "That-there's Lieutenant Myazinski's ship. He went in for what youse might call reverse luck."

"And what's that when it's at home?"

"Well, like . . . seems the Lieutenant he married some hot-pants dame in Texas where he trained . . ." Technical Corporal Flaherty grew confiding. "Only, turns out too late she's a well-known base bunny, right? No sooner he ships overseas than she's puttin' out for anyone that's askin'. So, when Myazinski he finds this out, he tells me to paint the bitch on his airplane . . . an' doll her up as a bride, see? Even gives me her picture so's I can get her just so. An' then he calls her 'Welcome Wagon' for the way she keeps showin' up at everybody's door wit' the goodies on display . . ." Technical Corporal Flaherty wondered then, "none o' youse got nothin' like that goin', let's hope?"

We agreed that we had not.

"Okay. So how's about we try out where youse come from?"

"I'm from New York City," I offered.

"Virginia," O'Connor said.

"Enid, Oklahoma." Andy Devine puffed out his chest. "An' mighty proud of it."

"Some cockeyed thing to be proud of," O'Connor murmured. "But we won't hold it against you, son."

"Up yours, Cap'n," Andy Devine told him.

Smithson came from Kansas, Deeks from Poughkeepsie, New York, Patecki from Washington State. Cohn lived in the Bronx.

"If I could make youse a suggestion?" Technical Corporal Flaherty eyed us. "Do what lotsa guys does an' shoot for the majority? Two from New York, plus one upstate, so youse got heavy represen-tation for th' Big Apple, right?"

We looked at each other questioningly.

Sergeant Cohn ventured, "well, I'll buy that."

"Comin' from the Bronx, I guess you would," Andy Devine observed dryly.

"Close enough to home to suit me," said Deeks.

The others were nodding slow agreement.

"Hey, it's settled then." Technical Corporal Flaherty rubbed brisk hands together. "Okay, so here's the deal. See how youse like it."

In the air before us he outlined a female figure, jutting bosom, wasp waist, full hips and flowing thighs. Nude, he suggested, or maybe just the bottom half of a two-piece. "Bare tits," he stated firmly. "Big knockers, sirs . . . guys." His expressive hands caressed them. "But colored so's they reminds youse of apples."

"*Apples?*" Andy Devine echoed, shocked. "For *tits?*"

"Cox's orange tittins?" Sergeant Deeks wondered, grinning.

Slowly, very kindly, Technical Corporal Flaherty spelled out his strategy. "Yeah . . . apple-shaped knockers, an' colored so's to heighten the effect. Big Apples for N'York, ya see? There bein' two o' youse from the Big Apple. We do it so, an' call your bird 'Big Apples'. Ya get me?"

"I think I see a problem," O'Connor ventured. "With that."

"So, what's a problem?" Technical Corporal Flaherty bristled visibly.

O'Connor explained in tones of pure reason, "three New Yorkers? Shouldn't that mean three tits?"

"That's all right, Captain." Deeks' smile was accommodating. "I'm from Upstate, anyway. Don't want no preferment."

"What's up with you?" O'Connor appeared nonplussed. "You don't *like* three tits?"

Sounding prim, Technical Corporal Flaherty informed us, "sorry, two tits is all youse get, like everybody else. Like I said already, what youse call *repres-ent-ative*."

"Oh, right." O'Connor nodded sagely. "I see it all now."

*

Technical Corporal Flaherty molded her so that, life-size, she would have been tall. Willowy, with long, long legs, a hand-spannable waist and welcoming hips. By general preference a redhead. She met our vague specifications, and the exacting ones of her creator, pleasingly. Her colors glowed. Her smile was confident and warming to our souls, and her green eyes were filled with enduring tenderness for us all.

The promised breasts were splendid, and not at all outlandish with their subtle blendings of flesh tones, green and golds and russets; half firmly-rounded breast, half polished and tempting fruit. She posed there between the cockpit and the bombardier's position: "close enough," as O'Connor observed thoughtfully. "To reach out for a swift grope whenever the urge is felt."

Her reclining body was turned in a way to reveal her outstanding assets most clearly. 'Particuliarity' Technical Corporal Flaherty had called it. Whatever 'particuliarity' might be, she could be said to have it. She placed 'Millinocket Joy-Girl'—naked but for a New England poke bonnet—far in the shade: she made a total non-starter of the 'Welcome Wagon' bride. We all loved her, and the way that she lifted us from facelessness, and placed us on the map.

"I do believe . . . in the words of the distant Sons of Nippon," O'Connor felt. "She'll bring us 'rots o' ruck'."

*

I see then the first darkening of land down there at the sea's edge, glimpsed through scattered cloud and ground haze. Eighty five air miles from the Isle of Wight to the Cotentin.

Which made me think again of the British propaganda film we had been shown called 'Enemy Coast Ahead', about just such a landfall. Now, there it was, up close and for real. There, where the land emerged, things would start to get serious. That was *France*: I had never been to France, and had always wanted to go there . . . but like this? A foreign place of color and contour, the pale threads of roads, huddling towns and villages, a rocky coastline as dark as iron. Indented coves filled with pale crescents of sand and splashed with surf; the long lines of the waves driving onshore. Much like other shores over which I had flown, although those had been friendly, Long Island and the Texas Gulf coast, the beaches of Wales and Devonshire and Essex. Although, as yet, nothing apparent on *this* coast to mark it hostile, a place where you could die . . .

Called back suddenly from these reveries by O'Connor's voice in my headset, the voice now of a stranger, hard and uncompromising. Taking command as we draw near to the I.P. From now until 'bombs away' I will fly only and exactly as O'Connor directs.

I peer ahead and out to the sides, checking on the positions of the other aircraft in proximity, slotting us into place, running in now on a parallel with the coast as, before us, the sprawl of the city opens out, with the wide basin of the deep water port, long pier arms thrusting into the sea. Cherbourg . . . the reality.

Now, around us, the first of the promised flak appears in black, blossoming smudges. Within the city, along the waterfront, from the harbor's breakwaters and the great red citadel above, scores of guns snap and belch and spark, delivering the high-velocity and deadly accurate eighty eights that everyone detests and fears.

All real now . . . not a movie.

*

O'Connor's voice again. "Coming on the I.P."

'Big Apples' is at the Initial Point where the bomb run begins, and, from here, O'Connor expects me to—demands that I *will*—hold a steady, mathematically precise heading. And may Christ look sideways upon me should it not be so. I fear the wrath of O'Connor more than I fear the flak, and maybe that's not such a bad thing . . .

"A-a-and ON!" O'Connor says.

Hold the heading, hold the height, flying the gages, centering the needles as O'Connor dictates. Pressure on the rudder pedals, skidding us left or right as needed in fluid air to pinpoint the exact gyro heading through the turbulence of massed slipstream and shell-burst. Pressure back and forth on the control yoke; a nervous tendency to over-control and compound error, the adjustments transmitted along taut wires to the elevators, rudder, ailerons. Locking the D.G. and altimeter into their ordered places.

"Hold *that* . . ." From O'Connor, rapt over the bombsight. "Just so . . . good."

It seems marginally better to be flying on instruments; I have no eye then for brutal realities outside, tied to the endless, shifting demands of needles and numerals; almost like basic training again—you can kid yourself—learning the gages under the hood in the Link trainer. Except that the Link will not kill, merely shame and embarrass. Flying thus, not having to see those winking darts of light below. Each releasing its hot steel projectile upward to tear you apart.

Flak *sounds*, though, cannot be blotted out; not that crack-whoomp! audible over the engines, piercing the shielding cups of the headset. Nor the terrifying hail of splinters from near misses against flimsy metal skin. Nor the savage currents from the bursts that shake the laden airplane from its tight slot of altitude.

"HOLD it, God damn it!" O'Connor furious and raging in my wilting brain. "Fly this tin and rivet hunk of junk like I TOLD you! You HEAR me . . . ?"

O'Connor committed and unshakeable for this seconds-long eternity of the run-in to target. A hateful stranger now who bears no resemblance whatever to good old easygoing 'Buzz'. Spitting mad as his exacting workmanship comes apart in the hands of a scared-shitless pilot still wet behind the ears.

"Stay on TRACK, asshole!"

Doing it for O'Connor, more terrified now of O'Connor than of any German with me in his sights and murder in his heart, or of determined, unsmiling German efforts to render me down to small scraps of pink meat raining on Cherbourg.

Back *on* track with a wild thrust at the right rudder pedal, crudely yawing the airplane like the most ham-handed student. Straight and level and rock-steady, right down the middle of Flak Alley.

As O'Connor tells me to, "hold *that*." Followed by, "bomb doors open." Hearing the roar and rush of two hundred knots-worth of wind into the exposed belly with its racked, downward-pointing load. From O'Connor, approvingly now, "real nice."

And holding it *so*, real nice, even though our now-perfect flight path should coincide with the trajectory of *that* particular eighty eight-millimeter shell. Thy will be done, O'Connor.

"Yeah . . . steady . . ." The bombardier's tense final-seconds utterance. "Steady . . . *Christ*! STEADY, damn it!" Silent protest, appeal . . . that was another near-miss, O'Connor. But O'Connor cares nothing for near-misses, nor for my endless struggle to meet his shrill, tyrannical demands. For O'Connor, frozen there in his own speck of time, there is no flak, no near-miss, no rocking turbulence, only those things which he views avidly through the bomb sight's cross-hairs.

Cherbourg, here we are, bomb doors open, a milk-run. Over your great port where, in better times than these, the liners would come in from New York: *Normandie* and *Bremen* and *Europa* and *Queen Mary* . . .

One prayer left, the only worthwhile prayer there is, miraculously answered as O'Connor cries, "bombs awa-a-ay!" Sounding like 'Amen'.

Feeling the lightened airplane soar under me, going fast forward on the yoke to correct, then re-trimming to compensate for the surge . . .

As O'Connor returns to the fold, reformed character: welcome home, Doctor Jekyll. "That's it, boys an' girls. Say your fond farewells." And, unbelievably, a pat for me. "You done okay, kid."

Banking steeply away, ducking and diving to throw off the gunners, heading out at full power for wide open blue water, freed from servile bondage to altimeter and directional gyro, able to look out and around. At flak, a carpet of black filth, and little comfort in the knowledge that black smoke represents spent force, that smoke cannot hurt you. It's the ones on the way up, all unseen, that bring on the hurting . . .

A B-26 flies, plodding, below us, one engine trailing fire and smoke. A feathered propeller, a shredded wingtip. Close enough to read the fuselage letters.

"'Rio Rita'," an awed voice says from somewhere. "Them poor bastards." "Still flyin', aren't they?" another points out callously. "What you expect for one thin dime?"

Because 'Rio Rita' would be duck soup if the Krauts had fighters up over Cherbourg today. They do not have: their Messerschmitts and Focke-Wulfs are far away in Germany, mixing it with the Fortresses and Liberators and dark-flying Lancasters. Which, selfishly or not, we do not mind at all.

Our good fortune—and the cripple's—to be flying off beyond the reach of the last, clawing perimeter guns. So that it looks as if 'Rio Rita' might make it.

Fifty safe miles out to sea, alive and intact, with one mission down from thirty five, and the dawning awareness after the full experience of that one of how vast a number thirty five can be. Wondering also, a question shared by the six of us who are beginners . . . how did we do first time out?

Holding course and altitude, then wildly evading to make our escape; no thought during that time of where the bombs had gone down, only delighted to be rid of them. Now, however, there is time to enquire, "how was it?"

O'Connor peering up from the crawlway, pipe in mouth, making a circle with thumb and finger. "Jim-dandy. How else with me on the trigger?" No false modesty with our lead bombardier. Tell it as it is . . .

Soon, once more, England, our homeward track bringing us up to Worthing, overflying Haywards Heath to Dartford, skirting round the London balloon barrage. Starting the let-down at Brentwood with Chelmsford in clear view off the right wing, heading in to the Tiverell Lacey landing pattern as O'Connor thumbs his throat microphone to remind everyone, " . . . of the next significant event in our charmed young lives . . . tonight's Squadron dance. Which, to cull from the vernacular of our English cousins, will be a jolly affair with lashings of booze and oodles of fresh country poontang."

Listening to the intercom chatter, I reflect upon how, before Cherbourg, no one had made mention of the dance. Because, although we had known of it, no one had dared to. To speak of it with a mission before us would have been to push our luck perilously. There could be no talk of dancing, drinking and getting laid until that obstacle had been overcome. Now, though, Cherbourg is history, reduced to a bomb symbol—our first—to be daubed under the cockpit window. It is okay now to talk of dancing. For a little grudged while Providence is sated.

THREE

And yet, after Cherbourg, it seemed grotesque, even monstrous, to be laughing and wisecracking about a dance. Fresh as we were from a deliberate and concentrated effort to kill people and destroy a city.

Here, though, was the evidence behind our unthinking words: Number Three hangar transformed into a makeshift dance hall, with flags and bunting, a trestle table bar and buffet, the improvised bandstand upon which musicians hired from London, sweating under the lights in their tuxedos, warmed up industriously. For one night only reality was to be expunged. Except for the one unavoidable reminder, a lone B-26, 42-9045— 'Dinah Might?'—parked behind the bandstand. Down for major overhaul, the left engine removed, flags draped across the exposed firewall, the plexiglas nose and fifty-caliber machine gun overhanging the big bass drum.

It's the after-effect of the mission, I was telling myself, and the way it had hit me. Standing there at the bar with O'Connor and Andy Devine, waiting for the trucks bringing the girls to arrive. Cherbourg, mere hours in the past, was too raw and recent with its fire and terror as sharp and sudden as electric shock.

Reality was not waiting like this, nursing a bourbon and ginger ale, but, rather, the report received of 'Rio Rita' belly-landing at the Tangmere fighter base with a wounded dorsal gunner. A write-off from which everyone had walked away.

Reality could never be this spotlit hangar interior, the music and colored bunting, drink and food, the horde of crowding, impatient khaki men hollering for WOMEN! This part had to be the dream: in a little while the wake-up call would come, and

briefing, followed by the draughty, bumpy ride to the hardstand.
Now *there* was reality . . .

There was the outbreak then of cheering and whistles to
accompany the muffled grumbling of truck motors from outside.
We watched the tide of men turn to go flooding toward the
blacked-out hangar doors, and O'Connor raised his glass, smiling
gentle mockery. "One presumes . . . the lovelies?"

They came, a first hesitant trickle that swelled into a rush
through a single narrow doorway, then fanned out across the
floor. In pairs and threesomes and bunches, simpering, waving,
their carmined lips and brassy hair-dos, their Cuban heels and
party frocks; others in uniform. A.T.S. and W.A.A.Fs, a solitary
Wren rounded up from somewhere, lots of breeched sun- and wind-
burned Land Girls. Flirting from the corners of their eyes, twitching
their hips self-consciously, surreptitious hands straightening hems
and seams. Blushing and giggling under the wolf whistles.

Until, all alone, the tall brunette came in her black ball gown.
One of the last as the brown tide receded, bearing off the early
influx of trophies.

She paused there, looking hesitant and unsure beside the
blackout drapes, gazing about her as if for a known face. Holding
her head well, with just a hint, it seemed, of challenge, or defiance,
under the concerted regard of men. I watched her with sudden
longing, and emptily, because there was about her an air not to
be mistaken of 'keep off the grass' discouraging haste or familiarity.

An immediate sharp desire for her prompted me to step out
there and seize the initiative . . . do it, make your move, introduce
yourself. Tell her welcome, and that everything we have is yours.
Before someone more pushy and less-deserving gets there. I did
nothing.

At my side, O'Connor murmured, "amongst the dross, dear
friends, we have the pearl. Something far out of the ordinary,
one might surmise."

"Holy shee-YITT!" Andy Devine, following O'Connor's
attentive gaze, offered his own brand of approval.

As Major Delaney, our non-flying Squadron operations

officer, stepped forward, smiling, offering his hand, taking her by the elbow, leading her off . . .

"Well, hell, somethin' that good . . . what you expect?" Andy Devine wore a sour grin. "It'd have to be spoke for by the high brass."

So much, I reflected, for ideas above my station. There had been a reason for that cool, poised air, the look of expectancy. Courtly Major Delaney, a well-qualified stuffed shirt, had exercised his *droit de seigneur*, easing the brunette smoothly into the swing of things. Which, I decided with prim irritation, was pretty damned disgusting. Major Delaney, the old bastard, was forty if he was a day, a wingless pen-pusher, a horse's ass, and he should be ashamed! Five would get you ten that he was married, and if I knew his wife, I decided, righteous and disappointed, I would be more than happy to regale her with a few home truths about her freelancing old man.

*

The English band was good, earning its pay with hits non-stop: 'In the Mood', 'Tuxedo Junction', 'Chatanooga Choo-Choo', 'Moonlight Serenade'. Playing them as they were meant to be played, the way they were written.

The floor was jam-packed: no shortage of girls to partner the eager, hungry men: you could squeeze a lot of girls into the backs of a dozen U.S. Army six-bys. All cheek to cheek on the hangar floor as a middle-aged crooner appealed, "'Won't You Change Partners and Dance with Me?' . . ." And I'd love you to, I thought, watching enviously Major Delaney strutting his stuff with the girl in the black ball gown.

Delaney's higher rank aside, I was held back no less by the knowledge of my poor dancing. *She*, I could see, was very good indeed. I would be hopelessly out-classed amongst all those skilled and agile people; English girls, their American partners, jitterbugging to every number, step for step, wiggle for wiggle. No place there for me.

Instead, I drank, and exchanged moody banalities with
O'Connor who appeared drowsily content to prop the bar for
the evening. Andy Devine, fortified by Jim Beam and Canadian
Club, had gone off to jitterbug energetically with a predatory-
looking blonde in a too-short dress.

I was aware of being dog-in-the-manger, a reflexive defense
mechanism; reverting to type, patronizing and hyper-critical, the
old, well-heeled Sutton Place snobbery. Into which I had been
born, and then raised. The invisible barrier between Them and
Us. Something of which I had not been conscious until I went
to Princeton. And Princeton opened my eyes, although the
university offered no cure; my spoiled brat attitudes persisting
with only the merest leavening of tolerance. Until the Army
beckoned, and absorbed me swiftly, and I was compelled first to
endure, then by some imperceptible osmosis, to accommodate
those from whom, otherwise, I would have recoiled.

The Army, with the power to level all to the common
denominator of its dictating, forced me to rub shoulders, offering
at least a show of amity, with people disdained until then. My
former values, the Army pointed out brusquely, would work for
me only if I was up there with Douglas MacArthur, George
Patton, Mark Clark or George C. Marshall. As lowly and
loathsome aviation cadets, we were informed in the first
bewildering days of basic training by a two-rocker sergeant with
many long-service hash marks, "we eat shit, ladies, we do it all
together, and we smile the while." I learned to eat the shit, *and* to
smile, because, detesting the Army, still I yearned to fly the Army's
beautiful and expensive airplanes. To achieve that end, some shit
must be smilingly ingested.

Habit died hard, however. Beneath the Army's applied veneer
of toughness and bovine acceptance, I remained the incorrigible
snob. And, in moments such as this one, the veneer could crack,
allowing the old and intolerant head to rear itself, stiff with
disapproval.

I felt it then, standing at the bar with O'Connor, and could
not prevent it. Looking at all those English girls herded into the

backs of trucks and delivered to provide willing diversion for foreign troops.

Feeling so, I pondered with something like disappointment the girl in the black ball gown. So clearly a cut above these others, she would not have been at all out of place at the Princeton alumni ball: how *could* she be one, and freely, with hardened, rough-talking country girls with their too-loud voices and shrieking laughter. Of the type found hanging out at American bases, in the company of off-duty, free-spending G.I.s. How could she let herself be driven here, bundled into a crummy six-by? And in a gown like that . . . ?

Imagination elevated her to a plane of my own assuming. She displayed without effort or contrivance the signs of . . . gentle breeding, *that* was it! Admiring her, hungering for her, I was, at the same time, reproving of her. For Letting The Side Down. Even if she *was* Delaney's date. Major-jerkhead-Delaney should have had the nous, at least, to lay on something better than a *truck* ride for her!

I searched the dance floor with my eyes until I found her, and . . . not now with Major Delaney. Instead, dancing with an unknown sergeant wearing gunner's wings.

I followed them, weaving my fantasies: just possibly she was not, after all, high brass material? Not if a mere sergeant could dare to muscle in! Whereas—and the craven side of me rallied with the realization—a first lieutenant *could* muscle in on a sergeant. A first lieutenant, moreover, who had flown that very day to Cherbourg and back. I did not consider for a moment the likelihood, strong, that the gunner sergeant might also have flown there.

I squared my shoulders, straightened a perfectly straight necktie, and, paying no heed to O'Connor's knowing smirk, went out to the dance floor to pull rank.

*

Her slender tallness placed us almost eye to eye. She was light on her feet, graceful, able with ease to make my shaky dancing

appear much better than it was. She told me that she preferred
the slower numbers, an admission which relieved me: her wish
to jitterbug would have relegated me at once to the bench.

Her eyes were clear and gray, in marked contrast with her
heavy, dark hair; her brow wide, the face heart-shaped around a
firm, even stubborn, chin. Her lips were full and, to me, very
inviting, and she used them to smile at me politely, the smile not
quite making it up to her eyes. She had a delicate nose that was
slightly thickened across the bridge, an attractive flaw, and her
teeth were white, even and well cared-for. Many girls in wartime
England had poor teeth; they would look fine until they
smiled . . .

Her name, she told me, was Heather Granger, and she lived
in the village of Tiverell Lacey. These details emerged from our
trite small-talk after the gunner sergeant—with remarkably good
humor—had yielded her to me. So far, I decided with caution,
things looked fairly promising. Just so long as Major Delaney
did not show up to re-stake his claim? " . . . Pardon *me*, son, but
(heh-heh!) you know how it is . . ."

Knock on wood, that had not happened: I was being give
the time to break a little ice. Impressed by her, I sought in turn to
impress. Because Heather Granger—I *had* been right—was not
of the crowd.

Bit by bit, I was coming to recognize English accents, and
what the refined English, the 'upper classes', sounded like. What
the English, themselves, called 'B.B.C.' or 'Oxford' or 'posh'.
Heather sounded all three. Mother, and Sutton Place in general,
I was certain, would have shown approval.

I chattered edgily, all the time tensed for that proprietary tap
on the shoulder: banal questions and proffered platitudes in place
of the worldly and witty things that I longed to say to her. In
response, I was given her name, approximately where she lived,
and the information that she worked at the horticultural research
labs of an industrial chemical company established since the war's
beginning at Tiverell Lacey, safely distant from the main, and
vulnerable, manufacturing plant close to London.

"Most of our stuff is war work . . . mainly pharmaceuticals." Heather gave a shrug. "But the war won't last for ever, and we'll be thinking of parks and gardens again. That's what the labs are gearing up for."

I asked, "are you a chemist?"

"No, no . . ." She laughed. "A mere assistant . . . very 'umble, Mister Copperfield, sir." She added, "that's Dickens, by the way."

I grabbed at my first chance to match her intellectually. "Uriah Heep."

She affected astonishment. "You've actually *heard* of him in America?"

"Not only that . . . he came over and lived with us for a while. *And* said how much he enjoyed it." I grinned back. "Dickens, I mean. Not Uriah Heep."

"Well, I never . . ." She looked at me wide-eyed, and I sensed her gentle ridicule of me, and felt even more of a fool.

Without appearing to do anything, she helped me to turn her through a crush of dancers, telling me, "I got my job on the strength of some decent science marks when I matriculated."

A good education, I thought. With high pass marks. My estimation of her moved up a few more notches.

She might, she allowed, try later on for a degree, then do more advanced work in horticulture, which she enjoyed. "That's if no better offer comes along." She looked into my eyes, smiling, and she had a lovely smile. "Sorry . . . I must be boring you stiff."

"You're not, believe me." And I was wondering just what 'better offer' she might have in mind?

It did seem to me then that she was warming beyond the merely polite stage, telling me of living at home with her mother, of biking to her job every day. No word, though, of her father, of brothers or sisters.

I enquired without any pretense of originality, "what's a nice girl like you doing in a place like this?"

"Now, how often have I heard Cary Grant ask someone that?" For the first time then, the smile reached all the way to her eyes. "Simple, really. Your dance was well-advertised. The inference was that one . . . and all . . . would be welcomed." She glanced around, taking in the other dancers whirling near us. "A bit of doing one's bit? Plus the fact that it sounded like fun, and there's not much of that to be had these days." Her eyes came back to regard me candidly. "When I asked, Mum gave me her blessing, and here I am."

A little rashly, I pressed, "but coming here in a beat-up truck?"

The smile withdrew then slightly. "Does that shock you, Lieutenant?" She said 'lefftenant'. Only the English, I thought, could contrive 'leff' out of 'l', 'i', 'e' and 'u'.

"No . . ." But the truth was that it did shock. All those others, okay, but not *her*. I offered clumsily, "but you're kind of special."

"Am I? How's that, then?"

"Well, sure . . . the way you look and speak." I groped for the right words, looking about me for inspiration. Seeing . . . lights, crowds, the laden food and drinks tables. Hearing the band thumping out 'Rum and Coca-Cola'. A song about G.I.s and whores in Trinidad. I saw the whirling skirts, the beefy legs and the exposed underwear of the jitterbugging girls. "You're not a bit like them."

"Aren't you being unfair?" she wondered, and then confessed quickly, "although I *am* flattered."

"I mean what I say."

"All the same, I do hope you're not giving me too much to live up to?" Her eyes were bright with amused malice. "And as for the lorry, I have to say that I was treated rather well."

The driver had invited her to ride up front with him. Heather declared that she thought him gallant. I would not have put money on it.

"He's promised me the same seat for the drive home." I did not like the sound of that at all.

Considering the unknown driver, I yielded without thought to a sudden, insane impulse, blurting out, "I'd like to do better for you, if you'd let me?"

"Let you what?" She watched me with wide and guileless gray eyes.

And then, like Casey Jones, I rushed on toward destruction. "Drive you home." Thinking, appalled, what are you *saying*?

"You . . . ?" A quizzical eyebrow went up.

"Well? Why not me?" Thus challenged, I was bound to go on. "If it's okay with you?" Adding swiftly, "you'd be perfectly safe."

"Oh, no doubt." And was that more of her dry mockery? "But, do American officers usually drive lorries?"

Numbed and disbelieving, I heard someone (it could not have been *me*?) saying, "I'll get us a jeep."

"Can you do that? I mean . . . do you have one?"

"Well, not exactly . . ." Her smile became knowing. "Fine. Okay . . . I know what you're thinking?"

"Oh? What am I thinking?"

"Here's this Yank trying to impress me."

"Well?" she wondered. "Aren't you?"

I laughed. "Yes."

"That's nice," Heather said. "It's much better when you laugh. You're not so stiff and serious then." She nodded. "All right . . . I'm impressed. Now, if you want to, you can retract without losing face."

"You mean about the jeep?"

"The jeep," she agreed.

Offered a way out, unhesitating, I blew the opportunity. "I'll get the jeep, don't you worry." Who did I think I was . . . Eisenhower?

Heather said thoughtfully, "we-e-ell . . ."

Only one possible further escape route presented itself now: if Heather were to thank me and, with courtesy, to decline. She must use the transport provided; her mother had insisted upon it. Her unmentioned father and/or brother(s) would be out looking for her with shotgun(s). Something of the sort to get me off my own hook. Although at what price?

"Can you really?" she asked.

"Of course. Absolutely," that other hateful someone answered for me. As if this were Manhattan, and all I had to do was whistle up a cab.

She arched questioning brows. "And no funny business?"

I vowed, feeling ill, "eyes on the road. Both hands firmly on the wheel."

My last poor chance slipped away as Heather told me, "I accept, then, and thank you very much." Confessing, "actually, I didn't care awfully much for that lorry. Even sitting in front."

The dance, a long medley, ended, and the buffet supper was announced. I invited Heather to join me, and she said that she would like that. My delight was, however, marred by the awareness of incipient disaster and humiliation.

At the buffet tables, Heather helped herself, wide-eyed, exclaiming over things not seen in England for the best part of five years. The plate I bore away for her held, she vowed, 'at least a fortnight's rations'. It made her feel uneasy. " . . . when others are going short."

I got her the requested soft drink, despairing over my self-generated dilemma, pondering what must be the dismal outcome of my eventual shamefaced confession that I had been shooting off my face, and that I had about as much chance of getting hold of a jeep as I had of flying her home in a B-26!

Humbled and contrite, I was at the point of taking Heather aside to confess all when I spotted O'Connor, still at the bar, and a faint flicker of hope returned. The possibility that, in old-hand, worldly-wise O'Connor, one might find salvation?

I introduced him to Heather, and he played with grace his role of Virginia gentleman, talking through supper, endlessly witty and charming. Until, made abrupt by anxiety, I must tell Heather that I sought a quiet word alone with my bombardier, and she could smile and take her cue: it was time to powder her nose.

When she had left us, the ever-perceptive O'Connor ventured, "you look like you got troubles, cousin."

"You might say that."

"What's up?" His brows wig-wagged ironically. "Won't she come across with the goods?"

"It's not like that," I informed him stiffly, and he gave me another of his smirks.

"So . . . suppose you tell me what it *is* like?"

I told him.

O'Connor sighed. "All this . . . and after only one dance?"

"Look . . ." I offered feebly, "she's a real honey."

"Seems that way." He nodded. "On the outside, anyhow."

"Come *on* . . . don't spoil it, Buzz. We do seem to be hitting it off." I managed a rueful grin.

"But you won't be if you can't come up with a set of wheels, right?" I nodded back wretchedly. "Ever stop to consider, kid, that a female that'd give you the air over a jeep ride maybe ain't worth the trouble?"

"It's not anything she's said." I defended Heather. "Just the way I've figured it."

O'Connor observed judiciously, "If there's one thing I've learned in this life, it's never to let my cock rule my head."

"Jesus!" I almost gave up then. "If you can't help, then say so. Only kindly spare me the sermon."

"When did I say anything about not helping?"

"Well, it seemed . . ."

"Just you never mind what it *seemed*, son. Don't you go frettin' your tiny brain." O'Connor lifted capitulating hands. "Okay, okay . . ."

"You'll *help*?"

"Only because you play so shrewdly upon my vanity." He shook his head, chuckling. "Attributing to me wiles I'd never suspected." We stood watching as Heather picked her way through the throng toward us. "You're right, I'll give you that. She's a honey."

I said, "thanks, Buzz." For the compliment to Heather as well as for the promised help. From the warm comfort to be drawn from my faith in O'Connor's certain ability—with an Air Medal and twenty five missions survived on B-17s—to succeed.

"All the same," he warned me. "Never forget the golden rule of continued existence in the A.A.F. Watch out ahead, both wingtips, and your very vulnerable ass . . ." Heather was smiling at us from twenty feet away. "Now, go dance with your girl.

Discuss lots of clean and wholesome things. Keep your pecker firmly in your pants. I'll get back to you all in good time. And, win or lose," he concluded with firmness. "My next drink's on you!"

*

I danced obediently, and, my continuing anxiety notwithstanding, enjoyed it very much. There had been no firm commitment from O'Connor, merely the non-specific pledge to 'do what he could'. I made myself dismiss all that, concentrating on the lovely girl in my arms, on the music, on the unfamiliar steps. With the background knowledge persisting . . . should O'Connor fail, she would probably not be in my arms for much longer.

As we circled together, a few seemingly lackluster attempts to cut in were rebuffed with ease. Major Delaney made no re-appearance; no one, in turn, tried to pull rank on *me*. I imagined the word making the rounds: Heather was 'with' me.

She declared her interest in my name. "Is Denney short for Dennis?"

I explained that Denney was my given name. "I don't care much for Dennis." And added quickly, "sorry."

"Why sorry?"

It was an opening not to be missed. "There might be someone . . . ?"

"There's no Dennis in my life, if that's what you mean?" Heather said levelly. "And no Tom, Dick, nor Harry, either."

I told her, much-relieved, "that's pretty hard to credit."

"Odd, though . . ." She turned aside from that proffered bait. "The name Denney, I mean. Not *odd* odd. Just a little odd to an English ear."

And here it comes, I thought edgily. The good old English-American game, pointing out the differences: 'we do it this way, you do it that'. "Well," I said. "Real sorry about that."

She peered at me closely. "And now I think I've made you cross."

"Cross . . . ?"

"You went all growly then." Her smile, now hesitant, questioned me.

"Only because you made me think," I offered swiftly, and grinned. "I find that painful . . ." But I had to ask, "so? What's odd?"

"Just that, with us, Denney's more of an abbreviation, or a nickname. That's all." She sounded apologetic.

Still a little ruffled, I suggested, "different countries, different ways, yes?"

"Oh, dear . . ." She looked away from me.

And who was I, I wondered then, to get picky? After the dumb stunt that I had pulled over the jeep. I recalled a fitting English word . . . 'churl'. I was a churl. "Please excuse me," I begged Heather. "I'm a churl."

"If you insist," she answered agreeably. "Although, really, I hadn't noticed."

"You should give horticulture the go-by," I suggested. "Take up a diplomatic career instead."

I explained how Denney had been my mother's maiden name, passed on to me. "The way it's done in some families." Families with pretensions, I thought wryly. "The first-born winds up with the maiden name tacked on, and the mother keeps it, too. Mine, single, was Joyce Carolyn Denney. Married, she became Joyce Carolyn Denney Pilgrim. And I got landed with Denney Marcus Pilgrim."

She said quickly, brightly, "they're wizard names."

I was getting familiar with the current R.A.F. slang. 'Wizard prang', the R.A.F. people would say, and 'wizard show'. 'Wizard' was all the same 'pretty damned good' . . .

Looking across just then, I noticed that O'Connor was back at the bar. Wearing an expression of sleepy contentment. When our eyes met, he nodded once, and my heart leapt; on the basis of that single nod, right now was suddenly looking . . . wizard! Because right now might have a jeep in it. Already it had Heather, and now with the real chance coming up of a nice slow drive to the village after the last dance. And whatever might develop from that?

*

The jeep was a crock.

A has-been and near write-off, employed now as a perimeter vehicle for the transportation of men and equipment—mostly dirty and greasy men and equipment—between the hangar line and the hardstands.

The transmission and gearbox were shot to hell. The clutch slipped, and the speedometer did not work at all. The carburetor leaked, and the thing stank of raw gasoline. There were no side screens, and the canvas top was ripped and flapping. It was decrepit, littered with old cigarette butts and candy wrappers. It was scabbed deeply with rust. It was, for all that, a jeep, and, to me, better by far than Franklin D. Roosevelt's official twelve-cylinder Buick limousine. It might just manage to save my face and reputation, and for that alone I loved it uncritically.

I found a whisk broom, and managed to sweep out the worst of the accumulated crud, then covered what would be Heather's seat with an OD blanket taken from my bunk. To save her dress. The fact notwithstanding that this sad old ruin was my life-saver and possible Open Sesame to better things in the future, I could not quite suppress the uncharitable thought that this might be O'Connor's notion of a good joke?

I returned to the dance to find that Andy Devine had acquired a girl, the same armor-plated blonde in the short dress. Who enquired of me without preamble, "got a jeep, 'ave you?"

"Well, yes . . ."

"Good-o. Gi's a lift 'ome, then? I on'y live down the village." She turned to grin with undisguised malice at Heather. "Shan't take you far out your way."

Heather offered no comment, but I was warned at once by her frosty expression. I studied the blonde doubtfully, and my immediate typecasting of her was less than favorable.

"Wouldn't mind, would you, pet? If this nice fella give us a lift?" She kissed Andy moistly, leaving a lipstick smear. O'Connor was smiling dryly. Andy, looking abashed, offered, "Skip . . . uh . . . this-here's Gladys."

"Hi, Gladys," I said.

"Hi, good-lookin'." She simpered back. "What's cookin'?"

I wondered how Andy might get himself out of this one? Gladys looked to be the limpet type. It was Heather's evident distaste which gave me my lead, "I guess there's a problem with that, Gladys. You see, I couldn't take you."

Gladys looked at me, looked at Heather, and winked bawdy understanding. "Oh, I get it. Three's a crowd, eh? An' four's even worse." She was laughing. "On'y a little *lift*, darlin' . . . not lookin' for none o' the old 'ow's-your-father. Jus' drop me an' Steve off. The council 'ouses on the Colchester road." Andy, I reflected, had discovered someone willing to call him by his proper name. But was the price worth it?

"It's . . ." I invented swiftly, "regulations."

"What regulations's them, then?"

Gaining confidence, I improvised further. "Only one civilian at a time may be carried in a general purpose vehicle."

O'Connor supported me, grave-faced. "At a time, that is."

"It's the insurance, Gladys," I explained. "You wouldn't be covered."

"An' she *would*, I s'pose?" Gladys eyed Heather who smiled back at her with great sweetness.

I said, "she's the one legal non-service passenger I'm permitted."

"'Ow bleedin' smashin' for 'er," Gladys retorted in a hardening voice, and then grew coaxing. "Look . . . about the insurance, I wouldn't mind, honest. I mean, nothin''s gonna 'appen, is it? An' even if it did, I'd never make a fuss."

"Gladys, sorry, but I just couldn't live with that on my conscience." At my side, O'Connor buried his nose in his drink. "It's Uncle Sam who calls the tune. And we'd have to drive past the M.P. post on the gate. They'd take one look, and we'd all wind up in the hoosegow . . ." Heather showed Gladys a look of sympathetic understanding. "I'd get busted down to private and have to spend the rest of the war on K.P." I launched an appeal to Gladys's better nature. "Now, you wouldn't want that, would you?"

Andy murmured in an aside, "way to go, Skip."

"Reelly?" Gladys looked suspicious still. "You're not tryin' to muck me about, are you?"

"Would I do that to you?" I asked.

Andy rallied to the cause then. "No kiddin', babe, honest to God. They'd turn round an' throw the book at the Skip for somethin' like that."

Gladys gave me her parting shot. "Bit much, I mus' say. On'y one allowed in a jeep, yet they stuff us in them lorries like soddin' sardines!"

"How it goes sometimes, honey," Andy soothed her. "Guess they ain't so particular about what gets carried in trucks."

*

"Such bare-faced lies . . ." Heather was still chuckling. "How will I ever know now if you're to be trusted?"

I was driving with slow care out of consideration for the jeep's age and infirmities. Following a tree-shaded lane, the masked headlights throwing their puny beams out before us. I could only answer Heather lamely, "I don't usually do things like that."

"Of course you don't," she murmured.

"Anyway, I got the feeling that you didn't object a great deal. And that you don't care much for her."

"I don't care anything at *all* for her."

"Is Gladys all she appears to be?"

"And quite a bit more," Heather replied grimly.

Gladys Gibbons, she related, was a village girl who had married a soldier early in the war. When he went away, she began playing the field with airmen from what was then the R.A.F. base. And I remembered . . . 'Welcome Wagon'. Another girl.

Another air base, in Texas. It happened everywhere, and all the time.

Someone had written a letter about his wife's behavior to Lance Corporal Gibbons. Given a special furlough, he came home and thrashed her, then thrashed the R.A.F. boy friend of the moment. Chastened, Gladys promised to behave, and did so until her husband returned to camp. Where, soon afterwards, he received another letter. But there could be no more furloughs: he found himself, instead, on board a troopship bound for Egypt. Later, at a desert dust-hole called Sidi Barrani, he had died in battle . . .

Heather said in a stony voice, "she didn't even try to keep up appearances. Just didn't care. And then, when you people arrived . . . well, she was right in her element."

I stilled the prickle of irritation induced by 'you people'. "Then I'm glad I gave her the bum's rush."

"Now," Heather directed. "Let's forget her, shall we?"

"She's already ancient history."

"I've had a really smashing evening." She smiled across at me, her face lit by the dim dashboard glow.

"Me, too," I said. "Smashing."

"It was all right, wasn't it?" she wondered. "About the jeep?"

"Oh, yes . . . just fine." And how much did she know, or guess. "Tonight, given the festive occasion, there's a kind of unofficial amnesty. As long as I have it back on base by daybreak."

"What happens if you don't?"

"It turns back into a pumpkin." Heather was laughing. "Which, considering its condition as a jeep, might not be such a bad thing."

"It *was* clever of you to get it." She had turned her face away to stare out at the dark trees drifting by. "Especially as I know you had to work a fiddle."

Had O'Connor, then, filled her in on the murky details, I wondered then, and decided that it did not matter. We had a jeep of sorts, and honor was satisfied. The means, surely, did not count. "Do you mind about that?"

"All that I mind, with approval," she told me. "Is that you tried very hard for me, and kept your promise." She was looking at me now. "But, one thing . . . ?" She put out a tentative hand as though to touch me, then hesitated. "If it's all right with you, that is?"

"What thing? Tell me."

"Just that you needn't try quite so hard in future."

I seized on that. "Is there to be a future?"

She countered with, "would you like there to be?"

"Depend on it."

"All right, then," Heather said. "Why not?"

We drove on in silence for a while as I considered this unexpected and pleasing development, and my response to it. "I'd like very much to see you again, of course."

Heather repeated calmly, "all right."

"Could it be soon? Please?"

"Isn't that more up to you?" she wondered.

"Sorry. I don't get you."

She pointed out soberly, "I have only my job to worry about. Whereas you don't have quite that level of freedom, do you?"

"That's a good point." It was a point, though, and a reminder, that I could have done without there and then.

"Simply fitting in," Heather said. "I'd say that's more up to me."

"Okay." I accepted the initiative. "Tomorrow? Would that suit?"

"Today tomorrow, or tomorrow tomorrow?" She reminded me, "it's after midnight, you know."

"*Today* tomorrow . . . every time!"

"Will you be able to get away?"

"The Group's on stand-down . . . it'll be at least twenty four hours." I laughed.

"After tonight's little shindig there'll be no one left sober enough for war. Beyond that I can't say." I asked, "and what about your job?"

"Today tomorrow is Saturday." I had forgotten that. "The labs don't work . . . we're no longer essential to the war effort.

So? If you'd care to meet me?" I thought that her eyes, soft-lit, held a deeper, unasked question.

"I'd like that more than anything," I answered.

We had left the trees behind, driving into open country with little hedged English fields that stretched away to the village. The jeep groaned and rattled over the old humpity-back railroad bridge, and then there was only a mile left to go. I picked out the row of identical ugly council houses where Gladys Gibbons lived. Just a little way past those, and all this would come to an end, I knew with regret. I was not ready for it to end, not yet. Even when there was now tomorrow. *Today* tomorrow.

*

Heather lived in a fine-looking house.

Big and dark and rambling, with half-timbering beneath the eaves, and dormer windows and tall chimneys. All set well back from the road and screened by a high hedge of laurel. A drive curved its way round to a portico'ed front door. With my eyes attuned to the blackout, I could see the house clearly in its acre of ground, its many windows and gabled roof, the big conservatory round to one side, and it made me think of houses described in the novels of John O'Hara, set in the 'Twenties, privileged and comfortable, steeped in generations of sexual scandal and country club blackballings, garage suicides with carbon monoxide; the car in the garage always an Essex. Which, in this eastern corner of England, would have been suitably fitting.

"Pretty nice," I said.

But Heather pulled a face. "It's not the happiest of houses, I'm afraid. A bit of a millstone, really." She gazed out somberly at her blacked-out and silent home as if seeing it for the first time. "I call it the House of Usher sometimes, just sitting there, waiting for its fall." Her tone was gently regretful. "It's far too big for us, and the upkeep's killing. Slowly rotting away because you can't get any proper work done in wartime. It's getting to be too much for Mum and me on our own."

I digested this piece of information, thinking of . . . no father.
Out patrolling, fuming, with his shotgun. No incensed, honor-
defending brothers . . .

"I'd ask you in for a drink," Heather was saying. "But it *is*
rather late, and Mum's tucked up for the night . . ." She made an
amused grimace. "Or what's left of it."

"That's not expected," I said. Although it would have been
pleasant.

"Such a gorgeous evening," she insisted once more. "A true
breath of fresh air." She put her head back, sighing. "One feels so
stifled sometimes. It would be lovely simply to fly away, but, of
course, one can't. Not like you."

"Although . . ." And the stark pictures of Cherbourg re-
shuffled themselves at the back of my mind. "Not always to
places I'd choose."

She was quickly apologetic. "That was a stupid and quite
thoughtless thing to say."

"Not really. Just me being needlessly touchy."

Heather stirred in her seat, and the worn-out springs twanged
in protest. "Oops!" She stifled a giggle, then asked, "could we sit
out for a little longer, and talk, do you think? That's if you're not
too exhausted?"

I supposed that I should have been. It had been a pretty long
day; eighteen hours since the wake-up call, the mental strain of
gearing up for Cherbourg, then flying the mission. The time of
reaction, drinking, dancing, meeting Heather. All the turmoil
stemming from my near-gaffe over the jeep . . .

"I feel fine," I assured her. "Let's make a night of it."

And then, naturally and easily, our hands reaching out, fingers
interlacing. Yet, when Heather spoke again, she caught me right
off guard. "Denney . . . do you ever feel afraid?"

"Flying missions, you mean?"

"Yes."

I needed a little time then in which to think that through: it
was pretty personal and high-powered stuff for a first meeting.
And yet, now that it had been invited, I found that I was ready to

talk of it to her, and tell her things. So that, hedging only a little, I said, "you have to know that I've flown only the one so far. Today, Cherbourg, was our first together as a combat crew. Don't think there's been time enough yet to figure out if I'm scared or not . . . it hasn't really sunk in." But I was feeling again, and in full, the tautness of the endless-seeming run in under fire from the I.P. "Although, if it's all going to be like that, then I guess I'll learn pretty fast."

She asked, sounding, I thought, almost eager, "was it really awful?"

"There again, I'm still not sure." I shook my head, troubled somehow by the intensity of her questioning. "They said it would be easy, a milk-run. But I've had no previous experience by which to judge. Simply that, if *that* was a milk-run, then I'm not looking forward too keenly to when things start getting rough." But that sounded too much like whining, and I was embarrassed and ashamed. "Hell . . . I'm talking like a damned sissy."

"No, you're not at all!" Heather grew sharp with me. "You mustn't ever think that. It's not wrong to dread things, only human. Believe me . . . I know this," she insisted. "I've heard those same doubts voiced before, almost word for word, by . . . by someone. A very brave and honest man. Who wondered about himself and his ability to cope exactly as you do. And just as mistakenly."

I would have liked to know then who was this brave man who shared my inner thoughts. Father? Brother? Cousin? *Friend* . . . or worse?

"Perhaps it might be better to talk about something else," Heather suggested then, and watched me in the dimness. "Something more comfortable and pleasant." It gave me a sudden shivery feeling: it was as though she had peered inside my head to read my most secret thoughts . . .

And so, instead, we spoke of the dance, and that *was* easier, and a whole lot more pleasant. She had, she said, loved all the music, the Glenn Miller and Dorsey hits, the numbers by Jerome Kern, Gershwin and Cole Porter.

"They're so wonderfully *alive*," she said breathlessly, and broke off to sing, "'Manhattan babies don't sleep tight . . . until the dawn. Good-night ba-by . . . *good*-night . . . milkman's on his way. Sleep tight ba-by . . . till the break of day. Lis-ten to the lull-aby of old Broad-way' . . ." In her sweet, clear English voice. And gave a small, strained laugh. "Sorry."

"God . . . you mustn't be! That was knock-out!" I said, "if we'd had any idea you could sing like that, we'd have had you up there on the stand. You'd have knocked them silly."

"What utter rot." But she was smiling. "I would've sounded like a crow."

It was my turn to smile. "What utter rot."

We laughed together in the dark, and she asked, "that's your town, isn't it? New York? Manhattan?"

"That's the place."

"And do you know lots of beautiful and exciting Manhattan babies who don't sleep tight until the dawn?"

"Not a solitary one I'd prefer to being here with you."

"That's very sweet." Heather glanced at me sidelong. "Even if, in your heart, you don't really mean it."

We talked on, endlessly, it seemed, as, around us, the spring night melted away. The first birds were breaking into their dawn chorus while we discussed George Gershwin. I had this considerable thing about Gershwin's music.

"He always created such incredible sound pictures . . . pictures of New York." Heather listened with all the satisfying signs of close attention. "I only have to hear the Piano Concerto in F, and I'm looking down on Manhattan at once, each and every part of it, no matter where I am . . ."

Speaking of it now, so far away from it, could bring it achingly back.

"That great orchestral swell after the piano introduction, and, straightaway, I'm there, up on the Queensborough Bridge, or across the Hudson in Jersey. And it's night," I told Heather. "With that whole vast skyline blazing with power. All there for me in his music. Or it can be like driving up for the weekend from

Princeton, the university I attended. Heading home over the Pulaski Skyway. It'll be sunset, and I can see all of mid-town off in the distance, with the sunlight on the towers. All those millions of windows looking as if they're on fire . . ." I let out my breath. "Guess I'm getting carried away."

Heather said simply, "that's a love story."

"That how it sounds to you?"

"It's what it *is*," she corrected me. "You were there then, weren't you? All those places with their wonderful-sounding American names. What was it again . . . Skyway?"

"The Pulaski," I explained. "An ugly elevated highway in New Jersey that cuts through the even more ugly industrial zones surrounding Newark. But it does give you that fantastic sunset view."

There was a sudden, sharp pre-dawn chill, and the sky was paling.

I said to Heather, "your mother's going to hit the roof."

"Don't panic. She trusts me."

"Sure she does. But does she trust *me*?"

"I do," Heather said matter-of-factly. "And Mum will find a way to."

"That sounds promising." I was thinking just then of my own mother, and making comparisons which, from my mother's position, were not altogether favorable. "And I guess that's what makes you so mature."

"Do you find me mature?" Heather looked intrigued.

"There's that old belief about women growing up faster than men . . ."

"You mean *age*?" Her eyes teased me.

"Not what I mean at all," I replied with sternness. "We were discussing maturity, and my feeling that you bear out the old saw about growing up."

"Oh, excuse *me* . . ." She was laughing again, and I thought how much I liked her laughter, and my seeming ability to make her laugh. She demanded then, "and what of you, Denney Pilgrim? Are you mature?"

"I used to think so, or moderately so, at least. Until yesterday."

"Because of your flight?" she pressed.

I nodded. "I'd figured out that I had a grip on myself, and could get the job done. You're supposed to be reasonably mature for that. They put you through heavy training, endless yelling and petty humiliations, all to weed out weakness and force maturity on you . . ." And, hey, I reflected, startled. I had taken off suddenly, airing my secrets without any pressure put on me to do so. With Heather, in spite of my usual reticence about myself, it seemed right, and natural, to disclose those things. "But, there, on the mission, when it came to the testing moment, all I wanted to do was duck under the bed-clothes."

"That's only self-preservation," she said. "Nothing could be more natural."

"Not under the U.S. Army's rules of engagement."

With a perceptible edge in her voice, Heather wondered, "is that what you all are, then? Heroes to order?" Put like that, any arguments of mine could sound corny, *and* immature. "Not even generals," she insisted. "Can deny human nature." And no, I thought. They simply have you shot instead. "I've felt the same way often, for all of my vaunted maturity." She was smiling reminiscently. "During the Blitz. I'd wake up with the siren going, and hear that uneven beat of engines that told you it was the Germans. They say that's done deliberately, to put the wind up us."

"You do it with the propeller controls." I trotted out my airman's expertise for her. "Twin-engined aircraft . . . you nudge one of the levers a little out of synchronization, and it gives you that drumming sound."

"Whatever . . ." She gestured dismissal. "But my stomach would do flip-flops, and . . ." Her slim fingers toyed idly with the gearshift. "I *did* hide under the blankets. Which was quite pointless, but still human."

"You're doing great things for my morale," I said.

"Well, that's good." She faced me, looking into my eyes. "I have to say, you don't seem old enough to be flying bombers."

"Catch 'em young, that's the secret." I said, "but I'm old enough . . . oh, yes." And quipped, "I've even got a cer-stiff-icate that says so."

"May one dare to enquire how old?"

"Old enough," I told her. "To have outgrown a once-great frustration."

"What a very strange answer." Heather looked thoughtful. "More of a riddle, I'd say."

"Indulge me. It's one of my little childhood fantasies . . . totally devoid of all logic, and quite lacking in maturity."

"You *said* it was a frustration," she pointed out.

"And so it was. Over my never being able . . . old enough . . . to speak with any authority of twenty years ago."

"I think . . ." She laughed once more. "I'm beginning to see now. Although you really must tell me more."

"You'll say I'm stupid."

"I might, if I thought you were." I was given the full effect of wide and melting gray eyes. "But I doubt that I shall."

Encouraged thus, I confided, "it was something that really bugged me as a kid . . . a teenager. Surrounded by know-it-all adults talking about their pasts, and never being able to say in my own right that 'twenty years ago I did this, or that'. Even if all I was doing at the time was getting born."

Heather asked, grinning, "and?"

"I've been able to speak with the necessary authority for slightly better than two years."

"My goodness . . . despite your appearance, you're positively ancient," she breathed. "Like the Picture of Dorian Gray. Do you have a grisly portrait of yourself hanging up in your cellar at home?"

"No. But I can show you a real scary I.D. photograph, if you like?" She shook her head and looked alarmed, and I challenged her, "so? Your turn now. What about you?"

"Oh, come *on!*" she protested. "That's hardly fair."

"What's fair got to do with anything? What we have here is a love and war situation . . ." It was out, and said, before I had time to think of consequences, and I wondered, holding my breath, about Freudian slips. Could that be the way I was starting to see things, and after such a little while? We had a war . . . okay, but love? Although the bare notion of it seemed pleasant. I added quickly, retreating, "in a manner of speaking."

"Yes, I imagine that we have." Heather held my gaze while revealing nothing, and the moment passed as she stated, "if you must know, I'll have been able to speak with the same authority for a year in August."

"Could I put in my bid now?"

"Bid for what?" She looked blank.

"A date with you to celebrate the occasion?" And, the hell with you, Providence, I decided. And all of the debatable, doubt-filled future. Like me, in this, they must take their chances.

"That," Heather promised. "Goes straight into the engagements diary."

I released some more pent-up breath. "Now, all of a sudden, and thanks to you, I have a goal in life."

By then I could see her face clearly in the growing light, and we looked at each other in silence for what seemed like a long time. Until her gaze dropped, and she suggested lightly, "perhaps we should consider the pumpkin?"

"You think of everything." I stretched my creaking limbs. "Could've gone on sitting here for ever."

She wanted to know then, "can you ride a bike?"

I had not been on one since childhood. "I guess so, but I'm way out of practice."

"It's like walking," she assured me. "Something you never forget."

"Is that what you'd like us to do?"

"If you fancy the idea?" Her eyes questioned me anew. "I think it's going to be a nice day, and I can show you the countryside. We could stop off somewhere for tea . . ." She faltered then. "Sorry again . . . I wasn't thinking. Would you be able to get hold of a bike?"

"I can probably manage that okay. I got hold of a jeep, after all." This time, I knew that my chances were better. All it should take was some leverage. "Should I call for you here?"

But she shook her head. "There's a spot I know."

"Okay." I wondered if that decision was based on concern for her mother, or on the possibility that the old lady might create problems? "Say where."

She gave me directions: I must turn left out of the base and go on for a mile, then make a right when I came to a concrete anti-invasion bunker. Go on down that road to the second tuning left, then a final quarter mile until I came to a crossroads. Heather vowed that she would be there.

"You're making it sound pretty tricky," I complained.

"No more so," she reminded me. "Than flying to Cherbourg."

"That was no problem. All I had to do was follow the others."

"You'll do it, you just see," she told me with confidence.

FOUR

At first, I did not recognize her, and thought with disappointment that she had cried off, sending someone else to make her excuses. Some flushed and unknown country girl, bent breathless over the handlebars. In a headscarf and one of those coarse, bulky white raincoats that the English called riding macs. Her feet in flat, 'sensible' brown shoes.

She wore no make-up, and her face, intent and shining with effort, appeared bad-tempered. Illogically, I had anticipated seeing again the poised, black-gowned young woman of the dance, which was stupid of me, and quite unfair to her. I blamed such musings on my lousy mood of the moment. Brought on by a bicycle.

In exchange for a carton of Lucky Strike, Staff Sergeant Tallichet, 'Big Apples' ground crew chief, had agreed to loan me his. A machine begged or stolen from somewhere, and used by Sergeant Tallichet to commute back and forth between the maintenance shops and the hardstand.

Pinning all my hopes on it, I was delighted when the sergeant clinched the deal. Until, for the first time, close to, I was able to examine the bike, an angular device of great antiquity, cast-iron heavy, arthritically stiff, and with only the one gear which would make of it a hard-hearted bitch on even the slightest upgrade. Worse still, it was a ladies' bike, wrought so as not to impede the free movement of voluminous, old-fashioned skirts. It was enough to dispel at once my earlier buoyant mood as I pictured Heather's immediate and loudly uncontrollable mirth upon finding me mounted on such a contraption. But, even though it embarrassed me horribly, I was now well and truly stuck with the thing. A no-holds-barred date with Princess Elizabeth of England could not have begun to compensate me for such mortification . . .

While following Heather's careful directions, I succeeded in getting myself lost twice, having to ask the way, then to suffer revised instructions delivered as if to a mental defective; that so very English manner of explaining the obvious to dumb, bewildered Yanks.

Arriving finally at the crossroads, I was actually relieved to find no sign of Heather waiting. I stood there, glowering at the now-detested bike; no *bikes* I should have insisted. And thought anew of Cherbourg, of how those Kraut gunners would die laughing if they could just see me now. A revenge infinitely more sweet than that of merely shooting me down!

I waited sulkily at the roadside as the minutes drew out . . . and just maybe Heather would not show up. Being stood up on our first date seemed to me then to be the lesser humiliation.

But now, here she came in her shapeless mac and peasant babushka and plain shoes. A stranger.

Until she saw me, and waved and smiled, and that smile could change everything for the better. "I wasn't sure you'd be here."

She stood before me, breathing hard, and was once more the princess of the Squadron dance. While I was the toad, and unlikely to be transformed by any number of kindly kisses, but, instead, fixed for all eternity in my surly and self-pitying place.

She dismounted from her smart sports model, and I smiled back, confessing, "I was thinking along the same lines."

"If I hadn't wanted to come, I'd have said so at the time," she chided gently. "I would never have let you down like that."

With that admission, pique went flying out the window, taking injured pride along with it. "Forgive my lack of faith," I told Heather, and handed control over to her. "Okay . . . you're flying lead. What's the flight plan?"

She remounted and bade me follow her, and offered not one word about my God-awful bike. I should have realized, of course, because Heather was English, and not materialistic in the way that we Americans were. I had anticipated as a matter of course her deriding of Sergeant Tallichet's antediluvian relic, yet, clearly, she did not care a hoot for it one way or the other. Rusty, creaky old bikes were par for the course after five years of wartime privation. They were not, I decided, governed by *things*, these people.

Back in the States I would have been loudly jeered and cat-called off the road by every passing driver. Here, it simply did not matter, a comforting realization that served well to restore my self-confidence. I was glad now that Heather had not stood me up.

She rode gracefully on, and I ground along in her wake, trying hard not to make too disparaging a comparison with Heather's sleek and gleaming Raleigh Sportster. Which had a gearshift and cable brakes, an air pump, streamlined headlight, basket and a little polished bell.

∗

Heather pedaled without seeming effort as I did furious battle with dry and creaking parts and a wretchedly slipping chain. I called after her, hot and panting, "whither are we headed?"

"You'll see." She slowed to let me catch up. "Are you suffering dreadfully?"

"Never!" I grimaced. "Stiff upper lip and all that, what?"

She giggled, and promised, "we'll stop and rest soon."

But we kept going for what seemed like miles through the Essex fields and woods, swooping around the curves, fooling about, no hands, on the downgrades, building up maximum speed for the inevitable hard run at the rising ground beyond. Some of the slopes were just too much for the old bike and me, and I would have to clamber off and shove my way to the top where Heather waited, smirking.

Until, as we freewheeled down a sunken lane, she cried suddenly, "look, there's a place!" Swinging in and braking. "In among the buttercups."

I slid off with relief. "Take care. They can be poisonous."

"Are you a secret botanist, Lefftenant Pilgrim?" She regarded me mirthfully. "As well as a hotshot pilot?"

I squirmed as I recalled my pre-dawn bragging. "Sorry about that."

"Why should you be, there's no need. One would have to be rather good to do what you do, so some simple and harmless boasting is permitted surely?" She took charge then, patting a place at her side, directing me to, "sit there, then you won't mess up your smart uniform."

"No big deal. Uncle Sam will provide." I lay back at ease in the mild May sunlight, and saw that she was frowning. "What's wrong, Heather?"

She was twirling a freshly-picked buttercup. "What you said then . . . about Uncle Sam." She gazed down into my face. "You Americans are so incredibly self-assured all the time, taking things for granted." There was disapproval in her tone. "Always so certain that things will work out."

I made light of it. "Won't they?"

Her answer was startling. "It makes me think of tempting Providence, that's all." She wondered, "does that offend you?"

"No. But it makes *me* think, too."

"May I ask what about?"

They were things, though, that I would have been happier not to ponder at that moment. Of how, on each day, we were paid to tempt Providence, and indeed expected—ordered—to do so every time we flew. Which was something that, with the blind arrogance of indestructible youth, I had been doing since dropping out of Princeton to enlist in the Air Corps. Through the days of flight training, the later conversion to bombers, B-26s, which were temperamental and unforgiving airplanes. And of how I—and we—went on doing so now in the E.T.O. I tempted Providence on a daily basis by being who I was, what I was, and where. Now, on a green bankside along a country road, I was being compelled to consider Providence anew. Recalling the ways in which I had set myself willfully to lock horns with that grim old specter when this war, for Americans, was just one more looming squabble between the always-squabbling Europeans. During the long, hot Eastern seaboard summer of 1939 . . .

Heather enquired mildly, "can it be that I've lost you?"

"Forgive me once more." I smiled apology. "I was just running through a quick review of my checkered, pampered American past."

"Checkered as well? My word!" Her mouth twitched.

"Not serious. Nothing they'd send you up the river for."

"The river . . . ?"

"Going to jail," I explained, and told Heather of the New York State Penitentiary at Ossining on the Hudson. 'Up the river' from the city.

"Sing Sing," she said.

"That's very good. How did you know?"

"Oh, we know all about Sing Sing. The place where they send the gangsters to the electric chair."

"That's right," I agreed. "Jimmy Cagney and Paul Muni and Humphrey Bogart and good old Edward G. Robinson."

"Now you're taking the mickey," Heather accused.

"Isn't that what Gladys said at the dance? Anyway, it makes a nice change for me to get the opportunity."

"We choose to ignore that," Heather declared. "And, instead, to make further enquiry into this famous checkered past."

But *would* she be interested in the rather tame story of how, in that summer, I had set out with malice aforethought to joust with Providence? Driving up Long Island with three college friends in an old Model 'A' Ford to the little sailplane club outside Amagansett. Which possessed three soaring aircraft and a battered Waco biplane tug. A hungry place that was eager for the business that four eager-beaver college kids could bring in.

I had learned quickly, going solo in under five hours and earning my first soaring rating at the same time—the humble 'C'—by staying up there, riding the weak thermals, for all of forty minutes.

I grew to recognize and understand the thermals; how to find and use their lifting columns of air, to pick out the puffballs of cumulus that marked their presence on fine, warm days. Feeling with delight their boot-in-the-backside thrust as I would roll the aircraft into its climbing circle, reveling in its spiraling response to pure lift.

Even as I wondered about boring Heather, I was telling her, finding in the recounting the awakening of old pleasures, still bright and sharp and good.

I told of staying on to fly more after the others had tired of it and given up. Because, by then, I was hooked, loving soaring with its disciplines, the constant need for swift response, with the demands it made on my wits, and the pleasure and endless satisfaction bestowed in return.

Until, on a December Sunday, it all went toppling as Japanese naval aircraft attacked from the early Pacific morning. Forget then the soaring club, and the junior year almost completed at Princeton. Instead, think *Air Corps!* To be able, and allowed, to fly anything the Air Corps might place in my hands, fighter, bomber, transport, troop-carrying glider, a tiny spotter plane. Just as long as I flew, it did not matter what . . .

Glancing up then from my yarn-spinning, attention drawn to the distant sound of aircraft engines, B-26s at take-off power. Spotting them as they climbed out over a low ridge. Three of them lifting westbound, deep-bellied, business-like and competent. Tall single fin, tailplane with pronounced dihedral. Dark against a clean sky with sunlight winking on their plexiglas panels.

And I must watch them, and could not do otherwise: I flew them myself, and knew them intimately, the feel and sound and smell of them: fuel and hydraulic fluid, hot oil, leather, rubber and superheated metal . . . the very *being* of them. A trio of sleek Martin Marauders, their engine notes dulling as the pilots throttled back, adjusting their propellers to climbing power. Wherever they went, something of you went with them always . . .

"I really must dream up a way to keep your attention."

Heather was grinning at me. "Should I take off my clothes, perhaps?"

"God . . . I'm so *sorry!*" Back to earth with a thud, and more Yank ill-manners she would be thinking. Mumbling back, abashed, something about it being impossible not to watch; a kind of compulsion. Any landing or take-off. "It makes you forget the social graces."

She held out an excuse for me. "A professional interest."

I seized it gratefully. "It's remarkable what you can pick up sometimes, simply by watching. Things to do and not to do." A last throb of receding engines drifted back from the west as I insisted, "you do have my attention. Like . . . what was that about your clothes?"

She gave a peal of delighted laughter. "There's still hope, then . . . what a mercy. You weren't totally lost. Although," she acknowledged. "Maybe that idea *was* a bit extreme." She toyed with her buttercup, holding it up like a trophy. "Instead, if you'd care to lean a little closer?" Not realizing it, I must have hesitated, for she promised, "I shan't bite."

"What are you going to do? Put a spell on me?"

Her brows went up. "But I thought I had already . . ."

"You have, and you do, and you can take that as read." In unquestioning obedience, I leaned toward her, conscious at once of her warm closeness and fragrance; even better than the closeness of dancing, or sitting, talking, in a parked jeep. My heart started at once to do a soft-shoe shuffle, and my breathing went all haywire.

"You must stay quite still, now," she warned, and held the little yellow flower beneath my chin, studying it with close attention.

"Okay. But mind telling me what you're doing?"

"A small scientific experiment . . . I *said* I wouldn't hurt you." She growled in a salty Marlene Dietrich voice, "you musst giff up now, Liebchen. Mein liddle schpell . . . how very cleffer of you to guess." She examined my chin through narrowed eyes, and announced, "yes, you do."

"Yes I do what?"

"Like butter."

"And how do you come by that gem of wisdom?"

"I held the buttercup under your chin," she replied calmly. "And got a nice yellow reflection. That told me all."

I protested, "that's not much of a spell."

"No. Only a childhood tease."

Feeling suckered, and foolish, I demanded, "so what *is* this famous spell?"

"Just this . . ." And she leaned close, close enough for our lips to touch lightly, and then, from her, with firmness and insistence, hers parting under mine as she found me with the little hard point of her tongue. My head was filling with the mingling scents of her, the sweet astringency of the cologne she wore, the fresh odor of strenuous, sun-warmed exercise . . .

And, *Jesus*, what was this? Although 'this' was terrific, and quite unbelievable. First date, first kiss, red-hot and French, and initiated by her!

And yet, an ingrained Yankee puritanism could mar full enjoyment. To be kissed so, without warning or by-your-leave, my puritanical side argued, could not be entirely proper or becoming? It could not, furthermore, be viewed as acceptable for her to make the pace? While my worldly, mid-town Manhattan side could respond to her eagerly and wholeheartedly, to her soft mouth and the sweet taste of her on my tongue.

Her lips were moving under mine then, and, weirdly and wonderfully, she was breathing words into me, baffling words that *did* seem like an incantation: "I'm glad . . . glad . . ." And what in hell did that mean? Or her urging that: "we can make this work, and we will . . . you wait and see." And I caught her urgency then, mouthing back that, "yes, we will . . . for as long as . . ." Having to struggle to hold back laughter because this, nice as it was, was *insane!*

Her hands were gripping me, fingers digging hard into my arms. "For all the time there is."

We might have been alone in the world. No one passed by

along the lane; no farmer on his cart, or rare English car squandering rationed gasoline. No jeep or deuce-and-a-half from the base filled with leering soldiers. Nothing to interrupt that long-drawn contact. Until Heather picked the moment to break it, and to sit back and survey me with a look of proprietary triumph.

"There, now. It's all done . . . signed, sealed, witnessed and delivered."

I found my voice. "I'd call that one humdinger of a spell!"

"And did you notice?" She grinned impishly. "I haven't turned you into a frog." We sat, holding hands, and my head was in a total whirl, and it did seem to me then that all the lights were glowing green. Although, was that really possible with a girl like Heather? An English girl of the kind referred to as 'top drawer'? The big question then . . . where did we go from here, and how? Pure instinct curbed the first gross urge to make a grab at her: I was bound by inexplicable taboos; the closeness, the intimacy, served paradoxically to set her apart, like forbidden fruit, not to be bruised or defiled.

I was painfully conscious, both physically and mentally, of my sexual arousal, appalled by what must be the all-too visible evidence of wanting, and, too, of my immaturity in that department.

There had been other times, other girls; at school, at college, or during the long Cape Cod summers. The moments of awkward and embarrassed fumbling, with little fun or pleasure in it, and no magic that was worth a mention. It had never been as Hemingway had written: the earth declined to move. And, afterwards, only the sour tastes of shame and guilt, the lurking fear of the ridicule of one's too-evident shortcomings.

Although, from those clumsy gropings, there were things to be learned. Like sensing the rightness of the moment, or not. The answering signals: 'Okay, here it is'. Or: 'Back off, brother!'

Right here and now, I thought, the signals *seemed* clear enough. At home, I might have grasped what was intended; with Heather, I could not. She had become like someone glimpsed through mists, enticing yet ill-defined, a mystery beyond comprehension. And the signal blurred, making me shrink from what might have been the next step. And the possible—probable?—ghastly mistake. Instead, inanely, I muttered, "Jesus!"

"Is something wrong?" Heather enquired politely.

"Anything *but*!"

"So what can have brought that on?"

"An honest expression of feeling, coupled with a limited vocabulary. Or else your magic spell leaving me speechless."

"Jolly good," Heather said.

"Was it a spell?"

"It could be. If you'd like?"

"Then I think I would. Please, and thank you."

"We'll have to see, then, won't we?" She sounded remarkably matter-of-fact.

"Why's that? Don't you know the power of your own spells?"

She toyed still with the buttercup; it was beginning to wilt, its brief moment passing as I dithered.

A jeep was coming slowly down the lane, and the occupants, two unknown lieutenants wearing pilots' wings, waved to us, the driver calling out, "how you makin' out there?" Then, as they laughed and accelerated away, "no . . . no need to answer that. We can see for ourselves."

They went on out of sight, and the brief diversion had allowed me some needed time in which to gather together my jangled thoughts. "You said . . . about being glad? And us having time?"

"Yes, I did." She watched me without expression.

"Care to explain that to a poor simpleton?"

"As I see it, we do have time, although, once again, that's only if you wish." Heather dropped her gaze. "If you do, then I'd like that very much."

"But what do *you* want?"

She answered quietly, "for us to have time together."

"Oh, yes . . . lots of it." I would not think of Providence.

She said, puzzling me once more, "it's better that you're new here." And asked, "how many raids do you have left to fly? If it's permitted to enquire?"

"That's no secret. Thirty five . . . what we call missions . . . comprise a tour. I've done just that one, so there are thirty four left."

Heather offered the enticing suggestion, "you could be finished, then, in thirty four days from now."

"I could, but don't count on it." I shook my head and laughed. "It seldom, if ever, works out that way. For starters, our high brass couldn't deal with anything so clear-cut." I tried to explain how the time of our lives was utilized by the Army Air Force. "We get breaks between assignments, like today. And aircraft go sick, and have to be grounded . . ." You get hurt, I thought. And you die. "They have periods of rotation between the Squadrons and Groups. Unless it's something really big, like the Invasion, whenever that comes. At which point I guess we'll all be on overtime . . ." I made myself ease up then. True, what we discussed was mere speculation upon what was already common knowledge. Still, it gave the uneasy feeling of sailing a mite too close to the wind of official secrecy. Instead, I went on lightly, "we might even rate a furlough somewhere along the way . . . you never can tell. Whatever, it'll be rather more than thirty four days . . ." And, once more, unbidden, unwelcome, the bleak reminder . . . *if* you make it. Because so many did not.

"It's probably jolly selfish of me, and I still don't care," Heather announced. "But I hope you stay here with us for as long as possible. With *acres* of days off between missions." She was beaming at me.

"And we'll meet on every one of them." Her candor could make me bold in turn, and it felt great just to say it. "Like you said, all the time in the world."

"Do you know," she said, sounding pleased, "I do believe my spell is working."

*

Riding on through the afternoon, I found, startled, that I was taking seriously this spell business. Reason dictated, of course, that it was only a silly, harmless kids' game, some garnish sprinkled on that incredible kiss, the sharing of small intimacies; foolish, then, to try and attach additional meaning to it. Which did not stop me doing so as the crazy notion persisted.

We were, each member of every flying crew, plagued relentlessly by dark superstitions. We would tell one another that it was pure hokum, and that we *knew* that, a declaration of defiance that failed to alleviate the affliction, or to prevent us from arming ourselves with every bizarre form of amulet, talisman and lucky charm. It seemed now that I, too, had caught the bug badly as I contemplated the possibilities of . . . a spell? My very own and personal safeguard! There was nothing to say that it should be something visible and tangible; merely the fact of Heather's having uttered it, and then wished it upon me, should suffice. Why could there not be as much protective magic in that as in any other device employed? Enough, maybe, to protect me in combat. Her spell working for me and, thus, for us all. Like a rabbit's foot or a lucky garter, a medallion: like the pair of lacy panties borne faithfully aloft on each mission by the bombardier of 'Kickapoo Express'. Hanging, swaying in the wind, from the butt end of the nose fifty-caliber. Like a doll, a handkerchief, or any of the other many gizmos in which airmen pinned their individual or collective faith for trip after trip. Could I—dare I—seek peace of mind from words that Heather whispered into my mouth? Something that was meant almost certainly as a gag, the means to enhance feminine 'mystique'. Yet, on the other, and more positive, hand, one possible way in which to see 'Big Apples', my crew and me through the next thirty four missions. And even as logic demanded to be told how I could begin to consider such a thing, something else was shouting logic down with a defiant why not? There was no harm in it, certainly, and all the logic in the world still lacked the essential power to save our necks. If there could be something, albeit wacky and weird to employ instead, there could be no risk attached to giving it a chance. Sure it was crazy, but then was not the situation we were all in no less crazy, the war and the whole wide world?

At the same time, there remained the others in the crew to be considered. What of them? How would they react, O'Connor, the incurable ironist, happy-go-lucky, don't-give-a-damn Andy Devine, the four phlegmatic sergeants, to my airy claim: 'not a thing in the world to worry about, fellas, we're all safely under a magic spell. Placed on us by this cute English girl I've got the galloping hots for. We can't put a foot wrong . . .'

And yet? With people as superstition-ridden as we, in an enterprise that could lead—and did all too frequently—to the full and premature realizing of one's darkest fear, why should they not be tickled pink by the prospect of an honest-to-God *spell*? The anti-hex!

But then logic, unfazed, came bouncing back: if it was all hooey as I half-suspected, then how could I, reasonably well-educated, supposedly rational, take serious note of it? Except that, with half-doubt there went also a counter-balancing half-hope, a deep-down readiness to acknowledge that there might be *some*thing there. Longing, fingers crossed against the Evil Eye of Providence, for there to be . . .

One heard of people like Heather, clairvoyants, mediums, prophets: not all of them charlatans necessarily; those taken seriously held in awe by many, even feared. Not all that long ago, in Massachusetts, and here in England, it had been taken so seriously that you could get yourself burned alive for it. Questions, and more questions: could Heather and her playful spell actually be our longed-for lucky piece? With me covered by her protective umbrella, might there not, then, be room beneath it for us all?

It was, when you stopped to think about it, no more wild than what went on amongst other crews. With their St. Christopher medals, their cherished photographs of mothers and wives, girl-friends, motion-picture stars. There were the guys on board 'Daisy Mae', genuflecting before every take-off to a kewpie doll figure of their heroine from the Al Capp comic strip. Who rode blithely through the flak and opposing fighters perched up on the instrument panel for all to see, dispensing her favors . . . her Power. Cherbourg, for 'Daisy Mae', had been Mission Thirty

Three, two left to go, and she had taken care of things just fine throughout; only minor flak damage and, once, an engine shot out. A pilot wounded and replaced. The pilot had been sent home from the hospital to complete his tour as an instructor in Arizona.

On board 'Millinocket Joy-Girl' there traveled always a pink brassiere of generous dimension: another Marauder crew swore by their shared silken garter, reputed to have belonged once to Mae West. The derisive counter-claim by an uninvited outsider that the garter had probably belonged to W.C. Fields had been more than sufficient to start a vicious fistfight.

And, in place of such trivia, I was thinking as I pedaled, 'Big Apples' would sail through it all under a real live magic spell. Enduring everything that Fate and thirty four missions might have to hurl at us.

*

I liked the tea garden.

The spring afternoon was warm enough for us to sit outside. "Please yourselves," the proprietress had told us with the stiff, distant expression that I, and most visiting Americans, were getting to know about over here. Never quite certain if it was calculated ill-manners, or mere cockeyed Englishness.

I noted the way that the proprietress took in my uniform. Not caring for us at all; 'overpaid, overfed, over-sexed and Over Here'. George M. Cohan's patriotic song of 1918 had rebounded on him pretty badly in this war. 'Yank', I imagined the proprietress to have tagged me with a certain emphasis, and to her complete satisfaction. 'Yank' and 'Yank's little gold-digger'.

All the same, it was a nice garden: the garden by itself could almost atone for the snotty proprietress.

War and 'Digging for Victory' had not despoiled it; no Government decree had transformed it into allotments for growing potatoes and tomatoes and lettuce and runner beans. Or destined to be horribly stewed to mush Brussels sprouts! It resembled still the gardens fondly depicted on those boxes of imported English cookies sold in the better New York stores.

It possessed apple trees, and a vast, gnarled mulberry: it had grass of an incredible greenness that millionaires in the Hamptons and Westchester squandered fortunes on developing, not always with success. Here, where people were hard-up and shabby with war, million-dollar grass ran wild under the apple trees . . .

Unlike the garden, the tea provided did not make a favorable impression. With its thick sandwiches of grayish bread spread with gritty margarine, a filling of cress and a salty, fishy substance which, Heather informed me, was bloater paste. A separate plate with four small, hard cakes.

I bit into one. "Holy Jesus!" Heather was laughing. "What *is* this? Britain's secret weapon?"

"They're not called rock cakes for nothing," she informed me cheerfully.

The tea, however, was strong and refreshing. Unlike the majority of my compatriots, I had no trouble with tea-drinking; tea was the frequent beverage of choice at my mother's Sutton Place establishment. In those privileged surroundings, tea was viewed as polite; it set one apart.

Heather was examining her sandwich filling. "It's rather awful, I'm afraid."

"It beats C-rations . . . by a nose."

"Whatever they are?"

"If you'd ever tasted them, you'd agree." I added, "the tea's fine."

She offered one of her baffling comments. "I can read you, you know."

"Oh, yes?" I eyed her, and was aware once more of a faint and inexplicable unease.

She was looking smug. "Just like the proverbial book."

"Which must make for some pretty dull reading."

"Your thoughts come through to me clear as clear." Heather went on in apology, "it's not that I'm being deliberately nosy. I can't help it."

"Okay, fine." I challenged her, "so tell me about me."

"You loathe this tea."

"No one has to be clairvoyant to spot that."

She continued, ignoring my jibe, "you're embarrassed, and feel that's wrong, and that you shouldn't be. You know all there is to know about rationing and shortages, and making do. But it *is* a rotten tea, and knowing that, and thinking it, makes you feel guilty."

"That's pretty damned good." I nodded, and asked, "where did you learn to do that?"

"It isn't something you learn . . ." She shook her head firmly. "It's simply there. Like my being able to sense this desire you have to *do* something. Like . . . offer gifts. Food parcels from your abundant American supplies." Her returning smile appeared wistful. "Like so many of your chaps do for their English . . . their Limey . . . friends."

I answered too quickly, "I don't call you that." But it was not true, and she would know it. We all did it, and all the time, whenever—frequently—we felt ticked-off with the English. Like when they called us Yanks in that way of theirs. Because there were Yanks . . . and *Yanks*.

"Why shouldn't you?" Heather asked as, once more, she delved disconcertingly into my thoughts. "We call you Yanks."

"Yeah, right . . ." I grimaced at her. "Even the Rebels."

She looked blank, and I told her about Southerners, mimicking—badly—a redneck Dixie accent. "If'n thar's one thang us good ol' boys jist cain't abide, it's gittin' called damn Yankee carpetbaggers." Adding, "Yanks, Yankees, are Northerners, technically New Englanders. The old enemy."

"I never knew that," Heather admitted.

"It's all right . . . there are no Rebels present. I *am* a Yank, an effete New Yorker." More and more curious, I asked then, "what else do you read in me?"

"Just the thought of gifts. You want to provide things, to help us. Because you're decent and kind, and you feel rather sorry for us. Although . . ." Her eyes questioned mine without apparent rancor. "You don't really like us much . . . not as a lump sum."

"It's not anything . . ."

"You find us snooty and stand-offish." She sliced straight through my weak attempt at protest. "And, of course, you're quite right . . . we are. It irritates you that we don't seem sufficiently grateful to you for coming all that way to fight with us . . ." I could feel my face growing warm: she knew it all, had it down pat. "You want to be kind and American-generous, and then worry about us being offended by what looks like charity, making us, thereby, even more stiff-necked." She tempered uncompromising words with a soft smile. "Correct?"

"I may only offer George Washington's apocryphal response to another loaded question . . . 'I cannot tell a lie'."

Heather nodded. "The cherry tree."

I was impressed. "Where did you learn about that?"

"In school . . ." The smile became a grin. "We do know about you . . . from a distance. It's only seeing you close to that's a shock."

"Ouch," I said. And, "I'm sorry. About you being correct."

"And *I'm* sorry for such shameless poking about in your private thoughts." She was looking contrite. "Are you furious with me?"

"More curious, let's say. Although it's all a bit scary."

"It needn't be," Heather insisted. "There's no malice in it, you know. Not with you . . . a friend."

"Well, that helps." I asked again, "how do you do it?"

"If I tell you, will you promise me not to laugh?"

"I never would."

She said quietly, "I'm supposed to be fey."

It was a term I had come across before, something from popular fiction, mushy romances. Old biddies in darkened rooms with tarot cards, reading teacups, holding séances . . . 'is anybody *there*?' Not quite what you hoped to hear from the girl who had captured your attention and imagination.

The slick, superficial side of me longed to come up with some smart-aleck response. Which would have been inexcusable. Even if Heather was talking hogwash, it was not my place to point that out to her, and most certainly not at this early and tentative stage of the game. Yet, an awareness of that could not halt the question forming in my mind . . . was there something that was not quite right about the lovely Heather Granger?

Instead, I wondered, "who says so?"

"Everyone who knows me." It was a flat statement, with nothing coy or affected about it. "Friends and relatives. Well-meaning but tactless aunts. Chums at school telling me, as though they saw it as a compliment."

She had been hurt before, and I was glad then that I had not shot off my face.

"The thing is . . ." she began, and faltered.

"It's okay, Heather," I urged. "You can say it to me."

"All right, then . . . it *is* so." But her answering tone was defensive now. "True, more or less. I know this."

"Well, yeah . . ."

"A child of nature, or so I'm told." Her laughter contained a shrill note. "Under the moon's influence. A wild, free spirit."

Once more I found myself locked in a struggle with my mean-spirited side, against the mocking comparisons: moon, lunar, lunatic . . . screwball? Until I could beat down such thinking, declining to accept that Heather, wacky-English or not, was insane with it. I did not mind wacky-English, an acceptable part of the package. There, though, it must end, the line drawn indelibly.

I drew it by telling Heather, "if that's you, then it's fine with me. Wouldn't have it any other way."

She frowned, her eyes moving over my face, and I made myself look back at her steadily.

Until she said very quietly, "Denney? Really?"

"It's been said, and every word was meant." I made myself go right on looking at her, revealing nothing of inward turmoil: soon, in time, I *would* come to believe, and to accept without question. And consoled myself with the thought that that was very much what I wanted to be able to do . . .

She leaned across the table then, offering her face, and, once more, our mouths met and joined. Her lips were parting, and I heard her breath catch . . .

Someone coughed.

We broke apart, and the proprietress was watching us with stony disapproval. "Will there be anything else?"

The sour face, the banality of the enquiry, induced immediate laughter. "Do you have anything better on offer?"

Heather, with shaking shoulders, averted her face quickly.

"There's a time and place, you know," the woman informed me severely.

Heather began to choke. "Oh, dear . . ."

"Care to tell us," I wondered. "Where and when?"

"We really don't appreciate that sort of thing here . . ."

"Whatever that sort of thing may be!" Laughter was gone: I was coldly furious now. "Which, we notice, didn't prevent you sneaking up to peek." I detested the woman and her smugly-bodiced hypocrisy.

"Kindly do not adopt that tone with me."

"No? Would you rather that I turned really nasty?"

She turned to stare accusingly at Heather. "You, at least, ought to be one to know better."

Heather, speechless, looked back at her, her eyes vivid with suppressed laughter.

Our bill was slammed down. From my billfold I withdrew a big white Bank of England five-pound note. The woman stared at it. "I can't possibly change *that*."

"Business that bad, huh?" Heather, forsaking restraint, giggled openly. "I can see why if this is the way you treat all your customers." I shoved the money toward her. "You want to be paid . . . right, I'm paying. Good, solid sterling currency."

She protested weakly, "it'll take all my cash float."

"Your problem, lady."

"No, wait. Here . . ." Heather felt in the pocket of her mac, and produced a ten-shilling note. "Please take this."

"Hey!" I objected. "I'm the one taking *you* out to tea, remember?"

"You can pay me back." She shook her head at me, a warning. "It really is better this way. Truly."

"I'll fetch your change." The woman stalked off, stiff-backed. I called after her, intentionally rude, "sure hope you're not looking for a tip." Her pace quickened. I said to Heather, "you're not to pay. That's just not right."

"It's cheap at the price." Her laughter rang out freely now. "Believe me, I'd have gladly paid much more for that little diversion."

*

We had cycled for a mile before Heather wondered, "are you still livid?"

"Some," I allowed. "With old Sourpuss, though, not you."

I stopped pedaling, and she pulled in beside me. "And you're not cross with me for paying?"

"I do feel several kinds of damned fool," I confessed. "Money in my pocket, yet you have to bail me out."

"It's something you couldn't be expected to know."

"What something?"

"That five pounds, here, is quite a lot of money," she replied. "For many, it amounts to a week's pay. Other people get less."

I did some swift mental arithmetic, and was shocked and humbled by the realization that, in 1944, in a war that brought a perverse kind of prosperity after the lean years of the Depression, twenty dollars a week could be a fair salary. "You're right. I didn't know."

"You don't see all that many fivers around. And then, when someone starts flashing them about . . ."

"I did not *flash*!" I was newly stung by the choice of expression. "All I was trying to do was pay my way, and that was legal tender in payment of a debt. I never once imagined that it would start a God damned international incident!"

"Keep your hair on," Heather advised coolly.

I sighed in gusty exasperation. "You try and do the right thing, meet your obligations, and what happens? You get told how dumb you are, and that you flash your money around!" I was in full stride, giving free rein at last to much bottled-up resentment. "What the hell do you people *want* of us? All we did was come to help out. And all because our President allowed your Prime Minister to sweet-talk him into beating the Germans first. We never had any real beef with the Germans. Germans didn't bomb Pearl Harbor. Yet we get treated like hicks . . ." A little startled, I reflected . . . you're really letting it all go, boy. "If you don't want us here, then just come out in the open and say so. Plenty of other places where we'd all sooner be. But don't be two-faced. Don't take what we have to offer, then turn round and kick us in the teeth!"

A silent half-mile went by.

I ventured, "guess I got a little het up back there."

"One might say so," Heather agreed with commendable tact. She glanced back at me without expression. "Feeling better now?"

"Once again it's time to say sorry."

"That's not what I mean, or expect. I don't find fault with you, Denney. You did exactly right. But you're not familiar with our silly, illogical ways." Her tone was very dry. "You see? I can concede that we are all those things, and more. Just that, for the future, you should know."

There it was again, her talk, so tantalizing, of a future. The kind of talk to help restore good humor. "I'd like to hear more of your ideas on this bright, shiny future, please."

"Just that, in it . . ." She gave me a glance of mock severity. "We don't use fivers to pay for a three bob tea. If you're snowed under with them, it might be better to change a few at the bank first."

"That seems really weird," I grumbled. "You go and mint the fool things, then act as though you're scared of them."

"But, with us, you see . . ." She remained patient with me. "Ten shillings is a sizeable sum, and a pound more so. Even in London, which is expensive, if you're careful, you can get through a weekend on a pound, and still have bus fare on Monday morning. Very few people find fivers in their pay packets. In fact . . ." She chuckled. "Those who might expect to are usually above such mundane things as pay packets. Fivers are only for the Ritz and the Savoy and Claridge's. Into which the majority of us Great Unwashed seldom venture." Her eyes were teasing now. "Unless invited by rich Yanks, or Rebels."

"I'll make a note," I vowed. "You and me, we'll penetrate those sacred halls."

"That would be lovely." But the response was merely polite, and I told myself, pleased, that she was indifferent to all that. Unlike so many girls anywhere and everywhere, out for all they could get. It was good to think of Heather as not being among their number.

She went on to explain, "people can get into a flap over anything larger than a ten bob note. Even with them, if you offer one to a bus conductor, he won't be awfully pleased with you. And then when they see you with a great handful of fivers . . ."

"One," I corrected her firmly. "*One* lousy fiver."

"All right, one then," she conceded. "But they'll still think, rightly or wrongly, here's one more Yank chucking his weight about." She met my gaze squarely as she stated, "I don't want other people thinking that of you. Because it wouldn't be true, or right."

While delightful to hear, that could chasten also. I knew very well of the many and frequent English gripes about us and our ways, and of the dismissive responses to them of my aggrieved compatriots. Not all of us gave offence, but enough did so to get us all noticed, then tarred indiscriminately with the same brush. To the indignant café proprietress, I would have been revealed beyond all question as just one more loudmouth, know-it-all *Yank* . . .

Heather and I went skimming side by side down a long gradient, freewheeling with the wind in our faces. Far off in the distance before us Tiverell Lacey lay sprawled in the late afternoon sunlight, looking tranquil and changeless to my unaccustomed foreign eyes. And that, I considered then, could well be our biggest stumbling block in this place: we *were* the foreigners. Something that was not hard for us to overlook; that, for all of the vexations and occasional abrasiveness, I had not thought much of until that moment. As a native New Yorker, I could find myself more out of place in West Virginia than in Essex, England. A citizen of one of two countries—I recalled the ironic quip—divided by a common language. Between Manhattan and West Virginia, one could question realistically that supposed link of language.

Where the English were concerned, I decided, a major troubling factor lay in the indelible awareness that we Americans had had the temerity to win our breakaway war, something that could not be forgotten by the defeated side, nor wholly forgiven. Never mind the legends of redcoats marching out of Yorktown with the honors of battle, played down to the waiting evacuation ships by the fifes and drums of the victors. In the end, all that stayed in mind—and lodged in the craw—was the certainty of having been roundly licked by a crowd of undisciplined, raggedy-ass Colonials, and the Crown humbled. Hard, always, for the vanquished to go on living with something like that.

The Germans, too, had stayed wild over the events of 1918-1919, which was one of the big reasons why we were back here in 1944. The French were said to smart still over the beating they had taken from the British at Québec. Enough, some said, to threaten the future undoing of Canada, that most amiable of nations.

We were no different, I remembered. Eighty years on, the coals of resentment smoldered still in the heart of the old Confederacy, and we damned Yankees, kidding or not, went right on calling them Rebels. While they flew their little defiant Stars and Bars banners that bore slogans like 'Forget . . . HELL!' The very fact of winning placed us forever in the victors' quandary. Cast down here in this latest conflict we paid the steep price demanded of brash upstarts . . .

Over beyond the village, the airbase was now in view, the camouflaged hangars and control tower, the spread of lesser buildings, a wide circle of dully-painted B-26s parked on their hardstands. Right down the middle, bisecting the whole, the dark ruled thread of the single runway.

There were three Marauders in the landing pattern with their wheels lowered; perhaps those which we had watched departing earlier.

The steady rumble of their throttled-down engines drifted over to us: in my mind's eye I saw the pilots busy over the controls, the crews strapped down tight, telling their beads, sweating out the approach and landing. Hoping for the best from the goofball in the driving seat . . .

Heather called back, "let's wait here and watch them land."

Dismounted, I placed my arm around her slim shoulders. "You'd better look out or you'll get bitten by the flying bug."

"I might enjoy that." She smiled at me, and we stood there together until the returned aircraft had reached their hardstands.

"A training flight, I should think." I explained, "there was no mission called for today."

"I'm glad. Otherwise, we wouldn't have had this."

"No . . ."

"It's been a lovely afternoon," Heather said.

"In every possible way."

"Even old Sourpuss?"

"Sure . . . why not? She was good for a few laughs."

The anger had drained away: I felt good, and close to Heather, experiencing a kind of inner glow that might have been the beginnings of love. I held her within the circle of my arm, and she did not try to withdraw; and *could* it be that I was falling headlong for this fey, oddball young woman? Certainly she would be—like the popular song said—so easy to love.

I was no stranger to infatuation, to puppy love, and this was not at all as those had been. This was sudden, and soon, but nonetheless real. And, given reality, what did soon matter? So what that it was less than twenty four hours since she had quizzed me about my name, and I had gotten all mean with her? In a war when one day could encompass a lifetime, and reach its end in a single blazing instant, was twenty four hours really too little, or, as I preferred now to see it, time a-plenty? That, in so short an interval, one could find oneself deeply smitten by a desirable female who worked her magic for you, and on you.

I would have liked very much then to sound Heather out by declaring my thoughts and feelings, and knew, dispiritingly, that I would do no such thing; that this moment was not the right one. Which led on the next worrying question . . . would there ever be a right moment?

I offered, poor substitute for what was weighing on my mind, "I really do regret that bust-up back there. Hope it didn't spoil things for you."

She pressed closer then, saying, "I enjoy being with you too much for that to happen."

"That's good for an old soldier's morale." I squeezed her shoulders gratefully.

She said, "it's not simply to do with your being American, and those things that attract us to you people . . ." 'You people', this time, did not rankle. "Just you, and it wouldn't matter at all if you were a broke English Tommy, or . . . a Hottentot. Only who you are, and what you are, and the things you do," she insisted. "All of which interest me."

I noticed the way in which she stressed certain words: 'what' and 'are' and 'you' and 'do', and for no reason upon which I could have put a finger, felt once more the stirring of that faint, inexplicable unease. And pushed it impatiently aside, telling her, "with that for a testimonial, looks like I can't go wrong. Just as long as I keep on doing those things."

"You will, and you'll have the time," Heather informed me with calm assurance. "All the time needed for flying your missions."

"That's pretty wonderful to hear . . ." I hoped that any lingering traces of doubt were not apparent to her, and that, in her unnerving way, she was not reading me 'like the proverbial book'.

She almost floored me then when she wanted to know, "do you often think about being hurt, or killed?"

"My . . ." I answered edgily, "you certainly don't pull your punches."

She had moved, unhesitating, on to some tricky ground where

all airmen feared to tread. She was, though, Heather, and she had asked me, and I could see no way in which to duck out of answering.

"Sure, it comes to mind, I guess. It's a war, and you're in it, and things like that happen to people." I drew a breath. "As I discovered over Cherbourg."

"Would it be all right now to ask about that?" She turned her intent gray gaze on me.

"Yes, okay . . . why not? It's been on the B.B.C." I paraphrased that morning's newscast. "Medium bombers of the United States Ninth Air Force carried out attacks on selected targets at Le Havre, Cherbourg and Brest, causing extensive damage to enemy installations. Three American aircraft failed to return." Adding, "those were other Bomb Groups. *We* all got back." 'Rio Rita', down and burning, written-off at Tangmere, counted as 'getting back' . . .

"And so you will," Heather affirmed. "You'll see."

I smiled at her. "Is that the feyness talking?"

"If you like." She returned the smile with particular warmth. "Mein liddle schpell, remember? There, watching over you."

"And jolly glad of it we are, too." I responded happily to her lightening tone.

"Don't you dare make fun," she scolded. "You have to believe and trust. Hold on tight, and never let go."

I said, wondering, "you really mean this, don't you?"

"Oh, yes."

"Then I'll do just that . . . hold on." Even if it was a load of tripe, it was well-meaning tripe, and that should count for something. "A grip of steel."

"That's good, Denney." She looked pleased, but then returned in the next breath to her earlier theme, asking, "but how *was* it at Cherbourg? I don't mean the B.B.C. communiqué. You."

I tried my best to recall it for her, but the pictures would not stay still, shifting behind my eyes, a blurred kaleidoscope of dimming impressions. Like trying to recall pain, or a dream. "It was . . . confusing. Strangely slow-moving, yet, at the speeds we fly at, all over in seconds. There was time for a few things to register . . ." I paused, wondering if Heather would see my words as boasting, something more that the English claimed to dislike about Americans. "Finding, once we were there and on the job, that I could function. I'd been worrying about that beforehand." She nodded seeming understanding. "How I might be when it came to the moment of truth. And finding that I was holding up pretty much the same as everyone else." That part, at least, could be recaptured: Major Ambruster's clean white cumulus, confidently prophesied, mingling with the flak smudges. Through which you were compelled to ride in to the target, every move and thought and response dictated for you by the irascible and inflexible O'Connor. Until, with his own relief undisguised, O'Connor yelled 'bombs away', revealing his frailty and humanity. Laughing aloud on the intercom, telling me, "now, Lieutenant, kindly fly our spry young asses outta here!" Delivering us for a while longer from evil.

"What sticks in mind," I said to Heather. "Is that first full realization that school's out, and this is the real world. Over the target is for real . . . no more practice bombing ranges. Those men down there using real guns and ammunition, and using them well. After all the practice *they've* had from here to Moscow and back. When all you are is the most raw beginner."

"But each time," Heather pointed out with simple logic. "You'll be more experienced and sure of yourself. The first time is always the worst. That rule applies in any situation."

It would still take luck, though, and lots of it. It did not matter a hoot how good and experienced you were if you were not lucky. The old-stagers who had ridden the road so many times were always quick to tell you that.

And Heather was saying, " . . . until the day comes when you don't have to go anymore."

Impulse made me ask then, "and after that day? When I'm free to go home. Will you and your spell still be there for me?"

"Oh, the spell will be," she assured me, and I wondered if she had missed my deliberate nuance, or, more depressingly, chosen to overlook it. "Once it's there, it's for keeps. I'm good at putting them on, but I haven't quite got the knack for taking them off again."

"Then I'll just have to learn to live with being a frog, or whatever." I made myself laugh, and tried again, pushing a little harder this time. "Which will be bearable if I can have you around."

And then, for the first time, her steady regard of me faltered. "I think . . ." She polished distractedly at her gleaming handlebars. "We'd be better off to wait and see. Don't you?" Her declared faith in the future, it appeared, did not run quite to those lengths.

I puzzled over this sudden withdrawal, the abrupt switch just when everything looked to be shaping up so well; what could have brought it about? She had been the one to raise the topic of futures, yet went coy on me at the slightest attempt to pin her down. And I wondered what it was that Heather feared?

FIVE

FLIGHT LOG.
DATE: 5/16/44.
AIRCRAFT TYPE: B-26C.
NO. or REG: 43-2693.
PILOT-IN-COMMAND: Self.
SECOND PILOT: Nil.
CREW: O'Connor, Devine, Cohn, Smithson, Deeks, Patecki.
FLIGHT ROUTE: T.L.-Antwerp-T.L.
FLIGHT HOURS: 2.35.
HOURS VISUAL: 2.10.
HOURS INSTRUMENT: 0.25.
HOURS NIGHT: Nil.
OBSERVATIONS: Target shipping and railroad center partly obscured, unable assess bombing results clearly. Flak heavy. Fighter opposition stymied by escorting P-47s. Two MEs seen shot down. Marauder 'Li'l Brick Outhouse' destroyed over target area, two parachutes observed. Marauder 'Abbie 'n' Slats' ditched in sea 10 miles off Orford Ness. Crew in life raft. Orbited crash site and directed R.A.F. Rescue to position. Returned T.L. Minor flak damage left wing, left propeller. TWO DOWN—THIRTY THREE TO GO!

*

'Dear Mother,

'One mission completed already, and now a second. I think with longing of numbers squaring; one, two, four, sixteen. My tour over almost before it had begun. Some dreamer!

'We have been once to Cherbourg in Northern France (I can tell you this now that it is fait accompli). About the same distance over water as across Lake Erie from Cleveland to Canada. Distances here can be confusing. The mileage we have made together in the past by car from home to Buffalo to visit with Aunt Sarah would take us from where we are here to Hamburg, or almost to Zurich in Switzerland. Over two, sometimes three, countries.

'Our second run was to Antwerp in Belgium, we really are getting to see the world all right! Across the North Sea which is wider than the English Channel, although the point where we crossed over was pretty narrow. Not long out of sight of land, although it seemed long, especially coming back. You sit there waiting for England to show, wondering if it ever will. Like Lindbergh over the Atlantic on one little engine, and with less than half our airspeed, hoping to find Ireland in all that water. I still wonder how he could set out deliberately to do that. I get itchy over a hundred miles of water with two engines and sixteen times the horsepower!

'Antwerp was, in A.A.F. vernacular, a milk-run. We went, we saw, and if we did not exactly conquer, then at least we came away again.

'What we found was a sooty city and port close to a tricky estuary choked with islands, mud-flats and sandbars, although, because of cloud, we could not see a lot. The Germans duly fired their guns at us, and some out-dated fighters came up for a quick sniff. We left our calling cards, decamped at a high rate of knots, and were back home before the pubs opened. (Pubs being public houses, all the same saloons or low taverns.)

'All said and done, not such a bad old war.
Three meals a day, bed and board, some
recreational flying now and then, and back for tea
and cricket on the village green. What they refer
to here as very jolly civilized.'

Reading my scrawled lines and thinking of the Happy Warrior
image. Which, for the Folks Back Home, was about as good as
you could make it.

There can be no easy or witty way in which to describe the
knot in the gut as the Dutch coast appears ahead; the pale, sandy
mouths of the Scheldt River with its islands checking in on time
against the map: Walcheren, Schuwen, Noord Beveland, Tholen,
Overflakkee. Listening to O'Connor, never one to pass up on a
good word-play, "any time now, girls, we're gonna be over *flak*kee,
and then some!"

Islands like broken plate shards on the kitchen floor. Each
with its batteries of winking guns popping out puffs of dirty
cotton batting. Over flak-kee . . . yeah!

How do you tell of that in your mother's weekly Happy
Warrior letter, and make it sound like good, clean fun? Answer:
you don't, because there is no way to, so that part gets left out.

Along with the high crossing of the Westerscheldt to the
Belgian frontier, to the target city ten miles beyond. With more
dangerous, soul-destroying straight and level flight at O'Connor's
command, the flak carpet looking thick enough to drop the
wheels and land on.

Likewise, there is no light-hearted way to recount the shock
effect of your first meeting with German fighters. Lean, sharklike
machines with darts of fire at their wing edges and around the
propeller spinners. So terrifyingly *swift*, and yet, with scared eyes
and mind going into overdrive, seeming slow, with time to note
small details, the crosses and tail swastikas, letters, numbers,
geschwardern emblems. The mottled camouflage on their upper
surfaces, then, as they roll away from the attack, exposing pale
bellies the color of summer skies. And one close enough for a

long-drawn microsecond's glimpse of the enemy pilot's face, our eyes meeting, locking on . . .

Assuredly, Mother, with her rigid perception of what is right and proper, would prefer not to hear the details of 'Li'l Brick Outhouse' taking the direct hit: one second an airplane and crew, the next a flame-dappled smokeball as the shell blew the ready-fused bombs in the belly. Seven gone . . . snap! Michelmore, the pilot, and Brewer, the bombardier: the navigator with a Slovak name that was all consonants. At least, if nothing else, quickly over . . . they would never have known in that infinitesimal gap between the quick and the dead. Something to be said for that . . .

Until, unbelievably, the two 'chutes opening and spreading to drift clear of the downward-tumbling wreckage, floating through the flak and the fighters, the ongoing, elephantine bomber stream. Doll figures suspended from shrouds and risers. As the last hot scraps of 'Li'l Brick Outhouse' went teeter-tottering into Belgium.

Mother, deploring vulgarity and the too-frankly physical, would not care to learn of her only son with bowels turned to water, and sour, dry-bones mouth, watching the Messerschmitt 109 as it flicked with contemptuous ease through the Thunderbolt screen. With himself in its sights.

Only to have the cannon tracer pass him by to slam instead into 'Abbie 'n' Slats' (Sutherland, Klein, Battersby, Killian, Le Maire, Fisher, Eberhart). Setting an engine ablaze, killing Klein on the spot, costing Le Maire his right arm, torn from him by a cannon shell. The 109 half-rolling on down, pointing its vulnerable fish belly to the sky. The distinctive clipped wingtips and externally-strutted tail of an early-model 'Emil'. Obsolete but still deadly, able to bypass the P-47s at three hundred and fifty knots, and shoot the shit out of you. And have shit shot in turn as a '47 from the high screen drops like a streamlined rock and blows the old-timer to rags and tatters . . .

How Mother would wince at the mention of sickness, bile in the throat, the swollen bladder and rancid armpits; the tongue gone thick as an old, dried-out boot sole. Or of the certain knowledge blossoming within of personal cravenness, the shameful relief amounting to something like joy that it had been 'Abbie 'n' Slats', and not oneself.

On the heels of that comes the reflex of guilt, the desire, strong and urgent, to make amends, leading in turn to quixotic action. On the homeward leg, out over the North Sea, I move 'Big Apples' in close to the stricken B-26, a little to one side, slightly behind, from where I can observe the feathered propeller, the fire not contained, a fierce white wind-torn glow inside the ring cowl. Worrying that the flames will reach the fuel tanks, or weaken the wing to the point of collapse. For those, and a hundred other reasons, I elect to stay there, close and watchful. In the main, though, it is because it *is* them and not us. Letting down in tight formation as 'Abbie 'n' Slats' loses height slowly, with all of us pooling our wills in the attempt to body-English the doomed Marauder as far as the home runway. Until, in its final exhaustion, it drops into the sea within sight of the friendly coast.

We stayed on then, paying our due, circling, calling on the distress channel for a rescue launch, or one of the R.A.F.'s tough little Walrus amphibians to land and take them all on board.

Turning and turning over the slow sinking, over the bright yellow raft being launched into slapping waves. Counting with relief the full seven of them in the raft; two limp shapes having to be dragged from the water. Thinking . . . they've got wounded. Not yet knowing that Klein is dead, and that they will not leave him to the sea . . .

Hearing gladly at last the cheery English voice on the frequency, "have you in sight now, Two-Six-Niner-Three."

A stubby, high-winged Westland Lysander of Coastal Command coming up at a bumbling hundred knots— Lindbergh's speed—to take over and circle in our place. Telling of the launch already on its way out from Felixstowe.

All the things that can never be written into the weekly Happy Warrior letter home to Mom.

SIX

Heather sounding breathless on the line. "Where are you calling from?"

"Somewhere in England."

Hearing her woman's laugher; such a nice sound after the all-male ugliness of Antwerp. "You *silly* clot!"

I amended, "from the payphone on the base."

"Are you all right?"

"I'm *always* all right." The Happy Warrior mood lingered still.

"And did you fly today?"

"Yep."

"Oh . . ."

"It was a snap . . . easy." Once safely back on the ground, you could almost kid yourself that that was true. "I can't tell you where yet in case Adolf's listening on the line." I added, "but the spell worked beautifully."

She laughed again. "What did I tell you?"

"That it would work beautifully. So now I'm even more of a believer. And I'd very much like to meet you, please, and demonstrate the full extent of my belief."

*

A deuce-and-a-half was making the run to Colchester. The PFC driver declared himself more than happy to drop me off in the village. Right outside the pub.

I sat in the saloon lounge waiting for Heather. It was early, and the door stood open to let in the evening sunlight. There were men in uniform there drinking, mostly Americans from the airbase, one or two British servicemen on furlough mingling with the darts-playing locals. The old place smelled cozily of wax polish, of decades of liquor soaked into seasoned wood, of a sweet, heavy tobacco called 'Digger Shag'.

It was great to be there, back, alive, from Antwerp. Secure . . . for now. Great also—the continuing shame for allowing such thinking notwithstanding—not to be one of the crew of 'Li'l Brick Outhouse', dead, or hurt, or traveling now under guard to some grim Stalag Luft in Silesia. Good not to be Le Maire . . . or Klein.

So sorry, I thought, waiting alone there for my girl to show up. So very, truly, deeply sorry for you all. But no less glad—forgive me—not to be of your mourned and honored company . . .

An outbreak of wolf-whistles; I looked up quickly, and she was crossing the room toward me, smiling, and my heart keeled right over at the sight of her.

Young, sparkling, and English-pretty in her pale blue sweater and tweed skirt. I rose to take her hands, and she reached across to kiss me lightly, which brought forth more whistles as the locals pulled slow noses from their pints. She told me pleasingly, "it's lovely to see you." Wondering, "have you been waiting very long?"

"Long enough to heighten anticipation."

"Hope it was worth it . . ." She flushed. "That I don't disappoint?"

"That could never happen."

I went over to the bar to get her shandy. When I returned, she said, "well, you're *looking* all right, anyway."

I put down her drink, and touched her hand. "I've got everything I need now to make me look just fine."

But she was shaking her head. "Actually, I was thinking more of where you've been today."

"It was Antwerp . . . I can tell you now. Der Führer's hung up. It'll be on the B.B.C. later."

"Are you allowed to tell me about it?"

"Oh, you know." I shifted uncomfortably. "In and out . . . boom-boom."

But her eyes were eager, almost avid, as she pressed, "was it like Cherbourg?"

"No, not like that . . ." Her seeming hunger to be told of those sordid things, I found, was ever-so-slightly getting my goat. I had no desire to recount it, because that only brought it all flooding back: the 109 boring in, firing; the man who might have killed me now dead in my place. 'Li'l Brick Outhouse'. Klein. Le Maire. My own sick terror and gutlessness. And yet, was that any reason to get ticked-off with Heather . . . ?

She was telling me, grave-eyed, "Denney, it's only my concern for you. And, possibly, my way of sharing? I can't be there with you, but, afterwards, I think of how you can talk to me, and that that may comfort you a little?"

It was the perfect explanation, and it disarmed me on the spot. "You can't be serious about wanting to share *that*?"

"If it'll help you, then yes, I am."

"All the same, it's not something you go around sharing with people."

"Then it must have been bad," she stated quietly. "Certainly worse than you've been pretending with me."

"Okay, let's face it . . . it did have some pretty mean moments." She had me cornered, and I tried to wriggle free. "Hey, what is this? We're meant to be here for a chat and a drink."

"But we're chatting, aren't we?" Heather pointed out reasonably. "We have our drinks."

There was, it appeared, to be no way out. "I give up," I said.

She made herself more comfortable, crossing shapely legs, resting her chin on her hand, watching me expectantly. "So?"

As with my mother's letter, though, I would not tell her of 'Li'l Brick Outhouse', or of the carnage inside 'Abbie 'n' Slats'. For her, only the diluted information that we had had two shot down. And of the enemy fighters, and how nerve-jangling they had been . . .

"The way they come at you head to head like that, and so incredibly fast." And they were there, then, back inside my head, like a blurred camera gun sequence. "Opening up to blast at you with everything they've got. Then gone, almost before you realize they were there. Our combined speeds must've been nigh on six hundred miles an hour. And that's really motoring."

"Yes, it is," Heather agreed with her eyes on me.

"You spot them, or else someone yells out 'fighters at two o'clock, or ten, or twelve'." I explained the clock system to her, the airplane's nose at twelve, the tail six, wingtips three and nine respectively. "Add 'high' or 'low' or 'level', then you know where to look, and aim your guns. At little hurtling dots like midges. Until they grow wings, and the wings are lit up by gunfire. And for what's the tiniest fraction of time, yet which feels like for ever, they fill the windshield, and you start to think they'll wind up in the cockpit with you . . ." I was in full spate, and could not have stopped, not once I found how good it was to talk it out of the system and into the open.

And Heather hung on every word, her expression rapt, eyes aglow, as I said, "then they're gone, and it's as though it never happened. There, and not there, leaving no sign behind . . ." Other than a spreading ball of dirty smoke and flame, two parachutes drifting in the massed slipstream; another B-26 with white-hot fire under one cowling. And what lay behind her deeply-earnest expression as I talked on: what did she see, and how did it affect her? At that moment, was she even aware of *me* as I rushed on to my close? "And so you sit up straight again, and try and take stock. Get your people on the intercom to call in any hits they can see, or report on anyone hurt. You take a look outside to check on how the other aircraft are making out."

"And what do you see?" Heather wondered softly.

What indeed? The memories were seared deep, and would be there with you for as long as you were permitted to live, short time or long. "Oh, this and that," I said, somewhat purged by then, and all through with talking, sick and tired of it now. "It'll be on the radio. Just tune in."

"I knew already that you'd lost planes," she said then.

I eyed her askance, wondering about *more* clairvoyance? "How did you come by that?"

"Denney, I can count. You either land or take off right over the labs where I work. One way or the other, we get you."

"You're very observant."

"And I remember things I'm told," she said. "And, being observant, I observe this minute that you're troubled, and perhaps you'll speak of that, and again, perhaps not, so I shan't pursue it. As long as you appreciate that I *do* see things, and register them."

"Okay, fine." I wanted to know, "what was that about counting?"

"I was at work when you left, and I went outside to watch . . ." Her face was somber. "I wanted to try and pick you out. And I was there later when you came back, and counted the aeroplanes circling to land, and that was when I knew." I nodded acceptance.

"We were the fourth to take off, and the last to land."

"That was some time after everyone else, wasn't it?"

"We'd been keeping company with a lame duck until they ditched off the coast. One of the two that didn't make it."

"Why you?" Heather demanded.

"Well, why *not*?" A sudden and unexpected spurt of anger hit me, leavened with the same sense of guilt felt before over the fate of 'Abbie 'n' Slats'; the half-belief haunting me still that it should have been us on the receiving end. It was gone almost immediately, although not fast enough to let me bite back the harsh retort.

"I'm sorry." She gazed down at her clasped hands. "I should have known better than to ask something like that."

"I'm still kind of edgy, that's all." In fact, the nerves were wire-taut, and I was having to work at it to still my trembling hands. To make it up to Heather, I explained the need to shepherd 'Abbie 'n' Slats' across the open sea, and then to wait when they went down, calling for assistance, marking the spot. But leaving out the details of Klein and Le Maire.

"And now, how are you . . . *really*?" The apologetic note remained in her voice. "I want to know . . . in fact I *need* to."

I admitted, "a little shook-up, as you can imagine." I laughed, although it was not one bit funny. "Your first Jerry fighter experience plays havoc with your grammar." And added dryly, "it's a thrill a minute, this business."

SEVEN

We all knew that the Invasion was imminent, although not yet when or where.

The preparations were evident wherever you went: tanks and guns parked in rows, trucks by the thousand, half-tracks, small mountains of artillery shells lining the country roadsides, concealed under spreading trees, in woodlands, behind hedgerows, or swathed in camouflage netting. So many airfields thick with parked gliders, tug aircraft, troop transports, all cheek by jowl. Every harbor, estuary and creek mouth jammed from shore to shore with moored assault craft.

The whole country was buzzing, charged with expectancy: 'any minute now' was the favored catchphrase. But the minute passed, and was followed by more that swelled into hours and days and weeks, and still we did not go. The waiting was possibly less arduous for the flying crews. We, at least, remained actively at war each day while the ground soldiers, and the sailors, trained and trained. In our Squadron, a batch of missions was called back to back, for 'Big Apples' and her crew numbers three through six. Two that were relatively easy, two more that fell into the category of 'tough'. L'Orient, on the Biscay coast, was one of the tough ones. Where they sent us to bomb the U-boat pens.

Much like Cherbourg, except that L'Orient was worse, and farther away. Where, once arrived, the flak was concentrated, deadly, and mathematically, almost beautifully, accurate. I took us in at O'Connor's command, willing myself to hear only his shrill, irate carping. Letting my eyes see nothing but the erring instruments. There was NO flak; there were NO vicious, hating Germans down on the ground with ME in their sights, trying their God damnedest to kill me. That was only the ugly dream from which I would waken, and then everything would be fine.

By a regime of willful and persistent self-deception I kept on going at L'Orient. Because the truth, all the way in from I.P. to target, was too grisly to be faced.

Until O'Connor gave us 'bombs away', and returned control to me, and I could stand 'Big Apples' on a wingtip to circle widely away around the Brest peninsula, heading back to Plymouth and Salisbury and Andover, avoiding trigger-happy London before the final long descent across the easy Essex flatlands. One of those who made it.

Of our number that day, from L'Orient, 'Over Easy', 'Tubbs' Thumper' and 'Dinah Might?' did not return.

*

We flew to St. Denis near Paris to bomb railroad yards, and there was some light flak directed at us from Abbeville, Amiens and Compiègne. Even so, the mission had a holiday atmosphere to it; a bright, clear day through which we sailed like a crowd of gabby tourists on a bus, every man loud on the intercom.

Over Amiens, Sergeant Cohn in the top turret appointed himself our guide, pointing out in solemn detail the old Somme battlefields of the earlier war in which he had a declared interest. There, he said, were the pale chalk scars in long lines that were the marks of filled-in trenches. A nondescript village in the near-distance was, we learned, Bellicourt. Where Cohn's old man, then a corporal of Infantry with Pershing's Rainbow Division, had been wounded in 1918 . . .

More light flak came up to greet us around Paris, but, with our recent raw memories of Cherbourg, Antwerp and L'Orient, this was, we agreed, a cakewalk. When O'Connor gave me the heading from the I.P., I cruised it like a training flight, straight down the slot. Turning away smoothly as we dumped our load, a four-mission veteran with not a care in the world . . .

Later, in the truck, riding in from the hardstand, I felt pretty pleased with myself. I had been cool. My stomach had behaved. The strange conviction came to me that I had almost enjoyed it!

*

Next day, they gave us Caen, and a needed lesson in humility. Where, in a hurricane of flak, the fair illusions of St. Denis were shattered.

We hit the Luftwaffe airfield at Carpiquet, and were hit back hard for our pains. No fighters came up, and maybe there were none there, but the ground fire made up for that deficit, relentless and malignant from Deauville to the target and back again. A shell—*the* shell—blew 'Earley's Bird' apart, killing Jim 'Jubal' Earley, Melcher, De Santo, Corbin, Pryde, Sullivan and Scripps.

*

And then, as though in apology, we were handed a gift: Number Six was the archetypal milk-run, fast and low-level, down on the deck from the Kent coast to the complex of rail junctions and yards that made of St. Omer a primary target.

We caught the Germans napping, leaving behind our bombs with their two-minute delayed fuses, then rocketing on through town, throttles wide open, the big radials howling. Down low like that we could strafe as well, each B-26 with eleven guns blasting away around the clock, and the wonder of it that we did not shoot one another down and do the Germans' dirty work for them.

We swung around St. Omer, hedge-hopping joyously back to the sea, gunning the Jerry transport strung out on the highways, waggling our wings at French farmers working in their fields. There was hardly any flak; a few flustered machine guns letting fly belatedly, and no feared eighty eights that we could see, hear or feel. We had ourselves a marvelous time, and managed not to lose a man. Agreeing happily that, if they could all be like that, we would not mind at all if they doubled up on the number of missions to be flown.

Listening to our empty, blowhard talk, O'Connor, the old soldier, shook his head at us pityingly. "Some day, should we survive so long, maybe you poor, sad bastards will learn . . ."

*

Back safe from St. Omer, and the Squadron awarded a blissful forty eight hours of stand-down. There was steak for dinner, with the loud accusation that the steaks were mule-meat, and old mule at that, being vehemently denied by the much-aggrieved and put-upon mess sergeant. Who alleged that we were all low-lifes and ingrates, and wondered plaintively why he bothered to bust his balls.

Well-fed and more-or-less content, we could rest awhile, and go to work on getting some of the kinks out, mental and physical. It had been a hairy four days, *we* felt, whereas the true veterans discovered vast pleasure and amusement in informing us that we had seen nothing yet.

But this stand-down, we responded with irritable defiance, was not a whit more then our due. We were tired warriors, and refused to deny that we had earned this brief interlude of almost guaranteed life.

For me, it meant that I could shower and shave, and put on my best soldier suit, then go and telephone Heather to ask her to meet me, and not one obstacle foreseen in my path to prevent it.

Thinking with anticipatory pleasure of these things when Andy Devine came smirking into the Quonset. "Hey, you guys . . . know what? Stand-down's been *extended!*"

A reclining cynic nearby advised him to, "blow it out your ass!"

Andy looked around, wounded and accusing. "Sons of bitches like you just don't deserve no breaks. I should've kept the news to myself, and left you to sweat it out." He declared with heat, "it's official, anyhow. Right up there on the bulletin board, large as life, so you don't need to go takin' my word for it . . ." He gave a disdainful shrug that encompassed us all. "Go see for yourselves." About to turn his back, he could not resist the urge to elaborate. "It's so's they can paint up the airplanes."

We jeered our continuing disbelief at him, and he defended the assertion with resentful vigor. "They's each one gettin' painted up with stripes."

"Ah . . ." O'Connor tapped his nose, and winked. "I begin to get the drift now."

I did not, and demanded, "what stripes?"

"*Stripes* stripes for Christ's sakes! Candy stripes! Barber pole stripes! How the hell would I know what stripes, and, anyway, who gives a shit?" Andy was laughing at my bemused expression. "You seen one stripe, you seen 'em all. They gonna paint 'em round the wings and fuselages. Gonna make us look like zee-bras." He gave an exultant whoop. "Best news of all, it's gonna take 'em awhiles to get the job done. So, how's about that?"

O'Connor, looking wise, was nodding slowly. "It'll be the Invasion. What else?"

Andy challenged him, "what'll be?"

"The stripes, you dumb prick! One more big fat nail in Herr Schickelgruber's coffin."

Now it was Andy's turn to look baffled. "God damn it, what the hell kinda difference'll stripes make?"

"Son . . ." O'Connor squinted up at him with patient understanding. "Try and see the big picture. How, when the balloon goes up over there, there'll be more flyin' machines toolin' around, ours and theirs, than you can shake a stick at. Likewise, no end of nervous young fellas with itchy trigger fingers, and none of 'em too choosy about who or what they blast. So . . . *voilà, mesdames et messieurs*, we get painted-up with nice, high visibility stripes."

"Oh, yeah . . . I'm *sure!*" Andy snorted derision. "And that won't make us all that much easier to hit, right?"

"Now, what kind of negative way is that to be thinkin'?" O'Connor regarded him now with disfavor. "Handed time off on a plate, and all you can do is fret about your mortality?" His eyebrows flickered in agitation. "Ever stop to think that by the time these slow-pokes get through with their zebra paintin', this-here war might be over?"

"Sure thing," Andy retorted. "An' pigs might fly as well."

"Indeed they might, kid." O'Connor nodded mild agreement. "Although, I have to say, every time I take a look around this over-ripe G.I. dwellin' of ours, I get to thinkin' they do already."

*

Heather sounded pleased. "*How* long?"

"Three days . . . maybe four."

"That's *mar*-velous!"

"We think so, too." I asked her, "could we spend some of that good time together?"

"Tell me how much you'd like to spend."

"What would you say to all of it?"

"You *muffin*!" She laughed, then admitted, "I wouldn't mind that at all." And added prudently, "although, of course, we can't."

"I guess not."

We were cycling again. Heather had managed to borrow a bike for me, a vastly superior sports model with dropped handlebars, light and fast and able to take the steepest upgrades with ease.

We pedaled in pale sunlight that was speckled across with little friendly dabs of cumulus, the higher sky traced thickly with the vapor trails of heavy bombers returning from Europe.

In celebration of the fine weather, Heather was wearing trim blue slacks and a white sleeveless blouse; the sensible shoes of our first bike ride together yielding to summer sandals. Freed from the earlier peasant babushka, her dark hair blew out on the warm wind. I rode behind her, watching her with pleasure, and empty longing.

Empty because, knowing her better now, and more receptive to her shifting moods, I could discern that the time for more than companionship, the contact of eyes and hands, the occasional

kiss, was still . . . not yet. Instinct dictated that I must await my
cue: so far, no cue, nor the hint of one. For now, I could accept
that. The pain of wanting remained more sweet than frustrating.

I worked hard at the business of convincing myself that such
matters could not be hastened: I must be patient and high-
minded; lots of uplifting thoughts and cold showers. Until—as I
prayed she might—Heather sent me her signal. It was a policy
that might just have been more tolerable had not the very real
possibility of sudden serious injury, or violent death, existed for
me.

I would wonder also if I was being too timid; the male, it
was claimed, was meant to set the pace. Females, the worldly-
wise cocksmen would insist, despised the gentlemanly type deep
in their hearts, and would swiftly lose interest and look elsewhere.
That might be so, I felt, with the types of hefty, easy-going girls
who had packed the hangar on dance night. Heather was—*must
be*—the firm exception to that rule. With her, the more forceful
approach could never hope to succeed.

Right along with that belief went also my awareness of her
complex and baffling nature; the way that, with her, I could never
seem to figure out the right moves to make until it was too late.
We got on fine; were close and affectionate. Always, though, as
matters seemed to indicate signs of progress, the barriers would
shoot up. And I would be left once more with the hope—and
little to sustain it—that, at some time, somewhere, the barriers
would be there no longer. And that I might live long enough to
know of that time and place.

*

In an unknown village miles from the base a man sold us ice
cream from a pedal cart. Watery stuff made with powdered milk
and corn starch, not much like the remembered wares of the
Good Humor Man.

There was a sunny green where we could sprawl on the grass
and slurp our messy, melting cones, and Heather could conjure

up two bottles of warm beer from her bike pannier. "I thought . . . instead of another staid and potentially explosive afternoon tea . . . ?"

"Ice cream and beer." The brown liquid foamed and overflowed creamily when the stoppers were removed. "A weird and wonderful mixture."

"That's because we're a weird and wonderful people." I was awarded an ironic grin. "As you Yanks so enjoy telling us."

"Touché . . ." We drank smilingly under the warm sun, and I said then, "what I'd really like to do is take you out somewhere special."

"To paint the town red, you mean?"

"That's the general idea. If you'd care to?"

"Oh, I'm all for that," she declared, and laughed. "Like what, where and when?"

"Dinner, maybe? Somewhere that's really good. With posh English service and fine wine. If there's any to be had still in this weird and wonderful, austerity-only country of yours?"

Her answering glance was cool. "We're not totally backward, you know."

"Well said, that lady. Okay, then . . ." I told her, "say the word and we'll do it."

"Consider the word said, my lord."

"Although we'd better make it pretty soon. While this free time lasts." I suggested, "tonight, or tomorrow? Whenever?"

"Tomorrow," Heather decided. "Sounds lovely."

"Have to leave it to you to pick the place. Your knowledge and your choice."

"Careful. That could cost you a packet."

"You have unlimited credit up to a single five-pound note. Or, if you prefer, ten ten-shillings ones."

She knew of a place, and believed that I would like it. "A rare foreign experience for you."

"Funny thing," I mused then. "How I don't get the feeling of being foreign here."

The comment earned me a smirk. "That's because we're doing

to you exactly what we do to all our invaders. Romans, Saxons, Vikings, Normans . . . Yanks . . . we simply soak you up."

I foresaw a sudden problem. "Not likely that I'll be able to scare up a jeep this time, sorry." I suggested doubtfully, "I don't see how we can hit the town on bikes."

"There's a perfectly good bus," Heather pointed out. "And it runs quite late, so we'll be able to get back . . ." She looked concerned then. "Oh, dear."

"What's wrong?"

"The bus only goes through the village, not out to the aerodrome." She was looking downcast. "You may end your big evening out on Shanks's pony."

"Don't worry about it. After an evening with you, I'll be floating home on air." I invited, "so tell me about this place you know."

It was at Banxted, a nearby market town. Where there was an ancient inn which still 'did a good evening meal'. "And there may be wine," Heather half-promised. "Although I can't be certain." The inn had been a posting house once on the old highway from London to Norwich. "It's a bit swish and, I'm afraid, correspondingly pricey. Where British officers from the camps and airfields can take their ladies for decorous nights out."

"What about American officers?"

"I do feel that they might make a single exception for you." Her eyes were dancing. "And you'll be relieved to know it's a place where you can flash that fiver to your heart's content."

"In that case," I vowed. "I'll remember to bring my wad."

*

It was one more startling difference between England and the States. In England, it was just jim-dandy to take a girl to dinner by bus.

An aged vehicle with hard leather seats and grinding gears, smelling of diesel and dust and stale humanity, its driver aloof in his little separate cab, the conductor standing on the platform, swaying, and fingering moodily through a rack of different-colored tickets, and jotting figures on a clipboard. The ten-mile journey to Banxted, with detours, took forty minutes, and cost us ninepence each.

Heather had briefed me on the history of the inn, and its great age. Looking at it, I got the feeling that it must have been pretty old already when the *Mayflower* sailed away to Plymouth Rock.

We ducked our way through dark-timbered passages and over tilting flagstone floors that had been smoothed and polished by the centuries of passing feet. On the wooden lintel above a fireplace tall enough to stand in, the date '1547' had been deeply gouged, and I mused over the likelihood—uncertain—that, in 1547, New York had even been called New Amsterdam. There, in 1547, Columbus had still been recent news!

Heather had pre-booked, and we were led to a paneled lounge with mullioned windows standing open to a garden so classically English as to appear contrived, like an elaborate Hollywood set for some old world romance. All that was missing, it did seem, were Jeanette MacDonald and Nelson Eddy caroling a love duet.

"Well?" Heather's eyebrows lifted in enquiry. "Does sir approve?"

"It's like a whole different world," I said, half-awed by the place.

"The old after the new?"

I gazed around. "Manhattan may have been like this once, but not for long."

The lounge was not crowded: a few military officers accompanied by wives or girl-friends; two Canadian pilots with girls, who smiled and waved, and asked us, "how's she goin'?"

There was an elderly British officer with red flashes on his lapels whom I was pretty certain was a general. I was the sole American in evidence.

Guests were called in turn to their tables: our order was smoothly taken, and, yes, there was wine, a hoarded half-bottle for each couple. We pondered, and agreed on claret.

*

Dinner was lamb and green peas and new potatoes, with sherry trifle to follow. The claret was admirable. It was almost possible, in Banxted, to imagine that there was no war, no shortage of any kind.

We went back to the lounge for coffee, and a choice of liqueurs was proffered. Heather asked for Drambuie. "Make that two," I said.

When the maître had gone away, she smiled a sleek and well-fed smile. "After which, I imagine, we'll retire discreetly to our suite with its antique four-poster which Queen Elizabeth may, or may not, have slept in, and then . . ." Her eyes teased me wickedly. "You'll sweep me off my feet, or something?"

My heart was hammering and, suddenly, it was difficult to speak. I managed to ask her, "is that the wine talking? Or at least prompting?"

"I wonder . . ." Her gaze held mine. "If I'd let you?"

"Baby, you're tempting the hell out of me to try!"

"Perhaps that's what I mean to do." She cocked her head quizzically. "Or is that being cruel?"

"Depends on how far we take it." I held my breath.

But her steadfast gaze faltered, and slid away. "I must admit, it *does* sound like tremendous fun."

"Tremendous," I echoed hollowly.

"And also horribly unfair to you."

"Perhaps a little," I acknowledged. "Considering."

She raised her eyes back to me. "Considering . . . ?"

"That it *is* only talk. Although of a kind that does some startling things to my libido."

She wondered softly, "what sort of things, Denney?"

"Do I really have to spell it out?"

"And . . . I actually do these things to you?"

"My God . . . and *how* you do them!"

She probed deeper. "And they excite you?"

"That," I got out. "Must qualify as the understatement of the year."

"Then it is cruel of me, and very unfair." She smiled into my eyes. "Although I have to tell you how glad I am."

And that, if we were not to pursue it to that most desired of ends, had to be that. It was clear that we could not, not in this place. And, if not here, then where else was there within an easy bus ride? I said, trying to conceal regret and disappointment, "it's such a beautiful idea, but, as we both know, there are some snags. Like, for instance, we don't actually have that suite. And I shouldn't imagine this is that kind of hotel."

"It's probably not, no," Heather agreed, and I thought that she, too, sounded regretful.

"And, of course, we mustn't forget your mother."

She sighed, nodding. "Which doesn't alter the fact that it *was* a lovely idea."

Our liqueurs appeared to offer timely distraction. I tasted my first Drambuie, and Heather wondered, "like it?"

"One more of your lovely ideas."

"It was Prince Charles Edward's favorite tipple, or so it's claimed."

"Good for him. Whoever he is."

"Was," she reminded me. "He *was* Bonnie Prince Charlie."

"Oh, that one." I tasted some more. "Have to give him credit . . . he certainly knew his booze."

And then, with sudden urgency, Heather said, "Denney . . . listen to me." She watched me closely, and her smile was gone.

I wondered, puzzled by the sudden switch of mood, "are you okay?"

"Never better. Only . . ." Her mouth tightened, then she went on swiftly, "what we were talking about . . . you know."

"You mean . . . *that?*"

"Yes." The shadow of a grin re-appeared. "That, indeed."

"I don't think . . ." I raised a warning finger. "My system can take much more right now."

"Not that per se," she answered. "Just, I suppose, a connection of sorts."

"Well, as long as it's not too close a connection . . ." She gave a little impatient shake of the head, and I dropped the subject. "Heather? What is it?"

She began with care, "if you think you can bear to hear them, there are some things that I feel I should explain. Especially now after . . . well, after what we've been discussing." She pulled a rueful face. "Unburden myself, as they say in sloppy novels."

"What could you possibly have to unburden yourself of?"

"Isn't that being naive, and rather too trusting?" She offered the reminder, "pedestals, and feet of clay?"

"If you say so. Although I can't see them from where I am."

"And yet, as *I* see it, there's a considerable amount of unburdening that needs to be done. And this might be the time and place." Her nervousness showed itself in the way that she twisted her liqueur glass by its stem.

"Drink some of that," I suggested.

Obediently, she sipped a tiny amount. "Dutch courage? Isn't that the term?"

"If it helps."

The lounge was almost empty. The general and his lady were gone. Two army couples sat by the fire, chatting. The Canadians and their girls had drifted to the bar. There was no one around to overhear us. I said, insisting, "only if you really want to. Otherwise . . ."

She nodded abruptly, not looking at me. "On the night we met, you were just back from your very first mission. You were a bit upset, it's fair to say."

"Upset, sure . . . you could call it that."

"You told me things, and I wanted so much to help and comfort you."

"You did both, and wonderfully well."

"Thank you." Now, a smile crept slowly back. "And I spoke then of having had a . . . *friend*." She began to fiddle with her liqueur glass again. "A . . . a close friend."

It needed no spelling out, and there was a sudden void somewhere down in the pit of my stomach. "And brave, too."

"He was, yes . . . very." The smile remained, a reflective smile, and her eyes were distant. "He came from Canada, from British Columbia." She moistened her lips with Drambuie, then resumed her fiddling. "He arrived here in nineteen forty one, with the R.C.A.F."

I asked, "was he a pilot?" Not thinking, I was following Heather's lead in referring to the unknown Canadian in the past tense.

"Yes," she replied, and elaborated, "he was attached to Coastal Command, and flew Beaufort torpedo bombers . . ." Her voice broke a little then.

"Take it easy," I soothed.

"Oh, *God!*" Her eyes brimmed, but she managed to hold back the tears. "I'm such a bloody crybaby." She dashed a quick, furious hand across her cheeks.

"If it makes you feel better," I offered uncertainly. "Isn't that what tears are for?" She grimaced in self-mockery. I asked, "was he killed?"

"Yes, but not flying." Her tone was flat. "That would have been bad enough, but still what one had come to be more or less prepared for." She said then, as though to explain away a lapse of good taste, "it could happen just as easily to me, of course. Or to Mum. Just a casual sneak raider in the night."

"Yes," I said, wondering.

"He died in London, during an air raid," Heather explained then. "Near Waterloo Station, waiting between trains. He was on a posting . . ."

Because his onward train had been delayed, he had gone to a nearby pub to while away the time. It was 1942, and the night bombers were hitting London regularly. And one seemingly casual bomb had destroyed the pub. The Canadian, trapped in the rubble, critically injured, had talked and joked with the Civil Defense men as they struggled to free him, and died there before they could. The story had trickled back to Heather along slow channels. After the long and hurting silence . . .

"Not killed on ops, the way you'd expect." There was wonderment in her voice. "They call them 'ops' in the R.A.F. Operations. Not missions, the way you do."

I said again, "yes." And thought of ops and missions, and a haphazard bomb in a London street. All the same in the end.

"I found it strange tonight," Heather confessed. "Seeing those other Canadians with their girls." Like an acknowledgement of her soft words, a drift of laughter came from the bar. "The 'Canada' flashes on their shoulders. As if there might be some obscure moral for me there? Which I don't see . . ." She was shaking her head.

Try as I might then, I could not have contained the sudden spurt of jealous resentment I was feeling for the dead Canadian. His day was over and gone: I did not want him dead, yet I could have got along just fine without his post-mortem intrusion. It was wrong to think and feel in that way: in the end I would have *wanted* to know of these things . . . although, in my own good time, I amended silently. And a man killed was no rival . . . was he?

"We'd known each other for a year." Heather stared back at places and events from which I was forever excluded. "He was here at Tiverell Lacey, in the R.A.F. days. For about two months. Until, one day, they packed up and left. Off to Scotland . . . somewhere near Aberdeen, I think it was." The words flowed with the sureness of familiarity with events gone over again and again in the mind. "I never did learn where it was he was going on that last posting. And it hardly mattered as he never got there." The note of reverie vanished, and she grew more matter-of-fact. "By then we were engaged . . . it was all very pukka, with the formal notice in *The Times*, and everything . . ." She was smiling anew, wanly, and it was not for me. "We received tons of letters from his zillions of relatives in Vancouver, Victoria, Toronto and Winnipeg and Montreal . . . he was from a huge family. Relatives coast to coast and wall to wall, he used to say." And then, seeming like an afterthought, she wanted to know, "is this upsetting you?"

I assured her that it was not, and was relieved when she appeared to take that at face value. "I wanted to hear about it."

She studied me frowningly. "You don't *look* awfully happy."

More sharply than intended, I replied, "it's not something to make you jump for joy." She inclined her head, acknowledging the rebuke, and I offered apology. "I'm just the listener here. And all of this took place long before I appeared on the scene."

1942, she had said. The year when I enlisted and went through an air cadet's basic training before being taught to fly the Ryan PT-22, the Vultee BT-13 and the AT-6 that, over here, they called the Harvard.

In '42 I had been chosen for multi-engine training, shown the ropes on the old Cessna Bobcat—the 'Bamboo Bomber'—and the more complex Beechcraft AT-11. Which, in turn, delivered me to the threshold of the bomber pilot's craft, boning-up on a tired and battered old Model 'A' Marauder. Screwing around, having great times in the peaceful skies of Illinois, Kansas and Texas. While Heather's Canadian was flying torpedo bombers in a serious war, and getting himself wastefully killed. An absurdity . . . on both sides.

For Heather, then, I had not existed.

"When the war was over," she was saying. "He wanted to take me back to Canada." She wore a quizzical look, as though perplexed suddenly by a possibility never seriously considered until that moment. Something remote and unlikely.

"Would that have troubled you?"

"I don't know really." Her brow creased in thought. "But it hardly applies now."

That seemed to me almost brutally dismissive. "You must've thought about it . . ."

"Of *course* I did!" Her eyes were snapping. "What do you think?"

"Sorry, it's nothing personal." I gave ground swiftly. "That must have sounded bad."

"Yes, it did. Very." Her face seemed set in stone.

"I wasn't getting at you . . . truly . . ." I tried to shrug it off. "Only wondering, kind of, about you going off to Canada, and that maybe you weren't keen? No reason why you had to be . . . this is your home, after all."

"It was something we never discussed much," Heather replied in muted tones. And reminded me, "there wasn't time, was there?"

"That's all I had on my mind," I said. Rounding out my deception carefully.

The small crisis passed as her expression softened. "I suppose I'm still far too touchy for my own good."

"After all that's happened, how else could you be?"

"Even now," Heather admitted. "I'm still not sure of what we would've done . . . we'd never got round to making firm plans. It didn't seem right to . . . then."

And, *Providence*, I thought. And of how, in the end, it had made no difference. They had tried not to tempt, and it had gotten them nowhere. Fate went sailing on in its own don't-give-a-damn way.

"I did care a great deal for him," she said then, and it occurred to me that she had not once spoken of love. She was looking at me. "I *did* feel that it was the right thing . . . to tell you, I mean."

"I'm thankful that you did." And maybe now, as it began to sink in, that was true?

She asked then, sounding almost playful, "if it was you who had died, you'd want me to care, wouldn't you?"

"Put like that . . ." It was a further jolting reminder amidst those peaceful surroundings. "But, please, nothing obsessive, or morbid."

She quoted mystifyingly, "'fetch out no shroud for Johnny Head-in-Cloud'."

I stared at her. "What's that?"

"A war poem . . . 'For Johnny'. A sort of requiem for a pilot who dies. What you said then about morbid, it reminded me." She wondered, "is that what I'm being? Obsessive and morbid?"

"No. But it *could* happen if you didn't take care." I tried a lighter note. "Although much would depend, of course, on whether you cared for me while I was still alive."

"*Would* depend, yes." And then, as I pondered the likelihood of further playfulness in that response, Heather let fly with her bombshell. "Denney . . . I'm afraid I'm not a virgin."

"You're *afraid* . . . ?" Goggling at her, I managed—barely—to hold my balance. "Well, I mean, who is these days."

A tiny smile crept into view. "Are you?"

Tit for tat, I thought. The chance to score a point. "No . . . I'm afraid."

She revealed nothing. "Never mind."

The maître appeared to enquire if there was anything more that we required, and I thought of the suite, and the four-poster, and glanced instead at my watch. There were twenty minutes still to squander before the last bus would leave. I paid for dinner with a five-pound note that failed to cause a stir, and Heather suggested, "let's sit and talk a little more."

I told her edgily, "don't think I could handle any more true confessions."

She ignored the irony. "Simply the final unburdening."

They had made love together twice following the announcement of their engagement. There had been no one since. I absorbed these facts which were delivered with a simple directness, and found that, yes, I could accept. What else was there to do? I envied the Canadian for having known her first, and claimed her, yet I could be more sanguine about the other. What did gall me was the knowledge that he had been first at the post. The way that Scott might have been galled by the earlier success of Amundsen. Without really begrudging . . .

For a while, after her loss, Heather had dated casually with an American master sergeant, but had called it off when the sergeant began getting heavy. There had been no one special in her life, she informed me gratifyingly, until I had come along.

"I promised a clean breast . . ." The words made me wonder if the torment was over at last, but it did seem that she was not through with me yet; there were to be no half measures. "We didn't go off to hotels, or anything deliberate like that."

"Heather, look, it's none of my business . . ."

"It happened in the late summer." She went plowing on as if I had not spoken, intent on her recounting. "The harvest was coming in, and the fields were full of stooked grain, rows of little straw cottages," she remembered softly. "And wonderfully snug when you crawled inside." I sat in sweating silence, wondering why the *hell* she was doing this to me. "What we wanted, at first, was simply to neck, and enjoy ourselves. Cuddle . . . and things. But you'll know how it happens." Willfully, then, she got in her little vengeful dig. "It's happened to you, hasn't it?" And all I could do was clench my hands and pray silently that I might be spared the round-by-round details: I didn't *care* if the earth had moved for them! But she said only, "it was in August. And, in November, he was killed."

*

She was demonstrably affectionate in the bus. Clasping my hand, leaning close to nuzzle my shoulder, and I wondered with lingering bitterness if all that was her belated attempt to make amends. When we got off the bus in the village, the conductor wished me, "good luck, Yank." It could have meant anything.

She hung on my arm, chattering and laughing as we walked the short distance to her home: it had been a *marvelous* night out . . . 'like a breath of fresh air'. I thought sourly of the way she had been batting the breeze with her detailed unburdening: surely a lot of air must have been circulated.

Outside the darkened house, she was sorry once more for not inviting me in.

"I didn't expect that . . ." I was stiff with her, and could not prevent it; the clean breast, especially unsought, could have that effect on you. "I didn't mind last time, and I don't now."

She peered into my face in the dimness. "You really are rather sweet."

"For a Yank." Was I as sweet, though, as the Canadian—so obviously—had been?

"I feel terrible now," Heather declared. "Here I am, thanks to you, safely home, and you've still got that long walk."

"Don't worry, I can always use the exercise. I spend far too much time sitting around in pubs and airplanes." She clung to my hand, laughing. "It's a warm night, and nothing to get up for in the morning. We're not going anywhere special."

"I'm glad," Heather said. "Of that."

She kissed me hard and long, and I was very aware of her closeness, her body's heat melting away the lingering dregs of my frostiness. I was in her hands, helpless, as she recast her spell with yielding lips that parted under mine, her tongue searching as, with pain and longing, I thought of the wheatfield, the secret snugness of stacked sheaves. Where they had gone together, intending then only some heavy petting . . . the hot excitement rolled through me.

We pulled apart, breathless, looking at each other with unconcealed intensity, although I sensed at once that this was not yet The Signal. Even as she admitted in a low voice, "I could almost be coming to love you, you know."

I hugged her until she gasped and giggled. "Wish you could . . . sure hope you can." And . . . jealousy was quite gone, out the window and away: I could resent the Canadian no longer, and even begin to hope that he did not resent me.

She murmured, "Denney . . . can you be patient with me?"

"Can be." I stroked her hair. "And am."

"You may need," she warned. "Quite a lot of patience."

"We've got patience we haven't used yet."

"And promise me you won't get cross?"

"Never will," I swore. Forgetting completely how cross I had been.

Her smile was hesitant. "I do worry so about upsetting you."

The ungenerous thought intruded itself . . . you didn't seem all that worried back at the hotel. I dismissed the thought as cheapjack and nasty. "That's a long, long way from happening."

In the moment of saying it, it could seem so.

*

The rain began as I was walking back to the base.

I had not brought a trench coat, although I should have been wise to the mercurial English weather. Soaked through, and with a mile and a half to go, I heard the car coming up the road behind me, saw its slitted headlights, a once-in-a-rare-while civilian car.

And would reserved English civilians provide succor for a half-drowned Yank? I offered a hopeful thumb, and heard the whine from the differential as the car slowed.

"Where are we off to, then?" A window rolled down, a dimmed flashlight, the male voice cheery, only a little guarded. Two men barely visible in the dashboard glow.

"The base?" I squelched dejectedly before them. "If I'm not washed away first. You couldn't . . . ?"

"'Spect we could." There was an answering chuckle. "Before you go down for the third time, lad." A rear door swung open. "Hop in, then."

"Thanks a lot." I was in, and the car's interior was warm, smelling of leather and tobacco. I saw then that the men were cops.

The spokesman wondered mildly, "it *was* the airfield you wanted? Not deserting, are we? Doing a runner?"

"The base, the whole base, and nothing but the base, so help me God." Dripping wet, my clothes were clinging to my shivering skin. I felt the massive sneeze coming, and could not hold it.

"There goes a five hundred-pounder," the spokesman said.

His companion, who was driving, offered politely, "bless you."

"Thank you." I informed them, "if I was going AWOL, I'd choose a better night than this. All I want is a hot shower, then to hit the sack."

"Don't want much, do you?" the spokesman said good-humouredly. "Here's us restricted to five inches of bloody water to scrub up in by the government, while you lot are standing under showers and running the country dry."

I knew that I was being ribbed, but still felt the need to put up a defense.

"Well, okay, but we do other things as well . . . now and then."

The driver laughed as the spokesman told me, "'course you do. I was only havin' you on, lad."

"Sure. I know that. But I had to go down fighting."

"You do your share for us, all right," he told me flatly. "So, while we may grumble a bit, because we all enjoy a good grumble, we certainly don't begrudge any of you a few comforts. Not when you've done so much to earn them."

The friendly and heartfelt words could warm me right through, and it seemed then the perfect way—short of a shared four-poster—in which to wind up an evening of rare pleasure, and the counter-balance of pain that went with it. Although the pain did not matter so much: pleasure and pain were, after all, the two sides of the same coin. And some appreciation warmly expressed could always help even when it did not come from the one from whom you would most like to hear it!

The policemen delivered me to the M.P. post at the gate, wished me 'best of luck over there', and called back "Cheerio" as they went puttering off in their little dated black car.

*

I had had my shower and was composing a letter when O'Connor rolled in from the Officers' Club, drunk and benevolent. "How you doin', kid?"

"Pretty good." Seeing his enquiring glance, I told him that I was writing to my girl.

"The fair Heather, one presumes?"

"That's my girl." It sounded fine to me.

He stood, swaying slightly, hands on hips, his hat pushed far back. "Didn't you just leave her?"

A little loftily, I explained, "it's a graceful note of thanks for what was an outstanding date. The way things are done over here."

"That's it, huh? We-e-ell. And very right and proper, too," O'Connor approved before adding, "especially as, for the next little whiles, your communicatin' looks like havin' to get itself done through His Royal Majesty's Mail." I was uncomprehending, and he spelled it out. "The whole base is sealed

up tight as a tick's ass from midnight, son. Once the last unhappy
stragglers are rounded up, hootin' and hollerin'."

Orders had been issued to expedite the painting of our aircraft
with their patterns of broad black and white stripes. Once that
was done, O'Connor believed, life would begin to get interesting.

"Invasion-wise," he opined. "I get this feelin' the shit's about
to hit the fan."

EIGHT

'Somewhere in England
(As the saying goes!)
June 6 1944.'

'Dear Mother,

'This has been SOME day! There is time now, though, as it nears its end, to catch my breath and think about it, then try and get these thoughts on paper.

'You will have heard by now. It is 7 p.m. here, which makes it early afternoon for you, and I can almost hear the radio newscasters: "We inner-RUP' this program to BRING you . . . !" Falling over themselves to spread the Good Word.

'And it is all true, take it from one who has been there. The INVASION is on, and we are ashore at last in honest-to-God France. What, here, is referred to as the Second Front, the first being the Russian. This is gospel from a very recent eye-witness.

'It began last night as the airborne and glider troops went in ahead of the main landing force, the British at their end putting their big heavy gliders down in pitch darkness, would you believe! Something that this one-time glider pilot would prefer not to try. While, at our end, the paratroopers of the 82nd Airborne and the 101st, the Screaming Eagles, were dropping. They had something to scream about this time!

'Then, this morning, all the battlewagons,

cruisers and destroyers in the world lying off the Normandy coast, blasting the Germans out of bed, covering the amphibious landings on a line of beaches code-named Utah, Omaha, Gold, Sword and Juno.

'There is so very much for me to tell you, and the poor old pen cannot keep up with my head; a feeling in the air such as I have never known or imagined, and could not begin to define. No matter how long I may live, I am certain I shall never know its like again. War is, of course, a bad thing, but it surely does have its moments! And this is one of them, this once-in-a-lifetime THING. Like electricity, a bolt of blue lightning, is the only way I can describe it. And we are all charged up with the current, and about ready to pop. Sheer excitement, I guess.

'I would seek a favor, please. DO KEEP THIS LETTER. Shove it away by all means, but do it, would you? Again, please?

'It is no earth-shaking document. The New Yorker or Atlantic Monthly would not give a plugged nickel for it, or allow it an inch of space. But it is MY document, my account through my eyes and brain and nerve-endings of this unique Event. There is the feeling in me that, some day, it may possess some significance or relevance. As one very small account of history in the making.

'Right now it does not feel much like history. That was something we debated once at Princeton; the inability of those making it to recognize history *in* the making. That it is something that reveals itself only later.

'Well, it is like that for us today. We will get the message eventually when we are old, and history is all we have left. In the uncertain belief that, then, it might be worth dusting off for another look-see. A topic to be rehashed down at the Legion post with all the other grizzled veterans and bores.

'You have mentioned in your letters at times that I am a frequent conversation piece at your regular coffee mornings. So, at your next happy foregathering, if you like, you can hold the ladies in thrall with your recounting of my doings of June 6. As dictated by God and Dwight D. Eisenhower—or should those names be in reverse order? Do I descry a pucker of maternal disapproval at my taking in vain the holy name of Dwight D. Eisenhower?

'When you do come together, please give all the ladies my best, and inform them that your soldier son has been in (however humbly) at the kill. Flying support missions: for the first time ever two in one day! If we keep that up, I could make it home for the Fourth of July!

'The first trip was to a place called Caen where we've been before, a city only a few miles inland from the Invasion beaches. If I have my earlier history down pat, Caen was home town for one Charlotte Corday who done Citizen Marat wrong in the bathtub. (And did she know that she made history as she wielded her wicked blade?) Now it is an important road and rail junction through which pretty well everything the Germans can find to bring up against us must pass. Also Carpiquet, a Luftwaffe airfield. They sent us there in some force, around a hundred airplanes, each bearing its ton and a half of bombs. Which meant a hundred and fifty tons with which to flatten Germans satisfyingly . . .'

*

I sat alone in the writing room we had inherited from the R.A.F., and lived once more the events of the day. Certain that it was right to set it down, and never mind that this account of mine was fuzzy and vague, naive and probably self-aggrandizing. I must, while it was fresh, store up and lock away the immediacy of it for other times and places where, should I survive to the end, I might seek to relive it through these by-then yellowing sheets of flimsy V-mail paper.

Late evening now of June 6. Back on the ground in England, yet wound up tight still, and humming. Still, as in every mind of every man among us who had flown that day, *THERE*. Wired up to it, and plugged in; all teetering on the high wire of our strung-out nerves with the current buzzing and fizzing in our heads.

No one could sit still for long; we paced endlessly and aimlessly, or went hurrying outside to study the empty sky, although for what none could have said. That sky, cloudy, stormy, with the evening light shafts lancing down through a tumbling deck of strato-cu. Windy and unseasonably cold for early summer. Not what anyone would call invasion weather. Under that sky men gathered in gesturing, murmuring groups as if seeking a sign, or walked singly, heads down, with edgy and hurried strides. Going nowhere. The questions hanging over us all, voiced or unvoiced: how is it going . . . how are we doing THERE? How have we *done*? On each uplifted and storm-lit face the shifting expressions of anxiety, eagerness, yearning, impatience.

This taut and thrilling end to the greatest day of our young lives; feeling that *some*thing in us that would be there for time beyond calculating, which surpassed all of our collective understanding, or the ability to figure out. The shared urge, following the doing of momentous things, to do more, no matter what. Or, simply, bust!

*

Assembling for the morning's pre-flight briefing, we had known already of big things in the offing, the biggest so far. *That* big could mean only the one thing.

The dark hours had been raucous with massed aircraft movements. Andy Devine, slipping outside the Quonset, had returned to report eagerly that British Halifax heavy bombers were passing low overhead, and that each one was towing a laden glider. "It's *gotta* be for real . . . right?"

The stripes painting had been completed in a rush, each B-26 sporting its bold markings: there was an additional air of drama and purpose about the new appearance, the visible evidence of mighty happenings that could not now be halted, in which we were all caught up without exception.

For our Squadron, that morning, it was to be Caen again, and the news sent my gastric system straight out of kilter. The memories of Caen were still too fresh and rough around the edges.

It was to be another low-level run, and we dropped to the wavetops beneath a tossed and drab sky, bouncing in gusty turbulence as we left the Sussex coast behind.

Eighty miles across a sea churned white to the first misty sighting of France between Fécamp and Le Havre. Making the precautionary detour around the port city to avoid its unfailingly diligent gun batteries. Hitting shore as we came up on Cabourg, and seeing them then, up ahead, a little off to our right. The Invasion beaches.

Picking out the two vital rivers on the eastern flank, the Dives and the Orne, and the vast areas between them that the Germans had flooded to make matters that much more difficult for the men fighting on the ground.

The British gliders, cumbersome and overloaded, had gone in on the Orne's far bank: as we hedge-hopped through, we found them where they had crash-landed, broken cruciform shapes lying at every tilted angle imaginable, and, from the state of some, it was clear that few, if any, men could have emerged from them alive. Grounded for ever now in small fields that were little more than garden-size. And how in God's name had they achieved that, and in unknown terrain on a blacked-out night? What kind of pilots *were* those men? Picked at random, at short notice, trained in haste.

While, beyond the glider landing zone, the land lay shrouded by the pale, wind-churned haze of battle, the smoke of fires and explosions, the dust in tons cast aloft from wheeled and tracked vehicles beyond counting, by tens of thousands of plodding infantry feet.

Deep within the haze lay the flashing guns, bursting shells and mortar bombs, the downward, fiery rush of rockets, the parabolae of tracer, and the flares in arcs of red, green, white and gold.

All edged by the white-scuffed, shivering-cold sea crammed to the limits of vision with ships of every kind and size, as thick as a Times Square traffic snarl . . .

"I'll be a sadsack son of a bitch!" Sergeant Patecki's gravelly voice traveling through the intercom from his ringside seat back in the tail. Patecki, at most times a silent man, taciturn and intolerant of empty chatter, who must be deeply moved indeed to countenance this lapse. "Never seen so many Jesus boats! Never knew there was that many God damn' boats in the whole Christly world!"

And in those moments of immense revelation, I found that I was . . . steady. The magnitude of what we witnessed down there could make me forget *me* and my little private fears: I was in thrall to the immense panorama of armed invasion. Beside all that what could *I* matter?

So much around us everywhere to be observed in the fleeting seconds it takes for us to fly by: the myriad specks of assault craft streaming shoreward in long lines, and butting back out to the waiting merchantmen and attack transports for their fresh loads. Cockleshell LCAs and LCVPs plowing through surf to the shore. LCIs, and the long, slender LCTs that would beach themselves to disgorge the tanks onto the land, Shermans and Churchills and Stuarts; fighting tanks, flail tanks, flame-throwing tanks, tank destroyers, tracked recovery vehicles, self-propelled guns.

There, far out, the encircling steel wall of the warships, cruisers, destroyers, minesweepers, the towering, castellated outlines of battleships—the *Texas*, we had heard, was there, and the *Augusta* on which Churchill and Roosevelt had met long before to begin sketching the plans leading up to this day. In company now with the British *Warspite*, with *Rodney*, her sixteen-inch guns hurling ton-weight shells deep into Normandy.

We watched the capital ships transforming themselves into rippling masses of flame and mushrooming brown smoke as the broadsides went out. More dramatic still was the firing from the rocket ships, converted assault craft working close inshore to spit out their multiple lightning-streaks, waves of high explosive missiles with white fire at their tails . . .

Seconds only in which to try and take it in, then there was O'Connor on the horn, all business, chasing me up. Down in the nose under my feet with the Rube Goldberg—the Flannick low-level bombsight. "Bombardier to pilot . . . okay, the party's over." The now well-known, but always chilling warning, "coming up on the I.P."

I went back to work, holding 'Big Apples' at the ordered one hundred and fifty feet. We would hit the target like that, the bombs fused for delayed detonation.

Lucky thus far with ground fire. We were making tracks, the aircraft well-spaced; there should be—in theory—little time for the Germans to get organized . . . the targets would be too many, too sudden, too swift. So it was reckoned by those who purported to know of such things.

What was good about low-level was that you were often not seen or heard until you were right *there*, riding your own sound waves to the spot. By the time a flak gunner had got it together, you were gone, more history. At hairy, scary Caen, though, could such predicted good fortune hold? Caen, even with the element of on-the-deck surprise, could be counted on as a twenty four-carat evil bitch.

O'Connor's cold, flat order had had an immediate and detrimental effect on my new-found complacency: the gut-wrenching ache of anticipatory dread was back with a vengeance. Like the return of pain after the anesthetic, fear came creeping into every nerve and fiber. 'We have nothing to fear but fear itself,' Roosevelt had informed us once. Coming up on horrible Caen at two hundred and forty knots earned us the right to reply, "Mister President, that is horseshit, *sir!*"

Fear I knew now, and intimately, as an ugly, endless cycle. Feeding upon itself, fear begat fear, which crapped more fear to manure fresh beds of fear . . . on and on, round and round.

"Five miles to go, son." O'Connor sounding easy and friendly in my headset. For now. "Kindly hold it just like that."

Like *that* is . . . one hundred feet above ground, fast and dead level, with Caen Cathedral, my given landmark, a big square Norman tower, immediately ahead. Like *that* is sneaking quick and furtive glances right and left, watching the converging lines of bombers and their distance from us, holding my spacing . . . hoping that O'Connor will not catch me out.

From trained and ingrained habit, a scan across the board: mixtures full rich, props set at high R.P.M., right hand tight on the twin throttle levers, and finding some small, spurious comfort from that familiar smooth hardness against the palm. Check all instruments, their readings of pressures and temperatures, the life-flow of vital fluids that keep us airborne recording themselves on the brain . . .

And, at once, O'Connor nails me. "I said to *hold* it, Tiger." Still, though, deceptively mild.

"Sorry . . . instrument check . . ."

"SCREW the sonofabitching instruments!" No longer mild. "We're flying, which is what counts, and the instruments can't change that! Now do as I tell you, and HOLD it!"

The sickness comes bubbling up inside, hot and pressing, although still within limits. The target is seconds away, but I have allowed the cathedral to drift left, and I skid 'Big Apples' back on track with a bootful of rudder. Stomach has gone into knots, and I'm breathing much too hard. Like a winded runner.

"Bomb doors open," O'Connor is saying now, and the old lurch hits the seat of my pants as air roars into the belly, and the pressure shifts painfully on my eardrums. Sensations to accompany the sudden startling awareness of . . . NO FLAK! We are bang over the middle of downtown Caen, and no one is shooting at us! Up ahead there is rising smoke and dust, legacy of the first waves to bomb. A few . . . a very few . . . black bursts appearing then, and one or two tracer streams, but none of them near to us.

The great square tower sliding in and under, then gone from view. "Coming *on*," O'Connor says. "Give me a touch left, and . . . EASY now."

The slick sweat of hands on throttles and control yoke, but it is only routine sweat. Sweat, but not muck sweat. Funk, but not blue funk. Because, mercifully, this is all too swift and chaotic for the nervous system and the cringing mind to keep pace with.

Fresh smoke and dust over the outskirts of Caen. Straight on, and a mile to go. But Caen is no bitch today as we slide down the final tight slot. Caen, this once, is minding her manners.

What flak there is is, at best, half-hearted: the Germans have bigger things on their minds this morning. When compared with what's going on ten miles down the road from here, all *we* are is a nuisance, a gnat's bite . . .

O'Connor reports 'bombs away', and 'Big Apples' performs her customary stiff-legged bronco buck, yawing and pitching her way through the smoke thermals from the fires below, and we boom right on through, down among the rooftops. Put your trust in God and Pratt & Whitney . . .

*

' . . . and, Mother, it was an easy run, pure clockwork. Knock, knock, and thank you very much, Ma'am. No time wasted, like the friendly Fuller Brush Man.

'The Germans at Caen caught on the hop, and no doubt they were pondering more pressing matters just then. We circled away, and O'Connor, our famous—or infamous, depending upon one's point of view—bombardier came up then with his lunatic idea . . .'

*

He knelt in the crawlway, wagging his brows at me in that way of his. "So? What say we have us a look-see, partner?"

I missed his point. "You can't mean circle the target again?" That *was* lunacy, and certifiable immediately. Even if the Germans had not got their hearts in their work today.

"Neg-a-tive, kid." He looked at me pityingly.

I glanced out, an automatic position check: we were climbing, passing through two thousand feet, the nearest visible aircraft a quarter mile distant. Still no flak worth mentioning. "Look-see at what, then?"

"The war, what else?" He gestured widely around. "The great overall tactical situation. A genu-wine bird's eye view."

"Now you want me to fly you over the God damned *Invasion?*"

"Can you call to mind any other worthwhile tactical situation hereabouts?"

"But," I protested. "We're supposed to head straight back."

"Only a coupla minutes, why not? All you need do is make an itty-bitty dog-leg."

"They'll have my ass if I do that."

"And a very comely one it is, too." He watched me in expectation.

"Sweet Jesus, Buzz, I don't know." I was still churning within, all I wanted to be was out of there. I had had enough of war. The Invasion appeared to be doing pretty well on its own, and needed no help from me . . .

"Skip . . . gimme two seconds!" Andy chipped in then, eager and helpful. "I'll plot ya a headin' . . ."

"Andy, you numbnuts, I see it right there!" I stabbed an irritable finger at the windshield. "By the time you'd worked out a heading that far, we'd be in Iceland!"

"Yeah . . . an' I love *you*, too!" Andy turned his back on me. There was little more that he could do within the limited confines of a B-26 cockpit.

"Mister Pilot, you're being obstructionist again, I can tell." O'Connor sounded disappointed with me.

"All I want is to go home. Why won't you let me?"

"Egad, sir . . . never be a faintheart." His quizzing brows grew more agitated. "Don't you want to have something heroic to tell your grandchildren?"

"There won't *be* any grandchildren once those trigger-happy pricks down there take it into their heads we're a Kraut."

"What's life," O'Connor mused. "Without the spice of a little risk?"

"The Krauts never got us over Caen," Andy Devine pointed out sulkily. "So what's your big beef now?"

I could not seem to grasp his reasoning, but responded, "they weren't trying, or hadn't you noticed?" I peered into the high haze of vast land battles. "Those guys down there are, and very hard. Anything that moves, and fair game . . . it's open season. Or . . ." I groped for ways in which to strengthen my case. "We could connect with a damned great shell from some battleship."

"After which, surely, no more worries, and off we all go to a better land I know." O'Connor was unmoved by my griping pessimism. "Just fly nice an' high, son. Cruise easy, look friendly. They're bound to see our brave new stripes," he declared. "You can't believe they'd shoot at one of their own zebras."

*

I wrote: 'we flew over Bayeux, the home of the Tapestry, and I could see a certain irony in that. Among the British soldiers there must have been many of Norman descent, and among the Americans and Canadians, too. And there they were, returning after nine hundred years to fight on the old home ground.

'And exactly what did we note from our lofty perch? That, in a few hours since dawn, tremendous progress had been made, the soldiers already well inland with many villages captured, and the lines edging close to Bayeux which is an important town on a major highway.

'The country around there is rolling and wooded, with little hedged fields and deep sunken roads that the French call 'bocage'.

Every road is narrow and twisting, making it difficult for mechanized warfare, and ideal for defending. It was plain that the tanks and half-tracks were having problems, and there were traffic snarls at the villages. What tanks we saw were halted, hemmed in, firing from what had become fixed positions. I understand very little of ground tactics, but it is evident even to me that armor needs open ground in which to function properly. They do not seem to be finding much of that in Normandy.

'I thought of how it might have been had we been a German bomber crew, what a field day we could have had! But another lost opportunity for the Germans, who don't have many bombers around now, and you wonder about no more blitzkriegs, the screaming Stukas we used to watch on the newsreels. No more Guernicas, Warsaws, Rotterdams, Londons, Coventrys? Let's hope so.

'We all got back with only a few scratches, and sat in the mess-hall eating lunch, and I got what has become my frequent post-mission feeling about the unreality of it all. Only an hour from THERE, back safe on the ground, acting normal, as though nothing much had happened, and all for show, how cool and nonchalant we are. Standing under the shower, or eating, or writing you this semi-coherent screed. Or simply lying back to stare up at the ceiling. Everything shifts and changes too quickly, and the mind cannot take it in: hitting Caen, then seeing the ground battles and the seaborne Invasion as it was taking place: hundreds of ships all crouched under little silver barrage balloons. And then sitting down to eat the Army's offering—I can picture the way you shudder—"Swiss Steak" (canned hamburger), mashed potato and stringy string beans, with cherry jell-o to follow. That's when Caen and Bayeux and the huge assault from the sea become surreal. Like after the movie, back out on the street and trying to re-adjust.

'Until reality is restored as they call us for the second mission. To Brittany this time, and a town called Rennes.'

*

Rennes was a wicked brute of a trip that brought back all of the sweat and odor and terror and physical sickness.

It was major road and rail junctions once more, and the bridges crossing the Vilaine River over which must pass German reinforcements flooding toward Normandy from the south of France. A simple and straightforward objective with nothing heavy to stand in our way, the briefers promised with characteristic glibness. *We*, at least, should have known better than to swallow that old line of malarkey. But, by then, everyone had gotten round to thinking that if once-deadly Caen could be such a push-over, then why not Rennes also? Were the Krauts not in all kinds of grief with our guys raising Cain in their backyard? Rennes? Some bridges and railroad tracks; the mixture as before. Like St. Denis, maybe, or another St. Omer.

The radar-coordinated flak hit us in full fury as we passed over Mont St. Michel, concentrated patterns of bursts in their scores and hundreds, the air filled with hot steel, ranges figured down to the inch. Already, off to the left, a B-26 burning, nosing down. Going into the terminal spin as one wing snapped off, and a 'chute popped, then a second, a final third. Three of seven, and no time left for the remainder as the dying airplane fell into fragments, smoking tendrils of wreckage curving out and down.

A voice on the intercom, shaken, "anyone know who that was?"

But no one did yet; the doomed machine had been a mile away, a greenish silhouette with zebra stripes, the ident letters too distant to be read.

Seemingly encouraged by the first kill, the flak stiffened and edged closer: this time, for all his furious demands and curses, O'Connor must be ignored, his meticulously-planned bomb run screwed out of sight. I would fly straight and level for the carping son of a bitch if and when I could, and *that* would be at the last possible moment. Now, with Rennes in view, I cared only to elude the guns and preserve our necks.

For the first time, I was more afraid of the Germans than of O'Connor: scared witless by their superb and inhuman marksmanship, their coldly-deliberate stalking of us, the efficiency of the beautifully-machined weapons that they controlled so well. Hitherto, they had been the marginally lesser fear; now the scales tipped, and I could defy O'Connor. If O'Connor wanted a straight-in through this shit, then O'Connor could haul his miserable, bad-tempered and trouble-making ass outside and walk it! And take his bombsight and his bombs with him!

"God damn YOU . . . I've got eyes in my head, and I know where we're going. I'll give you the last mile straight and level, and that's all! I'm not committing mass suicide just to provide you with a pretty bomb pattern!"

And O'Connor, because he *was* O'Connor, expressed sympathetic understanding at once. "Okay, fine, ace . . . do it your way."

Which wiped the floor with me more effectively than his reciprocal anger could ever have done. So that, still two miles out from the target, not able to credit that I was really doing this, I rolled 'Big Apples' level and held precise altitude, as steady as a stupid rock through the flak mat over Rennes. Telling the bastard, "right . . . she's yours."

For two miles and a thousand light years we locked into the groove, waiting for *our* shell. And, with all my accumulating experience, it was not getting one bit better: I was not toughening or growing accustomed, or coming to accept, and it was becoming increasingly apparent that I never would . . .

The millennium passed as O'Connor sang out, "bombs away!"

And I could hurl the airplane up and around then, away from the hating guns and the singularly unpleasant people who served them.

*

'Millinocket Joy-Girl' had been the one destroyed during the approach to Rennes. With Redvers, Carpenter, La Salle, Fishbein, Marks, Curwin and Benton. A cruel and bitter irony was attached to the loss: 'Millinocket Joy-Girl', named for a town in the State of Maine, met her fiery end in a Département of France called . . . Maine.

'Georgia on My Mind', a write-off, bellied in on the sands of Utah Beach with both engines dead. Everyone got out: Keeley, Majors, Zubko, Brownrigg, Rutheven, Faber and MacPhee. The difference of a few hours, a changed situation, decreed that they would return to us instead of becoming prisoners.

'Mickey & Co.' went into the sea south of the Isle of Wight. Taking Mickey Vaughan, Petersen, Callaghan, Bowyer, Nye, Heinemann and Hayes. The rescue launch found only wreckage and a single empty life vest.

'Big Apples' came back with a major hydraulic leak, and we had to pump down the flaps and landing gear by hand. The fin and rudder were peppered with splinter holes, and the left main tire went wearily flat as we taxied to the hardstand.

Sergeant Cohn was telling all who would listen of the shell splinter entering on one side of the fuselage and exiting on the other. Missing his balls, he vowed, by an inch at most. "I seen the Goddam thing whiz right by me like a bat outta hell." Informing us in his deadpan Jewish fashion, "you fellas are real lucky to have me around still." Looking nonplused and hurt when we doubled up with helpless laughter that was very close to the edge.

I lay on my bunk, trying to still my inner demons. But it was taking longer each time, and becoming more difficult. Could the day be approaching—my great and secret fear—when I would fail to do so?

NINE

The armies were ashore in Normandy: Bayeux was taken, the line edging closer each day to Caen. We were holding enough ground in which to lay out forward airstrips, runways hastily bulldozed and graded, then covered with perforated steel planking on which the fighter-bombers and transport aircraft could land, barely. It was beginning to look likely that, if not quite yet, the showdown was, at least, closer.

In support of this growing conviction, the radio and newspapers were loud with the optimistic jargon of the moment. June 6 had been 'D-Day'. Then it was 'D plus one' . . . plus two, three, four . . .

On D plus 5, every man at Tiverell Lacey remained confined to the base, no one allowed in or out except in the line of duty, and no reasons forthcoming from the higher echelons as to why this should be. For many, the sole way out of U.S.A.A.F. Base 909 lay in flying missions. Which was no way out at all.

We grumbled interminably and futilely about 'those brass-bound bastards': how did keeping us penned up safeguard security when, already, the world and his wife knew all there was to know about the Invasion . . . probably more than we did.

Meanwhile, bomber crews flew support missions: to Villacoublay and Amiens, Cherbourg and Evreux, back to Caen, which was proving a tough nut for the soldiers to crack. Back again to horrible Rennes, which stayed horrible.

While O'Connor, Andy, the sergeants and I, without an airworthy airplane, goldbricked shamelessly, lying late in the sack, playing cards, writing letters. With nothing better to do, we joined 'The Morbids', those who did not, or could not, fly; who, as the return time for a mission drew near, would drift down to the ramp, or the base of the control tower, to count the returnees, weighing those stark figures against the tally of the ones who had gone out two or three hours before.

In that time, 'Pinball Machine' was lost in flames at Villacoublay to a rare Focke-Wulf 190. Taking Stephenson, Gaye, Prescott, De Jong, Purdy, Bellamy and Regius. No parachutes.

'Lady Is A Tramp' took heavy flak damage over Pont l'Eveque, but managed to limp home on one engine, and with a two hundred and fifty-pound bomb on board that would not release. Then, when safely overhead, the landing gear refused to lower.

Millet, the pilot, circled the field gently, enabling Venter, Arbuthnot, Di Salvio, Williams, O'Grady and Manley to use their parachutes. Millet informed the tower that he would attempt a belly landing in the long grass on the field's far side. It was decided later that he had figured out already what was most likely to happen there.

Millet made a copybook approach, the fuselage bottom touching ground: to us watching it seemed as light as the drifting contact of thistledown. The airplane bumped along the ground for a hundred yards until one wingtip dipped into the earth, and it pivoted slowly, almost stopped, and we all let go our breath: Millet, that lucky stiff, had *made* it, bellying in with a fused bomb . . .

Which detonated then with a clap of thunder, a rushing, sighing gust of hot wind, and Millet was dead at the heart of the firestorm he had created. There was not enough left there to gather in and bury. Millet became one of the unaccountables, listed as 'Missing in Action'. He was there somewhere, but no one wanted seriously to look for him . . .

At hated Rennes we lost 'Patsy Popsicle' with Smoot, Kilbride, Theroux, Bayliss, Lonegan, Lindstrom and Holmes. Gone, too, was 'Four Leaf Clover'—her luck run out—shot down with Menzies, Carton, De Groote, Forbes, Greenbaum, Arnold and Glebers. The news came in later that both crews had been made prisoner, and, later still, that Lonegan and Arnold were dead in German hospitals.

Losses grew more heavy, and the replacement crews and aircraft flowed in, crews often reduced in number as drain exceeded supply. On the heels of the D-Day euphoria, as more men died or went missing, despondency set in on the base, deepening as the new crews got killed in turn, very often first-mission men whose aircraft had not yet been named. Gone from our midst before they had *been*. It seemed wrong, and savagely perverse: we were fighting each day deeper into France, said to be starting to win this war, winding up the watch on the Rhine. How could it be, then, that things kept getting worse for us?

Evidence of the growing manpower shortage was to be seen in the number of B-26s that flew now with reduced crews, their waist gun positions left unmanned, an action claimed as justified by the fact that we were meeting with few enemy fighters. Waist gunners could do nothing against flak, and were mere dead weight on already overtaxed airframes. *Should* any fighters manage to break through, there remained nine operational guns for self-defense in each aircraft.

My personal state of mind during 'Big Apples" down-time was not improved by our ongoing forced confinement within the base area. With nerves still ragged, I would become short-tempered and snappy over even the most insignificant of trifles. At times I would notice the way in which the others were watching me with curious disapproval, and I would try to shrug it aside, and get a grip. After all—the reminder was always there—they endured no less than I. Yet, with them, I could observe few outward signs of strain. If they felt as I did, then they hid it well. Much better than I seemed able to manage.

They had every right to demand to be told what it was that was spooking me so badly. I was their pilot; they rode with their lives in my hands, counting on my acquired skills, my alleged ability to deal effectively with most situations that might crop up unexpectedly in the air. And always, and without let-up, in what we did on each mission, there were so many damned awful situations to tax me, undermining those skills which, if I were to admit it honestly, were perilously limited.

Times there were when I would find myself envying emptily the dullards among us, those phlegmatic and unimaginative ones who, untroubled, unfeeling, flew blithely through the flak and the fighter swarms. Wondering afterwards, when quizzed about it, what all the fuss was about. No sense, no feeling, and that would have been a blessed condition to achieve.

Like someone gravely ill who pins faith blindly in the empty placebo, I would tell myself that all I needed was to get off base and spend some time with Heather: all my troubles would cease then, and vanish. Concealing from my consciousness the fact that I was creating a myth from another finite and fallible human being, a hornets' nest of neuroses in her own right. Turning her, instead, into my inexhaustible source of hope and peace and comfort, the certain cure for a war-induced malaise. Like the ever-deepening fear of combat flying, of being compelled to rise in those dawns in dread anticipation of the still-unnamed target. Sweating out the truck ride to the hardstand, the start-up and checks and taxying, then the take-off to wherever. The plain loathing each time of simply having to go. The long, low ache of private guilt that was mine when others went, and did not return.

Against those evils I held up my bright image of Heather, like the crucifix before the vampire: *she* was my fount and my solace, and would soothe away forever all my doubts and crushing fears. Heather, weaving her protective spell, and with *herself*, was the one safeguard that I must have to ensure that everything would work out just right. My girl the rabbit's foot!

But, thanks to the Army and its fatuous restrictions, at a time when I felt I needed her most, I could only telephone her. Which did help a little, but could never fully soothe my craving for her.

There was one payphone on the base, down at the gate beside the M.P. post. A quarter mile hike there, and a quarter mile back, in all weathers. When you got there, there was always a waiting line, all ranks, no privileges, take your turn like everyone else. There you would stand, chafing, hating each long-winded blabbermouth using the phone before you, being hated as a long-winded blabbermouth by those who came after . . .

"Gonna be long, lieutenant?" The staff sergeant next in line watched me in anxious appeal as I entered the booth. Behind him, a dozen more hopefuls shifted and muttered.

I could feel the way that my nerves wound up tight then, and I was shaking as I stared back at him. "As long as it takes, right?" It would have been nice then to haul off with my fist and deck the staff sergeant. "You have a problem with that?"

"Well, no . . ." He broke off eye contact. "Just . . . I got this important call to make, and . . ."

"You, me and everyone else." Staring him down, I asked myself why I was doing this. More reasonably, I pointed out, "if it had been you ahead, I would've been the one waiting."

"Well, yeah . . ."

"Jesus Christ . . . get *movin'!*" an irate voice yelled.

"Okay, Lieutenant." The staff sergeant nodded slowly. "Fair enough."

I relented some more. "I'll get it said, and get off. So stand by one, huh?"

I dropped two big English pennies down the slot, dialed Heather's number, then crossed my fingers, praying . . . *let* her be in. She should be home from work by this time. The receiver lifted, and she said, "three-nine-six."

I pressed the 'A' button, and my pennies clattered down. I had more pennies for when my time ran out. "My prayer was answered," I said, smiling.

"Oh . . . ?" She gave a little answering laugh. "What prayer was that?"

"That you'd be there."

"That's a safe one," she answered dryly. "I usually am."

"I'm glad. Even if that's selfish."

"Where are you?" she asked.

"Give you three guesses."

"Not *still* cooped up, surely?" I heard her sigh.

"I think they went and threw away the key."

"It's quite ridiculous."

"Would you be kind enough to point that out to the dimwit

colonel or general responsible? He might listen to you." Outside the booth, the waiting men rumbled and stirred, and I showed them my back. "I miss you."

"Miss you, too." It was what I had been waiting to hear.

"And I wanted to talk to you."

"You've done that," Heather reminded me. "Every day."

"I know, and it's driving me crazy, but talking to you is still good for me."

There was a pause, and then, sounding hesitant, she wondered, "the flying? Has it been bad?"

"Not for us. We haven't turned a prop for four days. The bird's still grounded for repairs."

"At least, in that case, you're spared all that's happening now," Heather pointed out.

But we could not be spared for ever. You missed out on one phase, but scored the next; everything evened out. There were still many missions to be flown. Now, under the cockpit windows, 'Big Apples' could boast an honest dozen bomb symbols, which pleased us, and impressed the rookies, but still left the small matter of twenty three outstanding with all their attendant hazards and risks. And the next in line would be Number Thirteen, a chilling prospect for men hag-ridden by hexes: none of us talked, or even cared to think, of that one . . .

The telephone warned of time up; I shoved in two more pennies, and would not look at the lengthening line of would-be callers outside. "Are you still there?"

"And where else would I be?" I could hear the smile in Heather's voice.

Heather smiled often, and in differing ways, her smiles reflecting her many and shifting moods. There were smiles for happiness, for contentment, politeness and uncertainty. She would smile at you gravely, and to tease, and always politely when she disagreed with something you said. A smile of hers could convey disdain and contempt, and the type reserved for those like Gladys Gibbons could freeze you solid at ten paces. I had run much of the gamut of Heather's smiles, although, so far, knock on wood, had been spared the more painful extremes. There was a straightforward rule by which to work: when the smiles reached to her eyes, you were okay. When they did not, then a degree of caution was advisable.

I said, "the fact of your being there makes these calls important for me."

"And all this time I thought it was me." The smile then, had I seen it, would have teased.

"Of course it's you. You have this terrific tonic value, and you do good things for me. Just the thought of you does."

"Jolly good," Heather said.

"Jesus, Lieutenant," a wounded, muffled voice exclaimed. "Give us a God damn' break!"

The staff sergeant, made bold by impatience, watched me in accusation through the glass. At his back at least twenty waited now; I faced their concerted hostility which informed me wordlessly—no need for words—that I was selfish, inconsiderate, a prick, a son of a bitch . . . an *officer*.

My choice; I could ream out the staff sergeant, or I could temporize. I thought then of long memories, of faces not to be forgotten, whether for good or evil: those men represented a cross-section of those with whom I must live and work, must trust, upon whom I had to depend.

I begged Heather to wait, and informed the staff sergeant, "listen, I'm not stalling deliberately . . . there are things that have to be said. And I'm pretty near through, so hang on." That would have to do, and I turned away to breathe in more of the booth's thick reek of old emotions, and my act of contrition was marred by the telephone's whickering for more pennies. I fed them in and felt the massed eyes boring into the back of my head . . .

"What you need, my dear," Heather advised. "Is a good talking-to."

I laughed. "Now you sound like my mother."

"Face to face," she added.

"I couldn't agree more. But the Army seems to think otherwise."

"I'm sure they'll lift their silly ban soon, it's only common sense, after all."

But who within the higher levels of command ever displayed any of that? "You'll see."

"I hope you're right, but I'm not holding my breath until they do." I speculated, "they've probably forgotten we exist." Except, of course, when there were missions to be flown.

"Perhaps I could come out and see you," Heather suggested. "You could buy me an American coffee in your canteen."

"How I wish you could. But it's no one in or out unless on duty. Although you could probably talk to me through the perimeter fence? Feed me peanuts like in the zoo."

Heather said then very softly, "we really should have that heart-to-heart."

"Suits me fine . . ." Hope had re-kindled. "And the sooner the better." I could picture fondly how it would be, this forthcoming tête-à-tête . . .

"I *do* want to be of help."

"Don't you understand yet how much you help already?" I reminded her, "plus, I have the spell."

"It's there always, whenever you need it. Never forget." She was insistent, as though trying to convince a backslider. "And, with it, my love to tide you over until your generals buck up their ideas."

I enquired hopefully, "think you could stick a spell on *them?*"

"Sorry . . . afraid not." She was laughing again. "Mine are always the friendly sort. I'm only fey, you know. Not a real witch."

*

'Big Apples' was signed out as airworthy on D plus 6.

On the next day we flew to Abbeville and caught some German transport, reinforcements from the Pas de Calais heading toward Normandy.

There was no flak worthy of the name, and not a sign of

fighters. We bombed pretty much as we pleased, and left many
of their vehicles wrecked or on fire.

Working with us was a squadron of R.A.F. rocket-firing
Hawker Typhoons, flying low for tank-busting, systematically
burning and killing at close quarters.

The Typhoon pilots flew like men with old scores to settle.
But then, from these same Pas de Calais fields *Adler Tag* had
been launched against England: Fat Herman standing on the cliffs
watching his bomber fleets make the swift hop across the Channel.
Now, four years on, it was payback time.

We circled above, watching as the Typhoons took their deadly
revenge at fifty feet and four hundred knots, and it was not easy
then to equate those coldly-efficient killers with the R.A.F.
pilots—'types' they liked to call themselves—we knew so well.
Casual and studiedly-scruffy, effete-seeming; occasional guests at
the base Officers' Club. Who had us back to their messes to
drink pints, play darts and sing dirty songs.

We flew home in time for the customary uninspiring G.I.
lunch, and nothing more was asked of us that day. Unlucky
Number Thirteen had been . . . no sweat. Still twenty two to
go, but Thirteen, we could agree aloud now, was a significant
stage safely passed.

Technical Corporal Flaherty vowed to have the thirteenth
bomb symbol in place ASAP, and asked if we wanted it a special
color, or bigger, or anything like that? Because of its being . . .
what it was? We declined with thanks all such suggestions:
Thirteen had been lucky, and we knew not to push things.

*

D plus 8, Mission 14, and our luck still holding on. We
went back to Caen which, for the Invasion planners, had been a
D-Day objective on the ground forces' battle orders. Following
the initial swift drive inland and the last-minute break out from
the near-catastrophe of Omaha Beach, the advance had slowed.

We were held still within the confines of the beachhead while supporting troops and supplies stockpiled along the shore. And Caen was holding out with grim persistence. Canadian and Polish troops were at the edge of Carpiquet airfield, unable to advance further against ferocious resistance, and fresh German units were streaming toward the city along every road in France.

For the Squadron, it was the now-regular format: destroy anew the roads hastily repaired since our last visit, knock out the fresh railheads established down-track from the yards and sidings blasted earlier.

The German air defenses were better-prepared than they had been on D-Day, although not back yet to their apocalyptic pre-Invasion level. Good enough, though, to knock down 'Eskimo Nell'. From which emerged five parachutes, and that was everyone: McGuire. Thibeault, Winscombe, Burnett and Sironi would spend what remained of the war in a Stalag. 'Eskimo Nell' had been flying short-handed.

'Big Apples' brought us home with a riddled aileron and a vibrating left engine. A shell splinter had bent a propeller blade. Aileron and blade would have to be replaced, which should be good for a day off at least.

Two easy missions, the classic 'piece of cake', although my piece had created further uproar in my gut. I must hold still during de-briefing, knotting my belly muscles, suffering the cramps in silence. Until released, and foregoing lunch, I could withdraw gratefully to the can.

The Quonset, when I got back to it, was jubilant. Andy Devine spotted me, and yelled, "hey, Skip . . . better get your butt in motion!"

I enquired, "what's going on?"

"What's goin' on is the barriers just come down! Them chickenshit sonsofbitches finally woke up. We're off the hook, an' on the Town!"

Eight days late, the gates had re-opened.

TEN

Three adjoining villages bore the Tiverell name: Tiverell Lacey, Tiverell End and Great Tiverell, forming a rough isosceles triangle with the airbase at its center. Each possessed its quota of public houses much-frequented by American servicemen. Tiverell Lacey boasted The Wheatsheaf, The Royal Oak and The Lamb and Mint, names that were curious and fascinating for men accustomed to doing their drinking in bars at home named McGinty's, The Starlight Room, or simply Bar & Grill.

The Lamb and Mint was our runaway favorite with its painted sign depicting a lamb roast on a platter with a sprig of green mint across its flank. The pub was unfailingly hospitable and tolerant of our frequently loud foreign ways. It was not long before we had re-named it 'The Sunday Roast'.

Where, on the evening of D + 8, I sat with Heather in the tiny saloon lounge. She with her glass of shandy, I, like a regular now, enjoying my pint of ale.

We had met at the end of her road where I waited with impatience for my first sight of her after far too long. Until she appeared, apologizing for being late; she had been stuck on the telephone with someone who would not stop talking. I replied that, after a week without her, ten more minutes was nothing, and was told once more that I was 'sweet'.

"Sweetness comes naturally to us Pilgrims," I said. "Didn't anyone ever tell you that?"

She took my hand. "Why must all Yanks brag?"

"Who's bragging? I'm simply stating the facts."

In the pub, however, she became quiet and withdrawn, staring moodily into the nearby public bar where almost all the drinkers were off-duty Americans. Puzzling, I followed her gaze, seeing only the usual darts game in progress, the people at tables, or propping up the bar. I recognized Gladys Gibbons, laughing loudly, all teeth on display, at something her companion, a grizzled master sergeant, was saying. Savoring her widowhood.

I asked Heather, "is it her . . . Gladys?"

She looked at me blankly. "Is it her, Gladys, what?"

"Who's troubling you . . . her being here, or something."

"Nothing about that woman can ever trouble me," Heather told me flatly.

"So tell me what *is* troubling you."

"Is it so evident, then?"

"You could say that . . . a little. You seem to have changed in the short time since we met."

"Sorry. I was just . . ." She shrugged. "Thinking."

"Dare I ask?"

"Of you," she said.

"Normally, I'd be delighted."

"Normally . . . ?"

"If thinking of me didn't give you such a long face."

That made her laugh, and she shook her head. "Not anything nasty. Just my silly imaginings."

"Shouldn't silly imaginings be fun?"

"That's the theory. It's just . . ." She studied the extended fingers of one hand. "I do worry about you."

"Who? *Me?*" I played the fool for her. "What's to worry?"

"If you must know . . ." Her eyes challenged me. "It's your alone-ness. Not lonely," she added quickly. "I don't think you're that, you're too nice to be lonely. But . . ."

"A loner," I finished.

"Yes." She nodded. "And that's worrying. Because it can't be good, not here and now. A war on, and you so terribly involved in it, and everything in you turning inward. Too much soul-searching and self-criticism."

She had nailed it again, precisely, and I could relate to it at once. "I guess I do tend to be a little hard on me." I gestured. "But then, you see, I've been living around me for quite a while.

I know all my own tricks . . ." But behind the show of lightness, I was thinking again of Heather's feyness, of that strange perceptibility of hers . . .

As she said, "so much brooding, and with the job that you have to do." She looked into my eyes, direct and questioning. "Are you angry with me now?"

"You've asked me that before, and the answer's still no. I'm just somewhat in awe of you."

"Then you mustn't be." She leaned closer. "Because I'm your friend, remember?"

I repeated it with deliberate emphasis. "Friend . . ."

She side-stepped at once with a reiteration of, "here to help if needed."

"And we've talked *that* over before as well . . ." I heard the testiness in my voice, and slapped a quick curb on it. "Heather, you *do* help. In only a month you've become important to me. Like a safe haven, I guess." That was as long as it had been, I realized then. One short, swift month since our meeting. Fourteen missions flown could make a long time out of thirty days. "You must know how often, and for how long, I've thought of you while I've been bottled-up on that crummy base." I reached out again to touch her hand. "And how wonderfully good this is now."

She stated bafflingly, "I would hate to disappoint you."

"Now, how could you ever do that?"

"There you go again." She sounded irritated. "Putting me up on a pedestal. Where you can see my clay feet."

"Like the way you see mine, and no pedestal needed." She did not reply. "You're right about the loner thing, it's the way I am. By nature and by preference. Which is okay, maybe, in Central Park, or beachcombing at Martha's Vineyard. But, right again, it has its drawbacks here and now."

"Exactly." Heather nodded.

"Big drawbacks when you're self-doubting, and scared half to death a lot of the time. And unable to talk about it to the people you work with . . . in case someone gets rattled by what you say, or group morale gets undermined. Plus the fact that the loner side of you won't *let* you talk . . . always too proud, and too ashamed. So that you simply clam up."

"But you know you can talk to me," she insisted. "And there's nothing with me, ever, to make you withdraw, or feel proud, or ashamed. As for being scared, well, if you were not, then I think that *would* be something to worry about. Because then, almost certainly, there would be something wrong with you."

I grinned at her without much mirth. "So that's the answer? Down off the high horse, and a little more humility and soul-baring?"

"It's one of the many myths of womankind . . ." Her mouth twisted self-mockingly. "That we're specialists in that sort of thing. The ever-sympathetic ear."

"You're the living proof," I said. "That it's no myth. I really *can* talk to you, and, when I'm with you, I'm no loner." As I made these admissions to Heather, the fresh belief was emerging that I was starting thereby to find my way closer to her . . .

Yet, as I considered that as a real possibility, she was telling me confidingly, "fears are always worse when the one who feels fear is in isolation. Someone who is private . . . secret . . ." I listened dutifully, willingly, as she set out her beliefs about me. "You picture the Germans and what they can do to you . . . what you've seen them do already to your friends . . ." Her voice was hushed, and her eyes were fixed on mine, and her words re-awakened in a rush the ugly images of airplanes burning, exploding, falling from the sky. Airplanes down in the sea . . . men bailing out, or not . . . As Heather wondered, "or is that *you* that you fear most?"

I gave a hesitant nod. "That's what bugs me, yes."

"And it's that deep, shameful fear that you spoke of?"

There was the uncomfortable awareness then that the initial spontaneity of our conversation was lost, ousted by a formal, almost defensive, stiltedness as I wondered afresh about the odd persistence of her questioning; like an intense post-mission briefing, or some kind of interrogation. I did not mind too much her questioning me, or answering her. What grated, I was finding, was the way that she kept on at it, worrying away like the dog with its bone, and for what? I said edgily, "I've admitted it already, I think."

"Listen, Denney . . . please." She leaned close, placing a soothing hand on my forearm. "Don't think I'm trying to make an Aunt Sally of you, I'm not. I would like to know, that's all. As long as you're willing to tell me."

"Well, something like that, that close to the bone, you know how it is." I mustered up a half-baked smile. "I'm a man, and men are vain." She bent her head in dry acknowledgement. "On the look out always for admiration and respect . . . all those good things. So how do I achieve them by admitting I'm yellow?"

"Do you truly believe that you are?"

I asked rhetorically, "what else is there?"

"There," Heather said, pleased. "Now do you see what happens when you're too solitary? A loner? All the doubts stuck in there, no outlet, left to stew and compound."

My prickly mood hung on stubbornly. "Anything else you can think of that might be wrong with me?"

She kept her composure, pursuing her theme. "You find it difficult to share, yet feel that you should be able to. You're very willful and, as you say, proud."

The grin returned, and would not be held back. "See any dark strangers in that crystal ball of yours? No need to mention long journeys, I know about those already."

"Only one particular dark stranger." She gave me an answering smile. "Who has long since left her crystal ball, and likes to view herself as no stranger now." She became severe then. "Think about it. You mightn't have got yourself into this wretched and needless pickle if you'd taken the trouble to *confide*."

"Okay . . . okay . . ." I shrugged capitulation. "I believe you, and respect your opinion."

"Really?"

"Cross my heart and hope to die. Besides which I haven't walked out in a huff yet."

"You might before I've finished with you," Heather warned.

"Keep talking, and we'll see."

"Only to add that, now, you *are* confiding. And, in doing so, finding that you're not alone after all."

"That's true . . ."

"And has your pride suffered?" she pursued relentlessly.

"What pride? Who has, or needs, pride?"

"Not you, certainly, when you're with me. All it takes is to be yourself, and talk things through, and feel that much better afterwards." Her fingers pressed into my arm as she insisted, "you're no coward, Denney. Believe me."

The darts game had ended. Gladys Gibbons, with hands wandering, was kissing her master sergeant as the onlookers whistled appreciation. I told Heather, "I don't think you should draw that conclusion from the fact that I keep on flying missions. I do that because I'm even more scared of the prospect of telling them where to shove their missions."

Although the paradox in that was that there was no real wish in me to default. I feared combat flying, yet was bound by a perverse and obstinate self-will to continue. A certain gallows humor under-scored the thought that I would sooner die than quit. Like the hurrying lemming, eager for the cliff-edge.

"That isn't what I meant at all," Heather declared. "It's that, rather, you talk to me about the troubling things in your heart, and find the means by that to face them and beat them. Doing that takes courage, more, possibly, than is needed to fly. And it rules cowardice right out." Her eyes, serious and level, questioned me. "Whatever cowardice really is?" With all my experience of it, I could offer still no definitive answer to that. "You worry about failing under those pressures that you're under already. And you feel alone, and uncared-for, and there's no relief to be had, and so your frame of mind just gets worse."

There she was, back again, ferreting about inside my head, and I was disturbed one more time by her weird gift, and by the notion of being so utterly *exposed* to her, with nowhere to run to and hide . . .

"Being solitary when your life is in such turmoil is simply one more cross that you're made to bear," Heather was telling me then. "One that you needn't bear, the weight of which can be lifted by something as simple and as good as having someone to talk to. Who might provide a different viewpoint."

"For someone," I said, smiling at her. "I read *you.*"

"That's right," she agreed at once. "Remember about troubles shared, and halved."

"Great for me, shedding the load," I pointed out. "But that means you taking it on, adding to your own."

"Does that matter when I'm willing to?"

"It's a fair handful . . . me *and* my neuroses."

"Let me be the judge." The laughter was in her voice again. "If it's too much, I can always renege."

"You do that," I said, not thinking. "Anytime."

"Which does seem to suggest that you'll let me help a little?"

I saw how, with skill and subtlety, she had backed me once more into a corner from which there was no escape. I could only temporize weakly, "the fact that it's you . . ."

My reward was an immediate up-to-the-eyes smile. "Would I let anyone else butt in? When *I'm* your friend?" Whether there was need for it or not, that unsatisfying word, uttered once more, could put a blight on the discussion. "Who really does rather love you."

That last part, offered without qualification, would have been close to perfect. But, again, Heather had managed to step aside neatly from any suggestion of commitment. Even when she added, " . . . perhaps more than is wise?"

ELEVEN

On June 16 we flew our fifteenth mission.

To Caen yet again for a strike on the heavy industry zones lying to the south of that battered and suffering city.

After so much early promise, it was beginning to look depressingly as though the Germans had succeeded in stopping our advance cold. Ten days after the landings, and the line had become static, confined still within the beachhead area. Many people, those in the know, and those who were not, were starting to question the leadership capabilities of the theatrical and over-exposed British general, Montgomery.

Each day the calls came in for more air attacks, the sure-fire means, it was touted about, to break the deadlock. Mission Fifteen was our small part of the overall response.

Caen lay in ruins, the city center all-but obliterated, surrounding countryside pock-marked by the rim-to-rim craters of our bombs, and by the shells of ground artillery and ships.

We would have to bomb with pinpoint accuracy within a tightly-defined area, and O'Connor went out of his way to be a worse-than-usual horse's ass. In fairness to him and his highly-nervous state, the proximity to the target of friendly troops meant that a small slip on his part, or mine, might cause us to slaughter our own people.

Mindful of that, I could understand and accept his vitriol; a state of mind made possible for me by the near-absence of all but some limited small-caliber flak. The true enemy that day was the weather which was falling apart about us as we flew on, and about which Major Ambruster had provided fair warning. The takeoff had been in strong crosswinds; heavy gusts had buffeted 'Big Apples' all the way across the sea, with visibility reduced in rain and fog patches. Over the French coast the overcast dropped lower, scudding lumps of strato-cu knitting their bases together at two thousand feet, keeping me for much of the time on instruments.

Sergeant Deeks expressed concern on the intercom over the possibility of losing his breakfast. Finding scant sympathy from the rest of us, he mourned, "these bastards over here sure got one cock-eyed idea of *summer!*"

All through the outbound leg we pitched and soared, prey to every skittish whim of the elements, the bottom dropping out from under us sickeningly in the vicious up- and down-drafts. As we approached Ouistreham, O'Connor stated peevishly, "Jesus Christ . . . surely you can try and do better than this?"

"Like to tell me how? Since when did I invent weather?" Sweating over the controls, I vented my frustration and fury at him. "Get off my back, God damn it!"

"Ho, boy . . ." He peered at me from the crawlway with an expression of comic concern. "Once more the biter bit." He yielded a little. "The best you can, then? Would that be all right to ask? And . . . one other thing?"

"*WHAT?*"

"Don't go 'way mad." He disappeared into his lair.

I did my best, cursing the evil-natured air, the drab and soaking cloud-deck, and I got good and mad, which helped considerably in suppressing the customary jitters. Staying mad until O'Connor dumped the bombs, telling us, resigned, "they could've hit Alaska for all I know. And who, in his heart of hearts, gives a shit?"

We climbed away from destroyed Caen from which came vengeful bursts of tracer that made me jink and twist in self-defense as I recrossed our stalled front line, a mere mile from where we had bombed.

Now, ahead, awaited a difficult crosswind landing. Tired, pissed-off, stressed-out, I made a sloppy, who-cares approach, bouncing us down on the asphalt with a jolt that earned me ironic cheers on the intercom, O'Connor summing-up in mild tones, "I'd be hard-put to describe that as a landing, kid. But it was sure one hell of an *arrival!*"

From Caen, on that occasion, 'Oakland Bay Baby' (Higginson, Pierce, Sully, Inman, Schramme, Weigand and McHugh) did not return.

That night, the Great Storm blew in from the Atlantic, a vast depression with isobars packed in tight to build winds with lashing squalls and mountainous seas. Which played havoc with the ships lying off the beaches, and wrecked the American Mulberry harbor on Omaha Beach.

The Great Storm grounded everyone and everything. Missions were off.

*

Heather hurried, dripping, into the Sunday Roast, muffled in her white mac, and with a scarf over her hair. She gave me her cold, wet hands to chafe, and I said, "I should never have dragged you out in this."

"No one dragged me." She shrugged out of the coat, and asked for her usual shandy.

The pub was quiet with the lousy weather keeping the locals at home, the airmen on base, all of them denied the treat of Heather in her figure-flattering gaberdine skirt and cashmere sweater. She was well-worth braving storms worse than this for.

We toasted each other, and she asked, "how are you?"

"Would you believe, fine?"

"You've flown, haven't you? Since we talked last?"

"Just the once."

"And how was it?" She leaned forward with her usual expectant look.

"The worst part was this." I pointed to the rain-streaming window. "We went just as it was moving in."

I regaled her briefly with the events of Mission 15, of attempting to bomb with precision from an aircraft that sought all the time to stand on its head.

"How did you feel?"

"Busy, and madder than a wet hen. With the weather and

my black-hearted bombardier." I talked of O'Connor's bitching, and she laughed. "Apart from that, blissful."

She patted my hand. "Well done."

It was praise that I saw as unearned: the fact was that we had been fortunate, and were still, the total of completed missions mounting steadily with, so far, only small damage and no one hurt. Shaken nerves, of course, but shaken nerves went with the job. Nothing that we could not handle, or had not already. Good fortune aside, however, the matter of Heather's claimed spell remained to be considered, because, smitten by her, I wanted very much to believe that there was more to our continuing survival than plain dumb luck . . . that she, too, helped to influence favorably the flow of events where we were concerned.

I wished, and not for the first time in my life, that I was really smart; mentally equipped to figure out the validity, or otherwise, of Heather's alleged gifts. Instead of being as I was— albeit willingly—able only to shroud uncertainty and ignorance in the convenient cloak of 'more things in heaven and earth'. The blind believer who, lacking evidence or credibility, was still content to believe.

Accepted that Heather was fey, although the word's meaning, applied to her, could be alarming if you let yourself dwell on it. When consulted, the Oxford Dictionary offered: ' . . . one disordered in mind . . . frequently with over-confidence'. Also (the part I hated) ' . . . like one about to die'. Over-confident? Well, okay . . . maybe. The rest, though, knowing Heather as I believed I did by then, I elected to refute.

There was, surely, nothing 'disordered' in her? Odd, or weird, yes, fine . . . rare, most certainly. As for 'one about to die', you could forget *that* straightaway! There, the Oxford Dictionary had called it wrong.

It might be that it was not true feyness, and that some other, more suitable, tag was called-for. Although, if she wished to be recognized as fey, then it was fine by me. Whatever it was that touched Heather with its strange fingers looked good in my eyes.

As long as she was on my side, and close, caring, then fine and dandy.

*

The Great Storm blew itself away after five days.

Doing so as the army divisions commanded by General Lawton Collins broke out from the Utah beachhead to cut straight across the base of the Cotentin peninsula, then swinging northward until, four more days after the storm, U.S. troops were in Cherbourg, and we had seized our first deep-water port.

The Squadron flew two missions in support of the Cotentin fighting, both deep into Brittany to attack more bridges and rail yards.

The first was a welcome milk-run to Angers where we succeeded in bouncing a long road convoy complete with a column of tanks, stuck there, sitting ducks. With those, the Bomb Group scored some of the designated bridges, and touched off an ammunition train with spectacular results. Back at Tiverell Lacey without a mark on us, we handed over 'Big Apples' to Technical Corporal Flaherty who stenciled our sixteenth bomb symbol indelibly in place.

*

Our seventeenth, next day, sent the Squadron to Le Mans, flying southward over the coast, and on by Lisieux, Argentan and Alençon at six thousand feet.

It was a heavy mission deploying numerous squadrons, and we were warned to expect much in the way of flak. The reality far exceeded expectation: what we faced was as bad, or worse, than anything experienced so far, more than enough—for all of Heather's assurances—to subject me to the full extent of my private hell of fear, sweat and tortured intestines.

It was a superb flying day, the sky scoured clean by the recent storms: from fifty miles out we could see clearly the great smoke pall hanging over the target, and the strings of blooming mushrooms that were detonating bombs. Also the black deck of flak that matched our approach altitude precisely.

We stared out, numbed and silent, at the too-familiar sight of a B-26 ablaze, leaving the bomber stream to drift tiredly down like a leaf in a fall breeze.

Supposedly to encourage our better performance, we had been given all the big spiel about the beachhead break-out, of the Cotentin cut off, our tank and infantry spearheads almost into Cherbourg. Caen was besieged, all-but surrounded: Le Mans itself almost within reach of the rapidly-expanding front.

Which appeared to faze the Germans dug in down there not at all as they shot at us with undiminished ferocity, precise, fixed and furious. Offering the impression that they would be there to give us more of the same whenever we chose to come calling. There for ever, and what did we plan to do about it? At La Mans, they were not remotely inclined to quit . . .

As, once again, O'Connor's crackly litany filled my headset. "Coming on the I.P. now, and . . . I have her. Hold that heading and altitude. Steady . . . so. Just like that . . ."

*

We came home with a large hole through the right wing. The direct hit we had been waiting for had found us. An eighty eight-millimeter round that tore through and kept going without exploding and shredding the wing. Through the outboard section, missing the engine, fuel tanks, mainspar and aileron.

We stood on the hardstand in a huddling group, peering up at *our* shell hole, each alone with his thoughts, none speaking for the moment. O'Connor with arms akimbo, his hat tilted back, nodding, faintly smiling. Andy Devine without expression, humming tunelessly. Deeks snapping spearmint, Cohn pensive, Smithson turning his head aside to spit.

Until the laconic Patecki broke the silence. "I'll tell you *this* for nothing . . . we are some lucky pricks." Everyone turned to look at him. "So lucky, I reckon that oughtta hold us awhiles, an' I don't give a pinch o' dried coonshit what anyone says otherwise." He stared hard at each of us in turn, challenging a contradiction which did not come. "Ain't no sonofabitch ever gonna touch us now. An' screw any asshole that tries to tell ya different!"

It was more in one go than Patecki had uttered since we came together as a crew. Patecki, one-time contract hand-logger from the Yakima Valley, a silent man of those silent Pacific Northwest woods and forests, had become our prophet. And even though his prophecy should provoke Providence to slap our insolent wrists, it still sounded pretty damned good.

And I had to forcibly suppress the sudden urge to blurt out that this was—*had* to be!—a whole lot more than luck. To tell them that we were being watched over, wrapped up tight and warm in the cocoon of Heather's spell. It would have been pleasant then to speak of that, but not at all smart.

*

Others had no such protective magic.

Le Mans cost the Group eleven aircraft, and two were from Tiverell Lacey.

'Roman's Ruin'—named, it appeared now, with grim prescience—went down in flames south of Falaise on the German side of the line. There were no parachutes. Roman, Wladawski, Greenamayer, Brown, Utley, Stemwedel and Keegstra had been on their thirty third mission.

On board 'Noontime Bandit', Simcock, Van Sant, Dwek, Grahame, Farley, Ahearne and Boquist simply vanished, fate unknown. Seen over the target, then turning away. After which . . . seen no more. Mission Twenty Six.

TWELVE

I came groggily from shallow, troubled sleep to find the unknown PFC standing beside my bunk.

I resented the way he watched me, his having caught me off-guard and vulnerable.

"You looking for something in particular?"

"Yeah, Lieutenant . . . sorry." He retreated an involuntary pace from my glare.

"If it's bad news, then you can't find me . . . and that's an order, okay?"

His grin was uneasy. "Wouldn't exactly call it bad, sir."

"Then what?"

"Ain't for me to say." He was the archetypal army clerk, short, pale and studious, with a nice clean fatigue uniform and spit-shined boots. Revealing nothing.

"But Major Delaney . . . he wants you like right away."

"You *do* know what for," I said.

"Well, I got me an idea, Lieutenant." His grin widened as confidence was restored. Listening heads lifted from nearby bunks. The full-throttle bellow of a Pratt & Whitney radial engine on a test run penetrated the Quonset walls. Puzzling walls; you could not work out exactly where they ceased being walls and became ceiling. The engine throttled down, fading . . .

"But you're not talking," I said.

"Sir, Major Delaney would really ream out my ass if I did," the PFC informed me earnestly. "I got the feelin' he's lookin' to keep this one for himself."

*

"Lieutenant Pilgrim, we picked your oh-so lucky name straight out of the hat," Major Delaney announced with all the appearance of jovial goodwill.

"Sir?"

"A special assignment . . . all for you." He twinkled at me and, at once, my gut knotted and went into overdrive. "Nice and soft and easy for a while. Some fun, a few laughs, maybe even the odd moment of illicit luxury?" He was toying with me, milking this—whatever it was—for all it was worth, and I willed him to . . . get it *said*, you old bastard. "Some chaps I know would murder for an opportunity like this."

In England since '43, Major Delaney had built up a collection of regional words and expressions like 'chap', 'piece of cake', 'wizard show' and 'bang on'. Following in the footsteps of Gatsby's immortal 'old sport'. But then, I reflected absently, Gatsby, in another war, had been a major, too . . .

"That's why we have to draw lots, you see?" Major Delaney was explaining. "To make quite sure all's fair and above board."

"Right, Major."

"We're sending you courier flying." He teased me with an arch look. "Unless you have any strong objection to that?"

I echoed him inanely, "objection . . . ?"

"To the job, dear boy . . . this favored assignment? I mean, if you'd rather go on flying missions, and let someone else . . ."

"Oh no, sir," I got in quickly. Before the chance slipped away. "No objections."

"Jolly good." He looked pleased. "Splendid."

I enquired politely, "when exactly is it we start, Major?"

"You've started." He turned brisk. "On the hook as of now."

"Could the Major advise as to the nature of the duties, and for how long?"

"The Major could not, because he doesn't damned well know." His mouth compressed in a sudden show of petulant disappointment. "Your fate rests for the unforeseeable future in the hands of those high enough in the command structure to be able to whistle up courier ships on whim. Your little lives are theirs to order . . . we have no say." He was sounding increasingly put out. "As for how long, it could be days or weeks. You may turn out to be such a shit-hot courier pilot that they just can't bring themselves to let you go. Or, again, they may fire your ass first trip. Generals can be fickle chaps." He allowed himself a sour grin. "Capeesh?"

"Understood, sir."

"Inform your crew, and your crew chief, of course." Delaney demanded, "who is?"

"Staff Sergeant Tallichet, Major."

"Clue him up, Lieutenant. Tell him his working hours and maintenance schedules are going to be up the creek for the next little while. Your own as well," Major Delaney added, smirking. "But then, war is hell, right?"

"That's *right*, sir!" And how would you know, I wondered.

"Well, that's it," he told me. "You can take a hike."

I threw him a big salute, and left.

*

No surprise to find that O'Connor was intimate with the ins and outs of courier flying. "At last, in my dotage . . ." He wore a contented smile. "The long overdue recognition of my selfless, devoted and exemplary service. The belated but welcome thanks due to a loyal minion."

I reminded him, "it was my name they pulled out of the hat."

He waved it aside. "Merely the gods and their mysterious ways."

Courier flights, he went on to explain, did not count as missions. When our spell as courier crew for the Bomb Group ended, we would return to full Squadron duties with the outstanding balance still waiting to be flown.

"No discounts, no rebates . . . a mere restful interlude, kid. From which, or so it's claimed in the manufacturer's manual, we return with batteries charged, outlooks improved, just itchin' to get back at the dastardly Hun. A notion," he added. "With which reality seldom equates."

Courier flying would, almost certainly, take us the length and breadth of the British Isles. We could anticipate, also, visits to the zone of the armies in France, landing at rough-and-ready forward airstrips.

"We'll be close enough to where the big boys are playing for keeps," O'Connor said. "And it's more than likely that we'll get shot at. But that still won't count." He smiled upon Andy and me with great fondness. "Should we have the extreme misfortune to get ourselves creamed under such circumstances, then we shan't have died in action, but in *service*. It's all a matter of semantics. Although the outcome, members of the jury, will be much the same."

*

We flew short hauls to neighboring A.A.F. fields, and to R.A.F. stations in East Anglia and Lincolnshire, and went further afield to Aldergrove, Prestwick, Turnhouse, Speke and Colerne; to Middle Wallop and Charmiedown. There were, too, the promised trips across to Normandy, landing on runways built of clattering, vibrating PSP sheeting that were barely long enough to receive a B-26, or to get one out of later.

In place of bombs, we carried people, freight, papers, the secret plans borne aloft by tight-lipped messengers wearing helmet liners, and with holstered .45s, their briefcases chained to their wrists.

We conveyed air marshals, the odd admiral and no end of generals with one star, two, or three. Who would call us 'son' (which made O'Connor snort), and demanded to know the names of our home towns, which they professed always to know well.

Sometimes it would be visiting senators or congressmen, shepherded by anxious-looking public relations colonels, who made no secret of their distaste for flying in a battered and paint-chipped combat airplane. At other times, we might be called upon to chauffeur a big-noise syndicated columnist or broadcaster. There for a look-see, first-hand, at 'the real war'. Getting the lowdown for the folks back home. Oozing bonhomie and insisting on first names all round . . . "none of this 'sir' bullshit with *me*, fellas." Who would become notably silent as we circled over yesterday's battlefields. Except to wonder, carefully-casual, about the possibility of ground fire . . . ?

There were times when, because of the number of visiting firemen to be carried, I would be compelled to 'bump' O'Connor and the sergeants, taking only Andy Devine along in his assumed guise of navigator.

The sergeants declared themselves well-pleased to be left behind. They had no duties outside of flying missions, and could goldbrick to their hearts' content. Nor did O'Connor object to being forsaken. From his sour and rumpled bunk, he would offer farewell and Godspeed, and urge me not to accept any wooden nickels. "I shall think of you with enduring kindness, and, occasionally, may laugh a little. But always without malice."

Our brass-hat masters were largely considerate of us, giving ample notice always of intended departures. Delays were kept to a minimum, and those which occurred would, sometimes, be explained with apologies.

They were liberal with time off. On completion of flights that had involved days away from home base, we would be told to stand down, often for an entire weekend. While everyone else was off flying missions.

It was dull in the main, and frequently irritating, although nearly always safe. No one that we knew of for certain was shooting at us, not even on the visits to France. I was feeling much better for the break, my mind quietening, my stomach growing more obedient. The pundits were right; courier flying *was* restful. I began once more to enjoy the simple experience of flying an airplane, working to improve personal standards which had been allowed to slip badly.

O'Connor, noticing the difference, offered acid comment. "You'll fly this good for some dickhead general or half-assed reporter. But you won't do it for *me!*"

*

All that generous time off enabled me to see more of Heather. Long, carefree hours spent together in the glorious days of mid-summer, with the sun still well above the horizon at nine in the evenings.

We took country walks, and hopped busses that bore us away, far from the presence of airmen and airplanes, and followed our noses through wide, smooth fields, through woods rich with birdsong. More than once we forgot about time, and there would be a laughing, breathless race to make the last bus, and, once, we missed it altogether, ruefully beginning the six-mile hike home. And were picked up by two amused British officers in a Ford staff car. Who told us, "we got this rattle-trap on lease-lend. The least we can do is provide some return hospitality."

Heather borrowed the smart bike for me, and we rode farther afield. It was British Double Summer Time with the clocks advanced two hours to allow the farmers, it was said, more time to get the crops in. It let *us* ride in sunlight until very late, and there would be light in the sky still at midnight, the hour at which, several times, we returned.

With further ironic conniving from O'Connor, I obtained another—and better—jeep one evening, and took Heather back to dine at the hotel at Banxted. They told us that they remembered us, and gave us grilled sole and another strictly-rationed half-bottle— a Sauterne from the Chateau d'Arche Lafaurie.

"My mother," I said to Heather. "Would pull a very sour face."

She eyed me across the rim of her glass. "Whatever for?"

"She's a lady of firm and definite views. One of those being that any white wine must be drunk within the year . . ." I held up the little bottle. "Nineteen thirty five. Don't know if that was a good year or not, but I'd never fault it. Which, to dear old Mom, would be heresy."

"Some day . . ." Heather watched smilingly as I refilled her glass. "You must tell me more about her. She sounds fascinating."

"That's one word," I agreed.

*

We stood down on the Friday afternoon following three days spent flying around in Scotland. There would be nothing for us to do until Monday, which pleased us all: office hours, and a July weekend beckoning.

I asked Heather, "anything you can think of that you'd care to try? Go somewhere else special, maybe?" I had been thinking of London, tickets for a show, supper afterwards . . . and whatever might ensue. In London, notwithstanding the blackout, rationing, the doodlebug raids, just about anything was possible . . .

"Why don't we go to Colchester?" Heather wondered.

I considered Colchester, which was certainly not London. "Do you recommend it?"

"Oh, I *do* . . ." She was grinning impishly. "Essex's answer to Manhattan."

We took the Saturday noon bus, and I wore my best Class 'A' uniform; olive-drab tunic and tan pants—that the English preferred to call pink. Wings, silver first lieutenant's bars, a suitably battered-looking fifty-mission hat. Heather was light and radiant in her summer frock and sandals, and had her thick, dark hair tied back with a length of velvet ribbon. She was lovely enough to bring a lump to my throat.

In the bus, she puzzled me by asking, "how well up are you on your British history?"

"You mean, like kings' names, and dates and things?"

"Those would do for a start, yes." Her dryest smile hovered.

"Well, as you'd expect, my personal bias is more American. I've got my presidents down more or less pat . . . then the Civil War and colonial wars. The Boston Tea Party, *and* some things outside America as well," I added quickly, noting her amused and knowing look. "But not so hot on your old kings." I thought for a moment. "Let's see . . . there was William the Conqueror, and Richard the Lionhearted. Then that other that Shakespeare wrote about . . ."

"Richard the Third, you mean?"

"Yeah, he'll do," I agreed. "And you cut the head off one."

"Poor Charles." She sounded regretful. "The First."

"Right. Then you had . . . Henry the Eighth, with his eight wives."

"Six, actually."

"Okay, six. But still a pretty good track record." I laughed then, remembering, "and Bloody Mary. After whom we named a cocktail."

"And you named Virginia after Queen Elizabeth, Mary's half-sister. The questionable Virgin Queen. Or, rather, Sir Walter Raleigh named it."

"O'Connor's a Virginian." I mused, "wonder if he knows about that?"

"I should think he does."

I groped further through the dimness of memory. "There were William and Mary, whom we commemorate with a pretty good university." I concentrated more. "Several Edwards."

"Eight," Heather pronounced, then corrected herself. "Well, almost. Number Eight did a bunk with a Yank." She giggled.

"Shows good taste," I ventured, and hurried on, "and all those Georges."

"Six to be precise, including the incumbent, whose name is really Albert. The Third, the mad one, was on the throne when you people got all disloyal."

"We'll skip that part," I said. "You had four Williams."

"That's very good," Heather approved.

"And one John." I shot her a glance. "Most houses do have these days, although some still have it on the outside, and call it an outhouse."

"That's rude." She looked severe. "*Our* John . . ." She began to grin. "Signed the Magna Carta, although very much under protest." She said firmly, "that's enough about kings."

"Oh, no," I protested dutifully. "I was starting to enjoy it."

"I've heard you Americans are great admirers of history," Heather said.

"Mainly because we have so little of it."

"Mustn't forget the *Mayflower* and the Pilgrim Fathers. Although I've heard no mention of any Pilgrim *Mothers*."

"There's my mother," I pointed out. "She's a Pilgrim mother."

"Oh, ha-ha . . . but that's not quite the same, is it?" She considered me for a moment before saying, "what I had in mind when I asked you about history was something that pre-dates all our English kings. *British* history was what I mentioned."

"So you did. Okay. How far back do you want to go? Although I can't promise you much in the way of answers."

"What about the Romans?" Heather asked. "And where we're off to today."

"In Colchester?" I felt my interest quickening.

"The Romans," she affirmed. "Built Colchester."

Inadvertently, with that disclosure, Heather had tweaked an eagerly-responsive nerve, because Rome and the Romans had been a childhood passion of mine. Where other kids went in for things like Little League, erector sets or collecting postage stamps, I was an all-time, all-American freak for the Roman Empire. I never knew quite why, only that I was. My mother, amused by my obsession, had concluded once that I must be the reincarnation of one of the Emperors. Nothing less than an Emperor would have done for my mother.

Whatever, by the time I was fifteen, I was something of a whiz on my chosen topic, having read and enjoyed Tacitus, and struggled more with Virgil, Marcus Aurelius and Caesar. Of the latter, I smiled still over the bawdy song attributed to the soldiers who marched with him on his triumphal return to the City.

> 'Home we bring the bold whoremonger!
> Romans, lock your wives away!
> All your gold you sent to serve him
> Went his Gallic tarts to pay!'

What had captured and held my greater interest, however, were the histories of Gaul and, coincidentally, Roman Britain.

I knew well of the 'bold whoremonger's' two landings in Britain, misnamed 'conquests' by some: more punitive raids in strength with an eye to possible political advantage. And of Gaius

Caligula's later empty farce and failing nerve on the Gaulish side of the Channel.

Also, the Claudian invasion, the true Conquest, establishing Roman rule throughout most of Britain for the next three hundred and fifty years.

I could speak with small authority of the garrison Legions, II Augusta under Vespasian, VI Victrix, XX Valeria Victrix, and of the great administrators like Agricola and Aulus Plautius Nepos. Of Hadrian whose Wall bound the farthest northern limits of Empire, and Septimius Severus who had died at York, a reigning Emperor far from home.

Where Ancient Rome was concerned, I considered myself to be not too much of a slouch.

*

We walked together, hands clasped, through the old town on a sunny Saturday with people around us shopping, queuing and strolling, soaking up the un-rationed sunlight for as long as it might last. Everywhere there were crowding uniforms and drab military traffic. Colchester, after so many centuries, remained a garrison town. Filled with purposeful, unsmiling British soldiers who threw me massive open-handed salutes. Which, in Heather's amused and watchful presence, embarrassed the hell out of me. Few of the Americans I knew were great on saluting: for citizen soldiers it smacked too much of career military horse crap. And, Heather, taken with the uncontrollable giggles, only heightened my discomfiture.

I was held in thrall, though, by the portions of surviving Roman wall built with flat, mellow-colored bricks, as strong and sound now as on the day they were raised. A place in which to drift and dream, my long-ago and distant passion made suddenly and wonderfully real as I ran fingertips over the weathered surfaces and pictured those who had stood once where I stood now, busy raising the walls, and a russet staining on my hands linked me somehow with those people, those times . . .

"I've seen groups sometimes in great cathedrals, or standing before famous paintings, and all with that identical look," Heather said.

I turned to smile at her. "What look's that?"

"Would 'rapt' do? Or 'spellbound'?" She gave a small, hesitant laugh. "Only, this time, the spell isn't mine, or me."

"Well, you know . . ." I nodded acknowledgement and apology. "This really is my kind of thing." I touched her cheek lightly with a fingertip, and left a little smear of dust from the old Empire. "Thank you for bringing me here. It was inspired."

We wandered slowly on through the lengthening afternoon, and Heather told me, "Colchester, you know, was once a *colonia*. And Queen Boadicea came one day and burned it all down."

With that, she wakened another memory; I searched for a name, running through an uncertain list: Glevum was . . . Gloucester, and Eboracum, York . . . *Old* York. Londinium . . . well, that spoke for itself. Venta Silurum, Venta Belgarum, Verulamium, Corstopitum, Caesaromagus . . . ? And then, it was there, and I said, "Camulodunum."

She studied me thoughtfully. "Who's a clever boy, then?"

"Just something I picked up." I affected carelessness.

"I'm impressed," she said with a smile. "Again."

There was the feeling then of having passed some kind of test, and even of doing quite well. Not knowing at the time that I had been sitting it.

*

Many times on our country walks and rides I would experience something that lay beyond my ability to describe or grasp fully. Something delightful and poignant, like the calling back of good memories from the threshold of sleep, accompanied at the edge of awareness by a hint of music that seemed like some cool, distant composition of Sibelius . . . 'The Swan of Tuonela', or 'Nuages', the Debussy nocturne. Inducing the longing within me for places and faces half-seen and all unknown. Which, when, metaphorically, I would turn my head, would not be there.

It would happen without warning as we turned a bend in the road, or crossed high ground with far horizons opening up. Sometimes it would come to me when I saw a weatherworn house, a patch of woodland where leaves flickered in a stir of wind. 'It' would be there then, in and around me, a faint drift of something like sweet autumnal woodsmoke.

It could not be *déjà vu*; nothing there to suggest the once-known. Rather, a delightful, ineffable sense of *returning*. And could it, I would wonder, be some form of throw-back . . . although, if so, then to what, for there was nothing in it that I could recognize, or point to with familiarity.

There was the unsure belief, too, that, whatever it was, was not distant from me, but something lying within the brief span of my own lifetime, pricking, while for ever illusive, at my consciousness. With it, also, a slow, gentle regret for what was lost irretrievably.

It came to me, I noted, only when I was with Heather: away from her I would try and try to re-capture it, always without success. And would find myself speculating on the likelihood of its being some hitherto unrevealed aspect of her magic, the weaving of more spells for my benefit. Done because she perceived my great need for inner peace and, in response, generated a quiet balm of time and distance, my hand reaching out for what could never quite be grasped, only sensed. By then, more than half-convinced, I wanted very much to see and accept what was happening to me as one more aspect of Heather's feyness.

THIRTEEN

As suddenly as they had begun, our easy times were over.

During the four weeks in which we had played tourist, the Squadron had flown mission after mission, with more crews lost, more aircraft down or damaged beyond repair.

Many of the old targets remained, together with a host of fresh ones, all taking their toll: Rennes, Le Mans, Brest, L'Orient, St. Nazaire, Nantes, Villacoublay and Amiens and Evreux. Antwerp and Brussels, Liège, Tilburg, Dordrecht, Breda. At each hated place, the Ninth Air Force took sharp punishment.

While winning on paper, the physical reality was proving less clear-cut. Seeing the empty hardstands after each trip, with their forlorn, unemployed ground crews, it became increasingly difficult to credit all the success reports, the grandiose claims of final victory in sight, almost within grasp.

In our absence, 'Rhode Island Red' had been lost, taking 'Red' Nicholls, the pilot, from Providence, and, with him, Blower, Willys, Forster, Flokk, Abbott and Burletson.

Gone were 'Begin the Beguine', 'Pony Express', 'Daisy T.', 'Gutless Wonder', 'Casey Junior', 'Minnie the Moocher', 'Bumble Beatty' and 'Rebel Yell'.

Shot down, force-landed, blown up, vanished, limped home for the single cold glance, the condemning finger across the throat: write off and cannibalize for spares. Bulldoze what remained into the graveyard dump over at the farthest, most out-of-sight corner of the field.

Gone to the grave, to the sea's depths, to hospitals and P.O.W. camps were Bullock and Viertel, Ghosh and Thomas and Walchek. Bard, Davidow, Schulz, Levinson, Caan, Frazier and McCarthy.

Penzias was dead, and Frisch, Hubble, Hughes, Loughead, Fackler, Tolliver, Bondi, Fiorini, d'Oliveira, Corey, Euler, Backus, Ward, Whittig and Yachmetz.

E.T.O. hospitals, and others in the States, admitted Whitley, Yoest, Scotting and Swantko, Urbach and Seiler, Troy and Ray and Powell: Richards and Phenix and Kennedy and Kirkpatrick; Buckholter, Crosby and Diggs.

Brezinski was a prisoner, as were Ames, Parker, Norman and Brandtmuller, Reskewich, Santana, Shaw and Pizarski.

Tyler, Venator, Winters, Kelleson, Fairchild, Wigton, Whitehead, Kelsall and Lebair were missing.

It was all very fine, just *great*, to have mastery of the air. The price paid for it, though, was an exorbitant one . . .

Everyone, when we returned, gave us a hard time about soft touches and ass-kissing, and said how glad they were to have us back. We were needed, or, as Major Delaney put it fittingly enough, "you chaps are off the bench and wanted in the scrimmage."

Although ground-bound Major Delaney would not, himself, be in the scrimmage. He was one chap who would remain on the bench.

*

We were, we learned, just in time for something called Operation Cobra.

"The name of the game," Lieutenant Colonel Friend announced. "Is breakout . . . and on the big scale."

He turned to the vast wall map of Northern France with its colored lines and little flags and symbols that marked the known German positions and our own, all the infantry and armor and artillery. The recognized and estimated and fondly-imagined enemy strongholds and concentrations. His busy pointer circled a spot marked with a neat swastika flag, and I wondered who it might be who had the task of creating all those flags and symbols: tanks, cannon, the cut-outs of little men shouldering carbines.

Turning those out at a quiet desk somewhere would be a pretty nice job to have in this war . . .

I heard Lieutenant Colonel Friend say, "St. Lô." His pointer stabbed aggressively at selected spots on the map. "Here, the Vire and Lozon Rivers . . ." The pointer described a ground-consuming arc. "Our line, the St. Lô to Periers road. The line of planned forward movement. Which you . . ." His stern and indomitable gaze fell upon us. "And the rest of the Ninth, together with plenty of the Eighth's heavies, will make possible. Now, men, the Army has a tough row to hoe out there. But you'll make things a whole lot easier for those dogfaces by bombing with perfect precision along the target line." His flushed face radiated confidence in us all. "A demanding task, men, but far from impossible. For you, in fact, I'd call it routine."

At my side, Andy Devine muttered furiously, "go stick it in your ass."

A ripple of mirth moved outward: Lieutenant Colonel Friend, an incorrigible gung-ho merchant, was not loved.

'Cobra' was to be the opening gambit of Omar Bradley's fresh campaign from the base of the Cotentin. Opposing it was the crack German LXXXIV Corps which included the highly-regarded (by both sides) Panzer Lehr Division, commanded by a tough old Kraut named Bayerlein. The initial assault would attempt to break the German line between the Vire and the Lozon, then, pivoting on newly-captured St. Lô, drive down deep into Brittany.

Before our arrival on the target, U.S. forces would retire briefly from their forward positions, allowing us an open bombing area.

"A strip of ground fronting on to the enemy positions, our line of withdrawal marked with smoke," we learned. "Beyond that smoke line, you have a clear field. Everything out there will be yours for the flattening."

A maximum effort, the biggest air mission so far into Normandy in terms of aircraft employed, some twelve hundred in all. Forts and Liberators of the Eighth, the Ninth's mediums.

Lieutenant Colonel Friend's tub-thumping aside, it sounded like heady stuff.

*

We took off on runway zero-nine toward the research labs where Heather worked, and, deliberately, I held 'Big Apples' flat at a hundred feet, looking down at the windows filled with faces and fluttering hands. More people stood in the open, waving. Heather would be somewhere among them . . .

I reached out to slide the propeller pitch controls back and forth, moving the whirling steel blades between high and low R.P.M., aware of the dramatic effect that the sound of it would have, the big props ba-rooming my thanks and love.

Holding level like that had allowed the airspeed to build up sufficiently for me to pull a show-off chandelle, racing up and away steeply to rejoin the climbing flights.

"What's this, Hotshot?" O'Connor was peering up at me with quizzical eyes. "Practicin' for some peacetime barnstormin'?"

"Merely," I informed him. "The cementation of Anglo-American relations."

His brows wigwagged. "So? Relations have reached the sementation stage, huh?" He saw my look. "Uh-oh! *Still* not like that?"

Heather and I had not: our wheatfield lay—maybe—somewhere in the future. It could be flattering, though, O'Connor's supposing that we had.

*

At altitude and holding position within the assembled formations: in all directions, at all heights, the air filled with a great, purposeful armada of aircraft. Way up, very high, flew the heavies in their tight Vees, streaming white contrails southward; so many that the vapor lines were intermingling to form a thin, ragged overcast. For the B-17s and B-24s, this would be a milk-run in the truest sense of the expression. Accustomed as they were to deep daily penetrations of Germany, Austria, Czechoslovakia and Roumania, a simple Normandy trip would seem barely worth getting out of bed for . . .

My comfortable reflections were interrupted then by Andy Devine on the intercom. "Hey, I just remembered! Today's our eighteenth mission. From now on, fellas, it's all downhill!"

And there, it was said. Out in the open, naked and shivering, the unmentionable. If Providence was to be goaded that one extra step, then Providence now surely was.

We greeted Andy's insane comment with silence, digesting the full significance of that unsought information. For God's sake, we all *knew* what mission it was, but only a meatball like Andy the Okie would have the temerity to voice the fact aloud. Now, we sat in place, hardly moving, waiting for swift evidence of divine wrath. A lightning bolt or an engine failure? A wing dropping off?

Nothing happened. We droned over Kent and into Sussex, angling toward the distant sea, the towns of Newhaven and Brighton, the curve of shoreline round to Selsey Bill where we would make the massed heading change to take us on direct to St. Lô.

And then, ahead, still far off, I saw the cloud deck. Solid stratus below our altitude, milky-gray and smooth, with dotted mushroom heads of cumulus poking up through. Cloud that, it was at once evident, was no local phenomenon, but spreading away south and westward to the very limits of vision. All the way, it looked like, across the English Channel. To France, maybe, and then deep *into* France?

We must, and soon, bomb precisely into a narrow strip of ground from which our soldiers had withdrawn a scant few hundred yards to give us a very limited safety margin. Into which several thousand tons of bombs must fall with pinpoint accuracy. For which we needed CAVU conditions—ceiling and visibility unlimited. To bomb through cloud under those stringent rules was an immediate and colossal recipe for disaster.

Watching as the stratus deck edged closer, picturing what we could find over on the other side, I very much wanted someone to hate for this . . . and there was *Andy*, that unspeakable idiot, who had flouted our cardinal and unfloutable rule about Pushing Luck too far!

Providence—laughing now at its own sick joke—had needed no lightning bolt or massive structural failure to humble us. Only a widening deck of solid, target-obscuring cloud.

Which I observed with deepening apprehension as we crossed over Selsey Bill and made the course alteration. Waiting now for what must be the certain and imminent recall message on the radio. Because recall, now, was our one safe option.

*

No recall order ever reached us: I would swear to that. Over the sea, heading south, fixed on track, we monitored all channels with agonizing care, as one in our belief that we were bound to turn back.

Below, no single hole appeared in the smug, smooth face of the stratoform layer through which some small thing might be seen, seized upon, recognized.

As our navigator, it was now up to Andy; not enough simply to follow blindly on with the other aircraft in company; their crews would be as mystified as we were, limited to the same poor guesswork. And maybe, after his inexcusable gaffe, it was fitting that the full load of responsibility should shift to his shoulders, a fitting punishment.

And how often in the past had we ribbed him without mercy for his evident—and self-acknowledged-ineptitude? Calling him a dumb-ass hick who, now that he had left the place behind, would never, *ever*, find his way back to his beloved Oklahoma.

Now, as inexorably the target drew closer, it became his baby.

Uncertain of what to suggest, I told him, "see what you can come up with."

Which, to me, seemed little or nothing, and no blame to attach to Andy for that. My own decision was made already:

with no recall order, I would fly on to the target area because that much, certainly, would be expected of me. Once there, should the target be obscured, I would exercise initiative by turning us around and flying home. The bomb load would be dumped in the sea, out of harm's way. End of story.

With that in my head, I could order Andy to, "get us as close as you can figure it, somewhere in the neighborhood. Then . . ." I held back my last card. "If it's still no dice, I'll think of something."

Andy nodded and, with unexpected conviction, promised, "Skip, I'll find us a way." And went to work with his map and slide rule and his yellow, beautifully-sharpened pencils. At all times he maintained at least the appearance of a navigator.

*

Only a little time passes before Andy presses his throat mike again. "You ready for this?"

"Shoot," I say.

Down there is the same monotonous flow of unbroken cloud. By elapsed time, though, we are nearing the Normandy coast. St. Lô lies twenty miles inland, another five minutes' flying time. Whether seen or estimated, we are close now to the I.P., and I note that we are not alone in our folly. There are airplanes everywhere, mediums and heavies, all on the same heading, and there is comfort of a kind to be found in that. In spite of an uncertain impression that . . . there are less aircraft out there now?

"Okay, I've got it figured," Andy reports. "Everything's in the mix . . . wind speed and direction, heading, drift and groundspeed. Track made good, *and* with variation and deviation applied." He sounds firm and self-assured. "I know I've got 'em just so."

"Fine, Andy . . ." But it is not at all fine.

No one else speaks, not even O'Connor, whose problem this may soon become. On target, O'Connor commands, I am only the driver. But O'Connor will be noting all that Andy says, forming his own conclusions.

I ask Andy, "what do you need from me?"

"Hold exactly one-niner-six. That'll bring you on."

Tact and trust should still my tongue, but do not. "You're certain of that?"

Andy's eyes go cold and unfriendly. "You asked for it, an' now you got it. An' I'll tell you dopes, it's pretty damn' good."

"Sure it is." I am contrite.

"Every God damn' thing checked an' double-checked," Andy insists, and holds out his stop-watch for me to see. "With this headin' an' altitude, you'll be on in . . . three minutes forty five from . . . *now*."

I fly the heading as given, and without difficulty. Here, above the cloud, the air is like silk, and I can hold one-niner-six with fingertips alone, not wavering by half a degree.

I am flying well, flying right . . . but still sweating it, nervous and scared all over again, but for differing reasons this time. Intent on directional gyro, altimeter, artificial horizon, rate-of-climb and turn-and-bank indicators. They all hold where they belong, exact dead center. Same time, flicking my worried gaze repeatedly through windshield and side panels. Seeking the elusive break, the crack, the tiniest hole in that blank surface that could reveal something of what lies below. The single scrap of vital knowledge that will dictate a more firm policy . . . bomb or abort. Seeing . . . *cloud*. France is down there; she hears us on the way, and she has got her head under the covers . . . that first conversation with Heather returns to mock me.

And then, from his top turret, Sergeant Cohn reporting, "aircraft ahead are bombing."

I look out, and he is right: from the deep bellies of B-25s and 26s strings of dark gnats are plummeting into the cloud, swallowed down soundlessly, gone.

"Bomb doors open," O'Connor says, adding, "just in case." And has he twigged that half-baked intention of mine?

Andy frowns at his stopwatch. "Two-five seconds."

"Coming on . . ." O'Connor calm, none of the traditional fire-breathing. "Hold it there . . . that's beautiful."

"Two-zero seconds."

Everyone else silent.

I begin, "we can't bomb through cloud . . ."

"I'll be the judge of that, Lieutenant." O'Connor turns sharp. "If we can't, we can't. Otherwise . . ."

"Ten," Andy calls.

One mile ahead a pair of B-26s are dumping their loads, beginning the wide clearing turn away. Still only cloud down there; no rising smoke or dust, no flak.

"That does it," O'Connor declares. "Eat your heart out, Andy. You're not the only hot-shit navigator in the E.T.O."

"Five," Andy says.

Others are bombing, so we will bomb, too. We are here, it is the job, there has been no recall. I hold heading, airspeed and altitude.

"Three . . . two . . . one . . . and ON!" Andy announces, and then lets his single chink of personal doubt show. "Far as I can tell."

'Big Apples' surges, freed of her burden . . . bombs away! I correct for the change of trim as the bomb doors close. I turn gently homeward.

*

Not one Squadron aircraft was lost on the first Cobra mission.

No one else in the Eighth or Ninth that we heard of had any shot down.

There had been no flak, and no fighters.

And, of course, no losses, or risk of them, for the majority who had received the recall signal and turned back well short of the target.

The news which greeted us on landing.

A furious greeting, all crews assembled to be informed that we were negligent, undisciplined, sloppy, insane and ripe, the damned lot of us, for court-martial . . . what in hell had we been thinking of?

Outraged, and furious in turn with our accusing superiors, shouting them down in open defiance: we had done their shitty job as briefed; there had been *no* recall, although all had expected one. Hurling our shrill barrage of protest and counter-accusation at the Colonel, at Lieutenant Colonel Friend and Major Delaney and all the other two-bit pen-pushers who were getting at us.

Reporting on the scores of other aircraft all bombing in turn on that self-same spot. Leaving the brass to stand before us, made mute, stuck for answers.

"That oughtta hold 'em." O'Connor with a deadpan grin. "As Marie-Antoinette once said, let 'em eat crap, it's their snafu. They can't hang us all. There'd be no Bomb Group left."

*

Later, however, it was made evident to those of us who had bombed that this was much more than some fresh foul-up to be dismissed with despairing derision.

Blind as we were, we had found the target, and managed to hit the Germans hard. Many bombs, though, had struck short of the enemy lines, in regions where U.S. units had pulled back in anticipation of our coming. Perhaps they had not withdrawn sufficiently far, and that was what we would never know. What we *knew* was that many of those short-falling bombs had killed our own men.

Andy Devine was inconsolable. "It's all down to *me . . . my* fault. I called us on . . . said we was there."

We strove to talk him out of it, partly from concern for his state of mind, but mainly because his lament, repeated and repeated, was driving everyone crazy.

At other times, over other, lesser matters, we would have yelled at him to shut up, but not now, for we knew what he suffered, and suffered no less with him. Blame, or the lack of it, counted for nothing. We were with Andy, and no one more than me, remembering my plans, unfulfilled, for a hidden target.

Andy had stated that we were in place, on target, and we had the awful, bitter proof of his claim right there before us, an outstanding feat of navigation. After a journey of two hundred miles, much of it blind, and his estimate had been out, if at all, by no more than yards. But what difference had those yards made?

We could not be sure that *our* efforts had contributed their share to the massacre; could only assume, burdened with our shared guilt, that they must have. It was enough, and more, that we had been there, and had bombed. Now, blame, self-apportioned, was our lot. Wallowing in wretchedness we sought objectives against whom or which to vent our sad rage. Finding only ourselves.

*

No comfort for anyone on the next day, hearing that the Eighth Air Force, re-flying Cobra, had bombed in cloudless conditions, with perfect visibility. That the heavies had pulverized the German front zone, destroying tanks, guns and fortifications wholesale, leaving the area a shattered and smoking moonscape. And also, due to one more perverse trick of fate (nature's snafu or bitter joke?), once more bombed our own side.

Yesterday's culprit cloud had retreated, leaving behind, like a booby trap, a capricious surface wind. Which blew the marker smoke laid to guide the airmen back across our lines. And fifteen hundred aircraft in relays, bearing seven thousand tons of explosive between them, had discharged unerringly along the treacherous smoke trail.

No official blame was lodged for what took place on July 24, although we went right on blaming ourselves, a mental self-torture which might diminish with the passing of time, but would remain with us in one form or another for ever, becoming a habit of guilt and shame.

It did appear to us then, and fittingly, that we were being punished when the next mission was called.

For 'Big Apples' and her crew with (literally) charmed lives thus far—Mission 19.

FOURTEEN

England
July 28 1944.

'Dear Mother,

'A quick line from the base hospital wherein I am currently held under restraint, although nothing, please be assured, to alarm you. By the time this piece of V-mail props itself against the toast rack, I will be long discharged and about my business. It is just that I am seizing this rare opportunity to catch up on my correspondence.

'I am not wounded, nor fractured from some spectacular demonstration of my less than masterly aviating skills. No scratch, no drop of blood, no Purple Heart, no cigar. So, sit back, relax, and enjoy your toast. Is it still rye toast thinly spread, with a dab of the Scotch marmalade? Two cups, black, no sugar, of Sanka? Ah, we creatures of habit.

'The ailment in question, the sawbones informs me, is exhaustion. Enough of it to get me put to bed for what is termed euphemistically "observation". I was given some tablets which zonked me wonderfully, and wakened, ravenous, to face rubbery hamburger patties and the inevitable string beans. After which, another merciful pill to drive out memories of the horrible meal, and repeat zonk. So much for "observation". Maybe they do that while I'm zonked?

'The cause of all this fuss and attention was a

slightly hairy mission to a place in Holland called Eindhoven, not far from the German border. Which meant that we encountered that usually rare bird of prey the German fighter. Yesterday, like today's hamburgers, not so rare!

'We took some damage, but obviously—as this is not a German hospital—were able to get home. One of the gunners was wounded, the classic million-dollar wound which guarantees him a Stateside trip. He is *not* complaining.

'It would appear, however, after landing, that I was taken by a touch of the vapors, sufficiently to perturb my fellow crew-members and to interest the doctor. So here I am, rested, fed (after a fashion), and rarin' to go.

'What may intrigue you to learn is that I am now dubbed (Government official) A Hero, and am to receive A Medal! All to do (I find) with the way they say I flew the airplane. Of which I have but scant memory . . .'

*

FLIGHT LOG.
DATE: 7/27/44.
AIRCRAFT TYPE: B-26C.
NO. or REG.: 43-2693.
PILOT-IN-COMMAND: Self.
SECOND PILOT: Nil.
CREW: O'Connor, Devine, Cohn, Smithson, Deeks, Patecki.
FLIGHT ROUTE: T.L.-Eindhoven-T.L.
FLIGHT HOURS: 4.25.
HOURS VISUAL: 4.25.
HOURS INSTRUMENT: Nil.
HOURS NIGHT: Nil.
OBSERVATIONS: Heavy flak plus fighters: FW 190s which broke

through the escort screen. On homeward leg, left engine knocked out by a 190, airframe damage severe, one man wounded . . .

It was a Focke-Wulf, the Kraut fighter we most dreaded and dubbed the 'Butcher Bird'. Making its single pass at us, hit and run, head to head, our matching speeds phenomenally high, and with the Mustangs angry on his tail. Its once-only opportunity to score, and, for that fact alone, we were lucky. Had the pilot been able to circle back for Round Two, the story would certainly have had a different ending.

I went rapidly through the emergency drill, trained and re-trained for it; always in practice sessions on those other occasions, for real on this one: fire extinguisher, feather the propeller and shut down the stricken engine. After which, tackle the asymmetrics: with the left engine out, she will swing to the left, pulled around by the good engine's off-center thrust. Retard the left throttle as I apply full opposite rudder to counteract the swing. Mixture to idle cut-off, starving the fuel flow. Watch the propeller as it windmills to a stop. Lots of whitish smoke from beneath the cowling, but no flame as the extinguisher does its work.

Set rudder trim against the good engine which lets me ease off the pressure under my foot as the compensating trim tab bites into the airstream. Re-select fuel tanks, set up the cross-feed, increase power on the surviving engine, adjusting its prop setting. Richen the fuel mixture. Adjust cowl flaps. Hearing the engine note louder now, but a thinner bellow, a soloist unaccompanied on this next long passage.

Check airspeed, and much has been lost, regrettably for good now with only the one viable power plant.

Check altitude, and . . . we are seven hundred feet down. That is sloppy and inexcusable. They drummed it into us in training . . . maintain *altitude*. She will keep on flying with an engine out, but height is like money in the bank, irreplaceable capital if you squander it. If luck holds, she'll stay where she is on one engine, but she will not climb worth a good God damn . . .

Try then, sneakily, to win back a few feet by lifting the nose, but, at once, a heavy toll is taken in diminished and precious airspeed, the needle of the A.S.I. dropping warningly.

The alarming discovery then, brought about by that rash maneuver, that 'Big Apples' will answer back pressure on the control column only so far before the column locks, although there should be much more free movement.

Tail-assembly damage . . . loss of full play on the controls to bring her to straight and level and hold her there? Try rolling in corrective elevator trim to lighten the controls . . . a half-turn, and then the trim locks as well, unable to budge further. Something, somewhere, has gone haywire, and that is making itself felt in the airplane's sluggish response to all attempts of mine at corrective handling.

Both the elevator and trim tab jammed tight, so that she wants to nose up unless held forward with firm pressure on the control column. Which must be maintained throughout the flight for, if I let the nose rise too far, then the wings will reach swiftly to the stall position, lift will be lost, and an inevitable—and fatal—spin will ensue. From which not all the magic spells in the world will save us.

It is now unpleasantly apparent that the 190's cannon, having knocked out the engine, have gone on to upset something vital back aft. To bring us back to England in level flight I must maintain that forward pressure by my own strength, not letting up for a moment against the full force of a one hundred and fifty-knot airstream. Yet, already, after a very few minutes, I am suffering the strain of that in my upper arms and across my shoulders, all the aching and shuddering when I have barely begun. There is still a lot of Holland to overfly, should the Germans permit, and, after that, the sea. A long, long trip.

As the aircraft commander, there is still more for me to attend to. Like getting on the intercom and finding out who's who and what's what . . .

"No sweat," from O'Connor, laconic in the nose.

"Likewise, Skip." Andy Devine speaks up.

From Sergeant Patecki far back in the tail. "Okay, Lieutenant. But several kindsa shit's been flyin' around these parts."

With so much more than the customary grunt from Patecki, things must be serious.

"What can you see?"

"Not a hell of a lot." But then, except for straight back, Patecki's outlook is limited, overshadowed by the tall fin and rudder. "More daylight than I'm used to around the left elevator."

Better to check it out with Cohn who sees more from the dorsal turret. Cohn, though, is not in his place; reporting in from the waist position where Deeks has been hit. Cohn and Smithson are working over him, trying to stop the bleeding and see how badly he is hurt . . . how much pain . . . breaking out the morphine syrettes from the medical bag, the combat dressings. Cohn drip-feeds me information as he works.

He and Smithson are okay.

Deeks has caught the fragments from a splintering cannon shell, and, at once, I recall Patecki's truculent assertion on the day that the eighty eight round went through the wing.

A Focke-Wulf's cannon shells are of twenty-millimeter caliber, heavy rocks hurled white-hot and at supersonic speed. This cannon shell which had fragmented without exploding, otherwise Deeks would now be shredded, dead, and Cohn also, and, very possibly, Patecki, back there in the tail. And, come to think of it, *all* of us. But that one round, possibly faulty, *has* fragmented, and Deeks lives, and is receiving care from his buddies.

Hit in the arms and chest, the multiple wounds dusted with sulfa powder and roughly bandaged. Cohn thinks the chest wound could be bad. "We need to get him on deck PDQ, Lieutenant."

I am strained mentally and physically, unsure whether I am doing all that I should in this situation, and Cohn stands right in my line of fire. "What in Christ's name do you think I'm *trying* to do?"

But bawling out Cohn helps no one and serves no purpose, and I fly on in shamed silence, biting my lip, holding forward with locked arms against the weight of the world outside, feeling my own pain spreading like slow fire, like a slower crucifixion.

Flying, piloting, activities which, hitherto, have been almost as routine for me as driving a car, but which now call for undivided attention and the utmost physical force. And my strength is waning, running out from my hot-fired shoulders, down my arms, dripping off my fingertips. An all-consuming ache that pounds and pounds, and makes me want to weep. Which I cannot do because I am duty-bound to fly this vicious circle all the way to England. And, in flying, I am alone here. A self-professed loner, I have no call to gripe about that. Except that, alone, in crushing discomfort, scared and worried stiff, with the evil specter of failure capering and jeering before me, I cannot think of Deeks; I do not have the time of day for *Deeks!*

I may only fly and try my meager best, and pray that the coefficients of my piloting skills and airmanship, and of flight itself—lift and thrust (much diminished) versus weight and drag (sorely aggravated)—of shifting weather patterns and barometric pressures, and, at the end, if such is to *be* the end of this, that my ability to complete successfully what will be, assuredly, a whore's bitch of an approach and landing, will all work out in Deeks' favor . . .

Now here is Cohn on the line again. Back up inside his cramping turret, and sounding apprehensive. We are still in Act One, Scene One of our tight little drama.

COHN: (HESITANT) Um . . . tail section's looking pretty rough, Lieutenant.
ME: (CRISP, BUSINESSLIKE, HURTING) How rough is rough?
COHN: (FOLLOWING CONTEMPLATIVE PAUSE) Right elevator looks intact, but only about half the left's still there. And something's jamming the stabilizer tab.

(DIRECTOR'S NOTE: SERGEANT COHN IS WELL-VERSED IN THE STRUCTURE AND WORKINGS OF THE AIRPLANE IN WHICH HE RISKS HIS NECK ALMOST DAILY.)

(PREGNANT PAUSE: THE PILOT DOES NOT SPEAK: A LISTENING AIR EVERYWHERE. SOUNDS OFF OF A SINGLE DRONING OVERTAXED & OVERHEATED ENGINE, THE DISTANT BARK OF BURSTING SHELLS.)

COHN: (TENTATIVE) I . . . uh . . . can see the tab okay.
ME: Tell me about it.
COHN: (A PLEASE DO NOT SHOOT THE MESSENGER VOICE) Kind of screwed . . . a whole lot missing. What there is is bent, and the hinge looks to be buckled.
ME: (WORST FEARS BORNE OUT) Oh, *great!*
COHN: Sorry, Lieutenant . . .
ME: (ONCE MORE NEEDLESSLY, BLINDLY, STUPIDLY FURIOUS) Jesus Christ, Cohn . . . why don't you just quit apologizing for the entire damned *world?* You've got enough troubles of your own . . . !

(THERE IS THE FEELING ABROAD AMONGST US THAT THIS PLAY IS NOT GOING TO RUN.)

I sit there for a while, shoving forward, pondering our mounting pile of troubles, and think then of the remembered punch line of a very sick joke: 'Apart from *that*, Mrs. Lincoln, how did you enjoy your evening at the theater?'

I am still laughing, actually *laughing*, when, far ahead, barely visible through summer haze, the edge of the pale sea appears, beckoning, smiling at me, yet still cruelly withdrawn. Neutral water, the final boundary of hostile lands; just get to them and it will be adieu to angry, hating flak and the last lingering risk of another rogue Focke-Wulf. A hurdle, a ditch, a great wet barrier to be crossed, depending upon how you view it. A hundred and fifty miles at laboring single engine speed, with the question always there . . . does that bland, innocent-seeming blueness conceal more treachery against a broken airplane on half power?

The North Sea is cold, wide and unpredictable, frequently—and swiftly—stormy. Whereas, if we land *here*, and manage to get away with that, there is the choice of life ongoing, medical care for Deeks, the dubious comforts of a P.O.W. camp. But . . . out there, in that?

The treasonable thoughts chase themselves around in my head, vying for my attention, my serious consideration of what, they whisper, are their distinct merits: two equally unattractive options which I cannot voice aloud. One more disagreeable aspect of the lonesome burden of command. My big trouble is, of course, that I am too young and green for any of this. Since when did any twenty two year-old jerk-off have the right to take on responsibility for a crippled ship and the six other unfortunates condemned to sail in her?

Pain that I believed could not get worse is doing just that: shudders that are like convulsions surging through me, each nerve and muscle screaming its enraged protest. Yet it's still ten minutes to the coast at this reduced-power crawl, after which there will be a whole hour more to be spent over the water. And how am I going to be at the end of that . . . if I *am* at all? In any fit state to land this recalcitrant beast, or even to control it? With each slow-passing second my doubts about that grow stronger.

Which is the right and good moment for the nick-of-time cavalry to arrive, galloping hard, bugles blaring, in the form of hot, hard anger with its flood of sustaining adrenalin. A strong, wonderful counter-current that flows unchecked into sinew and tissue, jerking the mind without mercy from its state of pewling self-pity, grabbing it by the short hairs. In a flash, then, I am fiercely and gloriously pissed off, and I will be GOD DAMNED if I'll let us fail! I shall NOT lie down and roll over . . . no! Not without, first, some sound arguments and seventeen different and valid reasons why I should do so, stamped and in triplicate. The Army way! Then, and only then, I might just think again about calling quits. But you, Providence, you mean-spirited old bastard, don't you count on it yet!

Anger is strong and very good, dark brown and chock full of

nuts; it fills me at once with fresh energy, and cancels out pain. Two contrasting forces, acid and alkali. So that, for a wonderful while (and may it endure), I feel no longer the Atlas-weight of a floundering B-26 across my shoulders. Anger is right here at my side, needling me, driving me on past Breda and Vlissingen to the clustering Scheldt islands, then up to, over, and beyond the outermost ring of flak ships . . .

To the emerging awareness that . . . flak has stopped. Looking down, wondering, to find blue everywhere, except where blue is bisected by a brilliant molten brass sun track. Blue that is darkly corrugated by the disciplined ranks of marching waves that trail white streamers, the unmistakable signs of a wind that blows *off-shore*, away from German Europe. An incredible, miraculous tailwind to drive us on home! Looking down and grinning like a damned fool, near to tears, studying the wave-patterns of what is at least a fifteen-knot blow. And dare one hope for twenty? To shorten the time spent over water, to get us there more quickly?

Tonic anger, though, demands a lot of fuel, and the fuel is limited: no one stays mad for ever. But now, on the evidence of that wind, something more positive and enduring can take over the reins from anger . . . *hope*, and growing optimism, which a blessed tailwind can nourish. Lending credence to the thought that now, just maybe, the corner has been turned, and that we are staying lucky, staying *charmed*.

Anger has sustained me to the sea. Now, calm and perspective are taking over as I start to plot the tailwind factor, deeply and humbly grateful for it, for the advantage in time and burgeoning optimism that it can provide. Not yet out of trouble, but, at least, far below, the irrefutable evidence of a helping hand.

With such support, I find that I can function, and that bodily discomfort can be accepted, lived-with. Already I am assessing our situation, gathering the sheaves of data available. Such as those from the warning of the still-laboring engine that keeps us aloft. Like . . . oil pressure, which is reading low, and its temperature, considerably above normal operating levels. Meaning? That the lubricating oil has been heated and thinned by the higher demands made upon it, by the added effort. Likewise, and for the same reason, cylinder head temperatures are creeping up toward perilous levels. I must weigh the readings against time and distance still to run, balancing the factors against the gained advantage of following winds. Drawing from those a working compromise, the command decision to retard a little the good throttle, easing the load of manifold pressure, then slicing off fifty revolutions with the pitch lever. Leave the fuel mixture at the full rich position; a rich mixture means a *cool* mixture. Net loss . . . five knots of airspeed, quickly justified by the evidence of lowering temperatures. And the wind on the tail more than makes up for the sacrifice of speed . . .

I attend to these things with a cool mind, without haste or flurry, no fear now, no shakes other than those induced by bodily effort. It seems that I have eased back also on my own throttle; I am detached, doing my job, doing it with care and interest, busy, deeply involved . . .

As I hear O'Connor's voice. "How you doin', son?"

"Pretty good, I guess." (No British stiff upper lip in that answer, it is actually true.)

O'Connor telling me, "while I'm not sure exactly what, anything I can do, you just holler."

"Thanks," I say. "I will." But it is not likely, I don't need him now. Everything is nicely in hand, thank you.

"Meanwhile," he suggests then. "You might care to treat yourself to a quick look out the window."

And, yes, there is a little time for that now. A moment off from the job, the small self-indulgence earned for good behavior.

My gaze is drawn at once to the dead engine with its frozen prop, its soot marks, the bluish heat discoloration of the ring cowl from which the paint has been seared away. Where the fire blazed most fiercely. There, too, the ragged tracks torn in metal by the Focke-Wulf's cannon shells.

'Big Apples' will need *another* new engine. The wing is horribly chewed up, and I feel sharp concern for the condition of the main spar; *can* the wing hold out just long enough . . . please?

It has done well so far; with the way our luck appears to be shaping, dare I hope for the one more hour needed to reach a friendly coast?

"Look up higher," O'Connor directs me. "And you'll see what I'm getting at." I obey, and there, fifty feet above us, to one side and a little back, riding the air currents with gentle ease, another B-26, mirror image of ourselves. With pale face blobs at the cockpit windows and in the nose position. All watching us as they match our crawl speed, keeping us company on the long haul home. As, once, we did for 'Abbie 'n' Slats'. Flying close enough, our guardian angel, to read the ident letters and tail number—4-17105. 'Liberty Belle'. A leggy dancing blonde in a skimpy Uncle Sam costume, one more of Technical Corporal Flaherty's masterpieces.

"Horner," O'Connor tells me.

Horner, who is from Philadelphia. Flying with Barrinton, Kreuger, Langlois, Trahan, Smart and Winsatt.

"Holy cow! I hadn't noticed." The lump feels huge in my throat.

"You've been a little tied-up, kid."

"How long have they been there?"

"Since Walcheren Island."

Deeply moved, I announce on the intercom, "Gentlemen, once back on the ground, we're going to invite those guys to the Sunday Roast. We'll set aside a sum from company profits to ensure liberal libation for all."

"Yeah . . ." From the tail, Sergeant Patecki barks one of his once-in-an-ice-age laughs. "An' we'll get 'em drunk as farts as well."

When we get back, I think. Believing in it now.

*

Flying high above the sea which reveals that the wind lies strongly in our favor still. Keeping steady in my seat with the aching in every dusty nook and corner of me; commanding myself to ignore that . . . there is no aching. Fix your mind, instead, on figuring the remaining odds.

But the thought, irrelevant to this moment and its many problems, intrudes, and will not be ignored: it has happened to us at last, the worst, or as close to it as makes not much difference. It has *happened*, and is now behind us for good; we have come through it together, are finding it possible to live and deal with. Knowing that can induce a feeling of satisfying warmth . . . something that seems like . . . happiness? So that, now, I can come back on the horn for a little more heavy-handed clowning. "There'll be drinks on the house also for the first seadog to sight land."

Smithson calling in with the welcome news that Deeks is in a morphine sleep, that the worst of the bleeding has been contained, that there is a decent pulse.

"If he wakes up," I tell Smithson. "Let him know we're almost there. Meanwhile, make him secure . . ." I remind everyone of the damaged tail, of my restricted ability to control the airplane. "The landing will probably be kind of hairy."

"So what's new?" O'Connor wonders.

*

And, indeed, what awaits us in England may be rough going: a tricky single engine landing complicated further by a vital control surface gravely impaired.

So, while time remains, ponder it, this elementary problem in aerodynamics with its unalterable—and indigestible—ingredients.

One sorely-tried engine to provide us with the needed power.

One shot-up elevator and trim tab which combine to disrupt the aircraft's normal flight characteristics, causing it to nose up perilously unless constant forward pressure on the control column is applied.

The asymmetric thrust of the surviving engine seeking to yaw us off course; that effect countered only in part by the heavy application of rudder and aileron trim, and whatever limited use can be obtained from the crippled elevator.

The sum of all these parts being that 'Big Apples' hangs limply in the air, held in a precarious balance that is sustained paradoxically by a worrying series of imbalances. All of which, while certainly farcical, could not be called even remotely funny.

Not when certain other factors and hypotheses are brought into the equation. Such as what happens when—as in due course it must—it becomes necessary to alter that balance? With the varying power settings, speeds and changed flight attitudes that attend an approach and landing . . .

Cohn, back on the intercom, breaks into these moody meditations. "If no one else feels like speaking up . . . ?" He hesitates as though to make allowance for the customary ridicule that greets his solemn pronouncements. "But, could that be England?"

There, *yes* . . . a hardening wedge of darkness on a hammered silver sea, taking on form and substance as we watch it hungrily. An estuary . . . the confluence of two wide rivers; a sizeable town and a port crammed with ships. South from there, a broad bay, then a headland lying out beyond another town. All close enough now to put names to.

Harwich. Felixstowe. The Stour River anchorage. The sandy shores of the oddly-named Naze. That farther town . . . Walton.

"Drinks on the house, my ass!" O'Connor's mocking laughter filling my headset. "Pilgrim, you two-bit, four-flushing cheapskate, you . . . you knew all the time our Mister Cohn's teetotal. Come on . . . 'fess up . . . you put him up to this!"

*

At last in comforting radio contact with the control tower, our troubles explained and understood: the crash vehicles and meat wagon will be there, ready and waiting, to cheer us in.

'Liberty Belle', still in company, will circle the field until we are down and clear. Or, should I succeed in lousing things up

terminally in the middle of the runway, she will fly sadly away to
her alternate landing ground at Mildenhall . . .

"Six-Niner-Three from Tower . . ." They talk to me steadily,
soothing me with their presence, their caring.

I acknowledge, "go ahead, Tower."

"Six-Niner-Three you're cleared for an immediate approach
on runway zero-nine . . . wind is from one-zero-five at two-five
knots and gusting . . ." Calculating swiftly the fifteen-degree
crosswind component that I must deal with additionally on the
approach and touch-down. A crosswind from the right to aggravate
further the off-center thrust of the engine. A tiny feeling of relief in
the realization that, by using zero-nine, we avoid passing over the
laboratories. Heather need not witness me sneaking home like this . . .

"Altimeter setting, one-zero-zero-five millibars," the tower
informs me.

"Six-Niner-Three checks." I make the required barometric
adjustment with the little knurled knob on the altimeter.

"Pattern and approach at your discretion, Six-Niner-Three.
The field is clear, and all yours."

"Roger," I reply. By the book. All businesslike with the field
in sight ahead. And *what* butterflies in the stomach?

Providence, as fickle as ever, has let us survive the flak, the
190's vengeful cannon, has allowed us to keep all our parts
together and fly home. With Providence, though, there is *always*
a price tag.

As, entering the traffic pattern, husbanding airspeed and
altitude and power; flying a right-hand pattern (Golden Rule
Number One: *never* turn toward a dead engine) with fifteen
degrees of flap extended, and sufficient play—barely—on the
stabilizer to part-compensate for changing flight attitudes, the
wheels refuse to lower themselves fully.

I have moved the landing gear selector to 'Down', and heard
the rumble of the nosewheel and main gear doors thrusting open,
the whining note as the lowering cycle begins. And stops long
before it should, leaving a 'barber pole' symbol showing on the
landing gear position indicator, ugly sign of hung-up wheels.

After the initial shockwave, it is first things first. Like *tell* someone. Not that there is anything anyone else can do. But a little expressed concern would be comforting . . .

"Tower from Six-Niner-Three . . . uh . . . we're having landing gear problems right now. We'll orbit, and pump down by hand, over."

"Roger, Six-Niner-Three . . ." The tone is suitably sympathetic. "Advise when ready to re-commence approach."

I'll *advise*, all right! Cross fingers, groundlings, and pray for wheels!

But all our furious pumping and cursing will only extend fully the nosewheel and the right-hand main gear. On the left side, Sergeant Smithson—who can observe the nacelle from his waist gun position—reports that the wheel is still jammed in its well. "She's part-ways down, Skip. I seen her move, then she stuck again."

"Check that okay . . ." Compel steadiness now in thought, word and deed as we chew over Smithson's news. Which is *not* okay, not one bit. Landing with everything down, or up, would be tricky enough. One wheel unavailable, though, presents a fresh and frightening dimension.

The Tower wonders politely what is happening. I advise my friendly interrogator, and resist the craven impulse to beg him to tell me what to do next. Because, now, as it has been throughout, it is all up to me. I know now, intimately, what lonesome is.

'Big Apples' circles in my hands emptily and aimlessly, helpless and beyond help, a one-legged duck. But one-legged ducks can land, they do it all the time, strictly routine, no sweat at all.

We try some more pumping, and . . . nothing. The wheel, half-in, half-out of its well, will not budge. We give up on pumping, it only makes us mad. Have to come up with something soon, though, because fuel is getting low. Do we go ahead and smash her down and in as is? Do we bail out? But what then of Deeks? What of local citizenry with a large lump of B-26 in their backyards? Or worse . . .

"Six-Niner-Three, do you read?" The Tower again. I had been miles away with my problems. "Are you experiencing radio failure?" An edge of anxiety now underlies the carefully-controlled voice. Like the operator querying a fault on the line. "If you're receiving, but unable to transmit, rock your wings to indicate . . ."

And *there* it is! An answer . . . even a possible solution, all in one little word. Rock . . . to *rock*, the kind of good solid verb that could save your bacon in a bind. Like someone went and switched on the lights . . . ROCK! And it has to be worth a try. When one considers the paucity of other options available.

"Tower . . . Six-Niner-Three, negative radio failure. Just busy here."

"Understood, Six-Niner-Three . . . how're you doing?"

"Tower . . . if you'll bear with us, we're going to try something new. Stand by one, over."

I explain to the others then my intended maneuver, one that has proved valid for fighter aircraft, notably the Mustang, a violent *rocking* motion designed to free stuck landing gear, locking the wheels down by their own weight. Whether it will work or not on a Marauder is a moot point, but now is as good a time as any for finding out. I will try it and, as I do so, try not to think too much of the maneuver's possible effect on an already structurally-weakened airframe.

I run a last check: everyone strapped down tight, including the unconscious Deeks. I hope very much that what I do will not rip the wings from our airplane. I inform the Tower and, considerately, the Tower wishes me luck.

Open the good throttle fully then, and shove forward with what strength remains against the jamming elevator, forcing 'Big Apples' into a creaking shallow dive to build up as much forward speed as possible. Heavy shuddering is coming through the airframe from the tail, and the tail can go straight to hell. If this is to work, then so must the tail . . .

Airspeed is rising across the dial, and, so far, we seem to be intact. Bless you, Glenn L. Martin, you surely do build nice rugged airplanes. I call on the intercom to "hang tough now!" as I let go the forward pressure, and let her soar into a steep climb. Without that restraining force, the nose lifts to an alarming angle, and if I were to do nothing about it, the aircraft would go vertical on me, then tail slide, or flip over on to her back. After which, the final stall and spin . . . inverted. And get out of that one if you can! I let her soar, but keep it within bounds until, with the nose at forty five degrees above the horizon, the bottom dropping out of the airspeed indicator, I push the control column ahead once more, just as far as it will go.

From somewhere along the rear fuselage comes a loud and terrifying crack, and my heart seizes up . . . that's *it*. I have torn the tail right off in mid-air! Haven't I?

But no, not yet, because the nose is starting back down, accepting unwillingly my brutal demands, and it would not, *could* not, if there were no tail left. I suffer the hot, sick sweatiness of negative 'G' as 'Big Apples' lurches heavily over the top of the clumsy arc I describe in space, and things are floating free in the air around me, a pencil, a map, loose and fluttering, O'Connor's forsaken pipe, all hanging there, weightless. Somewhere behind me more loose gear is clattering, and I hear Andy Devine's shrill, scared cry of "holy SHIT!" We are back once more then in a steepening dive, and I must make myself wait as the angle increases, with the bleak thought for company that, if this fails, then we are bankrupt. Have to go in then and land as we are, trusting to . . . what? It cannot be luck.

Until the moment comes for the deciding move, back on the column once more to snap us out of the dive. Tons of weight squeeze down upon me as another screech of metallic protest echoes, followed by a heavy thud that feels like a massive boot thudding into the base of my seat. The feeling then of additional weight on the airplane, but not that; the weight was there already. What we have now is *drag*, the negative co-efficient of weight, an effect created by sudden mass outthrust into high-speed airflow . . .

"Sweet Jesus Christ . . . she's *down*!" Smithson is yelling. "All the God damn' way . . . like a whore's drawers!"

"Fully extended?"

"Far as I can tell from here she is. Lookin' good." A pause. "Can't make out if she's locked or not, but sure *looks* locked."

There is one way only that we can know: proof of the pudding is in the landing.

O'Connor, at his most dry, takes Smithson's place on the intercom. "We got the prayer beads out, kid. We just know you're gonna do right by us."

I get this choked-up feeling then and the hot sting of tears filling my eyes to accompany something close to love for the whole cruddy lot of them. It is a moment when I can trust myself to speak only to the Tower. "Six-Niner-Three is on right-hand base for zero-nine. Turning long final approach . . . landing clearance, over."

"Six-Niner-Three, roger . . . we have you in sight plus all three wheels. You're cleared to land. Gear appears to be down and locked, over."

"Let's find out about that," I say.

*

The approach feels all out of kilter, and barely under control as I crab 'Big Apples' down the glide path to counter the crosswind drift. She feels leaden in my hands, and sluggish in all control responses. I feel the wind's effect on the nose, and in the way that the wings shudder in the gusts as I struggle to keep us lined up on the runway center line.

I must be firm, and double-quick in my responses, to keep her in check; she tries to nose up on me with even the slightest easing of forward pressure, although, mercifully, the tendency is less-pronounced now at our lower final approach speed. There should be little need for me to flare and flatten the glide in the moments before touchdown; she will do that for herself.

A half-mile out with three hundred feet in hand, but a high rate of sink is making us under-shoot. Put on more throttle then, sucking up the dregs of power to keep us barely in the air for as long as it takes. If I blow this one chance then we cannot climb away for another try. 'Big Apples' just will not do that any more.

At a quarter-mile, we are hanging on, just, and the threshold is drifting up to meet us. Time to end the crab-wise approach and line up squarely for the moment of contact, remembering to lower the upwind wing as the final means of opposing wind drift. And a wing down will keep the suspect left landing gear off the ground for a little longer.

I have to make first contact on the right wheel only, keeping the left off until it drops from lack of forward speed and lifting airflow over the wing above. Right gear first, then nosewheel, rolling in enough compensating down aileron to hold the left wing up. Should the left gear fold on contact at that low speed, then the outcome may not be too shattering . . . ?

The runway threshold slips out of sight under the nose. Fifty yards more, and we are *there*. A good moment to relax forward pressure, allowing the nose to lift above the flattened glide, and there *is* less inclination to nose up now that we are close to stalling speed, hanging at the brink ten feet off the ground. A slight touch forward on the control column then to keep it just so. Pull the throttle closed, and the engine rumble gives way to a whispering whistle from the idling propeller, a burst of back-firing, then the old familiar floating feeling. What an instructor of mine described once as 'the hush before rigor mortis sets in'.

Let the nose up a fraction more . . . keep the right wing down, the left wing well clear. 'Big Apples' lurches to the left as a hard gust hits the wing, and I feed in some rapidly-weakening aileron to correct as I feel the first very gentle bump of the right wheel meeting the asphalt, with the weight of wing and engine coming on, a slow sagging, but that wheel, at least, accepts the load. Too slow now for the rebellious elevator to act up seriously; I can hold back some more to keep the nosewheel off for as long as possible. Slowing further by ground friction until, in utter weariness, the nosewheel drops on and holds. Hard over on the control yoke then, all the way, scraping the bottom of the barrel of aileron control. Until that, too, is spent, and the control column goes slack and unresponsive in my hands. For better or worse, we are ground-bound, and the left wing comes down upon the suspect wheel.

Rolling ahead slowly enough now for the crash truck on one side, the ambulance on the other, to match our pace, the men out there in that world beyond reach watching all the time, grave-faced, attentive.

A last lurch, and then the soft rumbling of the left wheel touching and taking hold. Moving gently forward, and I can toe the brakes gingerly, seeing the nose dip in response to the pressure. Bringing to its end the best landing of my life. If I live a hundred years, and fly a million hours, I will never make a better one.

As though confirming that belief, I hear a voice in the headset, whether from within 'Big Apples', from the control tower, or from 'Liberty Belle', still patiently circling, I cannot tell. A voice that offers the single word . . . "Olé!"

FIFTEEN

"I can't talk for long," I explained to Heather. "It's a Department of the Army phone, and they get upset about private calls and bills, and things."

"Just tell me, please . . ." She was insistent. "You *are* all right?"

"Never better. Not a scratch."

"Then why are you in hospital?"

"They call it observation. They'll throw me out soon."

"What is there to observe?"

"That's a very good question." I heard her answering laughter. "Combat fatigue, they reckon. It seems that I may have flipped a little."

"How are the others?"

"They're all fine . . . but nice of you to ask."

O'Connor, Andy Devine, Smithson, Cohn and Patecki were shaken, but okay. Deeks was hurt badly enough to have put paid to his 9th Air Force career. A fact which did not appear to depress him greatly.

"Will you kindly explain to me," Heather demanded. "What 'flipped a little' means exactly?"

I had clambered down from 'Big Apples' filled with a bizarre sensation of disappointment and let-down. As if . . . there should have been more to it than that?

Then, as my feet touched ground, the shakes began, and, with those, the babbling; oral diarrhea without sense or meaning, and lots of shrill laughter.

Shock, I was told later, and exhaustion. The word from a captain with medical insignia whom, I suspect, was trying to humor me.

Spouting garbage, giggling uncontrollably, fighting back the tears as I saw Deeks on his litter being lifted into the big Dodge meat wagon. Deeks, awake once more, trying to smile through the morphine fog. Telling anyone who will listen that he is okay, fine, and that we must not worry . . . he will be back soon . . . he will not let us down. Thinking, as the shakes got worse, I'm going to fall on my ass any second now. Finding the thought of that hilarious!

Until O'Connor and Patecki had me by the arms, holding me upright, and the doctor came over to take a look, and at once ordered me into the meat wagon with Deeks.

None of which I felt like explaining to Heather over the phone. "I felt a little woozy," I said. "So they gave me the rest of the day off, and threw in some tender loving care."

"You! You worry me, you know."

"Not half as much as *I* worry me sometimes. You're too young and lovely to worry, and I shan't want you if you start getting worry lines."

The medical orderly who had accompanied me to the telephone was looking pointedly at his watch.

"Looks like it's time to go time," I told Heather.

"Is there anything you need?"

"What about a large slow dose of you?"

"Don't be silly," she commanded me.

"I'm really busting to see you."

She acknowledged pleasingly, "I'd like very much to see you, too." And spoiled the effect then by adding. "I want you to tell me all about it."

"The mission?"

"Of course . . ." She must have sensed my hurt, explaining a little too quickly and glibly, "what *you* do fascinates me."

The orderly coughed discreetly.

"They're trying to tell me something," I said to Heather. "I'll call you when I'm out of here."

"I'll be ready and waiting." She laughed again. "I've told you, I always am."

*

When next I wakened, Major Delaney was there to inform me that I was being awarded the Air Medal.

It registered slowly; I was still groggy from the medication. "You mean . . . like O'Connor's?"

"Exactly like, Lieutenant." He gave a little indulgent chuckle. "In fact, it's Captain O'Connor who's gotten you yours."

It made no sense at all. "How did he manage that? What did I do?" O'Connor was a noted string-puller with influence, but, even so, there were limits . . .

"My *dear* chap." Major Delaney went all English on me then. "What didn't you do? We have Captain O'Connor's combat report on the Eindhoven mission, and your exemplary handling of it. With his recommendation, supported by others of your crew, that your outstanding feat of airmanship be suitably recognized. A recommendation with which, I might add, we all concur."

I said, "thank you, Major."

"No . . . thank *you*, Lieutenant Pilgrim." He gave another 'all pals together' chuckle, adding waggishly, "although Captain O'Connor was, perhaps, a trifle over-zealous on your behalf. He actually proposed you for the Medal of Honor." His brows went up in playful astonishment. "A super job of work, of course, but hardly one to merit such extreme acknowledgement."

"Oh no, sir."

"Whereupon, discouraged from that belief, he went on to propound an alternative award of the Distinguished Flying Cross," Major Delaney said as I listened in thoughtful silence. He pulled a paper from his pocket. "Now, I've read up on the subject, and made a few notes." He consulted the paper. "Had it been a British D.F.C., then it might have been worth considering. An officers' award, one that, by their own admission, tends to come up with the rations these days. So many allocated . . . handed out at the C.O.'s discretion." Major Delaney, I decided dreamily, certainly knew how to make a fellow feel of some value. "Whereas that of the United States . . ." He read directly from his notes. "Established by Act of Congress in nineteen twenty six . . .

awarded to any person who, while serving in any capacity with the Air Corps of the Army, Navy or Marines, including the National Guard and organized reserves . . . distinguishes himself by heroism or extraordinary achievement while participating in an aerial flight." He looked up, watching me expectantly.

"Well," I said. "It was that, all right."

"I beg your pardon, Lieutenant?"

I explained, "an aerial flight, sir."

"Oh, yes . . . quite." He smiled thinly. "But, of course, while your achievement does, to some extent, meet those criteria, the duty element may not be overlooked."

"Duty," I murmured. "Right."

"What you did was, in effect, no more than your bounden duty. To pilot your airplane to the target, then pilot it back again . . ." The way he phrased it, it reminded of the one about the Grand old Duke of York. "Not so, Lieutenant?"

"Oh absolutely, Major."

"You did what was, quintessentially, your job. Which, in itself, is laudable," he added swiftly. In case he was worried, I was not at all offended, but simply happy to have him drone on. His voice was having a pleasantly soporific effect. I hoped that he would not be upset if I nodded off. "You did your job jolly well, but we can't really view it as a D.F.C. thing."

"That's okay . . ." I could not suppress a cavernous yawn. "You can buy me a beer instead."

He gave me one of those looks reserved by high school principals for the more unruly members of the student body. Blame it on fatigue, I thought. Fatigue would cover more or less anything.

He announced with formality, "in view of these considerations, and with Captain O'Connor's concurrence, the Colonel and I agree that you should receive an immediate award of the Air Medal."

"I'm happy," I told him. "That Captain O'Connor concurs."

When he left, looking huffy, I decided to write to my mother.

In the uncertain belief that getting it down on paper might make sense of it . . .

*

"That asshole." O'Connor shook his head, grinning. "That dyed-in-the-wool dickhead."

The hospital had let me go in the evening, and O'Connor came to collect me. "Let's go wet your medal."

We sat in the Officers' Club, and I filled him in on the details of Major Delaney's bedside visit. O'Connor, in turn, told of locking horns with the Major over the proposed award.

"Some slangin' match, kid . . . you'd have been proud of me. I fulminated at some length about desk-bound supernumerary personnel dictatin' the affairs of us intrepid birdmen."

I asked, awed, "you actually said *that*?"

"Maybe not in those precise words," he conceded. "But I'd lay you even money he got the gist."

"Putting me in for the Medal of Honor? Are you nuts?" I laughed.

"Oh, I never meant none o' that," was the unabashed reply. "Just joshin' the old bastard, tryin' to get his goat. But, hell, you shoulda seen them heels of his dig in then."

"Now I know," I acknowledged. "How it feels to be a pawn in another man's game."

"I meant it, though . . ." He considered me frowningly. "About the God damned D.F.C. You deserved nothing less, and the prick should've agreed instead of beatin' me down."

"I'd say you did okay."

"Why, thank you, Ma'am," O'Connor said.

My own feelings were mixed, and inclined more toward the negative. Okay, it had been a hairy trip, and we had lost Deeks, our first casualty. A new waist gunner, if one was to be found, would take his place, an outsider, not one of 'Big Apples" now tightly-knit crew. I, while not disgracing myself completely, had, as I saw it, gone to pieces in a kind of way. Although it had been difficult, and could have meant the deaths of us, it remained that Major Delaney was right. It was my duty, my job, and not much out of the ordinary given the flying conditions that we endured daily in the E.T.O. Nothing certainly, O'Connor's truculent declarations to the contrary notwithstanding, to merit a D.F.C. Nor, by my reckoning, an Air Medal. It was quite enough to have the concerted approval of my crew; to know that I had not done too badly, and had managed, when the crucial moment came, to face down my own inner demons.

"For all you've done," I said to O'Connor. "I'm deeply grateful, and I shan't forget it."

"Aw shucks . . ." In answer, he played the fool. "'T'warn't nothin' nohow." He lifted his glass in toast. "Anyhow, we needed another medal. Mine's been lookin' for some company."

*

Reaction soon set in to dim the effulgent mood. I felt better for the stay in the hospital, but was still shaky, tired, and unashamedly relieved to find myself on an extended stand-down. 'Big Apples', having avoided condemnation by a hair, was in the heavy repair hangar, and likely to be there for some time; what seemed like a near rebuild was in the cards before she would fly again. My surmise about a new wing was proven right, together with an elevator, trim tab, engine, propeller, cowling and a considerable amount of patching here and there.

I could not rid myself of the feeling that the medal was a sham, some phony-baloney excuse for publicity purposes to pass me off as a tinpot hero. It would not have been that way, I believed, if they could have looked inside my head in times like those. Then they would grab back their medal, and probably forbid me, on pain of court-martial, ever to go near one of their valuable airplanes again. With the blues sitting heavily, I viewed my shortcomings in the most harsh light, all the fears and terrors, the shakes, the cold sweats, gut rumblings and yelling nightmares. I was a mess, and no medal or citation could ever alter that.

*

We were to be given a week's furlough.

Jubilant, we made elaborate plans which included, of course, the traditional and obligatory crew drunk at the Sunday Roast with our guests, the men from 'Liberty Belle'. What Sergeant Patecki declared would be 'the chug-a-lug contest to end all chug-a-lug contests'. Although, to placate Providence, we would conceal these activities under cover of a tribute to the departed Deeks, who had flown out already to the States.

Each of us was in crying need of respite from walking the thin line of collective superstition: Sergeant Smithson summed it up in heartfelt manner, "bullshit like that's enough to piss off Pope Pius." Now, we were off the tight wire for a whole week, set free from airplanes, flying and war.

We had flown nineteen missions and were now well past half way with sixteen remaining. While not stating so too loudly, we felt that we had earned the right to give the finger to Providence.

Just this once.

*

"Now," Heather commanded. "Tell me all."

"Tell you all what?"

"Don't be obtuse, Denney." She gave a sigh. "It's been three days while you fiddled about at the aerodrome. I've been on tenterhooks."

"You know I was in quarantine . . . I told you that. The flight surgeon restricted me in case I bit someone and started a rabies scare."

She smiled forgiveness. "But now that we *are* together . . . ?"

"You can't wait to hear the gory details." I wished that

gratifying this hunger of hers for war stories did not irritate me so. I had no desire to feel irritated by her.

"*And* the medal," she said. "And all about the hospital."

It was another fine evening, one of the last of July. When we met at the end of her road, she had taken my hands in hers. "Welcome back . . ." Her grin teased me. "My hero."

I kissed her lightly. "You can cut that out for a start."

We ended up, inevitably, at the Sunday Roast.

There was a quiet corner, and we had our drinks. I told Heather how much I had missed her, and the compliment was returned. She pressed me then for news of the Eindhoven mission, and I was reminded, suddenly and unpleasantly of Madison Square Garden; the newsreels of the big heavyweight title fights, Joe Louis or Walcott, or Billy Conn. Dempsey and Tunney. And of how, between rounds, the cameras ranged over the massed spectators, and you would see the women there with their smiling lips, parted and expectant, their eyes eager for mayhem. I hated to see Heather in that light, yet the image would not go away. And, still, I let myself be cajoled by her, and got myself into a telling mood as it all came flooding back. Until I ended, "and that was it. Standing there shaking like a leaf, not sure if I was punched, bored or counter-sunk." I made a face, feeling cheap and soiled, although I could not have explained why that was.

Heather raised her glass to me. "Casablanca."

I did not get it. "How's that again?"

"The film, remember? Humphrey Bogart's toast to Ingrid Bergman . . ." She put on a lisping growl. "Here's lookin' at you, kid."

I laughed. "You sound exactly like O'Connor."

"It's supposed to be Bogart!" We drank, watching each other. "Welcome back," she said again. "My dear, doubly welcome."

"That alone makes it worthwhile having gone," I said, and admitted, "when we got hit, there was a moment when I wondered if we had pushed your spell too far . . ." She began to frown, and I added in quick explanation, "we really *had* pushed. You can see how someone might think that when the chips are down . . . all those things we'd dreaded so much starting to happen . . . the world coming apart. I mean . . . how much can over-abused magic be expected to take?"

But her gaze on me was cool and disapproving, no trace of an answering smile there. Seeking to minimize a gaffe that I was not fully aware of having committed, I spoke of the way that realization had come to me belatedly: of *course* the magic had been there to see us through; it was just that I had not been aware. Had it not been, where would we be now? Deliberately ignoring those still-skeptical regions of my mind which had never been stilled. "I don't claim to be perceptive, but I usually get it in the end."

"What was it, exactly," Heather demanded in frigid tones. "That you *got?*"

A moment or two earlier she had been aping Bogart. Now it was my mother she sounded like, and at her most disapproving.

"That it was there, looking out for me . . . for us."

She became very slightly more friendly. "Did something in particular happen to change your mind?"

"Just that I realized that I wasn't as wound-up and scared as I've been before," I replied. "Scared, yes, but able to handle it okay. And there was the feeling that being scared helped then rather than hindered . . ." Had that been adrenalin? The chemical secretion to induce one of two responses, fight or flee. If you fought, adrenalin lent you strength, fleeing, it provided speed. I had elected to do both: cocooned within the airplane, compelled to stay put and fight. Yet, in staying, I had been enabled to flee . . .

In the trite, shabby-comfortable pub surroundings, I tried to re-live that part for Heather. "Like situations I've heard of where you're caught up in conflicting, confusing circumstances, and you pass a point where you find yourself committed, one course of action, one direction to travel, one thing left to do . . ." When that moment came then all else counted for nothing, the fear and doubt and hesitation. No matter that you might not make it; only that you had tried, the outcome becoming diminished, the empty prize at the end. And I remembered the brief moment back on the ground before the heebie-jeebies set in . . . thinking then, is that all there is to it? "You settle down," I said. "And get on with things." Heather nodded understanding. "My mind was sharp, and I was interested in what I was doing, almost enjoying it in a weird kind of way. I could see better, and take things in . . . pick up on every opportunity that came my way. Like the word 'rock'," I added, and Heather looked blank. "The control tower people thought we had radio problems, and told me to rock my wings. And rock was the reminder needed of a way to get the wheels down that worked when I tried it."

In my usual funk, would I have remembered that without prompting?

"Yes," Heather said matter-of-factly. As if, once again, she had known my exact thoughts.

"I believe that ability to think and act came from you." It was what I *wanted* to believe, as I had wanted to from the start.

"Well, if you insist." She laughed lightly, her good humor restored.

It was complete and abject capitulation: to please her I took hocus-pocus, a light-hearted game, as though they were gospel, and pictured that skeptical inner me raising despairing hands as I went blindly on. "I thank you for it, and apologize if I seemed to doubt."

"What you have to see," Heather said then. "Is that I do this for *you*. Not for your crew or plane." Her uncompromising tone made it clear, as nothing had fully before then, that she was serious. As convinced of her claimed powers as any witch preferring the flames to rebuttal. "With the best will in the world, those others can't be my concern, and the aeroplane is only a machine. If they benefit indirectly, then well and good, and I'm happy about that. But that's as far as it goes."

It seemed so starkly dismissive, and I had to voice protest. "These are fellows I fly with, Heather. They support me, and give me their trust. I'd be nothing without them."

"Like D'Artagnan." Her smile was calm and assured. "I know that. But I can't feel for them as you do."

I did not have to like it, but I could accept. Cravenly, I turned aside.

"Could we skip the war talk now, please? Move on to things that matter?"

She nodded, taking her cue. "What things are those?"

"You. Me . . ."

"All right, then." She invited, "elaborate."

"Things like spending time together."

"But . . ." She gestured a question. "We do that anyway."

"I had in mind another kind of together." I had been dwelling on it almost without cease since the notification of our week-long stand-down.

Now Heather looked guarded. "You're keeping something back, I think."

"Okay, I'll come clean. We're getting a furlough, the whole crew."

"And you deserve it." She was beaming.

"It's to do with the mission, and the airplane being sick . . ." I grimaced. "*And* their stupid medal."

"Now, now," she chided. "No false modesty."

It was time to take the plunge. "What it amounts to . . . O'Connor, Andy and me, we're planning a celebration . . . you know, a weekend in London. To paint the Town. A show, dinner . . . the usual thing." Now came the awkward part. "And to put up at some posh hotel . . ." Feeling exposed and foolish, I watched Heather, and tried to shift the blame. "O'Connor's seeing to it all."

"A resourceful chap, your Captain O'Connor," Heather said thoughtfully. "Last minute jeeps in an emergency . . . bookings for West End theaters and hotels? My word, where does it all end?" I sat on the receiving end of her most smug and knowing smile. "And how does all this affect me? Or is it as I'm starting to imagine . . . ?" She tipped her head enquiringly to one side.

I said ruefully, "I *knew* you'd do that."

"Do what?"

"Guess right first go."

"The assumption to be drawn is that this bun-fight is not to be an all-boys together sort of thing . . . but that little girls are invited to play as well?"

"You've got that part already, but, yes, little girls are."

"And *are* there girls?"

"In two instances, yes . . ." My heart was beating rapidly and nervously. "O'Connor knows someone from his last tour. Andy's got a date locally . . . they'll be meeting in Town."

"Wonder who that can be?" Heather eyed me again. "And here's poor you . . . the odd one out."

"Got it in one," I confessed.

"And you were wondering . . . ?"

"Please let me say it," I begged her. "If only to preserve the illusion that this is my idea."

"But, my dear . . . of *course* you can." Her expression could be best described as ingenuous, the effect spoiled a little by the quirks at the corners of her mouth.

"Right again, I *am* the odd one out, and I'd like to rectify that . . . and with you." It came out in a rush, and I wondered if it sounded as imploringly desperate as I was feeling. "All above board, Heather . . . like the first ride home in the jeep," I reminded her quickly. "You can depend on that." That earned me a nod and a fleeting smile. "Or, if you say no, then I'll just string along on my ownsome, and try not to wreck the party. What I won't do is look around for a substitute." Heather's nod then seemed to indicate that she would have expected no less. "That said, I'd like very much for you to be my date, and under any conditions you care to name . . ." I let out my breath. "And that, I guess, is it."

"Wasn't so difficult, was it?" Heather asked.

*

Heather stopped at the side of the road, and turned, to face me. "I said at the pub that I'd like to think about it."

Following what I saw now as my London bombshell, her response had been to suggest that we take a walk . . . somewhere quiet. I felt immediately anxious; if she needed time to *think?* What was that rule . . . the more you thought, the greater the doubt? Until doubt suppressed impulse, and I would be on my own on Saturday . . .

There in the evening light, she said, "what you ask is rather out of the ordinary."

"If it's no dice, just tell me and it's okay." I held up accepting hands. "There'll be no heavy pressure, and no sulking."

"I didn't mean it like that," she assured me then. "Out of the ordinary is, after all, something special. That requires honest and careful consideration." I was given one of her searching glances. "And if the decision was no, would you be content to go alone?"

"I'd hate it. But I mean what I say about no pressure."

"A little time was all that I needed," Heather told me again. "And to be out here, away from all the noise and smoke."

It was a perfect hour for walking side by side through a long green tunnel of overhanging trees. Until she gave a nod and gripped my hand, and said, "all right. I've finished thinking now."

"Okay . . ." I offered up a last, quick prayer, and braced for rejection.

"I'd love to come to London with you, Denney. I would have been hurt if you hadn't asked me."

Delight, vast relief . . . and the moment of confession. "I almost didn't."

"Why's that?"

"My failing nerve. I was worried that you'd get me wrong, and be offended. You know . . . not that sort of girl?" She stood there, laughing at me. "Then you'd tell me to go take a running jump, and that you never wanted to see me again."

"Such wild imaginings . . ." She was shaking her head despairingly. "Whatever are we going to do with you?"

"Just make it humane, and quick."

Heather started me worrying anew then as she said, "there's just one thing, and . . . please . . . you mustn't be upset."

"You mean . . . you'd like to go, but you can't?"

"Not that at all. But there *is* one condition, and it can't be avoided. One that I hope you'll understand and accept."

"Sure, anything . . . just name it." Over-eager to please, I placed myself recklessly in her hands.

She nodded and said, "I must speak to Mum about it first." And there goes the weekend, I thought. Dead in its tracks.

Her mother, Heather was telling me, was wonderfully tolerant and understanding. They were the closest of friends, with absolute trust between them. And I listened, thinking . . . maybe. But there must still be limits to understanding, tolerance and trust. No mother worth a hoot in hell would not fight tooth and nail to prevent her daughter going off for the weekend with a man, a stranger, a soldier, a *Yank*!

No, I realized sadly, that does it. I must respect and acknowledge Heather's honesty, her unwillingness to deceive, that put the kibosh on any hopes that I might have dared to entertain. Mother, bless her little cotton socks, would put the skids right under those. And Heather, being *that* kind of girl, would listen to Mother.

At the same time, I could not simply throw in the towel. "Now, that's a very good thing," I agreed. "But is it such a good idea?"

She squeezed my hand, watching me closely. "What would you have me do?"

I knew exactly what, but did not dare to suggest it: that, willfully, she should deceive. Yet, if I hedged, the deception became my own. I tried, clumsily, to compromise. "I wouldn't want you trying to pull the wool over your mother's eyes . . ." And, *wouldn't* you jeered the hateful voice of my inner Puritan.

"That's good," she replied levelly. "Because I wouldn't."

Pointless, I saw then, the poor, last-chance suggestion that we say nothing, and simply go, hoping for the best . . .

Heather asked lightly, "what was that about not sulking?"

"Right." I worked hard on a grin. "Was that what I was doing?"

"A right little pout." She asked, "you think that speaking to Mum will spoil things?"

"I don't think. I'd bet money on it."

"What *would* spoil it," she declared. "Would be if I didn't. She would know if I simply upped and went to London." And there, she had been ferreting in my mind again, drawing it all out, the subterfuges poorly thought through, the cheap, sly ways and means. I should have known better, in her presence, than to let those enter my head. She went on in appeal, "Denney, something like that, it's bound to be a late do. God knows what time we'd get back, *if* we got back at all." There was the one argument that was beyond answering. "Can't you see how cruel that would be? Mum not knowing . . . going frantic."

"We wouldn't have left it at that," I offered lamely. "We would have telephoned her."

"Like Manhattan babies?" she wondered. "Is that what they'd do?" She promised then, "Denney, it's all right, we'll go, really. You mustn't worry."

"How can you be so sure?"

"Because I do know my mother."

"And if she chooses to put her foot down, what then?" I reminded Heather, "you're not twenty one yet, so the final say is hers." And went on sorrowfully, "that's another thing. It's almost your birthday, and we've had a date planned for that since May." Old Man Providence would be busting a gut laughing at that moment, I thought. I had managed to stay alive, and for what? A let-down like this? "We could have combined that with the general binge."

"Now, there's a charming afterthought," Heather observed dryly. "As for age, I can promise you that Mum never goes by dates and numbers. She's treated me always as an adult who can think for herself, and tell the difference between what's right and wrong. And it will be both right and adult for me to talk this over with her. As long as I'm open and honest, I know she'll agree."

But that seemed to me to be asking a mite too much of good nature. I demanded once more, "and if she doesn't?"

"Then if, and it's a very big if . . ." Heather sounded then like someone explaining the obvious to a dullard. "I shan't go.

Which would not change my wanting to go, and being glad that you'd asked me. I'd have to hope then that you'd understand and forgive. And promise you that I'd be there in spirit." Her hand squeezed mine once more in re-assurance. "Don't panic. It won't come to that."

*

"You're Pilgrim, right?"

He was a second lieutenant wearing navigator's wings. Summoned by him from my grumpy reverie, I was not prepared to be nice. "Right. Who wants to know?"

It was the evening following my inconclusive and unsatisfactory debate with Heather. She had promised to call me about the proposed weekend. Now, it was late, yet I hung on grimly at the Officers' Club which had a telephone on which incoming calls were tolerated. Instead, here was this unknown second looie. Who, gaging my mood, offered, "sorry to trouble you."

"It's no trouble." I put down grouchiness. "What's up?"

"M.P.s at the gate told me if I seen you to give you this." He held out an envelope. "A silly-vilian on a bike left it." He sketched an uneasy smile. "A good-looker, the M.P.s say."

I took the envelope gingerly: instead of telephoning, she had chosen to write. And what could be so awful that she must do that? I wished that the second lieutenant would take off so that I could find out. I said pointedly, "thanks a lot."

He stood his ground. "Nice work if you can get it."

"Yeah. Nice . . ."

"Don't suppose she's got any sisters?"

"None that I've heard of." I looked up at him. "But there's her mother if you'd care to try your luck?"

"Oh, shit . . ." He laughed, and nodded at the envelope. "Sure hope it's not a Dear John."

I hoped so, too, very much.

*

The envelope was addressed to 'First Lieutenant Denney N. Pilgrim, U.S.A.A.F., Tiverell Lacey Aerodrome'. In clear, firm handwriting that was not Heather's. I drew out the single sheet of headed notepaper: 'Hadleigh House, Mill Lane, Tiverell Lacey, Essex. Tel: Tiverell Lacey 396'.

> 'Dear Lieutenant Pilgrim,
>
> 'If convenient, could you come to tea with us tomorrow afternoon at four? In order that we may enjoy what I see as our long overdue meeting. Heather informs me that you are on leave at present, and this does seem an opportune moment to meet. I hope that it will not clash with your plans. Should that be the case, would you be kind enough to let me know?
> 'With kind wishes.
> 'Yours sincerely,
> 'MARGOT GRANGER.'

And . . . Christ, I thought. The lion's den. And forget all about clashing with any plans of mine; I knew a summons when I saw one. For this, any and all plans of mine went straight on hold!

*

Heather answered my phone call; it was as if she had been awaiting it. I said, "I've had a nice letter from your mother."

"I know . . . I delivered it. My penance."

I smiled into the mouthpiece. "Our military police were most appreciative. You've been classified 'a good-looker on a bike'." I asked, "what's this about a penance? Hope I didn't get you in trouble."

"Not at all. Mum couldn't have been more aware or sympathetic."

"Does that mean you get to go?"

"Well . . . that depends," Heather said.

"Let me guess. On how I measure up and behave when I come to tea?"

"To some extent, perhaps," she allowed, and wondered, "does that mean you'll come?"

"Wouldn't miss it for the world . . ." The truth was that I dreaded the encounter, and yet, perversely, looked forward to it, curious about this English lady who invited me, sight unseen, to her home. A dragon, or . . . ? "Please thank her for me, and say how honored I am . . ."

"It's all right." Heather's happy laughter echoed down the line. "There's no need to overdo it."

*

It was not difficult to bribe the mess sergeant into providing a K-ration carton filled with assorted mess-hall goodies: canned pineapple, peaches, luncheon meat, pancake mix, a big jar of Canadian maple syrup, sugar, butter, two dozen eggs. Things tightly rationed in England, or wholly unobtainable. A crude gift—or inducement—but still, I hoped, given the imposed stringencies of war, an acceptable one that might serve to smooth my way to the heart of the formidable-in-prospect Margot Granger.

In return for my bottle of PX rye and two cartons of cigarettes, highly negotiable currency in themselves, the mess sergeant had been generous. He could afford to be; such illicit gift packages for the English friends of American airmen provided him with a lucrative sideline: whisky and cigarettes were top value black market cash earners. His generosity extended further to a place of concealment for my carton in a supply truck leaving for Colchester, and in which I had arranged to hitch a ride to the village. As the mess sergeant pointed out, "can hardly leave you to walk out the gate with that-there under your arm, Lieutenant. Not and get asked no questions."

Four o'clock was the designated hour for tea. The truck dropped me off an hour early with my carton, no place to go, and the pubs closed at that hour. Which, when considering a strong craving for Dutch courage that I was feeling then, was probably just as well.

At the price of a can of cling peaches, a man in a hardware store agreed to take care of the heavy carton, leaving me free to wander about Tiverell Lacey for forty five slow minutes, feeling furtive and conspicuous as I peered through the windows of the few small shops, the public library, and into a schoolroom at rows of small, bent backs until fiercely quelled by a schoolmarm with hornrims and a bun.

I went to read the names on the war memorial, the corps and regiments: 'Essex Yeomanry', 'Royal Horse Artillery', 'Coldstream Guards', 'Royal Flying Corps', 'Rifle Brigade', 'Royal Naval Reserve'. So many names for so small a community. Until the church clock rang the three quarters, and I could retrieve the carton and make my way with thudding heart toward the big, daunting house in Mill Lane.

*

Heather was at the door to meet me.

I offered apologies for the carton. "Hope you're not offended? But they're scarce for you, and we have so much."

"Gosh, no . . . it's smashing!" She examined a catering-size can of Dole pineapple. "We haven't seen anything like this for ages. And all the way from Hawaii . . ." She eyed me sidelong, smiling. "Is it another little fiddle like the jeep? Or shouldn't I ask?"

"Some give and take," I evaded. "It goes on all the time." And reminded her, "afternoon tea? Otherwise, your mother will hand me a demerit for being late."

Heather scolded, "you know, you really do worry too much."

"Who's worried?"

"*You* are!"

I laughed. "Right."

"Mum, I promise, won't give you the dreaded third degree."

I made a motion of mopping my brow. "It's simply getting acquainted, and some small matters to be cleared up." Heather tugged at my hand, drawing me into the house. "And I can promise you a much better tea than that first one we had."

She led the way across a wide, high-ceilinged hall of dark wood paneling, past a staircase with an ornate newel post, and, again, I was reminded of my long-ago mental images of the somber, atmospheric houses in John O'Hara's novels.

There were hanging portraits of glum-looking people, seemingly made so by their banishment to this place where no one lingered. We followed a passageway that bisected the house to a salon where the afternoon light poured in through tall windows; a room as cheerful as the hall had been gloomy, filled with good, solid furnishings made shabby by much use. More paintings, mostly landscapes, and a baby grand with its top raised, sheet music in position, waiting to be played. There were fresh flowers that looked as if they had been culled that day from the garden, and silver-framed family group photographs with one that caught my attention at once: a woman in a print summer dress, a tall, balding man, a child—a girl—grimacing in direct sunlight. Who must be Heather.

The salon was empty, although it seemed the perfect place in which to take genteel tea. Heather, though, was moving on to the open french windows, the big conservatory beyond. Glimpsed once before in pre-dawn darkness.

It was warm in there, too warm for my wool Class 'A's, and I thought at once of a sweat ride . . . in more ways than one. Wondering if the choice of the conservatory as our meeting place was calculated to *make* me sweat . . .

I saw Margot Granger for the first time, and she was the woman in the photograph. Very, *very* attractive, and the more so that moment as she smiled up at me in quizzical welcome. Her eyes were like Heather's, same shape, clear and gray, the heavy hair as dark, only lightly touched with silvery threads. Seated before a glass-topped table set for tea.

She rose to shake hands, a slender woman of instinctive grace and elegance: I was reminded of Greer Garson, or Katherine Hepburn in one of her less-strident roles . . . the same cool poise, the small, delicious leavening of polite irony. Margot Granger's figure remained youthful and excitingly rounded, an effect heightened for me by her dark dress of that classically simple, to the point of near-starkness, style perfected by Coco Chanel. Worn with a single rope of pearls and the silver facsimile of the down-turned wings of an R.A.F. pilot. Until I noticed the letter 'C' entwined about 'RAF', the wings, then, of the Royal *Canadian* Air Force. *He* would have given that to her, perhaps to butter her up as, now, I sought to do. A better gift by a country mile than my battered box of canned food. The food would be eaten, commented upon, and forgotten, whereas the wings would endure from hand to hand . . .

Margot Granger said, smiling, "I was beginning to wonder if you two would ever stop whispering out in the hall?" Her voice was a warm contralto, and, as anticipated, posh. She released my hand. "Lieutenant Pilgrim, you're most welcome in our home."

I mumbled back thanks, and that it was a pleasure.

She had Heather's laugh as well. "We must all try hard to see that it is." Heather and she exchanged a brief, confiding glance. "Mustn't we?"

*

We sat around the glass-topped table in the still, warm air, amidst the scents of green growing things. Tea was poured and passed, and I listen uncomfortably as Heather extolled the virtues of the gift box, and it did seem then that the Canadian wings mocked me gently: ' . . . you'll need to do a mite better than that'. I was thanked for 'spoiling us so'. With the smiling admission that, "it does all sound rather scrummy." Major Delaney, I reflected in passing, would certainly cotton on to 'scrummy'.

It was, as promised, an excellent tea, with smoked salmon sandwiches the salmon, I learned, 'buckshee' from a Scottish relative, a slender but steady supply. "We're really jolly lucky," Margot Granger insisted, sounding exactly like her daughter.

I began, gradually, to relax in her presence: she was not at all formidable, I was finding, although the atmosphere remained formal during those first maneuverings and taking-up of positions. It was undeniably pleasant, as well as flattering, to be the solitary male basking under the attentive gaze of two extraordinarily attractive women, eating homemade Victoria sponge cake, and tasting the hoarded egg. Feeling better then about those two cartons of eggs. Twenty four eggs represented twelve weeks' rations for Heather and her mother.

I accepted a third cup of tea and, responding to restrained quizzing, explained that I always drank coffee and tea without milk.

"Is there a particular reason for that, Lieutenant?" Margot Granger enquired with polite amusement.

"Milk skin," I said.

In a strangling voice, Heather exclaimed, "oh, *God!*" She clutched theatrically at her throat. "Just the *thought* of it!"

Her mother was laughing again. "Now there's something else you two have in common."

"I only have to see it on top of the cup," Heather confided. "And my tummy heaves."

"We're all quite sure it does, dear," her mother murmured.

We compared notes on the topic of milk skin, and I spoke of my childhood loathing. "It probably scarred me for life."

"I've always called it 'carpet'." Heather shuddered fastidiously. "Quite disgusting."

We talked of the house, and I made reference to the fictional dwellings created by John O'Hara with which I compared it, and Margot Granger confessed, "there are times when I almost wish it could be fictional. Although it's hardly up to the standard you describe." She gazed about her conservatory with an abstracted fondness. "Poor old pile. It's getting to be something of a burden, I'm afraid."

I faced questions about my own home, and told carefully,

playing them down, of the Sutton Place penthouse, the summer residence on Cape Cod. Making the penthouse sound more comfortable apartment, swanky Sutton Place . . . a place. Squirming under Heather's dry gaze; I had been rather less reticent with her. It seemed to me important not to be viewed by the astute and restrained Margot Granger as American-boastful.

But she said only, "how fortunate to be so at the hub of things in New York." So it continued until the time for tea and chit-chat was past.

As though a signal had been given, Heather rose, murmuring of things to be done. A quick smile to me: did I mind awfully being abandoned . . . the clear indication that the softening-up process had ended. I smiled back, concealing fresh apprehension, and vowed that I had no objection. Heather warned her mother, "not to jaw his ear off," and was gone.

I watched her go with regret, and her mother made the gentle suggestion, "if you can bear a little chat?" She must have gaged my feelings, for she added, "I do promise you, nothing alarming."

I answered, "I'd like that, Ma'am."

Her questioning smile widened. "You know, I'm not entirely at ease with 'Ma'am'. It does date one so . . ." She cocked her head. "Much nicer if you could call me Margot . . ." She chuckled infectiously. "Or anything else but 'Ma'am'."

"It's a bit sudden," I acknowledged. "But I can spare you that."

"And, in return, might we dispense with Lieutenant?"

"Gee . . . yes." I told her, "usually, when we get called that, it's by some colonel getting himself ready to bawl us out."

"That won't be the case here." Her brows lifted in that way of Heather's.

"May I call you Denney?"

"I wish you would."

"Well, Denney . . ." She sat back, crossing slender legs, smoothing her skirt, captivating, feminine movements, sleek and almost feline in their grace, that aroused an immediate and startling feeling of lust. Naive and inexperienced, I knew nothing of the strong attraction that young men can feel for older women; for all of its sharp, electric thrill, this was unbidden and unconscious. She was, I decided, extremely beautiful, and it was a beauty which time and maturity had served only to enhance. I knew then, confused and guilty, that I would have responded if Margot Granger had offered the slightest suggestion: I had the image alive in my brain of going to bed with her . . . with *both* of them! Together, at the same time! Jesus! And my face flamed as I thought that—like her daughter—Margot might be reading these thoughts right there and then! But all she said was, "you will have gathered, I feel sure, that this is not entirely impromptu?"

"I did get that idea, yes." I met her cool and level gaze with difficulty. Was she also fey, gifted in the quick interpretation of the thoughts of others?

"Heather told me she'd be speaking to you."

"About London." It was the simple statement of something known.

"Yes."

"I shan't offend you by demanding to be told what this proposed weekend entails," she said quietly. "Heather has explained where you'll be, and what you'll do." She watched me, nodding slowly. "I imagine that you've spoken the truth, and I know my daughter, and believe her."

"It's just as stated," I answered earnestly. "If we get to go . . . if it's okay with you . . . then she'll be looked after and treated with respect. And if you'd prefer not, then, as I promised Heather, there's no argument."

"Thank you," Margot Granger said. "That's perfectly acceptable."

Something prompted me to ask, "but you have doubts."

Her mouth twitched. "That's perceptive of you."

"Anything you want to know . . . um . . . Margot . . . then please ask."

"I don't think there's much where London is concerned," she answered frankly, and dryness returned. "I've heard about you from Heather, and at some considerable length. The picture she draws is a complimentary one." The gray eyes revealed fresh amusement. "The reality now does appear to support the assertion . . ." She paused then before offering her benediction. "I don't object at all to Heather's accompanying you. Nor shall I presume to impose conditions. You appear to have done that very sensibly for yourselves."

"You'll never believe how happy I am to hear you say that."

"Well, I'll try to," she assured me, smiling. "But, you mentioned doubts, and that prompts me to ask . . . how much do you *know* of Heather?"

I had a mental image of the wheatfield as I replied, "she's been very candid with me."

"The other young man . . . before? Tim?"

Unable to meet her eye at that moment, I looked instead at the brooch. "You wear his wings."

"It was his gift to Heather. But . . . afterwards, she couldn't bear to wear them herself, and asked me if I would. So I do," she added simply, and enquired, "you know what happened, I take it?"

"Yes, I do."

"And that they were engaged?"

I risked a smile. "It was published in *The Times*. All very pukka, Heather called it."

"As, indeed, it was. Although it was he who insisted on that." She wore a look of reflection and regret. "As for Heather . . ."

"She's fey," I chipped in. "She has a gift for reading just about anything that's going on in my mind. Which really rattles me sometimes."

"It would seem . . ." Margot Granger was laughing softly. "That you've been given the full treatment."

"Certainly have, Margot."

"And what did you think of it?"

"That it's fascinating . . . as well as alarming."

"Do you believe in it, Denney?"

"I was skeptical at first . . . forgive me, but, feminine wiles, you know?" She laughed once more. "But, since then, there have been too many little things . . . the mind-reading and shared thoughts." I wondered if I should mention the strange and haunting visions—still beyond my understanding—that I had known in Heather's company, and decided not then, unable to find the suitable words. Nor would I speak of spells, of protective mantles cast over me, my crew, my airplane . . .

"Has she," Margot Granger asked. "Mentioned her father?"

"Not a word."

"No. That would be left to me."

I began, "I wouldn't want to intrude . . ."

"You don't, and you won't." For a moment, she was almost brusque with me. "But there are matters concerning him that . . ." And then, for a moment, she faltered. "It might be in your interest to know of them."

"Anything you tell me will be respected."

"Oh, I don't doubt that . . ." She was looking vexed. "I'm afraid I'm not doing this awfully well." Her smile, hesitant now, returned. "Heather has picked up a number of your colorful American expressions. Like the one that fits the bill now, which is . . . I should put up, or shut up."

"Oh . . ." I laughed awkwardly.

Margot Granger examined her hands, slender, well cared-for hands. "Heather's father, a loving, kindly man . . ." As she paused again, I was conscious of the absence of tense to indicate the father's place in the scheme of things . . . 'is', or 'was'? She gestured at the conservatory around us. "All this, the house and grounds, our comfortable living, are due to him. Heather's and my safety and security, all liberally provided." The affectionate words emerged in a carefully-controlled voice. "His unconditional gift, although one tinged with a certain guilt. Which he and I shared."

I listened, fascinated, to the story of Bernard Granger, successful architect, one time friend of Edwin Lutyens, and of our own Frank Lloyd Wright. Who, in 1915, had volunteered for the Army, although he was well over the age for military service.

"He was with the Essex Yeomanry," Margot Granger told

me, and I thought of the war memorial outside the village church, of the Essex Yeomanry names. There had been no Granger among them; I would have spotted that at once. "He served in France as an acting-Captain. On the Somme."

But Captain Granger's war had been a short one. Badly gassed at somewhere called Courcelette, he had lain out in a shell hole under the full fury of the German barrage. I knew something, myself, about German barrages and their fury . . . "His lungs were badly damaged," Margot Granger said. "Phosgene gas. He was also . . . it was the term of those times . . . shell-shocked. He spent a year at a hospital that specialized in neurasthenia cases. Until he was invalided from the Army. Which all took place some time before we actually met. Although," Margot Granger went on puzzlingly, "we knew *of* each other."

Their first meeting had been in 1918. "It was here, where he was living with his widowed mother," she explained. "Still convalescing."

She had found him to be charming and considerate, and there were few obvious indications then of the way in which the war had scarred him physically and mentally. He showed no anger or violence; the gentle, kindly nature was not impaired. Rather, his family and friends feared *for* him, concerned by his, to them, sudden and inexplicable shifts of character and mood. All knew the war to be the root cause, but what, or why, or how remained beyond their grasp just as those things remained beyond the grasp of their victim, Bernard Granger.

In the good times he could be quietly droll, and was an entertaining conversationalist, never more so than when discussing the subject of the T'ang Dynasty, which was his abiding passion.

"In what he referred to as his 'down side', he would become restless and reclusive," Margot Granger said. "There was a need, a driving force it seemed, to be off by himself. What possessed him then must be left to run its course, and in its own time . . . those dark tides allowed to recede. There was no other way then, and no available drugs or treatment that might short-circuit the attacks. When they came, he knew always what was happening, and would be so apologetic . . ." She gave me a searching glance. "Denney, there *is* a point to all this. Can you bear with me a little longer?"

I said, "I'd hate it if you stopped now."

Bernard Granger, struggling with the grim legacy of his war, would feel an irresistible compulsion to shut himself away from those close to him, or to escape from them, shunning all contact, taking himself off, walking out, solitary, over the countryside in all seasons and weathers to wherever the twisted whim of the moment might carry him.

"Sometimes there would be days with no word from him," Margot Granger recollected. "Then a telephone call . . . at any time of the day or night . . . from Sussex or Devon or Shropshire. Once, even, from the Ring of Kerry."

Financially comfortable, Bernard Granger could afford with ease the expense of his eccentric wanderings. Nor were his resources adversely affected by them: his professional skills had not deserted him, and there was a continuing steady income, albeit at a reduced level, from commissions and consultancy work.

"Although the old prewar vitality was gone," Margot Granger accepted. "And one does wonder also about the possibility of some innate, unsuspected flaw in my husband's make-up. Which his war experiences exposed and exacerbated . . ."

Margot Roberts and Bernard Granger had married in 1922.

"I wanted to be with him, close to him, imagining that I could be of help, a possible source of peace and stability . . ." Heather, too, expressed frequently this desire to help; an inherited trait? "Bernard was always, without fail, gentle and attentive . . . only in the bad times withdrawn, and so terribly sad and regretful because he could never seem to find with me the comfort I longed to give him." She drew a deep breath and closed her eyes for a moment, gathering herself together. "I took all that into account, or so I believed. I was twenty three and so, of course, knew all that there was to be known . . . such a little bossy-boots . . ." She smiled wistfully back at her long-ago memories. "Bernard is eighteen years my senior," she explained, and I latched-on at once to 'is', the first indicator that he was alive somewhere. "But I didn't allow a minor detail like that to stand in my way, and never imagined for a moment that I might fail with him . . ." She turned away to stare into the early evening garden, telling me, "Heather's father isn't dead, and we're not divorced. Merely separated by mutual agreement, heartbreakingly but amicably."

"Is he in England?"

"China," she replied. "Pursuing his passion . . . what he views as his lifeline, or his grip on sanity. Since nineteen thirty two."

I was shaken. "Twelve *years?*"

"China, Denney," Margot Granger pointed out reasonably. "Is somewhat farther off than the Ring of Kerry."

"Will he ever come back?"

"He could do, I suppose." She considered the possibility, then looked at me squarely. "And, yes, I would welcome him back, and so would Heather." She shrugged then, a defeated movement. "But I think it's unlikely."

For a time there had been the hope that Bernard Granger's mental state might improve or, at least, stabilize. It was a hope that faded as the bouts of depression and withdrawal became longer and more frequent.

"The hospital in Edinburgh closed soon after the war," Margot Granger said. "And any existing facilities for the treatment of neurasthenia were quite inadequate. Shell shock, you see, was viewed as something shameful, a nice, convenient euphemism for cowardice." Her voice hardened with anger. "The considered opinion of those who never knew the trenches, but who passed judgement anyway. People who make my blood boil."

Uncertain of quite how to respond, I said, "we have people like that, too. We call them 'rear-echelon rangers'. That's one of the more polite terms."

She smiled distantly. "There was a man who had helped Bernard, whom he trusted and admired. Professor Rivers, a leader in his field, whom we might have sought out. But he had died in the early twenties, and there seemed to be no one to take his place." Left to his own meager and dwindling devices, Bernard

Granger became obsessive over what he foresaw as the eventual loss of his reason. "There was a young soldier in that war called Ivor Gurney," Margot Granger continued. "One of the outstanding war poets like Graves and Owen and Sassoon . . . or Rosenberg . . . Blunden. Gurney published a volume of poetry from the front, and called it 'Somme and Severn'. We have a copy. I'll lend it to you if you'd like?"

"I'd enjoy reading it, Margot."

"It was always a favorite with Bernard, although probably not the best choice, given his fixation, that he could have made . . ." She tailed off, blinking and swallowing hard, then asked abruptly, "I don't suppose you know what happened to Gurney?"

I shook my head.

"He, too, was badly shell-shocked. Although there was talk of his having been a little odd in the first place, before the war. After it, and his experiences in the trenches, he became even more odd, unable to keep a job, going off to wander about the country, begging, living like a tramp. And then, at about the time Bernard and I were married, Gurney was committed to an asylum where he died years later." She finished broodingly, "and that was Bernard's great fear . . . that the same thing could happen to him."

Bernard Granger was driven deeper into hopelessness and despair. Until, in the spring of 1932, he informed his wife and young daughter that he would be going away once more, this time for keeps . . .

"He made full provision for us . . . the house put in my name. There were ample funds which, with judicious management and investment, would ensure that we never went short . . ." She was looking into the garden again, bleak-eyed, perhaps seeing there the events of twelve years before repeating. "The severance was made. He was going, and this time it would be China . . . Bernard's panacea with which I could not compete," she said in level tones. "He felt that China, and the T'ang Dynasty, all his studies and research, could help him to retain his sanity, and would not be persuaded otherwise. And if they could not, then Heather and I would not have to suffer the stigma . . . which mental illness was in those days . . . of a madman in the family, one whom we might have to have committed to an institution."

Speaking, Margot Granger maintained the appearance of calm control, no indication there that these things she told me might be tearing her apart. Within days, her husband was gone. She had failed in all her attempts to make him reconsider. "He hated to leave us, and admitted as much, but believed that he must."

I wondered, "how did Heather take it?"

"Quite amazingly well," she said at once. "So incredibly adult about it . . . you have to remember that she wasn't even ten years old then." A small smile came back. "I was terribly proud of her. Not for the first time, nor, I'm sure, the last."

Inwardly, though, I rebelled at that claim, and at the seeming triteness of Margot Granger's expressing of it. The English, even in matters so disruptive and agonizing, always had to be so God damned *English* . . . must not make a fuss, never grumble . . . maintain the stiff upper lip, even if they choked on it. I went on listening with irritation and deepening skepticism of Heather's bravery, her self-control and adaptability . . . how she had appeared to take it all in her stride. But then, with these people, *appearance* was everything. I wanted to ask then . . . what of *inside*? What of the certain hard core of hurt and disappointment and scarring bitterness? Did Margot Granger imagine truly that those would not be present in the aftermath of the father's seeming betrayal? As a family, they had been lovingly close, with Bernard Granger a paragon, the dutiful, caring husband and father. So, how in hell could his wife and child stand there, being adult and brave as he signed away everything, packed his grip and vanished for ever to China . . . ? I simply could not buy that. As Heather herself might have said . . . it was not human.

And could these things in her past provide some explanation for Heather's hitherto inexplicable coldness and evasion, for the way that she would shy like an animal in fear from any suggestion of commitment. *Was* it that Margot's claimed attributes of adultness, self-control, adaptability were, in reality, the ingredients by which a protective shell had been formed? A shucking-off of involvement and responsibility as the means to avert the risk of further pain? And, some day, would the shell split apart from pressures within too long contained?

And Margot Granger was telling me then in a tone that was light, almost playful, "that really is enough scene-setting, and I must get to the point." Still feeling testy, I gave her a stiff smile. As she said, "which is that Bernard and I are cousins." I recalled at once what she had mentioned earlier: not knowing him, she had known *of* him. "Nor are we all that far removed, which *is* the point." Her eyes searched mine. "Are you with me so far?"

"Not entirely . . . no."

She stressed, "*cousins*? Surely the significance isn't lost?"

"Well, no . . . I guess not." I had heard vague things; of such marriages lying within a gray area of opinion in society, law and the church. There were cousins and, again, cousins; distant ones virtually unconnected, the blood lines tenuous to near-breaking point, and those who stood one small step sideways from the closest of familial ties. And, somewhere in between, the region of conjecture and debate: when is a cousin not that much of a cousin, and so permitted . . . ? Like angels on pinheads, or which came first, the chicken or the egg . . . ?

Margot Granger provided the answer to my unasked question. "Sufficiently far removed to enable us to marry without incurring magisterial wrath . . ." Her lips curved in wry amusement. "Not enough, though, for the unhappy cleric who bound us together not to suffer mild palpitations." She broke into hard laughter. "How that poor man must have prayed for divine guidance, or at least for a small, protesting voice from a dim corner when he got to the bit about lawful impedimenta."

Somewhere out of sight in the garden, signaling the lateness of the long afternoon, a small English robin was making its sharp 'tic-tic' roosting call.

Margot Granger said, "and, of course, there were all the anxious relatives and supposed friends. The doom merchants, Bernard and I called them. Happily prophesying imbecile offspring, or misshapen monsters whom we would be compelled to keep fettered in turret rooms . . . my God fathers!" Her jaw clenched. "We should never speak of the Dark Ages as history . . . they're with us still." She gave me a look that seemed to blend appeal and defiance. "But we confounded them, and how we rejoiced, and I rejoice still . . . over Heather."

I murmured, "amen to that."

"You have another marvelous expression about people being made to 'eat crow'? Which I find so much more evocative than plain old humble pie." There was good, honest mirth in her laughter now. "I still relish the idea of the doom merchants having to do that over Heather. Gristly old crow . . . having to eat it all . . . fleas, feathers and everything else." I laughed with her then. "We have Heather, who is no driveling idiot, and no monster. Although . . ." She sobered quickly. "The difference in her cannot be denied."

"Her being fey?"

She countered my question with one of her own. "How much do you know of that?" Asking it in a way that made me suspect that she had been waiting for such an opening.

"Well, as I mentioned, she's talked of it. And I found it enchanting . . . the things she told me."

"But enchantment may wane, Denney," Margot Granger warned. "Following enough repeat performances." She fell silent again, and I waited until she said reflectively, "a rather pretty word . . . fey." I would *not* think of the Oxford Dictionary's definition. "The hint of mystery to cover the small multitude of our sins?"

Unsure of how to respond, I volunteered, "I'm grateful that you've told me . . . the things you have." It sounded, and was, totally inane.

"Does knowing alter your opinion of Heather?" She considered me soberly. "London, for instance? Could this make a difference?"

'King's. Row', I thought then.

The big weepie movie of 1942. All-star cast: Claude Rains, Robert Cummings, Anne Sheridan, Ronald Reagan, Nancy Kelly . . . floods of tears all round.

Small-town America—King's Row—at the turn of the century. High summer and laughter, straw boaters and parasols. Young people, young love, great hopes . . . and stark tragedy.

The foredoomed love affair between the hero and the town doctor's daughter. Whose mother was incurably insane, and confined to an upstairs room of the family mansion, peering out, wild-eyed, through parted drapes. *Had* there been something more than coincidental in Margot Granger's taut joke about turret rooms?

The lovely daughter had inherited the gene of madness.

The doctor warning off her suitor and, when the warning went unheeded, killing his wife, killing his daughter, killing himself . . .

Thinking of 'King's Row', I asked, "are you warning me off, Margot?"

"My dear friend . . ." She looked perplexed. "Would I go to all this trouble? The invitation, this, for me at least, pleasant meeting? Do you think me so two-faced?"

"No . . . no, of course not."

"Before you took over at the aerodrome," she related then. "One of your senior officers, a most smooth and persuasive character, beautifully-rehearsed, came to the village hall to give us a pep-talk. To explain just how we would be . . . safe-guarded?" I listened without comment. "Among much useful information provided was the simple series of steps to take if and when people made nuisances of themselves."

"Oh, I'm *sure*." Irritation stirred anew.

"Denney, be fair," she reproached me gently. "People do."

"Well . . . yes." I nodded. "Tell me about the steps."

"A call to the Commanding Officer . . . anything that gave offence . . . I'll always remember the phrase he used . . ." She began to laugh again. "The C.O. would, it seemed, 'lower the boom so hard and fast it would make the offender's eyes water'."

Laughter was shared now, and laughter dispelled annoyance; the Americanism sounded especially funny in her refined English accents.

"So you see," she concluded. "There was never the need for subterfuge. All I had to do was to ask your C.O., very nicely, to lower the boom."

"Well put," I said.

"Although I have not the slightest wish to do any such thing."

"I'm glad to hear that. Because, for me, there's nothing casual about this. I feel involved, and want to be."

"Which is why I offer you this most kindly of warnings," Margot Granger answered. The warning of the 'King's Row' doctor had also been kindly. "That Heather could cause you pain and unhappiness."

I echoed like a fool, "pain . . . ?"

"By all means, if it's your wish, then do persist," she encouraged. "But, at the same time, be prepared."

"All right. But prepared for what?"

"Heather has changed since Tim was killed," she said musingly. "Had you known her then, and seen the difference, then it might have made it easier for you to grasp my meaning now."

"Can you explain that for me?"

"You know . . . I'm not sure that I can." There was embarrassment and apology in her glance at me. "I don't understand it all that well myself. Just that there *has* been change . . . perhaps a hardening of sorts. And more overt evidence of what she terms her feyness."

"Is it okay to ask what evidence?"

"The fact, for one, that she spoke of it to you. When, before, at all times, it would have been concealed." She gestured. "For instance, I don't believe that Tim ever knew."

"That makes me feel kind of privileged."

"One would like to see it in that way," Margot Granger conceded. "But it might be better not to rely too heavily on that interpretation."

It had been a long discussion, and a blackbird had now joined the invisible robin as the garden filled with horizontal blue and gold light.

"Might Heather not want to see me any more?" I wondered. "Is that it?"

"It could happen . . . if she felt herself threatened somehow." She added quickly, "that's not meant in a nasty way, Denney. More of a feeling of being . . . what . . . hemmed in?"

That was a possibility with which I could equate; each time when I had sought in even the smallest way to pin her down, she had taken fright at once, and backed off.

"There are other things that could happen . . ." But Margot Granger did not disclose the nature or extent of those things, saying only, "or again, nothing. Full stop." She considered me with the same candor that I had seen so often in Heather's eyes. "I'd be delighted to be proven wrong about all this. It could be that you'll become the steadying influence that Heather needs."

"I'd be very glad to try."

"Nonetheless, Denney," she stressed once more. "Do, please, be on your guard. I would hate it if you were hurt by Heather when you're proving to be such a true friend."

There it was again, and from a different and telling source, the word that fell so far short of what I was seeking. I said, "thank you, Margot."

"Dare one read between the lines?" The gray eyes appraised me. "Do you love my daughter?"

"Yes, I do. Very much."

I received my reward then. "One might hazard the belief, from the way that she speaks of you, that love is returned."

"That's the very best thing I could hope to hear."

"But remember always that she *is* different." No maternal smugness underlay the claim. "Her values and beliefs, by her nature, are not always like yours and mine. She would hate herself for making you unhappy, and be miserable that she had. Not comprehending fully how she had done it in the first place."

SIXTEEN

"Everything's fixed," O'Connor announced. "Tooken care of with my unfailingly delicate touch and savoir-faire." Andy Devine and I exchanged resigned looks. "Always, as the Marx Brothers would have it, be arrogant, be elegant, be suave."

"Cap'n, sir . . ." Andy threw him a derisive salute. "What in hell you talkin' about?"

We were together in the Officers' Club, discussing O'Connor's preparations for the forthcoming weekend.

"Pardon me all to hell, son." O'Connor surveyed him with a jaundiced eye. "I should, of course, render the information down to your customary level of Neanderthal grunting. So . . . what you need to do is take plenty money. Go railroad station. Board train heading in right direction. Reach London. Get drunk. Get laid. Do not drink from finger bowls or spit in spittoons. Do not scratch nuts in public when dining in better-class London eateries. Got it?"

"Oh, all *that*." Andy grinned back at him. "I know that already."

"What did you do . . . read a book?" O'Connor turned his attention to me. "Whereas you, Pontius the Pilot . . . first, partner-wise, have we resolved our problems yet?"

"Is Heather going?" My nod was emphatic. "Heather surely is." Margot Granger might warn, I thought. But even the best-intentioned warning must come a poor second to that wonderful, now unalterable, fact.

"My goodness gracious me . . . *what* a relief! Been sweatin' blood with anxiety over it." O'Connor consulted his list, then stared at me in shock. "You really meant it? *Separate* rooms? When your fair companion is nubile, shapely, and seemingly willing?"

"I've said already . . ."

"Still not made it yet?" He held up placating hands. "Okay, okay . . . *two* rooms with facilities. Grosvenor House, one swish joint located on Park Lane, heart of a precinct called Mayfair. Where you will be warmly welcomed upon production of suitable I.D . . . like cash. Reservations from noon Saturday to noon Sunday. If in doubt, the mere mention of my name opens all doors."

"Roger," I said.

"As for you, Meatloaf . . ." O'Connor peered doubtfully at Andy. "I have succeeded against fanatical opposition to track down a lowly tavern that's willing to accommodate your unruly Oklahoma ass . . ." He re-checked the list. "One big bed. Breakfast within same costs extra."

"Don't you worry 'bout that. I'm takin' breakfast in bed along with me." Andy leered. "Where's it at? Same flea-trap as the Skip?"

"A flea-trap is as much as you merit, paisano."

Andy indicated his groin with a thumb. "Blow 'Taps' on this."

O'Connor, shaking his head regretfully, directed, "present your sorry self at the Piccadilly Hotel. Which is on a street likewise named Piccadilly, and close by the same-named square, which they call a circus where multi whores strut their stuff around the clock . . ." He was smirking. "Should your sweet companion elect sensibly to decline your grubby advances."

"Ain't about to happen, Cap'n," Andy declared. "But I'll bear the info in mind."

There were theater reservations; Andy and his date had scored a musical, and there was a play for Heather and me, a comedy with fair reviews. O'Connor had thought of everything, right down to the carefully-marked subway maps. "In case you two bastards, as I suspect, are too cheap to spring for a cab."

*

I hitched an early ride to Colchester where I waited for Heather who was coming in on the mid-morning bus.

On a blustery Saturday that threatened rain, she wore flat shoes, a headscarf and her unflattering white mac. She carried a suitcase, and smiled at me like a conspirator. "My glam things for tonight . . ." One hand brushed down her mac. "To make up for my immediate plebbie appearance." She reached up for a swift kiss, telling me, "Mum helped me to choose and pack. She has much better taste." The train came in, and we found an empty compartment.

"First class?" She gave me a look. "Third would've done perfectly well."

"Nothing but the best for my girl . . ." But, was I overdoing it?

"Yanks!" She shook her head pityingly.

As the train ran on through Chelmsford and Brentwood and Romford, I filled Heather in on the arrangements; of the separate rooms, the evening play, the planned get-together at the Savoy later. "You said once that you'd like to go there."

"It sounds super." But a shadow touched her face. "Also fiendishly expensive. I'm sorry, I shouldn't quibble, but London's awfully dear. And Grosvenor House? The Savoy . . . ?"

"Just this once?" I jogged her memory. "Your birthday and our nineteenth mission, *and* the medal? Plus the fact that O'Connor has tastes far beyond his means. I swear, after this, it's back to the Stage Door Canteen."

"Then I'll say no more." Heather took my hand. "Simply be grateful."

"Not even that. Just enjoy."

"In moderation, though," she insisted. "I shan't chuck my weight around. You won't know I'm there."

"Where's the fun in that? You're meant to kick up your heels. Manhattan babies in Mayfair . . . going home with the milk."

"You tempt me wickedly." She kissed me once more, more warmly and intimately this time. There was no one around to see us.

We pulled apart, and I said, "wow!"

"A token of true appreciation." The train was slowing for the Liverpool Street arrival as she added softly, "there's another token, if you're interested?" I watched her in the gray light over the city. "A way to save some money." She sounded nervous as she went on, "those two hotel rooms . . ."

Wheels screeched against tortured steel, a sooty arch was sliding over, a long, grimy platform crowded with people, servicemen, railroad employees. Carts and bags of mail. Tattered posters advertising Stephens' Ink, Bovril, Benger's Food, Fry's Chocolate. 'Careless Talk Costs Lives'. 'Guinness is GOOD for you!' I rose to take down our bags from the rack. We would find a cab: none of O'Connor's penny-pinching subway rides . . .

Heather said, "cancel one of the rooms, Denney. A second one's only a waste, really." I stood still, no longer thinking of cabs. "We only *need* one."

*

We sat with our bags in the lounge of Grosvenor House. A waiter had taken our order for coffee. Initial excitement over Heather's startling suggestion had yielded to caution, and some misgiving. "You really think so?"

"Oh, absolutely. Certain of it."

I gazed with less confidence around the lounge which seemed to be filled to bursting with well-heeled, influential people and heavily-braided uniforms: a Royal Air Force officer with the broad stripe of an air commodore on his sleeve, the equivalent of an A.A.F. brigadier general. In one corner, a rear-admiral of the United States Navy sat in frowning conversation with a craggy-looking colonel of Marines. I was painfully conscious of the single silver bar of my first lieutenancy. "But how can you know that?" I muttered at Heather. "Here."

"There's no need to whisper . . . we're not in Westminster Abbey." She was assured and at her ease, clearly enjoying herself.

I protested, "we could never hope to palm ourselves off as married. And, anyway, the reservations are in both names. How can I just stroll up there and cancel, and blithely tell them we've decided to shack . . . to *share*?"

"You can say shack up if you want to." She was grinning with happy malice. "After all, it's what we've agreed to do."

"Well, I guess . . ."

"A spade is a spade, my dear." The waiter brought our coffee with the check neatly folded. Heather picked it up. "Mine."

I began, "hey . . . !"

"You can't pay for everything. Leave a girl some pride."

I smiled at her. "Thank you for the coffee."

"Don't mention it. Now drink up and tell me your troubles," she invited.

"All right. For starters, I don't imagine they'll be too tickled about last-minute cancellations."

"Yes? And?"

"It's not that kind of hotel."

"I'll bet you anything you like it is." She looked around the lounge. "And that we're not the first to do it by a long chalk. As for cancellations . . ." Her shrug was carefree. "Hotel rooms are at a premium these days with all your pampered and polished lot in town. They'll be queuing up for any spot going to kip in."

*

The room would be cancelled at once; there would be no inconvenience whatever. Nothing was revealed in the cool, professional eyes meeting mine. Fingers clicked, and a youth materialized with a handcart. If I would indicate Madam's and my luggage?

"You won't need that." I pointed at the cart. "We're traveling light."

The youth looked knowing. He ushered us to an elevator, then led the way down silent, carpeted passages to an ivory door edged with gold . . .

As the door clicked behind him, Heather came into my arms. "What did I tell you?"

"You were right, of course. As always."

She was laughing. "I keep seeing all those desperately

important generals and admirals squabbling over who'll get my room."

"You're beyond hope, you know that?" We kissed, and the last of my unease left me, yielding to something more compelling . . .

Heather wondered, "are you a restless sleeper?"

"I'm not sure. Why do you ask?"

"If you are, or I am, we'll soon know." She pointed. "A single bed."

Awkwardness came right back then, leaving me without answers. Heather seemed perfectly capable of taking everything in her stride. I, it seemed, could not.

*

At once sensing my fresh unease, Heather suggested, "should we go out for a while? A walk . . . see the sights?"

"Where would you like to walk to?"

"There." She stood at the window, pointing. Our room overlooked the Park Lane traffic five floors down. With Hyde Park beyond, all summer greens and massive old trees. The clouds were breaking to let the sun through. "It's lovely now." She turned to me, eyes alight. "We'll make it a perfect day."

We walked to the artificial lake called The Serpentine to watch the rowboats with shirt-sleeved men at the oars, and the people swimming at the Lido, then on, unhurried, toward Kensington Gardens. Heather pointed out the palace and the Albert Memorial with the pale dome of the Albert Hall beyond. The sounds of traffic, like a distant river, drifted down from Bayswater Road.

"Oh, look . . ." She indicated some empty deck chairs. "We can sit there until the ticket collector comes along . . ." She wore an urchin grin. "Then we'll skedaddle, and let him shout insults at us about Yanks and their tarts." She assured me, "he'll enjoy that much more than collecting the money."

"You mean they *charge* you for sitting down?"

"Threepence a go. This is London. Nothing's free."

We stole our illicit breather, and Heather asked me, "what about after the war?"

"A pleasant, if remote, possibility." I stretched, yawning. "What about it?"

"It's just that I never hear you speak of it."

I thought of Providence waiting out there somewhere, watchful, for ever poised, and confessed, "I haven't even let myself *think* about it."

"But there's going to *be* an afterwards . . ." She made it sound nice and cut and dried. "And you'll want to do something."

"I know what I'd like." I eyed her guardedly. "But if I tell you, it'll probably bore you stiff."

"Let's find out, shall we?" Heather put on her good listener face.

Once more then, and with unexpected ease, I spoke of inner things shared with no one else until then. Of vague hopes and dreams that had taken root in that summer when I learned to fly sailplanes, and was encouraged by an instructor who believed that I was a natural pilot, and should persevere. Notions which gained substance from the experience of flying the powerful and complex bombers of the 9th Air Force. "What I'd like to do most is go on flying."

"Won't you have had enough of it by then?"

"Of the kind I'm doing now, yes. If I never had to look at another B-Twenty Six . . ." I shook my head. "But not of flying . . . of being in the air."

"What would you do," Heather wondered. "And how?"

There, for me, was the fascinating choice, and the most uncertain part of an ill-formed plan. I told of commercial flying in America: the international and trans-continental airlines that would operate the big, war-spawned transport planes. "Then there are the smaller feeder lines with aircraft like the DC-3, the one that you call the Dakota. Connecting between cities and the smaller urban areas. Those, and bush-flying," I said. "For which the Canadians and Alaskans are best-known. Small aircraft on floats or skis flying into the really remote areas."

"That sounds rather like fun," Heather thought.

"It's a hard grind for those who manage to grow old at it. Bush-flying creates some of the most adept and resourceful airmen there are. All up to you, by guess and by God . . . no airports or fancy navigational aids. Just the nearest creek or lake or clearing."

"Would you like to do that?"

"It has its attractions," I allowed. "Let's say, I'd like to be that good a pilot. But, being a typical city slicker, I guess I'd be pining for the bright lights." I revealed then, "best for me would be running my own feeder line. Alone, or in partnership with someone who could fly and put up some extra capital. Get in on the ground floor, you see . . ." Heather listened with the appearance of close attention as I prophesied the boom in postwar aviation.

"Everyone will be looking to fly, all those people for whom trains and cars and steamships are no longer good enough. And there'll be plenty of cheap airplanes up for grabs, all war-surplus. Many of which were designed as airliners anyway, then converted for military use. A couple of those and I'd be in clover . . ."

The life of the big park flowed around us as I talked. Children played; toddlers reeling on shaky legs, watched by mothers in summer cotton. A British sailor and his girl fed scraps to flocking pigeons.

Heather enquired, casting a sudden shadow over my dreams, "and what would your mother have to say?"

"I can tell you now." I made a face. "She'd hate it."

"Does she have *plans* for you, then?" I was conscious of that dry emphasis.

"All kinds of plans, and then some. Mostly she wants me to finish college and get a degree. Another year." I said in acquiescence, "I'll indulge her that far."

"But no more than that?"

"Not without a fight." A toddler toppled, and waited placidly to be rescued. "She'll have to accept that I'm no longer the kid who went off to the Air Corps."

"And who'll win?" Heather was smiling.

"I'm not sure I'd want to put money on that."

"What is it that she'd prefer you to do?"

"Business or law," I replied glumly. "Better still, for her, business *and* law."

"Like your father."

"Exactly like."

"Is there a family business for you to go into . . . ?" There was a perceptible hint of the sardonic in her tone as she asked that. "For you to take over when the time's ripe?"

"Not any more." Not for the first time when in conversation with Heather, I wondered what or where all her questions were leading to. "Dad was an attorney, the senior partner. The firm still carries his name." She nodded. "He retired early because of his heart . . . he had more than enough put by. We got off lightly during the Depression." I chose not to elaborate further upon the way, like many law firms, that my father's had thrived upon the endless litigation cast up by that global catastrophe. While others sold apples on street corners, starved, or threw themselves off tall buildings. "If I were to take post-grad law, there'd be a place for me in the firm. Which would make Mom happy."

"And you?"

"I'd be miserable, and bored to tears," I replied without hesitation, and justified that response with, "it's not as if there's a need. My mother's comfortable, and set up for life. And she can't have all things her own way."

Heather surprised me then by saying, "good for you, Denney." As on a previous occasion, there was the sense of having passed a test . . . or side-stepped a pitfall. "So you'll fly?"

"I'll certainly try hard to."

"And do you have the money you need to start your airline?"

Right there was one more potential sticking-point: I would have enough, with the inheritance from my father, untouched so far, to afford at knock-down prices two ex-A.A.F. C-47 Dakotas. Rugged aircraft with proven engines, capable of carrying good-sized payloads: freight, or twenty passengers in comfort, thirty if one dispensed with the frills. With C-47s it should, in theory, be difficult to go far wrong.

My remaining funds, I had calculated, would enable me to pay for airframe and engine inspections, the mandatory modifications that bureaucratic authorities would demand. With some hard bargaining, I might also pick up one or two spare engines and propellers; enough to get started. Calculations based upon the principle of going it alone.

With a flying partner who could match me dollar for dollar the horizon widened considerably. We might run then to three airplanes, more engines, props and parts. Or pay to have our spartan warbirds prettied up to meet more demanding civilian tastes.

Even having achieved that much, there would remain a multiplicity of problems to be faced and, somehow, overcome.

Like Government certification which pre-supposed airworthy aircraft; the minimum acceptable ground crew, aircrew and support staff requirements. Likewise, approved arrangements for servicing and overhaul, an operating base, hangarage, fuel, catering and credit facilities. A whopping annual insurance bill. Crew training and testing. Back-up lawyers, because damaging lawsuits lurked always in the wings.

I/we must find—against stiff competition—flight routes, landing rights, stop-over points, and establish turn-around arrangements. Facilities held with the knowledge always that if I/we did not measure up full time, then the Government could be counted upon to step in and shut me/us down.

All this I explained to Heather.

Who said with approval, "you've certainly done your homework well."

"Some of it, anyway."

"You'll need a terrific amount of money."

"You could say that," I agreed.

"What will you do?"

I gave her a wan smile. "Couldn't touch you for a small loan, could I? Pay it back with free flying lessons and guaranteed employment?"

"I'm almost tempted." She laughed at my chagrined expression. "But my few National Savings certificates wouldn't make much of a dent, I'm afraid."

"It's for me to do," I said then. "And there's the rest of the war in which to try and figure out the answers." And to stay alive, I thought. There was that, too. Providence, Providence . . ."I might be able to soft-soap the bank manager. Trading on the family's good name."

"Mightn't your mother help?" Heather wondered then.

"You mean . . . *back* me?" Now *there* was a notion to stir the imagination! "Okay, we're not exactly short of cash, but that's still a lot to ask."

"Just a thought in passing," she said.

"And a very good one, too," I offered in swift apology. "However, I do see this one minor flaw."

"Oh, yes?"

"My mother."

"Are you so very afraid of her?" The question seemed guileless.

"Call me cautious," I suggested.

"It does seem a terrible shame," Heather mused. "To come through a world war only to get knocked down back in Civvy Street."

"There's a lifetime job for you," I vowed. "In public relations and morale-boosting."

"I wasn't suggesting that she should actually give you the money," Heather made clear then. "Only lend it, or something of the sort. Perhaps offer to be your guarantor when you see the bank manager?"

"Suggesting that would be sure to bring on another fight," I said with regret. "She's going to be mighty displeased already when I bring up the subject. Asking her for a hand-out, or to go good on my signature, isn't going to help matters. And she'll be using all her formidable powers of persuasion to steer me away from such foolishness, and back in her preferred direction."

It remained, though, that Heather's suggestion had made an impact. The idea of being grub-staked by my mother in a venture which she was bound to view as hare-brained and uneconomical had not occurred to me. Now, encouraged by Heather's cool reasoning, I felt my viewpoint shifting. It was easy enough to become sanguine from the comfort of a safely-distant London deckchair . . .

I had not exaggerated to Heather my mother's willfulness, nor her autocratic ways. Yet, in fairness, she had never been the Medusa that I might imply at times. It was true that she liked to call the shots always. As her only child, I had been cosseted and much-indulged, and was still, but made also to toe a firm line of her dictating. Something which, living under her patronage, I did, albeit—at times—in rebellious mood. The terms of her line-toeing were seldom onerous, although, to me, immature and carping, they could seem so.

There *had* been times, nonetheless, when I could recognize and accept the wisdom and foresight of her hopes and plans for me, the path that she mapped out, and the love and caring that she contrived to conceal behind that high-handed manner. Most of her demands were reasonable, like the expensive—and I thought horrible—Connecticut prep school, which had provided me with a first-class grounding education. Princeton, too, had been at her firm suggestion, and I had greatly enjoyed Princeton, although in many ways, and frequently, that were unforeseen by my mother.

It was unjust to gloss over or belittle her tolerance of many of my foibles. Like becoming a sailplane pilot, or enlisting in the Army Air Corps: Mother would have much preferred the Navy . . . more 'gentlemanly', and 'such a smart uniform'.

Yet, she declared always an avowed respect for drive, initiative, ambition, innovation. Supported by the, to her, shining example of my father. While I, awed by her, allowed time to fritter itself away as I sought without notable success for ways in which to innovate and display ambition, initiative and drive. It was always so much more pleasant to follow the path of least resistance, and, anyway, my mother had sufficient drive, initiative and ambition for us both.

Until this moment, when, prompted by Heather, I could begin to visualize the possible ways in which Mother might be swung round to my kind of thinking. For instance, could she in honesty deny that, in desiring to start an airline of my own, I was at last displaying those characteristics which she so admired? And by virtue of that, be willing to help get me—literally and figuratively—off the ground?

It would be, of course, a no-holds-barred head-butting contest, but then, my mother had always enjoyed those. She could be, also, a generous loser, if an infrequent one, memory warned. But, with a wide ocean between us, it became plausible to indulge myself in visions of her losing this one. "There would be some pretty heavy conditions attached," I told Heather. "For a start, she'd be looking for a participating directorship, which would be hell on wheels."

She replied with severity, "what a dreadful thing to say of one's mother."

"You're biased," I reminded her. "You imagine all mothers to be like your own. Mine, you have to understand, is a whole new ballgame."

*

We retraced our steps across the park. The afternoon had turned warm, and people were out enjoying the improved weather, servicemen with girls, hordes of children running and shrieking. Two stiff and pipe-clayed British military police threw me regulation, muscle-wrenching salutes.

I complained to Heather, "I'm hungry."

"We'll get some lunch soon."

"Where away, this beanery?"

"A place I know that's cheerful and cheap."

"Heather, that's not important . . ."

"Tonight . . ." She cut me short. "You may spend like the

famous drunken sailor if you wish. But for now, we'll economize. A perfectly decent lunch for only a few shillings." I was picturing some London equivalent of the New York Automat. "Lyon's," Heather said. The name meant nothing. "The Marble Arch Corner House . . . it's very popular, and not at all bad." She gripped my arm. "I can practically guarantee a cup of English coffee that won't send you into shock."

*

The air raid warning began to sound as we neared Park Lane, a rising and falling, all-pervading wail that punished the eardrums, and bringing with it the realization that this would be my first time on the receiving end. How would it be? How would I be . . . ?

Rising above the monotonous sound, we could hear it coming.

A low, throbbing growl, alien and hateful, a sound wholly new and unimagined, deeply menacing, yet seeming almost unhurried, like a motor well throttled-down. Filling the air completely as the sirens gave up and fell away. Getting into the blood, like poison.

"Buzz-bomb," Heather said. She stood still, searching the sky.

Around us, however, I could see no evidence of haste or visible alarm. People standing stood. Those seated stayed put. The imperturbable military police had paused to gaze solemnly skyward.

A police constable in a blue steel helmet came briskly down the pathway, calling out amiable advice. "If the motor stops, lie down and cover your heads. And some of you start gathering up them kiddies." Calling to a knot of children, still and silent with their heads thrown back. "Come along, you nippers . . ." He was good-humored, avuncular, his voice up a little to hold its own against the enemy sound. "Where's your Mums an' Dads, then? Hop it now, and find 'em. Shouldn't need me to tell you . . . you know the drill . . ."

Heather pointed suddenly. "There he goes, the bastard."

Something midge-like and appallingly swift: automatically I was calculating the speed . . . around the four hundred mark. As fast as a Mustang or a Spitfire with the throttle wide open. Hurtling over the rooftops with its bizarre take-it-easy growl. I had been expecting something slow and bumbling, like one of our little L-4 Cub spotter planes.

The midge raced over Central London, taking on shape as it went, torpedo body . . . clipped, un-tapered wings . . . squared-off fin and rudder. A weird-looking propulsion unit mounted above the tail, spouting white fire. My first sight of a V-l flying bomb . . .

Heather stood on, unmoving, eyes raised to the sky. I asked edgily, "what did the cop mean about the engine stopping?"

"It happens just before they come down." She did not look at me, and I noticed how bright her eyes were, and her lips were parted: palpable excitement made her more beautiful than ever as, with growing disquiet, it dawned upon me that she was getting a big kick out of this.

The V-l was right over our heads, flying at five hundred feet. Pilotless, self-controlled by gyros and spigots and circuitry, blind . . . inhuman . . .

Until it coughed once, and the motor stopped.

The long tail flame dying away, then a silence as crushing as the sound of it had been. The great city frozen, waiting. The nose of the V-l starting to dip . . .

And Heather, smiling, watched it. "*That's* what the bobby was talking about."

People had begun to move, a concerted and considered movement, everyone knowing what must be done now. Gathering the children close, looking around, taking stock . . . last looks, maybe? Flattening themselves to the comforting earth, clutching their kids.

The military police, their massive dignity forsaken briefly, crouched behind a great oak. The steel-helmeted cop had gone upon his unhurried way, out of sight.

And, God in Heaven! . . . Heather standing there, smiling all the way up to her eyes at the plunging missile, and I was furious with her then, almost hating her, thinking . . . God damned stupid little *bitch*! What in hell was she thinking of, or trying to prove by this? As I reached out and grabbed her. "For Christ's sake . . . are you crazy?" Dragging her to the ground beside me as she uttered a little astonished cry.

The silence drew out across the bright sky, clawing at taut nerves, a waiting that was like pain. Until, almost like an afterthought, the explosion came, a rolling rumble, the ground beneath us briefly shuddering.

All over then but for some gasps and nervous laughter, a child's thin, baffled cry. People sitting up, brushing themselves off with embarrassed smiles as eye met eye. And a distant mushrooming of smoke and dust, ochre and saffron, lifting above and beyond the cream-fronted buildings lining Edgware Road.

Sounds of falling glass shattering, and of a vehicle hurtling too fast for the gear selected . . . the silvery clangor of an emergency bell.

More distant then, the growl of a second V-1 off and away to the east. Until it, too, cut out; another breathless wait . . . the detonation like remote thunder.

There were just the two.

Everyone was standing and talking, gesturing, comparing thoughts and impressions of this latest attack. Far overhead, sunlight glinted on the silver barrage balloons that had failed that time to stop the intruders. The M.P.s strolled on in strict step, loftily amused by the silly civilian chatter.

"You were angry." Heather watched me with frosty eyes.

"You're damned right I was . . . yes. Still am for that matter."

"But why?" She seemed genuinely puzzled.

"You really don't *know*? Standing there with that thing coming down!"

Her face had set. "There's no need to get into a flap."

"Who's flapping . . . ?"

"I'd say that you are." Disdaining me, she turned her back to watch the dust cloud slowly thinning on the wind. "It landed a good mile away, over towards Paddington. And you know what they say . . ." She flicked me a single icy glance. "That a miss is as good as a mile."

But her seeming foolhardiness had been only part of it. What was really getting under my skin was the vivid and ugly memory of her expression of exultation as she followed the falling V-1. As though loving it, the obscene thrill of it.

As I watched her, she seemed to make an effort, forcing a smile for me, reaching out to take hold of my arm once more. "Come on, you. Don't be such a glumpy old Jeremiah. The worst didn't happen, did it?"

The air shrilled again with the long, steady note of the 'All Clear'. Two flying bombs, a pinprick in the vast, spongelike fabric of London. But a deadly pinprick: *we* were all right, but how must it have been for other unknown people at somewhere called Paddington, a mile away? The dislike, and a kind of revulsion, rumbled inside me . . . *that* had excited her!

As we went on our way, I found myself watching Heather in a way that was no longer appreciative, but guardedly, and with suspicion. In the way that I might look at an odd and unnerving stranger. Finding an unpleasant comparison that refused to be dismissed to be drawn with those in the Squadron who confessed frankly to getting *their* kicks from the bombing and burning of towns, from the flak and fighters. Total weirdos who boasted of what they had seen and done, relishing each minute of it. With that look on their faces that I had just seen on Heather's.

SEVENTEEN

The play did not match its reviews, the writing pedestrian, the humor labored and predictable. The cast bowed to limp applause, the curtain came down, and we could escape with relief into blacked-out and crowded Shaftesbury Avenue.

I had only the vaguest idea of where we were; we had arrived by cab from the hotel, and I found London confusing with its winding streets shooting off at all angles, so unlike New York's precise grid system. Out in the noisy dark, I did not know where to go, nor how. We were due at the Savoy: O'Connor had explained it in idiot-proof detail. The Savoy was on a street named the Strand, and close to Charing Cross, a big railroad terminus. We could not go wrong. Which still left me feeling lost and hopelessly perplexed in this surging, heel-clattering, cigarette-glowing, flashlight-stabbing melée.

*

Following the air raid, we had agreed, after all, to skip lunch. Appetite was lost; Heather's to nervous excitement, mine to edginess and lingering annoyance. While hating it, and myself for it, I was feeling still the dislike of Heather engendered by her behavior in the park.

We returned to the hotel; Heather wanted to wash. "After having you roll me about in the dirt."

I lay on the bed, waiting for her, wondering what the next step was to be.

The V-I experience had left me shaken, as had the stolid acceptance of the attack by those around us. An air of resignation, almost of surrender, it had seemed, to the real possibility of death arriving right *now*. Like—and I could conjure up no more apt comparison—sheep waiting for the slaughter.

Could five years of close proximity to war do that to a city, a nation, of people, rendering them numb and indifferent to the greatest, and final, experience of life? Or was it to do with appearance, that English obsession that was so much akin to oriental concerns over face? I pondered these matters gloomily, listening to the sounds of traffic in Park Lane, to the soft rush of running water from the bathroom.

And what of Heather . . . *had* that little performance of hers been bravado with intent to create an effect, to gain attention? If it were the latter, then it had worked, although perhaps not in the manner sought. Recalling the way she had looked then, the smile, the avid eyes, much as I would have liked it to be one of those innocuous aims, I felt that that could not be so. The thought of it could be . . . frightening.

The air raid had been my introduction to the experience of being on the ground during an attack. Never mind that there were only two bombs by comparison with the scores and hundreds that we dumped on them. Those two were two too many.

In flying missions there was, always, a saving sense of detachment, the target remote and impersonal, a dot on a map at the end of a penciled line. You flew, as ordered, from your dot to that dot, then pushed a button. Whereupon the bombs released and vanished until they metamorphosed into rippling lines of smoke and dust far below, the intricate patterns of intermingling shockwaves appearing no more harmful than those of rain drops on a smooth pond.

From a mile, or two miles, high, you saw no people transfixed, pressed to the earth; you overheard no expressed concern for the children in the shadow of your wings. You never felt the trembling ground beneath you.

I lay back on a bed in a pampering hotel, and considered the likelihood that, from then on, I would be haunted by today's memories each time O'Connor triggered the bomb release. Something to tack on to all my other troubles . . .

Heather emerged from the bathroom, not speaking, and I went off to freshen up and brush my teeth. I straightened my necktie, and put on my tunic with its Air Medal ribbon. Awarded for doing at Eindhoven and other places what the V-l had done, no more heartlessly and mindlessly, at Paddington. That thought through to no logical conclusion, I rejoined Heather, who gave me a strained smile, and wondered what I would like to do.

"Could we get out of this place, please?"

She appeared nonplused. "Don't you like it any more?"

"Oh, I love it to bits . . ." I sketched an insincere smile for her, and said something quite crazy. "But, while we're out, maybe the maid'll look in and dust away the ghosts."

She nodded at once, seeming to grasp a meaning that was not at all clear to me. "Let's go sightseeing. That should sort you out."

At the entrance, I saw the doorman peering at my wings. He grinned at me, unabashed. "We could've used your services a little while ago, sir. You'd have given that nasty bit of work what-for."

For a moment, his meaning was lost. "You mean the V-One? Not much I could have done. I'm a bomber pilot."

"Never mind, sir." He looked sympathetic. "Next time you're over that way, you can give the baskets the old one-two from us." The pictures flickered again: a target, dots on a printed map. No involvement . . . nothing personal.

The doorman wondered if we required a cab. Heather, taking my arm, informed him that we were practicing wartime economies. I was to be introduced to red double-decker busses, and the subway.

"You'll enjoy that, sir." The doorman winked. "No end of thrills if you're not too fussy."

I tipped him a coin, and he saluted. When we were out of earshot, Heather wanted to know how much I had given him.

"A two shillings piece."

"That's far too much." She was frowning. "Sixpence would have done perfectly well."

The hectoring tone induced resentment. "I didn't have a sixpence as it happens."

"You only spoil them," she scolded. "And when you're gone, we'll be left to pay the price."

She led the way briskly, and I tagged along, thinking of 'when you're gone'. In my negative frame of mind, I wondered if that was how she saw the eventual outcome for us? I would go, and that would be that. Leaving her to pick up the pieces.

*

We rode busses and I had my first encounter with the London subway, which I was directed to call the 'Underground' or 'Tube'. "When in Rome," Heather said.

"Yeah, but this is London." She gave my poor quip the go-by.

We emerged at Knightsbridge, and walked to a large, ornate department store.

"This," Heather announced. "Is the world-famous Harrod's."

World-famous or not, I had never heard of it. I did not tell Heather that.

She showed me all of it, floor by floor, department after department, and invited my considered comparison with the Fifth Avenue stores. I answered with care that Harrod's compared well, which it did not: how could fair comparison be made with Sak's, Bloomingdale's, Altman's, Abercrombie and Fitch, or the brash, cheerful jumble of Macy's in a land rationed to the bone, its available merchandise home-manufactured to prescribed government austerity standards. When you could not buy a pair of shoes, a necktie, socks or underwear without surrendering coupons from a grudged personal allowance?

Harrod's was not a success. It would have been unseemly, though, even in my sour mood of the moment, to tell Heather that, or that I could find better choices at the London Post Exchange for U.S. servicemen and women. Or that, on principle, I loathed all department stores, the legacy of interminable dragging around the emporia of New York and Boston with my mother. For whom shopping was an obsessional hobby, and who could never pass up a sale.

A relief to escape to more busses, drifting along on the top deck through late afternoon London. Until, as the great clock boomed five above our heads, we stood on Westminster Bridge looking at the Houses of Parliament, and I thought of Winston Churchill in there, perhaps, at that moment, uttering one of the famed speeches about giving the business to the 'Naahzees', making the V-sign, smoking a cigar, wearing that weird wartime garment of his that looked like a kid's romper suit. With a Homburg hat!

I gazed down at the fast-flowing brown river, at little coal-burning tugboats hauling strings of lighters, tipping their smokestacks as they sailed under the low bridges. Heather told me that the river was tidal there, and for some distance farther upstream. " . . . to a suburb called Teddington, which is a corruption of 'Tide End's Town'."

I essayed another feeble joke. "Does the King approve all this corrupting of his English?"

Heather's answering smile was, at best, polite.

*

The slender obelisk, blackened by decades of London soot, soared into the pale sky to finger among the barrage balloons. Our day was drifting away, and I was getting a little tired of playing tourist.

"This, then," I observed on the right note of deference. "Is the great Cleopatra's Needle?"

"Brought from Egypt in a special barge . . . a gift to Queen Victoria."

I studied the phallic shape, and considered the possibility that the old girl had been thrilled? And wondered then why one of the flanking bronze sphinxes was peppered with small holes.

We found the plaque at the column's foot, commemorating the German bombing raid of 1917; a bomb plunging into the Underground beneath our feet, hitting a passing train, killing some passengers. Flying splinters had gouged the sphinx and chipped the Embankment wall, where the stonework was still speckled with the patches of pale cement used to plug the holes.

Everything, everywhere seemed to remind me of my reason for being here: twenty seven years earlier, and a frail Gotha biplane overhead. In its cockpit had there been a scared pilot unsure of what he did, or some dedicated and irascible Teutonic version of O'Connor? I shivered.

"What is it?" Heather asked.

"Nothing. Only a thought . . . a kind of memory."

"Not more ghosts?" When I did not reply, she laid a gentle hand on mine.

"Sorry."

"Why sorry?"

"Two reasons. One . . . that that was a silly, thoughtless thing to say. And, two, I think you've just about had a basinful."

"No, it's been really interesting. I wouldn't have missed any of this."

"But enough's enough for all that. And we had no lunch," she remembered. "I should think you're starved. When did you eat last?"

"Early breakfast . . . if you could call it that." I grumbled, "reconstituted eggs, canned ham, cold toast and wish-wash coffee."

"My God, you Yanks!" she exclaimed. "You're un-*believ*-able. What would you do if you really had to go short?"

"Then I guess we'd all grow stiff upper lips."

"Home, James . . ." She tugged at me. "A bite to eat and a rest. Then we'll go out and have some fun."

I insisted, "this was fun."

"Hilarious," Heather agreed with irony. "I can see that, all right."

*

Room service sent up sandwiches and a big pot of remarkably good coffee. After eating, I felt better about things in general.

While Heather showered, I let my mind drift, and probably dozed, coming back with a start as I heard her giggle, and say, "oh, dear." She stood beside the bed, wearing her robe, her hair damp from the steam. "Denney . . . you *snore*!"

"I never snore. Do I?"

"We'll be charitable," she conceded. "And call it heavy breathing." She bent down to kiss me, warm and fragrant from the shower.

With my earlier misgivings erased by her nearness, I reached out for her. "You should know that I could eat you right here and now."

"Better not . . ." She skipped nimbly aside. "I'd be sure to give you heartburn."

"You do things to my heart already."

She took that without comment. "Have another snore while I dress."

To order, I closed my eyes and let some more time pass.

Until she announced, "it's all right to look now."

I looked. "Terrific! Fan-TAST-ic!"

"Thank you." She pirouetted before me.

She was fully made up, and had put up her hair in a way to make her appear more adult and sophisticated. Wearing a silk dress of cool summer blues and greens, full-skirted, and pinched to flatter her waist, and there was nothing utility or austerity about *that* dress. She had put on patent leather pumps with high heels, and silk stockings that had been my gift to her from the PX, and the seams were straight.

"My Lord approves?"

"You're right off the cover of Vogue."

"Circa about nineteen thirty six . . ." Her fingers traced the skirt's material. "It's one of Mum's, actually. We spent a frantic couple of days doing it up."

"And an outstanding job you've done." I sat up and took her hands, close to her again, loving her. "The dress is beautiful."

"Well, it was pre-war." Doubt clouded her face. "I do hope I shan't be too much of an anachronism at the Savoy?"

"Take my word for it . . . you'll knock 'em dead."

She kissed me again, and I was aroused at once, seeking to draw her close, but, once more, she evaded me. "Steady! You'll crease me."

"Oh for the chance!"

"Later . . . just be patient." She considered me, smiling. "Can you be, for a little longer?"

"With difficulty." My heart had contracted. "Okay, I'll behave . . . but it's going to be a real chore."

"Can it really be," Heather asked lightly. "That you've got over your grump?"

"Grump? Me? I don't recall any grump . . ." But, of course, I did, and felt fresh shame: how could I have even begun to think of her in that way . . .

"All better now?"

"Worlds better, and bloated to the gills with carbohydrate. My mother swears by carbohydrate."

"What, Mom again?" Heather mocked. "With the low-down."

"You," I chided her. "Have been hanging out with too many Americans."

"Only one. One who matters, that is."

She chased me off to the shower. I stood under the scalding jet, paying no heed to the Government notice about bathing in a maximum of five inches of water. It appeared that, somehow, five inches aided the war effort. How was not explained.

I had my second shave of the day, and paid for that with a nicked lip, and skin that felt as though it had been sand-papered.

I had brought along a fresh shirt and spare necktie: I shined my shoes and brushed my tunic which was rumpled after the long day. A rumpled tunic would have to be my gesture to the war effort.

*

In the blackout, with the theater crowds milling around us, I decided on a cab as the best and only method of getting safely around stygian London. Cab drivers had all the answers, like how to track down the Savoy Hotel in the dark.

My attempts were unavailing; repeated forlorn cries of "Taxi!" earning only faceless scathing laughter, and a voice from the gloom, "fat bleedin' chance, mate!"

It would have been quite easy at that moment to develop an anti-British bias and go over to the enemy. I could hear Heather's laughter. "*Et tu, Brute?*"

"You'll never get one now."

"That's beginning to sink in."

"Anyway, it's only a ten-minute walk."

"Not *more* walking?"

"Bear up," Heather urged. "Be stoical."

She produced a small flashlight, shining its wan beam carefully downward, one among hundreds that bobbed and stabbed in the blackness. "What every nice girl should have about her person."

"Right. Now navigate," I said. "And I hope you're better at it than Andy Devine."

She went unerringly, and without hesitation, through a labyrinth of streets, naming and explaining each one. "Wardour Street, which brings us into Coventry Street, then on to Leicester Square. We'll cut through into Charing Cross Road, past St. Martin's, then along William the Fourth Street . . ."

I was impressed. "That's pretty good for a plain country girl."

"Watch it!" she warned, and told me, "when I was little, Dad would bring me with him on some of his trips to Town. He was a tireless walker, always on the go . . ."

Could that be what was termed a Freudian slip, I wondered. "After those excursions, it still surprises me sometimes that I had any feet left . . ." She faltered, and her breath caught before she finished hurriedly, "but he taught me . . . made me learn . . . and it's all stayed in my head."

She had not forgotten that, I reflected. Just one more among so many things that she could never forget.

*

O'Connor, a little drunk, was there to greet us. With his date, a tall, elegant and very beautiful Wren officer whose name was Jeanne. Jeanne and Heather weighed each other up silently as the introductions were made, and then smiled as if in shared approval.

"This . . . is my lovely lady. My one an' only . . ." O'Connor enfolded Jeanne within the circle of a beefy arm. " . . . my sole an' solitary . . ." He slurred a little. "Bombardier to pilot . . . stan' by one. Now, tell me, where was I?"

I prompted, "shole an' sholitary."

He eyed me loftily. "You're too much of a smart-ass by half, kid. Sole . . . and sol-it-ary reason for returning, uncomplaining, to this-here green an' pleasant land. For *chère Madame*, a second tour is cheap at the price. Maybe even a third . . . who knows?"

"Oh, please . . . not *that*," Jeanne was laughing, and her voice was soft, low and very posh. "My poor shattered nerves couldn't stand it."

Old dark horse O'Connor, I was thinking. Who for all his verbosity and banter revealed little of himself ever. Always solo, holding back, a little aloof. Courtly in a mildly-mocking way when there were women present. Never with one of his own.

From certain sources there had been veiled suggestions that O'Connor might be queer. The rest of us in 'Big Apples', although frequently mystified by him, believed that we knew better. O'Connor was simply a man content with himself, beholden to no one, needing no one. So we *had* believed. Until Jeanne, and the way that Jeanne and O'Connor looked at each other.

The Savoy was jumping, packed to the rafters with uniformed officers and their dates. I had read the books: the Savoy, traditional London wartime gathering place and watering-hole. Where, in the old war, subalterns with popsies and flappers had lived it up on the last night before the trenches of Ypres and the Somme. Those boy officers, the survivors, were middle-aged men now, and the Savoy traditions had passed down to their sons, their daughters, too . . . I noted the many young women present, like Jeanne, in British and American uniforms.

At one big table of six couples, the men were all Canadian aircrew: I wondered if Heather had noticed them, and if she might be troubled by their presence. But she was smiling broadly, apparently intent on something that Jeanne was saying.

There were Free French uniforms, and Polish, Czechoslovakians, a table of beery Australians. I smiled at the thought of Saturday night . . . Stompin' at the Savoy . . .

O'Connor was saying, "we got here a little while back."

"Andy not make it yet?" I asked.

"Believe you me, Andy *made* it." He laughed aloud. "And how!" Jeanne was looking amused. "Just wait till you see who with. Poor old Andy . . . if ever there was a sucker for punishment . . ." He was watching the crowded dance floor, the small orchestra, very smooth and well-rehearsed and professional. "He's out there somewhere, buried in the scrimmage."

I followed the dancers, among them an elderly British sea captain who could have been one of those in attendance in that earlier war. Jitterbugging valiantly, beaming, having a whale of a time with his—I supposed—wife, as portly and rubicund as he.

I spotted Andy at the heart of the throng, dancing at full throttle, sweating and grinning, but could not make out his partner's face. I watched as he reached out, heaved . . . and saw a flying skirt, fleshy legs, the flicker of underwear as the girl was spun across his bent back. There was a squeal from her, much laughter, some derisive cheers.

O'Connor reported, "they were here, doin' aerobatics, when we showed up. Him an' the light of his life."

"We shan't be unkind," Jeanne warned. "The poor girl can't help it."

A wine waiter approached with champagne in an ice bucket. "I took the liberty of ordering up," O'Connor explained. "So's we'd waste no time gittin' struttin' at this-here bar-bee-cue."

The waiter was filling glasses. "Champagne?" I asked him. "In strictly-rationed England?"

"The provisions, sir," the waiter replied. "Of special emergency legislation, as I always inform our guests."

"What legislation's that, son?" O'Connor enquired affably.

The waiter smiled with the merest hint of polite condescension. "The Ways and Means Act, sir." He waited as we tasted the wine, and O'Connor tipped him a ten-shilling note.

"My small but respectful tribute to the just and honest laws of old England."

The waiter bowed. "I shall convey your compliments to the Prime Minister, sir, on the occasion of his next visit."

When he had left us, O'Connor declared, "I'll bet he meant that. Wouldn't surprise me if the old fart was a regular."

The music blared to its end, and the band leader announced an interval. As the dancing crowd dissolved, O'Connor leaned forward to murmur, "bandits at two o'clock level." And called out then, "here she comes, our great big bundle o' joy!"

Andy Devine was picking his way toward us among the tables. Grasping the hand of his dance partner . . .

"Oh, Jesus!" I exclaimed. "The merry widow!"

Heather forgot herself sufficiently to say, "bloody *hell!*"

Jeanne let out a peal of delighted laughter. "Now I know what's meant by thunderstruck."

Heather whispered in disbelief, "Gladys Gibbons?"

"Do I take it," Jeanne enquired. "That you've met?"

"You have to hand it to Andy . . ." O'Connor, his shock effect achieved, wore the grin of a successful conjuror. "Never strong on finesse, but sure as hell knows how to take it on the chin."

Andy began the introductions, but Gladys stopped him. "Save your breath, love, we been through the intros before, remember?" She and Heather eyed each other without enthusiasm.

"Terrific." Andy looked hot and happy. "Leaves us more time for some serious drinkin'." He punched my arm lightly in greeting. "How ya makin' out, Skip?"

"Pretty good." I was watching Heather and Gladys bristling.

Gladys told everyone loudly, "the dance, 'member? Last spring?" She jerked a thumb at Heather. "But I known *this* lady much longer."

Sweetly, politely, Heather enquired, "and how are *you*, Gladys?"

"Mustn't grumble." Gladys laughed, showing her teeth. "Who'd listen?" She flopped, sighing, into the chair that O'Connor held for her, telling me, "you're the one that wouldn't gi' me a lift."

I met Jeanne's interested glance, and reminded Gladys, "regulations."

"Oh, we know all about regulations, don't we?" She smirked across at me. "You'd never believe 'ow many people seen you two followin' regulations outside that 'ouse till all hours."

"And now that that's settled . . ." O'Connor looked around at us all, emitting waves of inexhaustible bonhomie. "I reckon it's time for me to propose a toast or six."

Gladys had spied the contents of the ice bucket, and squealed pleasure. "Bubbly! Smashin'!"

O'Connor looked at her with fondness. "So glad you're glad, Glad."

There were toasts to Heather's now-imminent birthday, and to our furlough. To nineteen missions completed (and Providence could take a walk), and being together and alive, and to happy times. O'Connor held back my Air Medal until last.

Heather kissed me to applause, and so did Jeanne, murmuring, "jolly well done. Jamie has told me all about it."

I thanked her, and wondered, "Jamie?"

She stared at me, momentarily puzzled, then glanced in O'Connor's direction.

"Don't tell me you didn't know?"

"That's *him*?" I was startled, and tried clumsily to joke. "We've been pretty busy. Not much time for picking up on first names."

The funny part was that the joke was true. O'Connor was simply O'Connor, or Buzz. Andy was Andy, but only because he was Devine; it was more than likely that everyone in the crew had forgotten long ago that he was Steve. I was Skip, while, with the sergeants, it was the Army's way, last names all round . . .

Jeanne said softly, "funny old world we live in."

"We've got four sergeants in the crew . . . well, three now," I amended. "To my shame, I couldn't name one of them. Not first names."

"Jim, Ira and Wladislaw," O'Connor, who had been listening, said. "That's Smithson, Cohn and Patecki." He added, "Deeks was Elmer."

"Which puts *me* in my place." I asked him, "how did you know that?"

"*Noblesse oblige, compadre* . . ." He struck an attitude. "One's responsibility, accepted with due gravity, for one's less well-endowed brethren."

"*You?*" Jeanne concealed mirth behind a discreet hand. "The Irish reprobate?"

"Reprobate, *liebe fraulein*, I'd never deny. Not, though, simply Irish, but of blooded Celtic stock, if you please." He gazed haughtily upon us all, getting into his stride. "Us O'Connors, you should be aware, were the closest confidants of Brian Boru himself. We marched with Emmett and Wolfe Tone and the great O'Connell himself, b'Jayzus. We had the ears and hearts of Eamonn de Valera and Carl Marx and Groucho Marx . . . so many ears and hearts . . . a truly messy business."

"*They're* not Irish," Gladys said. "Not them las' two."

"Ma'am . . ." O'Connor looked at her with respect. "Yo' book-learnin' sho do you credit . . . yes *suh*. Ah guess they rightly ain't, at that . . ." The over-exaggerated Virginia drawl teased her wickedly. "But Ah'll match yuh anythin' y'all care to lay on the table . . . they sho wish they *wuz*."

Gladys simpered back at him. "*Any*-thing?"

"Long as we can git it on th' table, honey-chile."

The maître d'hôtel arrived with the menus. Allowing for all the claims of severe shortage, the menu could surprise.

"Ways an' means." O'Connor tapped his nose knowingly. "Making due allowance for the standard of clientele. Ourselves . . . Mister Churchill . . ."

The prices could surprise also: I was glad then of my hoarded back-pay. Heather had given fair warning; even so, our billfolds would take a caning on this night. For the first time, I found myself regretting having turned down my mother's offer of a monthly allowance, made before I shipped overseas. To supplement what she dismissed as my pittance of a salary. That extra would have been a comfort now.

We ordered in turn, and Heather was watching me, a look blending statement and enquiry: 'I told you so' and 'will you be all right?' I winked to re-assure her; I would be . . . just about.

Waiting for supper to arrive, we finished off the champagne. Andy, seeming puzzled, told O'Connor, "Buzz . . . way you was talkin' back then didn't sound like no Irish to me."

"Well now, y'all tell me, son . . ." The brows wig-wagged. "What li'l ol' thang it sound lak?"

Jeanne was giggling helplessly. "Sorry, all . . . but it absolutely slays me when he talks like that."

Gladys, silent and bored, wore a scornful look.

O'Connor's eyes rested on Jeanne. "Don't you care for it, lovely lady?"

"I adore it, you know that. It simply makes me go to pieces, that's all."

"What Ah'll up an' do then," O'Connor promised, laying it on thick. "Is lay it on thick. On account o' we don't get near enough o' the thangs we jest *adore*."

He tuned back to Andy. "Now, suh . . . what wuz y'all presumin' to say?"

"How that Irish o' yours . . ." Andy raised his glass. "Sound more like good ol' gut-bucket Dixie to me."

"I'll drink to that," O'Connor said mildly.

Andy wanted to know, "whereabouts you from in Virginia, anyhow?"

"Historic an' picturesque Newport News, son."

"You say *where*?" Andy guffawed, and looked around the table. "No one, but *no* one, b'longs in Newport News. That's some burg everyone stays away from."

Laughing, having fun, Andy failed to notice the way that O'Connor's face had hardened with anger. "It's where the cruddy

Navy hangs out. Where ships dump cargo, an' light out from PDQ. Can't get away fast enough." O'Connor watched him in silence, without expression. "No one in his right mind ever went an' *lived* there!"

O'Connor asked him in level tones, "and what would you know about it, you landlocked Oklahoma dust-bowl dimwit?"

There was a strained silence: the atmosphere around the table had become electric. We looked at one another questioningly, all but O'Connor, who watched Andy.

Who appealed, baffled, "*now* what did I do?"

O'Connor drew a breath as if about to speak again, then closed his eyes tiredly, and shook his head. "Forget it."

"I was jus' joshin' ya along," Andy tried to explain, hurt and bewildered. "Wasn't gettin' personal . . . I wouldn't do that. An' where's the harm in kiddin' about some ol' town? You fellows are always givin' me the gears for comin' from Enid." He added plaintively, "I don't get sore about that."

"You're quite right, and I'm sorry as hell, Andy." O'Connor was frowning, chewing on his lip. "I was way out of line."

"Me an' my big mouth." Andy, seeming cowed, tried to smile. "Always screwin' up . . . everything I touch."

"No, I'm the one that screwed up," O'Connor confessed. "In more ways than you can count."

"Perhaps," Heather ventured. "Everyone's simply trying too hard?" Her smile for O'Connor was sympathetic and understanding. "You're all very tired, and that's when things get blown out of all proportion. Mountains and molehills."

"Yeah . . . sure . . . that's it." Andy watched O'Connor cautiously. "Just some little itty-bitty molehill."

"Hear, hear," Jeanne agreed quietly.

Gladys said nothing.

"Thank you, Miss Heather." O'Connor bowed his head to her. "For pointing out the glaring error of my ways."

"I didn't mean to . . ."

"But I *do* mean." He shook his head once more, looking rueful. "I'm in the wrong, and you help me to save face." He grimaced at Andy apologetically. "I'll never know what made me say that, kid. I didn't want to. Just a sudden feeling. Let it out, or bust."

I looked at Heather with renewed respect, thinking of her prescience, and timing, and tact.

O'Connor met Andy's troubled gaze. "I beg your pardon . . . humbly."

"Well, shoot . . ." Andy gestured. "We're all on the same side here, right?" He offered his hand, smiling. "No hard feelin's?"

O'Connor took the hand. "None ever where you're concerned."

The next course appeared, and the wine waiter came to fuss over our glasses.

*

Too much wine made Gladys confiding.

"Steve's the firs' real officer I ever been with . . ." Heather's noncommittal gaze held mine. Jeanne toyed with her chicken salad. O'Connor watched Gladys with courteous attention. A quarter hour had passed, and the strain of the brief quarrel was gone, if not quite forgotten. "Although, I mus' say . . ." Gladys sounded plaintive. "Buggered if I can tell the diff'rence sometimes in your mob between officers and other ranks." She waved her fork in emphasis. "Only the other day, me an' Steve was in the pub . . ." I pondered anew the possible root of this unlikely-seeming alliance: *was* it that, in Gladys, Andy had discovered someone finally who would acknowledge and use his real name? " . . . an' there was these two, a captain an' a sergeant, callin' each other by their *christian* names!"

"My!" O'Connor breathed in awe.

"I mean *reely* . . . what's the world comin' to?" Gladys sounded outraged, and Heather hid her face.

"Then, dear Madam, I would opine that either they were lovers," O'Connor offered thoughtfully. "Or you were being shown first-hand evidence of our great democracy."

Gladys gave him a hard stare. "You takin' the mick?"

"Gladys, would I dare?" He spread abject hands, and quoted, "'They walk with kings, nor lose the common touch'." He looked around. "Kipling, folks . . . in poor paraphrase."

"You'd get bleedin' common touch in *our* Army," Gladys declared with heat. "They'd 'ave the tapes off that sergeant's arm quick as you like, an' a bollickin' for the captain, an' all."

"Mercy *me*!" O'Connor looked stricken. "Tell me, Gladys . . . do they still flog in the British Army?"

But Gladys had become thoughtful. "Do you really think so 'bout them two? That they was poufs?"

The band interval ended as a roll of drums led into 'Deep Purple'. Andy leaned close to me. "Been watchin' your face, Skip."

I eyed him uncertainly. "Haven't you got anything better to do with your time?"

"It's just that . . ." He was looking abashed. "Reckon you don't set much store by Gladys, huh?"

"I'm sorry," I said. "It shows that much, then?"

"Some," he acknowledged. "A little."

"Forgive me, Andy. It's not . . ."

"That's okay . . . no big deal." He smelled of wine and fresh sweat. "I guess when it comes to the head count, she's more wooden spoon than jackpot." He sounded sad, I thought. And quite uncritical. "But you take what you get . . ."

"What you two on about now?" Gladys was there, sharply-suspicious.

I said, not thinking, "talk of the devil."

Her brows drew together. "You *what*?"

"Secrets o' war, honey," Andy soothed. "Guy talk."

She snapped at him, "oh, *spare* me . . ." I had a sudden vision of Gladys twenty years hence, the bitter and disappointed ageing woman.

I told her, "Steve was saying about how you'd saved his bacon."

She frowned at me, not yet ready to trust. "'Ow did I manage that, then?"

"By agreeing to be his date . . ." I improvised with haste,

"without you for company, he'd have had to miss the fun." Which could have been the better option, I added silently.

She swallowed it at once, willingly, her expression softening as she looked at Andy, and I took no satisfaction from my petty deception. For just a moment, I could almost feel sorry for poor, screwed-up Gladys Gibbons.

"Been on your tod, would you, dear? That's a shame." She looked fondly at Andy.

"Whatever that means, I guess so," Andy agreed, and I hid a smile as I allowed that, after all, Gladys might be the better option? Rather than the Piccadilly Circus hooker Andy could have brought to the Savoy. "Okay," he asked Gladys. "Wanna dance some more?"

She twisted her face at him. "Thought we was goin' clubbin'?"

"Later. The night's still young." Andy rose. "At the prices they charge in this joint, I want me some mileage."

"Anybody mind?" Gladys enquired of the table. "Me an' Steve knows some good clubs. Thought we'd make the rounds . . . know what I mean?"

Jeanne offered agreeably, "that sounds like great fun."

"Come an' all if you want."

"Well, we'll see . . ." Jeanne's features remained carefully composed.

"Same with you an' yours," Gladys told Heather less affably.

"*Thank* you, Gladys."

Andy demanded, "you gonna dance, or you gonna gab?"

Gladys stood, slipping a possessive arm around him. "Mustn't tire yourself out with all this dancin'. Need to keep up your strength for later." She winked at us.

As they made their way back to the dance floor, Jeanne murmured, "oh, *dear*." And wondered, smiling, "was I being an arch-bitch?"

"If you were, then you're extremely good at it." Heather was laughing. "And you've got me for company."

*

Supper was over, but there was still plenty to drink. The Savoy could meet our needs and demands.

I danced with Heather, and with Jeanne, but was spared that requirement with Gladys: she and Andy had begun a marathon jitterbug session from which all others were exempted.

I led Heather out again, and she recalled laughingly, "when we first met, you had to be dragged on to the floor. Now, nothing can stop you."

We circled our decorous way through the gyrating, perspiring throng as I savored Heather's closeness, and the movements of her body against mine, and what that was doing to me as the silken dress emphasized her lithe softness.

To keep my mind off *that*, I said, "I've had nothing but the best instruction since those days."

"From me *and* Jeanne?"

"She's very good," I conceded.

"As good as me?"

"No one," I stated with firmness. "Is ever as good as you."

"Go straight to the top of the class," Heather said.

Gladys and Andy hurtled past, jitterbugging to 'That Old Black Magic', and Gladys's skirt whirled higher, and my Puritan began to rumble. Andy twirled Gladys with effortless ease, and I could not have done that to save my life.

He called across, "how's she goin'?"

"Just fine, Andy."

"Y'oughtta try this-here," he suggested, beaming. "Sure gets the kinks out."

They twirled away with Gladys smirking.

"Tart," Heather said.

"Now, now . . . suppose we talk about Jeanne instead?"

"Do you like her?"

"She's what O'Connor said . . . a lovely lady. The operative word being lady."

"I was merely wondering . . ." Heather pressed closer, and I thought of the night ahead.

"I admire Jeanne in the way I would . . ." I sought a comparison. "The Mona Lisa. Able to enjoy without the need for possession."

"Really?" she asked in a little-girl voice. "And truly?"

The question, and her way of asking it, made me daring. "It's *you* I want to possess."

She looked into my eyes. "Could we leave soon, do you think? Whenever good manners permit?"

"Any time we like," I promised. "That's part of the agreement."

"O'Connor won't mind, will he?"

I glanced over at our table where Jeanne and O'Connor were sitting with their heads together. "I believe O'Connor . . . and Jeanne . . . would be more than pleased to have us disappear. So that they can get on with the pleasant business of being O'Connor and Jeanne."

*

I sat with O'Connor. Gladys and Andy were still dancing. Heather had gone with Jeanne to powder her nose, and I speculated on whether or not I was the first male to ponder why it was that women seemed to enjoy going to the can together.

It was late, and the Savoy's night was beginning to get rough. People were drunk, the talk and laughter very loud: there had been a noisy argument at the Australian table with flushed faces and raised fists, and the waiters had moved in to hover discreetly. From the Navy captain's corner of the room came the crash of breaking glass, and much boisterous mirth.

O'Connor observed with a show of prim disapproval, "they should be more choosy about who they let in."

The band had forsaken the smoochy numbers, playing the big hits hot and loud, while, nearby, in raucous competition, the Canadian airmen had launched into song as a pilot beat time with a spoon.

"'Away, AWA-A-AY with fife and drum,
Here we come, FULL of rum;
Looking for girls who'll peddle some bum
To the North Atlantic SQUAD-ron' . . . !'"

I considered the possibility that Tim might have sung that on long-ago nights on the Town.

O'Connor appeared morose and subdued, and I asked, "are you okay?"

"When wasn't I?"

"That's no answer."

"No significant change in the overall situation." O'Connor shrugged indifference. "All quiet on the Western Front."

"And no change permitted," I warned, smiling. "You're our rock, and, therefore, changeless." Reminding him, "something you said the day we all met for the first time."

"I say many things. Usually a boxcar load of balderdash."

"This I remember well." I quoted for him, "I am a ROCK. A two-fisted, brawling, bruising lead bombardier who never takes no for an answer." I laughed at the memory. "You were somewhat in your cups at the time."

"And I actually *said* that?"

"Among other things. Word for word."

He shook his head in disbelief. "What a complete horse's ass."

"All the same, we needed a rock just then. Still do."

"You want to know about rocks? There's that song . . ." He sang it croakily. "'The Rockies may crumble . . . Gibraltar may tumble . . . they're only made of clay' . . ."

His eyes, watching me, were sardonic.

"Something's really got to you, Buzz." His sudden and puzzling shift of mood was setting me on edge. With their song ended after many verses in like vein, the Canadians whooped and pounded the table. I asked with care, "like to talk about it?"

"I've just said. The rocks parable."

"That's not you."

"Well, who knows . . . maybe, maybe not." He switched to a stage Irish brogue. "Sure an' begorrah, 'tis the drink. Get a few gargles inside, an' I go to the hoolies."

I said, "thank you, Barry Fitzgerald."

"That good, was it?" He cocked his head. "Okay, since you're insisting, I'll try and come clean . . . just for you."

"You do that. I'm a good listener."

"Not a hell of a lot to tell, really. Snap diagnosis . . . I'm good and bushed. Forty four missions in the E.T.O., all told, and I'm getting old and raggedy-assed. Scared, scared-er, scared-est."

"Sure, Buzz . . ." And the chill within me deepened. It should have been a comfort of a kind, finding that the dedicated and unflappable O'Connor suffered no less than I, but it was not. There was only the awareness once more, bleak and unavoidable, that, in the end, we were all alone, little frightened islands caught up in the rip-tides of war.

"My God damned gut aches without cease these days," O'Connor complained dryly. "I feel decrepit. Only the other day, in the shower, I found gray pubic hairs . . . can you beat that?" I said nothing. "I dread each mission, and keep praying for engine failures. Even though that won't change a single damned thing . . . we'd still have to go and make up their shitty numbers. But, at least, that'd put it off for a while." His eyes, bleak and empty, stared at nothing.

"You're not alone," I said then. "Right from Mission One . . ."

To that point, though, was as far as I was prepared to take it. O'Connor had his own inner monsters to struggle against; one soul bared was enough for one evening.

But he looked up at me, nodding. "I'd figured as much . . . from things you've said or done." He startled me by adding, "but you're good, I'll give you that. You never let it show . . . other than when you kick a little ass at times . . . like mine when I need it."

"And yet, that's exactly what I've always thought of you . . . all of you," I blurted. "Admired you and envied you so much for the way you handled things, it's made me hate your guts sometimes."

"Only sometimes?"

"A lot of the time, then."

"*That's* more like it." He grinned without mirth. "Well, we're nothing if not hateable."

"I've often wanted to ask you what the secret formula is?"

"Ain't no such thing."

"Then what ingredient's missing from me?"

"I'd say none. Because every time, depend upon it, every one of us . . . not just you . . . is soiling his BVDs." O'Connor leaned toward me to confide, "about the only way I have left now to keep myself going from the I.P. is to get good and hopping mad. Whereupon, I take it out on you."

He fell silent, and we watched the dancing. The band was beating out 'Pennsylvania Fifty Five Thousand' as the Navy captain and his lady, with their impressive bulk, cleared the decks around them, looking as though, at any moment, one or the other, or maybe both, would suffer massive and joyous coronaries. And, did that hefty and jovial sailor, up on the bridge of his ship, ever feel as we did when the U-boats and torpedoes raced around him? Was all this performance now, the hilarity, the frenetic dancing, simply his way of covering up the fear and the ugliness?

O'Connor said, "I've always just about managed to deal with it . . . this far, at least. Keep it on a tight rein. And then, along comes some little piece of pure chickenshit like Andy riding me earlier, and *bam!*" He punched his fist into his palm. "I come unstuck at once, and all I want to do, there and then, is beat the crap out of him . . ." He wore a look of chagrin. "And then the graceful Heather has to step in with the cool compresses."

If some good-natured leg-pulling was all it took, then O'Connor must be perilously close to the edge. And, if that was the case, what of the rest of us? Was it, these days, that 'Big Apples' flew with a bunch of crazies on board? Would Deeks's replacement spot at once what we failed to see for ourselves, and beg Major Delaney for re-assignment to another crew?

"There are times during the run-in," O'Connor confessed then. "When I'm sorely tempted to tell you the hell with it . . . that I'm just not interested. Tell you to do it your way, or not at all. Just turn around and fly us out of there."

"And all this time," I told him. "I've been thinking it was just me."

"You, me, the other guys, the entire Bomb Group, and don't try and convince me it's any other way." O'Connor waved an all-encompassing hand at the surrounding tables, the jammed dance floor. "All these clowns, not a care in the world, they'd have you believe. Showing the brave face . . ." His heavy brows went up, but there was nothing comical now in the movement. "And always, in the secret places that can't be shared, wondering about what's waiting around the next corner. While those *waiting* there are wondering the same thing." He gave a long, exhausted sigh. "I'd say we're in trouble, Denney." It was the first time, ever, that he had called me that. "And yet, really, what's the big beef? All we have to do is fly sixteen more missions. Doesn't sound much if you say it quick . . ." We spied Heather and Jeanne returning, and he shaped a smile of welcome, starting once more to make the effort. "Isn't that some peachy sight?" But a final chink showed in the armor as he told me, "without that unbelievable woman, I'd have come apart at the seams long ago. Back when I was with the Eighth." And then, softly, just for me, "there's just one thing I'd wish for you with all my heart. That, woman-wise, you're as much of a lucky son of a bitch as me . . ."

The two young women were fresh-cool, powdered and perfumed; something dark and musky that, it seemed, they had shared. They wanted to be told what we had been discussing that made us look so self-important and serious?

"Money, power and sex," O'Connor replied promptly. The mask was back in place. "The simple, basic, decent things of life."

EIGHTEEN

It appeared, like most other unobtainable items, that cabs could be conjured up at the Savoy no matter what the hour.

We waited as the doorman, with dimmed flashlight, asked the driver to deliver us to Grosvenor House. The driver gave us a quick glance, and nodded.

"They get a bit choosy after dark," Heather explained. "If we'd wanted Hackney Wick, or Bethnal Green, he'd have been off like a shot, and Shanks's for us."

In the dark back of the cab I drew her close and she kissed me hard and long before thanking me breathlessly for the evening. "I *do* like your O'Connor." She had fallen naturally into our way of naming him. "He's so droll."

"That's one description among many."

"And you," she informed me. "Are a sarcastic bastard."

"It does amazing things to me when you talk dirty."

She dug me with an elbow, and I yelped. The driver called through the partition, "you say something, Guv?"

"Indigestion," I explained.

"And I think Jeanne's absolutely super," Heather went on. "I'd love to be like her."

"She's probably having similar thoughts about you right now." I laughed, and added, "then there's what's-her-name."

"Don't let's spoil things. The less said about her the better," Heather felt.

"And kinder as well." But she felt a need to ask, "how *could* Andy have got himself mixed up with her?"

"Andy *is* mixed-up . . ."

The cab lurched as the driver ground his brakes. "You silly SOD!"

Clutching Heather, I called out, "are we okay?"

"We are now." He sounded grimly mirthful. "Nearly wasn't, though. Some git in a jeep." He said pointedly, "one o' your mob, I should think."

I agreed diplomatically, "could be."

"Thinks 'e's playin' cops and robbers." The driver enquired dolefully, "that 'ow you drive them aeroplanes, then?"

"Top secret . . . my lips are sealed," I said, and asked, "where are we?"

"Bruton Street. Not far now."

I peered into impenetrable blackness. "How can you be sure?"

"Learned Braille," he said.

With the near-collision, I had tightened my grip on Heather, and she made no objection when my hand rested on her thigh. Instead, hers covered mine, holding it there.

She wanted to know what O'Connor and I had been discussing. "You both looked so frowny. Was it the war?"

I answered rhetorically, "what else is there?"

She stiffened momentarily, then laughed and switched topics. "We didn't say goodnight to Andy and what's-her-name."

"I doubt they'll notice we've gone."

The gentle pressure came once more on the back of my hand. "And who'll pay that whopping great bill?"

"O'Connor, the ever-resourceful, is taking care of it." I told of chipping in to a pool. "Anything over the mark, he'll meet it, then we'll square up back at the base."

The cab came to a final halt as the driver announced, "'ome sweet 'ome, and all right for *some*, I'd say."

*

Alone with Heather in the room I suggested a nightcap, but she declined, saying that she had had more than enough already. Constraint had set in, and we sat in silence on the narrow bed, not touching now; the tactile daring of the darkened cab interior had deserted us.

Heather was looking down at her hands in her lap. "Denney . . . would you mind awfully if I undressed in the bathroom?" She smiled in an embarrassed way, and would not look at me. "Sorry, but I'm not used to . . ."

"Yes, of course. You must."

She went to her suitcase and I caught the quick, noiseless flicker of a pale garment, then she was gone, the bathroom door closing behind her with an all-excluding click.

I sat on alone and tried to work out how to handle things when my turn came. I had not thought to bring pajamas or a robe: the Army had gotten me into the now deep-rooted habit of sleeping in my G.I. underwear. Which was fine for a barracks Quonset or a BOQ. Government-issue skivvies, though, for the big Mayfair seduction scene, were hardly conducive to sustainable romance.

I was still chewing at this problem when Heather called, "please don't look yet."

"I promise."

Not looking, I could still hear: rattling clothes hangers, the soft shirring of silk as she hung up her dress. Her case snapped, then . . . silence, nothing . . . until a waft of perfumed air touched my face. "Now's all right."

I opened my eyes.

She had freed her hair to rid herself of the studied sophistication assumed for an evening at the Savoy. Her face, scrubbed clean of make-up, seemed almost childlike.

I let out my breath slowly. "Now you look the part."

"Part . . . ?"

"Fey. The nymph in the woodland glade . . ." I shrugged and smiled. "Something I read somewhere once, but it applies."

"Thank you."

She wore a pale negligée that fell from shoulder to ankle, and was ruffled at the cuffs and throat. I wondered if it was her own: like the dress, it seemed a little too artful somehow. Like a carefully-calculated sidelong glance of invitation.

The light from a table lamp rendered the sheer material

translucent, outlining the curves of her body as she said, hesitant and small-voiced, "I've nothing on underneath."

"I can tell."

"Is it . . . all right?"

"Funny thing to ask . . ." I vowed, "it, and you, are beautiful." She seemed still to doubt, standing there, and I watched her, loving her with my eyes until, self-consciously, she lowered her hands to smooth the material over her belly and hips. "I've never seen or imagined anyone so lovely. Other than you, I wouldn't want to ever again."

Her face was still. "One doesn't know quite what to say." The very English turn of phrase contrasted almost amusingly with what was taking place between us. "It's simply that no one's told me anything like that before." The sly, unbidden question shaped itself . . . not even Tim? At once, Heather demanded, "why have you withdrawn?"

"Didn't know I had," I lied swiftly. "Sorry. It didn't seem like a moment for talking."

"You're not troubled, are you?"

I crushed down brutally all lingering notions of Tim: I could conceal nothing from her. I reached out toward her, saying, "as a matter of fact, I am."

"What is it?" She shivered as my fingertips played lightly over her breasts.

"Some feelings of concern over my inability to match the entrance you've just made." I offered confession about my G.I. underwear, and she began to laugh, agreeing that that could be something of a passion-killer. "If we switched off the light?" I suggested, caressing her warm smoothness. "Then I got undressed and sneaked back in the dark?"

"Here's what we'll do." She placed her hands flat against my chest, and took charge of the situation. I was to undress in the bathroom and come quickly back to her. The lights would be left on. "I want to see you exactly as you are . . . nothing on, no uniform or wings or decorations. And there'll be no shyness, not with me, because there's no need for it . . ." She began to sound breathless. "I want to see you *big* for me, wanting me. Like this . . ." She opened the negligée to reveal herself, and stepped closer, and I breathed in her sweetness. She murmured, "just one thing."

"Anything at all."

"The thought that . . . you might be worried about Mum?"

I nodded on cue, although there had been no thought for hours of Margot Granger, of assurances and promises, or ready platitudes trotted out over the tea table. "Well, the thing you must know is that she's a realist . . ." Heather drew back, smiling, to twirl before me, and the delicate garment floated out and away around her. "And very much a woman."

"Yes, I know."

She stroked the negligée once more. "This is hers, actually. Like the dress."

"I did kind of wonder."

"She practically insisted that I take it . . . in case, you know?" She came back to me, taking my arm in a firm grip, turning me toward the bathroom. "Now, will you please go?"

I looked back at her from the door. "That is one unbelievable mother you've got there."

"Yes, isn't she?" Heather agreed.

*

Undressing, I thought with amusement of the quite unexpected way in which this was going, and that while Heather might retire gracefully to re-emerge and perform her seven veils routine, the part assigned to me was to strut back like a bare assed bull moose in rutting season with my dick (it was to be hoped!) at the high port. It was, I felt, a state of affairs that O'Connor might have placed under the heading of *noblesse oblige.*

While undeniably delightful to do, it was still not easy to step out and face Heather, then march over to her stark naked and to order. With the clear evidence of extreme sexual arousal boldly on display. And never mind that she had wished it so.

She was in bed, leaning on one elbow, her face turned to me. The abandoned negligée lay across a chair. She appraised me with her usual frankness, and I struggled against an urge to drop my hands. "You told *me* not to look."

"I mean this lovingly, so don't be embarrassed," Heather said. "But thank you for *him*." I could only nod acceptance. "You told me I was beautiful."

"And so you are."

"And *you*," Heather said. "Are a gorgeous man." Her eyes, lighted by her best smile, examined me. "*My* gorgeous man."

"I'd like very much to be him." I could *feel* the pounding of blood through my head.

She held out a hand to draw me down to her. I slipped into the bed at her side, pressing close in that restricted space, and her other hand found me at once, a surge of current that made me gasp. "He takes orders well . . . a good soldier." Her butterfly fingers developed a thread of possessive steel.

I got out, "he enjoys his work."

"*Work* . . . ?" My breath caught again in my throat as the fingers gave an admonitory squeeze. "I think," Heather confided. "We should call this a mission. Complete with . . ." The fingers moved and stroked, teasing. "Pre-briefing?"

*

The air raid siren shocked us into stillness: that animal howl of long-drawn anguish across the night sky.

Before it had faded, we heard the bark-crack of anti-aircraft guns that grew louder as they pursued the raider, and the high whoomp! of bursting shells. Then that other sound, like a fresh instrument taking up the ugly refrain, of the little pilotless planes holding imperturbably to their pre-set track.

Heather whispered, "they're more to the east this time."

"How can you . . . ?"

"Sshhh . . . listen." A finger rested on my lips.

A V-1 coughed and fell silent as others flew on, growling.

The explosion came, and the building shook slightly. I asked, "would you like to find shelter?"

"Would *you?*" I sensed the challenge, and lobbed the ball back.

"Only if you do." I watched the rise and fall of her breast.

"No."

That shared decision brought immediate fresh arousal . . . and screw the doodlebugs, I was thinking as I turned back to Heather. I said, "there'd be none of *this* in a shelter."

"My thoughts, exactly." She smothered laughter, and her hand found its way back to me with familiar ease. "And if we die here tonight, it will be so much better this way." She looked into my eyes. "I shouldn't mind at all them finding us just *so,* down amongst the rubble." Her fingers caressed.

It was wacky, fey, and, in all probability, completely insane . . . and none of that mattered. I was part of it, and with delighted acceptance . . . the whole thing, no holds barred, and the hell with what the neighbors might think! I answered her readily, "the best possible way to go."

Her brows went up in enquiry in the soft light. "Who's afraid of the big bad buzz-bomb?"

"Not us, that's for sure."

Her face revealed her excitement, a look that was like rapture, the same look seen earlier that day in the park. Now, no less excited than she, I was not repelled as I pictured the way it would be . . . the motor cutting out, the final earthward plunge. The world disintegrating around us even as we . . .

There were four of them, and they were all distant. We listened to the last explosion, and to the night becoming quiet again. Soon, the All Clear wailed over Mayfair.

We turned to each other.

*

Everything we had done together seemed so right, scorning the air attack, at peace with the prospect of sudden death, the added fillip to an already wildly erotic state. It could have happened; it *had* happened to others only hours before at Paddington. Let it all go, and the hell with bombs and dying, and Providence. Catch us if you can, and, if you do, then thank you for making it just so. Instead of as it could have been . . . burning over Le Mans.

We played a sweet and poignant game then, Heather and I, first she asking, "did the bomb come and get us, do you think?"

"I *do* think, yes. That, or something equally and wonderfully cataclysmic."

"And we died," she told me very softly. "Together, and it was joyous, and now we've passed without pain into Heaven."

"And they're digging us out now, and then finding us . . ."

"Exactly like *this*." And her hand began to play again.

Bodies mingled with no awareness at all of time or place. Fusing and becoming one as she guided me and made me welcome. From somewhere, in far distances, her small sharp cries . . . my reflexive anxiety at the thought of giving *pain*? And I may have hesitated, for she seized me fiercely, crying out in what seemed like anger, "NO!"

Drawn back and on and down . . . the long rushing of great rivers, the head filled with their sound, down to a dark, unseen sea . . . and, not *yet*, not too *soon*. Wait . . . ! But those forces gone far beyond any puny attempt of mine to control; the rivers running out and away to . . . grayness, deflation and emptiness . . . the heart's slowing trip-hammer . . . the realization of failure.

Whispering, wretched, "Heather . . . I'm so sorry."

And she held me, damming with herself the flood-tide of dejection and remorse. "Nothing for you to be sorry for, ever." Telling her soothing lies for me. "It was . . . wonderful." But that tiny, and unintended, hesitation betraying her. Looking up, smiling, with tears in eyes that understood and forgave. "That was for you . . . your need. Next time, it'll be for *us*."

*

"Now talk to me," Heather commanded. "While I play." Her hand moved down.

"How in God's name can I when you're doing *that*?"

"Persevere," she advised. Her fingers tormented sweetly. "I'm sure you'll think of something worthwhile."

I burst out laughing. "Anyone ever tell you too much play is bad for you?"

"Place yourself in my hands," she purred, stroking and squeezing, and began to grin. "But then, you've already done that, haven't you?" And, ever practical, "we have all night, and tomorrow morning . . . *this* morning, actually. This room, this bed, this . . ." The strong, slender fingers possessed. "Ours until noon."

*

As, obediently, I talked, I imagined that I saw Heather's purpose: to divert me, exposing my mind in those moments to the benefits to be drawn from simply talking.

She quizzed me anew about my mother. "What would she make of me?"

"She'd like you a lot. Also *your* mother. Who could teach mine a thing or two."

"Why do you make her sound so awful . . . she can't be. I think you're just laying it on." She softened the indictment by kissing the tip of my nose.

"Maybe so." I shrugged. "Now, about what she'd *make* of you."

"Yes?"

"The choice of expression is apt. Because, while approving, I know she'd do her damnedest to re-shape you to a pattern of her own. Right or wrong, you have to know that *she* calls the shots . . ." I sought, and found, an example. "Like the allowance she was determined I would have before I came overseas." I smiled at the memories. "Which, I'm pleased to report, is one of the few battles with me that she lost . . ."

*

"Darling boy, you're being mulish," my mother informed

me. "And there's absolutely no need. The arrangements are made already with Morgan Guaranty. All they're waiting for is my go-ahead."

"Mother . . ."

"A monthly banker's draft . . ." She beamed at me. "There for you whenever you need it."

"But, don't you see . . . I shan't. And, at the risk of sounding an ingrate, I don't want it."

"So very like your poor father, dear." She sighed theatrically. "Willful, stubborn, and almost always wrong."

"If he'd been as wrong as you seem to enjoy making out, it's not likely that we'd live as we do."

"That was *not* what I meant." The atmosphere became chilly.

"Okay then . . . it's a terrific offer, and I appreciate . . ."

"Good. Now . . ." Any further objections of mine were blocked in their tracks.

"Tell me how much you'll need. Two hundred dollars? Three?"

"Nothing, Mother. *Noth*-ing!"

She stared at me, much-perplexed. "But you can't live on nothing."

"I don't have to. There's my pay, and my flight pay on top . . ."

Disdainful fingers snapped, dismissing my pay. "Barely enough for socks and neckties."

"Mother, they provide all those . . . everything, including ten thousand dollars' worth of G.I. life insurance. They feed me, and give me a place to sleep." I offered my most persuasive and disarming smile. "Entrust me with a quarter of a million dollar airplane to fly around in . . ."

"I think you're being flippant, dear."

"Maybe that's what I should be." I was getting teed-off with this, and with her. "Because it's getting too serious." I begged her, "can't you see? My pay's pocket money, all clear, honest profit without strings."

"But . . ." She could not bring herself to let go. "Surely . . . something, perhaps, for the occasional little luxury?"

"No time for luxuries, Mother . . . this is *war*." I laughed. "I'm waiting now for orders overseas. If it's England, then everything's much cheaper there. And if it's to be some Pacific island, then I won't have much use for money, anyway." I pointed out to her, "Morgan Guaranty Trust may be big-time in London, but I shouldn't think they hold much sway on New Guinea or Guadalcanal . . ."

*

Heather lay on top of me, laughing . . . and she *was* making things happen to me again. "I admit, she sounds a little formidable."

"She's okay, but she does get crackpot ideas." I acknowledged then, "although, when I saw those Savoy prices, I had belated second thoughts about turning her down."

If it had been her design to do so, then Heather had succeeded wonderfully in diverting my mind from post-coital wretchedness. Between gentle words, laughter and melting eyes, and aided and abetted by her wickedly skillful hands, it had been possible to pull things back together, feeling the welcome return of strength and desire. To the point where I could suggest, "isn't that about enough of the chit-chat?" And kiss her, and feel her quick, willing response.

She took my hand and placed it over her breast, over the raised, hardened nipple. "*There* . . . yes." I teased the nipple tenderly. "I love your hands on me, especially there, and having you deep inside me . . ." I bent my head to kiss the nipple, touching it with the tip of my tongue, hearing her breath catch. "That's lovely, and it *does* start me off . . ." She stroked down the length of me. "Like you just now . . . vast, incredible things that are impossible to stop." The descending hand searched and found. "Like *him*."

My own hands journeyed on, learning her deep in the warm darkness where the rhythm began, shared and swelling, in absolute harmony now, no clash, no discord. Going with her into regions for which there were no maps, yet within which I found my certain way, in balance with her, tempo increasing to . . . a single sharp cry, a protracted shudder against me . . . then stillness.

After a moment, she breathed, "divine." In the lamplight, there were damp curls on her forehead; the carotid throb pronounced against the tautened skin of her neck. I kissed one breast, then the other, and she held my head close to her.

"You didn't," she said.

"And you did." My heart was slowing.

"Oh, *yes*. And now I'm the one to be sorry."

"Let's hear no sorry. Not for a beautiful debt . . . I hope repaid?"

"Never a debt." She hugged me. "But repayment was glorious."

We held each other, not wanting to sleep, and talked some more then of my mother. Mother, as was her wont, could crop up at some unlikely moments.

"I'd love to meet her."

"I'm sure it could be arranged," I said. "Following a period of intensive combat training."

"You really are a miserable toad." Heather pinched me hard, and made me yell. "She sounds super."

I rubbed the outraged buttock. "How do you figure that?"

The answer seemed studied in its artlessness. "Like mother, like son?"

"That's pretty cagey," I accused. "Doesn't my father get any credit?"

"Of course he does . . . a little. But Mum's always the greater influence."

"You could have a point there."

With smug assurance, Heather stated, "women know these things."

"*I* know this . . . she'd adore you."

"Now, steady on," Heather warned.

"*I* adore you . . ." Now, at long last, I could say it. "So? Like mother, like son?"

GLENN HAMILTON

"That's taking unfair advantage," she said, but her eyes were warm.

"With you, never." I said then, testing the water, "I do love you, Heather."

And, at once, she was back on guard. "How much do you love me?" She watched me, unwinking.

"All I've got. Which I've told no one else, ever." I plunged on in explanation. "More than enough to want you to meet my mother."

"In New *York*?"

"That's the general idea."

"You seem so certain."

"Trust me. I know her *that* much."

"But, going all the way there for . . . ?"

"Why not? And it won't be much longer . . . it *can't* be. I'll be back in the States, my tour completed . . ." And, get thee behind me, Providence!

"What about the war in the Pacific?"

"That may not happen to me . . ." I brushed the Pacific aside. "We'll wait until the *Queen Mary's* released from troopship service, and bring you over in style."

"And where, exactly, do we find the money for that?" Her tone was mischievous. "When Uncle Sam is no longer there to provide, and you're mortgaged to the hilt with your new airline?"

Along with feyness went the hard steel of practicality. "You think of everything."

She sensed my disappointment at once. "Darling, it's an awfully big step."

"I guess it is." I could smile again. "But 'darling' helps."

"This can't be more important than your hopes and plans."

"It's a major part of those, and every bit as important."

"All this . . . New York . . ." She hesitated, frowning. "Would be more than just a social visit, then?"

I had managed to talk my way this far, to where there could be no turning back; now it was going-for-broke time, the vital words waiting to be uttered. "I was hoping we might announce our engagement there?" And, rushing headlong, "marry me in New York, Heather. There, or anywhere else you care to name. That's the point I'm trying to get across. Get the war over first, so that we can dare to make plans . . ." She frowned again, and I silently cursed my thoughtlessness, picturing too late the re-surfacing of dark memories about the making, or not making, of plans. I feared to go farther than to add, "and then do it."

The room was still, as if it, too, awaited her response. Until, outside somewhere, an early thrush began to sing. And she was smiling, telling me, "I do so love that sound. It reminds me, would you believe it, of January. January in July . . . isn't that silly?"

She gave me one of her candid looks that promised I'll-never-deceive. She would meet my gaze like that, I reflected unhappily, when it was a thrush that we talked about.

"That's when you hear them for the first time each year," she said. "January, and a first hint of spring."

And so, neatly, almost painlessly, the topic had been switched, and I was filled with a sudden ache of despair, and the knowledge that I had blown my chances. Heather, committed fully to this long summer's night with me, was not yet ready to face commitment.

*

I came from a shallow sleep, not aware of having slept at all. Cramped on the edge of the narrow bed with my weight on my deadened arm.

Heather was quietly asleep at my side, as poised and controlled in her rest as in her waking hours, and as heartbreakingly withdrawn.

My watch showed seven-forty. The room lamps were still on, but daylight intruded through a chink in the blackout drapes. Muffled, querulous voices passed in the passage outside.

I lay quite still, and felt the waves of anticipatory sadness that presaged the now-imminent ending of our brief and, for me, inconclusive idyll. We would have breakfast sent up, pack our belongings, then go back to the station to board the grimy train to Colchester. And then what . . . if anything? Wide awake and dwelling on fresh evidence of Heather's evasiveness with me, I had all the ingredients required for a severe case of the early morning blues. Although, had I been asked to explain why, I would have had nothing concrete or specific to offer in support; my mood and feelings, I could recognize, were based on mere hunch. The lingering unease aroused by an innocent remark about a thrush. Something to be laughed to scorn by the one who questioned me.

I eased my way off the bed, careful not to disturb her, and, in the bathroom, threw cold water on my face, as though to shock myself back into channels of logical thinking. But the feeling of regret and loss persisted: it had been going so well—*perfectly*—until, with no warning, it stonewalled; no explanation, no reason that was evident. New York? Engagement? Marriage? Let's talk instead about the birds . . . but not the bees!

No outright refusal, but a swift, none too subtle evasion, the quick switch to the discussion of inconsequential matters that seemed to me in my depressed state tantamount to one. The precursor to the full and flat rejection to be offered up at some later time and place of Heather's choosing. In the park, or on the train; on the next bike ride through the country? Only a foolish, empty hunch . . . that would not be dismissed.

She was awake when I re-entered the room, and, yes, she had slept beautifully: she thanked me, expressing the polite hope that she had not disturbed my rest. I was told that I had not snored, and was given a bright smile to go with that. "You looked very peaceful."

I said grumpily, "you make it sound as though I'd just died."

"That might not have been surprising considering yesterday's exertions." Her tone was dry. "Together with a fair proportion of today's."

"And you?" I ventured.

"Out like a light." And that was as much as she would reveal of the immediate past; no ongoing reflections, no decisions reached after due consideration. Instead, I was asked, "are you in a hurry to get dressed?"

I was wearing a Grosvenor House bath towel. "No hurry."

"Then, if you feel like it . . . are willing?" Her brows lifted in enquiry, and, at once, the blood was surging, and I was very willing, and it was a secret that no bath towel could keep. As Heather, affecting astonishment, observed in a creditable Scarlett O'Hara voice, "why, Ah *do* decleah you *are!*" Laughing at my flushed and eager face, she ran lightly, naked, across the room. "Shan't be a sec . . . promise." The bathroom door closed.

Puzzled by her action, I listened with disappointment to the shower's rumble: it had been one more of her teases, another last-moment turning away to frustrate me and get my goat. She would finish her shower, then dry her hair and dress, and all it would have been, for *her*, was another little game . . .

The bathroom door re-opened and the vestibule clouded with steam. She stood there, outlined in curling vapor, and she said my name, just audible over the hissing rush of the water, and held out her arms to me in fresh invitation.

*

We played together under the hot torrent with no thought for waste or war effort, and she gleamed in the flow, flashing with every sinuous movement as she pressed herself to me, swaying and provoking. I was aroused to the point of near-pain, yet managing somehow to stay in control . . . there was no haste, not yet.

Although there must be limits, the moment when the shared cataract could suffice no longer . . . and running then with her weightless in my arms, leaving my wet footprints across the thick carpeting of our expensive room. Back to our tumbled, still-waiting bed.

*

She enquired very softly, "what did you do to me?"

Difficult to find an answer, to shape the words. "I don't think I had much say in it."

"I feel wonderfully *ravished*." She clung to me. "If we haven't begun a baby, then I don't know what."

"You make it sound as though . . . you'd like that."

"Perhaps I would." Her eyes searched mine. "Is that outrageous?"

"No, just amazing." But I had been caught hopping once again by an unimagined turn of events: from coy side-stepping to an unruffled acceptance of the very real possibility of parenthood . . . ? "But how could you face . . . ?"

"With ease, should it happen . . . complete equanimity." From the way she said that, we might have been discussing some minor, passing inconvenience. "No fallen woman . . . not me." Smiling, she let her fingertips trace over the length of my still-wet flanks: what had seemed endless and eternal had involved only the most brief passing of time. "And ours, I know, would be the most beautiful baby."

"You're not simply amazing," I told her. "You're beyond belief."

"And I suppose I shock and appall you . . . ?"

"Heather, you delight me endlessly, baffle me most of the time, and scare the hell out of me with it. But it's a good kind of scared, one that I wouldn't want to miss."

"That's good," she said calmly as her hands met and gripped, and I gasped, and gave myself up to her.

When I was able to speak again, I insisted, "you can't just thumb your nose at the prospect of a child . . ." I amended, "a possible child."

"Possible . . . probable . . . already *fait accompli*? Who can tell yet? Just have to wait and see." I had a glimpse of her urchin grin before she turned her face away, saying, "but, if so, then a baby to keep."

"I'd be there for you," I said at once. "I'd never walk out and leave you."

She murmured, "that's lovely of you, Denney." But when she turned to look at me, the grin was still there. "And you'd really want to make an Honest Woman of me?" And there it was back again, the smokescreen of playful words, and . . . *damn* it to hell!

As ever tuned to me, Heather said, "you just went quiet."

"I do that when I'm thinking of you."

"You shouldn't if it makes you unhappy. That's something you told me."

"I was thinking, too, of babies . . . *and* honest women." Steeled for the fresh rebuff, I said, "I'd want us to marry, and have it."

She hugged me again, and I could not see her face. "There's one thing, of course, that we're overlooking, isn't there?"

"What's that?"

"That, at the moment, all this is speculation, and not yet a happening." She had gone back to being matter-of-fact. "And people, as often as not, do get away with it. More than you might think." She laughed suddenly. "Just listen to that." This time, not a thrush, but the shower which we had left running. I mumbled, disconsolate, about turning it off, and Heather said with urgency, "not yet. Shall we put it to use, instead?"

"Again? Now?"

"If you're up to it . . . in a manner of speaking? We're ready, after all," she pointed out, and glanced across at the open bathroom door, the swirling steam. "The temperature looks about right."

*

"Funny," Heather said absently. "The tricks that time can play."

"What brought that on?" I glanced at her.

"I was thinking of what you've told me about the final seconds when you're nearing the target, with the ack-ack going off all around you . . . and how they seem like eternity." I gave a wary nod, uncertain of the direction the topic was taking. "Now, this weekend . . ."

She was speaking close to my ear. The only other passenger in the train compartment, an elderly civilian, dozed in his corner seat, the Sunday newspaper forgotten on his knees. "It seems like an age since yesterday, yet, at the same time, only minutes."

"For me as well."

A landscape stripped of color drifted past the window; shabby suburbs, smoke and steam drifting back from the plodding locomotive. We went through a glum station without stopping, a name board—'Harold Wood'—gray people waiting without hope, their shoulders hunched . . .

The civilian got out at Shenfield. No one else got in, and the compartment was ours for the final few miles. We necked breathlessly, hands roaming, but this gritty coupling on worn cushions seemed shoddy after the intimate bed and the hot showers; more reminiscent of best-forgotten gropings in the backs of automobiles. We drew apart. "Maybe we should wait for the wheatfield?"

Heather was patting her hair into shape. "Do you want there to be one?"

"Very much."

"But . . ."

"Yes, I know. Tim." She nodded once, avoiding my eye. "But you made it sound wonderful . . ." Jealous, I thought. Who's jealous *now*?

"The famous clean breast." She sounded embarrassed.

"Not regretting it, are you? Telling me?"

"No . . ."

"I respect everything you said," I asserted. "You took me into your confidence, and evoked some incredible images . . ."

"And Tim is dead," she finished for me.

"I didn't mean to . . ."

"And," she continued, grimacing. "After a suitable period of mourning?"

"Heather, it's been two years. And life goes on."

"I'm not some Gladys Gibbons!" she retorted. "Please remember that!"

I tried to soothe her. "You wouldn't know how to be."

The brakes were grinding for the Colchester stop.

"Thank you." A faint answering smile replaced the hard stare. "As for the wheatfield, it *is* getting close to harvest time . . ." The train crawled, dragging out the last mile, as Heather changed tack once more, hitting me with another of her startling questions. "If there were to be no baby, would that disappoint you?"

I thought about it for a moment. "Yes, it would."

The train stopped, and I held the door for her. On the platform, she took my arm, confiding, "I *would* love to have your baby."

"That beautiful child we made together." The picture danced before me, tantalizing, and out of reach. I could not rid myself of that conviction.

*

We had forty minutes to wait before our bus would leave.

Stranded at a stained table amidst the steamed cabbage smells of a cheap café. Where we could not be close or talk with any freedom over the thick cups of stewed tea. Wasting in heavy silence the little time we had remaining. In which many vexing questions might have found answers.

The bus, like the greasy café, was full; we sat together like strangers as London receded down the miles.

At the village I said, "I'll walk you to the house."

"There's really no need, you know." She was polite and distant, and I had the feeling then that I could not have explained or justified, that I was being warned off. Bafflement made me snap back at her, "damn it . . . I know there's no *need!*" It was going wrong, slipping away, and I could not fathom why. "There is, though, this silly wish of mine for a few more minutes of your company." There was no valid reason for disquiet; Heather had not actually given me the brush-off. She was simply being . . . difficult, being *Heather*. But the hunch, the bad feeling, would not go away.

I offered lamely, "don't take any notice of me, please. Guess I'm just a little rattled."

"About what?" Her expression was remote.

"Hell, I don't know. That God-awful café, maybe, or taking you there. That, or some damned thing."

"You can't blame the café, it's that sort of place." She demanded impatiently, "what's really wrong with you?"

"It'd be easier to ask me what isn't. Being back here . . . the big weekend over . . . the blues in general, things I don't seem to be able to understand. Everything seeming to turn upside down for no reason." And yet, while not understanding, I did, at least, *know*, and I wanted to shout it at her . . . you say you're happy to have a child with me, but you won't become engaged, you won't marry me, or so you make it seem. Can't you see it, I wanted to beg her. That this is starting to drive me out of my head . . .

"Oh, Denney, come *on!*" There was a rasp in her voice. "There'll be other times, it's not the end of the world, is it? Try and have a little faith in yourself . . ." The intonation softened a little. "I'm sorry."

"Don't be. We're both pretty bushed . . . that's probably the real cause." I reminded her, "we didn't get much sleep."

She nodded, accepting that. "I do feel a bit shattered." She kissed me without passion. "But worth it . . . it was magical."

"Unforgettable . . ." I searched her face for . . . what? And said, "I'll call you."

"Please do . . . and take good care." A smile came and went. "Remember the spell."

"Right here, next to my heart." I patted the place. "Like you."

NINETEEN

No sooner back on base, and there was Sergeant Tallichet, 'Big Apples" crew chief—the man who really owned the airplane—out looking for me. Wearing a shit-eating grin. "Okay weekend, Lieutenant?" He had the good grace not to wink.

"You'll hear few complaints, Sarge."

"That London's some burg, huh? I'd stack it against anything we got down my way."

I asked, curious, "where are you from?"

"Muncie, Indiana."

"I see what you mean," I said. "Now, was there something particular you were looking for?"

"The bird, Lieutenant. She's all set, ready for air test."

"Good news." Did my response sound as lackluster as I was feeling? "You willing to ride along?"

"Sure will, sir." He met my eye. "We stand by our work . . . Good Housekeepin' Seal o' Satisfaction."

"Okay. First thing in the morning, you and me and the wild blue yonder . . ."

It was the acid test of maintenance standards: that the crew chief who signed out the work rode the acceptance flight, a hostage to fate.

"Just one thing, sir," Sergeant Tallichet said.

"What's up?" I smirked at him. "Not going chicken on me, are you?"

"No, not that." He spread his hands. "Just that, seems, the air test can't wait till mornin'."

"Oh? How come?"

"That Major Delaney, Lieutenant . . . he comes by the hangar and sees how we're doin'. I tell him we're all through bar checkin'

the tires an' wipin' the windshield. Then he says to tell you he
wants the air test done like ten minutes ago. On account of in
the mornin' . . ."
    "A mission's been called."
    "Got it in one," Sergeant Tallichet said.
    "So what would have happened if I went AWOL? Would
Delaney have flown the test, and the mission as well?"
    "In a pig's ass, Lieutenant!" Sergeant Tallichet guffawed,
enjoying the joke. "No one wouldn't send that dickhead solo in
a kiddy car." His shoulders went up in regret. "All the same . . ."
    "Give me a half-hour, Sarge," I said. "Draw yourself a 'chute
and a headset, and meet me at the airplane."

*

    The first sight of the restored 'Big Apples' could capture my
immediate interest, helping to dispel some of the gloom I was
feeling over Heather and being back. The heavy maintenance
crews had worked their round-the-clock wonders to make our
airplane look almost as good as on the day of first delivery. She
crouched there on the hardstand, band-box new, gleaming and
powerful, ready to fly . . .
    Sergeant Tallichet, like a dedicated used car salesman, extolled
her rejuvenated virtues. "There's still some o' the original left . . .
little here, little there. But you got the new wing you was wantin',
and a brand-new zero-time engine an' prop." He peered up with
critical affection at his charge, running through the list of repairs
and replacements. " . . . landing gear, hydraulics, fuel tanks, pumps
an' lines . . . a rebuilt tail . . . the works."
    "You've been busy, Sarge."
    He grinned, and said slyly, "well, someone needed to be."
    Along with all the new installations, the aircraft had been re-
painted from end to end, after which Technical Corporal Flaherty
had stepped in to provide the vital finishing touches; nineteen
neat, bright bomb symbols stenciled in place, and 'Big Apples',
herself, after a face-lift and trimmings, glowing afresh, her

generous breasts proudly jutting, her smile for ever warm and welcoming. An honest, passive and uncomplicated female. A myth.

"Whaddya think of 'er, Lieutenant?"

"Just beautiful, Sarge."

"Yeah . . . you bet." His sardonic gaze followed mine. "An' how's about the *airplane*?"

I laughed. "And, after all this, will she fly?"

"Like a homesick angel, she'll fly," he assured me with pride. "I kid you not."

I hoisted my parachute. "If that's so, there's a bottle with your name on it from my next liquor ration."

Sergeant Tallichet looked pleased. "She'll perform, Lieutenant, if I have to haul my butt outside an' shove!"

*

As much as of the airplane, it was to be a test of me: the first time I had turned a propeller since Eindhoven.

I did everything strictly by the manual, taking my time, double-checking like a raw beginner as I lifted 'Big Apples' to ten thousand feet in a wide, gentle circle that encompassed parts of Suffolk, Cambridgeshire, Bedfordshire and Hertfordshire.

Testing each item on the repairs list as we went; the systems, flight controls, flaps and landing gear, fuel tank selection and booster pumps, then running both engines through shut-down and full feathering, and back to re-start.

We had scored new flight instruments, and one of the latest model radio compasses. The magnetic compass was freshly swung with the new compass deviation card slotted into its place. I could call our airplane near-perfect, and told Sergeant Tallichet, "you've earned your bottle."

Feeling more at ease, I played around for a while, getting back the feel, finding that, for all her brand-spanking newness, 'Big Apples' was as familiar and comfortable as a pair of old, good shoes.

Over Luton, I continued the turn back toward the east, beginning an unhurried let-down, getting ready to hit my throat mike and ask the Tower for an approach . . .

"Jesus CHRIST!" Sergeant Tallichet yelled.

As something flashed, lightning-swift, across the nose, seeming no more than inches away from collision, and was gone: I peered after it with wild eyes, shaken to the core . . . seeing the Spitfire as it rolled from inverted back to level flight: the Spitfire I had *not* seen when it counted, but too late. And what if that had not been a Spitfire? As the Focke-Wulf at Eindhoven had not been . . . A fast-dwindling shape now, with graceful crescent wings mottled green and brown. Pulling up into a near-vertical climb, hard-glinting in the early evening sunlight, then making a dramatic stall turn off the top, the long, sleek nose rolling over, back down toward us, 'Big Apples' locked in its sights, lining up in the classic head to head attack posture . . .

Like Eindhoven repeating, the enemy fighter boring in, its cannon pumping flame and shells . . . with every nerve screaming in raw panic, I must scream back soundlessly at my inner self . . . get a GRIP, you sonofa*bitch*! It's a Spitfire, British and friendly, meaning no harm . . . its pilot horsing around, having some fun. Not easy, though, to accept that, watching the beautiful machine expand in the windshield like an explosion. Like facing a firing squad with no blindfold, watching the bullets on their way.

Yet, no destroying burst of fire; instead, the wings rocking in final salute, and the Spitfire gone for good in less than a split second, its full-throttle Rolls-Royce roar audible ten feet above us, slamming us down hard with its slip-stream . . .

"That Goddam crazy son of a whore!" Sergeant Tallichet, slack-jawed with shocked disbelief, trying weakly to laugh it off. "I can tell you, Lieutenant, I was all fired up to kiss my ass goodbye that time."

Only a game; it happened all the time, the slightest opportunity. No bored fighter pilot on a dull patrol could pass up on the chance for a crack at a lumbering bomber, no matter whose.

But the Spitfire pilot could not know how he stirred the still-warm ashes of my private nightmare, or made me more painfully aware that the short breather was over.

I exhaled long and slow, and tried to keep up the appearance of calm and unconcern before Sergeant Tallichet's watchful eyes. "Did Delaney offer any hint of what's on tomorrow?"

"Nix, Lieutenant." My crew chief gave another strained laugh. "Mind you, for a little whiles back there, I was figurin' how tomorrow wouldn't matter a hell of a lot to me an' you." He shook his head. "All's I know, a big mission's on the cards . . . the whole Group. Anything that can get in the air's gotta git."

Over Bishop's Stortford, descending and in contact with the Tower which gave me a long straight-in approach on zero-nine.

It could only be zero-nine, I reflected briefly. That and the Spitfire to round off my Sunday. But then, I could not avoid zero-nine for ever: it was probably better now, at the end of this safe, inoffensive flight, with a fresh, sound airplane in my hands, to get to grips and start laying a few ghosts.

The effect, though, was weird: an impression that would not go away that I flew not one but two approaches to Tiverell Lacey. One with this splendidly-refurbished 'Big Apples', the other a pale reflection, like the fainter, outer rainbow. Coming down the glide path straight and smooth in quiet air, hardly any wind, holding easily to the runway centerline. While, stuck there in a corner of memory's eye, I flew that other approach once more, with its aching exhaustion, the nervous feeding-in of compensating aileron, fighting elevator and trim and crosswind, keeping the untrustworthy wheel off the ground until . . .

"Sarge . . . give me full flaps, please."

No need to ask for that, I could do it myself, did so all the time. Said and done for personal re-assurance; to see if my voice sounded okay. To discover if I was keeping control, concealing the returning sweat and shakiness, the nerves strung close to breaking point between this reality and *those* phantoms. Feeling the flaps bite into air while trying not to see at the periphery this mirroring of me, of 'Big Apples' afflicted, slowly dying in my hands. The tense thought that . . . if I look out to one side now, I'll find that other me out there off my wingtip, looking back.

I did not look out, but found my refuge in the job in hand, working away at it to bring us floating down to the asphalt to hit on the numbers with a soft, cushioning rumble.

I turned off, taxying back to the hardstand, and Sergeant Tallichet, his aplomb restored, confirmed, "pretty damn' nice landing, Lieutenant."

"Thanks, Sarge. Pretty damn' nice airplane to make it in."

But Sergeant Tallichet had not been aware of the true situation: he had had to ride out only the one landing.

TWENTY

August 1944.

The long beachhead stalemate broken at last, the rampaging armies thrusting deep into open country; the Germans falling back to evade the threatening pincers of Normandy and our flying columns moving up from their unopposed landings in the south of France. Columns that raced non-stop to the Loire and on into Brittany. Lisieux, Argentan and Alençon all taken, along with our two *bètes noires*, Rennes and Le Mans. Where we need never go again with our bombs to tiptoe across the flak carpet.

August . . . the month of harvest, and much industrious stooking from dawn until after dusk in the fields of Essex. The month, too, of the killing harvest, the mechanized and fire-blackened slaughter of Falaise as the Germans struggled to regroup their remaining resources and pull back to more secure positions behind the Seine River. And Falaise was where we trapped them in the strangling Pocket, killing them like penned sheep as we bombed and shot and rocketed and burned, wiping out their tanks, their trucks and guns, the panzerfausts and nebelwerfers; the Mercedes staff cars filled with the charred cinder bodies of their colonels and generals. Their riddled and ditched and overturned kubelwagens.

Turning about then to thrust on to Paris, with spearheads going out into Lorraine, George Patton leading noisily and flashily from the front, vowing that his Third Army would be across the Rhine and heading up the Berlin autobahn 'before you could spit'. So it was reported in the daily communiqués, and 'spit' was the word used.

We came up like a tidal wave through Chartres and Rambouiliet and Evreux and Passy and St. Germain—so many

of 'Big Apples" old targets—right to the Porte d'Orleans where a
halt was called to leave the liberation of their capital to LeClerc
and his Free French. And for Ernest Hemingway, for ever playing
soldier on the fringes, to commandeer the Ritz Hotel and rescue
Elsa Maxwell's hapless, elderly Japanese former butler from a
furious lynch mob.

As Paris fell, and Patton streaked eastward, and the British
and Commonwealth and Polish armies moved into the old
Flanders battle-grounds, we, too, were keeping busy. Where the
armies went, we went with them, and often preceded them with
our waves of medium bombers.

*

With the war reaching into the heart of France and Belgium,
we must now, for days at a time when so commanded, shift our
base away from Tiverell Lacey.

The men on the ground demanded unceasing air support,
wanting it right *now*, carping over the delays in strikes mounted
from England. They wanted to whistle, and there we would
be.

Flights, and sometimes the entire Squadron, would be briefed:
pack a toothbrush and head for some newly laid-out airstrip in
the front zone, there to make ourselves subject to the beck and
call of whichever divisional or corps or army commander was
expressing the most urgent need. We went, unquestioning, not
complaining too much, all the while never knowing for how
long it would be . . . days, weeks? For ever?

Thus did 'Big Apples' bear us, safe and intact, through
missions twenty one to twenty six. From a forward strip outside
Senlis, thirty miles north of Paris.

This must be, we made up our minds, how it had been flying
in the other war. Those old air fighters in their Spads and
Nieuports, Camels and De Havillands, had taken off from muddy
fields like this one, plowing along through the ruts. With tent
hangars and open air dumps for fuel and bombs and ammunition,

some nearby dilapidated farmhouse converted into a headquarters and mess.

For us, a generation later, there were the 'improvements' of rusting and malodorous Quonsets, and wider areas of mud and collected water to accommodate B-26s. Also the luxury, unknown in 1918, of a single runway built of PSP.

Each day, we took off and landed over the center of cobbled, medieval Senlis with its spired cathedral and enclosed, secretive buildings of pale stone. Low enough, a mile from the runway's end, to see the people looking up, watching us go by, and some— a few—waving. Not here, though, the spontaneous, unflagging support of the Tiverell Lacey research station.

The yelling and kissing, the waving flags and hoarded champagne of Liberation Day, had passed on to other places. Now, in Senlis, people wished only to get on with their lives, and could not do so with peace of mind while we remained at the edge of town. We were the ongoing reminder that the war had not gone away, only receded. The loathed German, out of sight, remained in mind, and possibly within reach, still. Our presence was the reminder to those French people that much remained to be done, and that the tide of war might yet turn against us. They stood in their streets and squares and gardens, watching us come and go, never quite able to believe . . .

Few of the missions from Senlis were difficult. Flying from French soil enabled us to penetrate more deeply into the still-occupied zones, where we bombed mining, smelting and railroad installations far to the east around Longuyon and Longwy, Sedan, Mézières and Charleville. And, for the first time, hit Germany proper.

The frontier region of the Pfalzer Wald, a synthetic oil plant outside Neunkirchen. As we flew homeward, passing over Saarbrucken, Sergeant Patecki reported from the tail position that the Neunkirchen fires had really taken off. "Lookin' good back there. That synthetic shit burns every bit as good as the McCoy."

O'Connor spoke of his pleasure at flying over Reich territory again, his first visit since the Eighth Air Force days. "Does my heart a power o' good seein' it gettin' the bejesus kicked out of it."

Neunkirehen was our twenty fourth mission, and the fourth away from England. We had been eight days on detachment at Senlis, and were coming to accept with resignation that our sojourn there would be, at best, indefinite. The pessimists declared that Senlis was *it* from now, and we could write off Tiverell Lacey as history.

I was not willing simply to roll over and accept that: the Essex village had become a kind of home, made so by the presence there of Heather. It was the one place where I wanted to be, and never mind that the Army of the United States might dictate otherwise. Heather, I felt, gave me certain claims and rights.

But the days away drew out, and no word was forthcoming about a move back to England. Endlessly troubled by unanswerable questions about the indefinable 'something' which seemed to have marred our relationship since the weekend in London, I began to consider the glum likelihood of my becoming, by my absence, a dimming memory for Heather, or even that that absence might afford her secret relief. It was deeply upsetting, and especially because, to my way of thinking, it just did not make sense. How could it be—the same question came back to pick at my mind—that a young woman who could display such apparent unconcern over the prospect of conceiving an illegitimate child, could, at the same time, duck an offer of honest, and saving, marriage from the one whom she had chosen as the possible child's father?

I was hurt by it, much-confused, and my ego had been dented. It was my belief that I had much to offer to 'the right girl', and that Heather Granger was that girl. It figured, then, that that belief should be reciprocated, that Heather should view *me* as the right man.

Now, here was the Army, as usual, adding to my difficulties. Had I been able to be with her, to talk and explain, and for us to make love again, then surely I could have quelled any fears or continuing doubts that she might still have. Above all, make her accept at last that Tim was gone (if it were so that he and his fate were what made her hesitate still), while I was there for her, and loved her no less than he had . . .

And for just how long, Providence taunted at my elbow, can you hope reasonably for that happy state of affairs to continue? What's this, wise-guy, Providence demanded mockingly. Do you know something I don't? How long is it going to be before you push that little fraction too far, and find yourself out on a limb, with no way back. *Always* consider that, boy, Providence urged slyly. And, as for your girl, what is she if not a realist? She'll be very much aware that I've got you by the short hairs . . . this way, or that. And haven't I, Providence pointed out cruelly, already run her through the bereavement mill? Now, like in the movies, *you're* where she came in.

So much negative thinking, almost without cease, could bring me to the point where I imagined that my total disappearance, be it to death, hospital, or simply on a permanent basis to a series of ramshackle European airstrips, might, indeed, come as a blessing for Heather, the lifting of the burden of her own fears which I had re-awakened. Away from her, with her not knowing my eventual fate, I could become another fond memory, one of those might-have-beens that it was better to accept as a never-was.

Question and answer, question and *no* answer; all these things chasing their tails inside my head, and the deepening conviction that I was quite likely to go completely crazy if I did not *do* something, then casting around for what there was to be done in my immediate situation, and coming up with the one unsatisfying option of . . . letter-writing. Writing to Heather, comforting and re-assuring her, proving to her my undeviating loyalty. Starting in at once, scribbling page after page, all about missing her, thinking of her; about loneliness—and the belated confession that, yes, the self-styled, seasoned loner *could* get lonely. Each evening after flying, or not flying, stuck in the Quonset with the pen growing hot in my hand. Explaining with apologies that my absence might be prolonged, begging for her understanding and patience and trust.

Loving letters in which I must be mindful always to hold back hard on the too-wild declarations of love, emotions carefully restrained, everything light-hearted and jolly: love seasoned with cool irony . . . 'whatever you do, don't take any of this *too* seriously'. In case the airing of my true and most deep feelings should succeed only in spooking her even more. When, inside, held down firmly, was the overwhelming desire to tell her that I wished her to take every scrawled word, and more, *very* seriously.

*

Mission 25 was to Liège, close enough to Germany to be able to recognize the distant smoky sprawl of Aachen, the pall of haze hanging over Cologne. And to excite attention and furious response, fighters coming for us across the border, 109s, Focke-Wulfs, new top of the range Messerschmitt 210s.

The Little Friends were with us, P-47s, P-51s, Spitfires with American markings, all primed to meet the Germans head-on. Dog fights everywhere, the air cluttered with broken burning airplanes and drifting 'chutes, the radios shrill with excited cries, warnings and appeals. A P-47 disintegrating in a ball of flame as a 210 blew up its ammunition, then the 210 wiped out an instant later in full tilt collision with a Spitfire. Over in a flash, and no parachutes.

For once, the escorts were out-numbered, almost smothered by the streams of enemy fighters breaking through to get at us. O'Connor crazy-jubilant on the intercom, shouting that this was like the good-old, bad-old days with the Eighth. His cries accompanied by the shudder of his fifty-caliber in the nose spraying out rounds at Germans.

Dead ahead then, an old twin-engined Messerschmitt One-Ten: O'Connor firing, his tracers reaching out to send pieces flying off the Me. Cohn's tinny, exultant shout then, "he's hit *bad!*"

But the Messerschmitt went on by with both props still turning, the pilot in control. Cohn's top turret slamming out more rounds, then Patecki joining in from the tail. "I *nailed* the cocksucker!" Cohn yelling. "I just know I did!" Patecki reporting in, "he was trailing something, coolant or fuel, from the right engine. Prick's still flyin', though . . ."

"Forget him!" Snapping the angry command into my throat mike. "There's more where he came from, so get on the ball and watch out!"

A dozen of them at least closing in . . . and then 'Big Apples' lost and trapped in a hard white core of shuddering thunder. Soaring, a wing dipping, going out of my control now, and, even as I fight to hold her, only the one clear thought left . . . no more spells, no more magic . . . THIS time . . . this is IT! Bringing . . . acceptance, and an accompanying feeling—quite wonderful—of great calm and peace, and curiosity, too; the deep desire to find out and observe, for however little time I might have, the cause and source of our deaths . . . just how it is for us all. Craning around for the last time in my seat to see . . . all that remains of another B-26 that had been holding loose formation off our left wing . . . now a vast and spreading smudge. Thick oily smoke, solid-seeming, and blazing metal shards at the ends of hot, lengthening tentacles extending from the obscene and bloating body. And then, again, raw reflex, the terrible relief that it is some other poor bastard . . . that we were merely rocked down to our souls by the yards-away blast of his ton and a half of detonating bombs. So glad that he, close as he had been, was still not close enough to take us with him . . .

The German fighters gone then: a single wave attack and their bolt shot; now you see them, now you don't. The flak returns in all its spreading, booming fury, but, following a fighter brawl of that magnitude, normally-feared flak has lost its edge. And O'Connor, eternal, indestructible O'Connor, for ever *there*, warning of the I.P. ahead, calling out the heading.

We bombed through the flak, doing it to whomever or whatever was down there to arouse the ire of our leaders. And turned, leveled out, and flew back to Senlis, with everyone listening to Cohn telling of the blown-up Marauder. "Another rookie crew . . . first God damn' mission. They hadn't even figured out a name yet for their ship."

Gone for ever, five men whom we had not met.

*

Sergeant Cohn stated with rare aggressiveness, "well *I* think we ought to take a vote on it."

"Ah, yes," O'Connor murmured. "The old, true-blue democratic way."

"You'll pardon me, I hope, Captain?" Cohn gave him an aggrieved look. "But, isn't that what we're supposed to be fighting for?"

"So our masters and shining examples are pleased to inform us." Reverently, O'Connor inclined his head. "F.D.R., John Wayne, Irving Berlin."

"Well, I say nix on votin'." Patecki glowered around, bullish and belligerent. "What's there to vote? Some cruddy Heinie we never seen go down in the first place?"

For once, as a crew, we were divided. O'Connor, who had certainly scored hits on the Messerschmitt One-Ten, remained noncommittal. Cohn, claiming further hits, believed the big fighter to have been mortally hurt. Patecki confirmed a thin white trail of fuel or glycol coolant from one engine. That was all. "Prick was hurtin' bad, sure, but that still don't mean he went down."

For O'Connor, it was simple. "If he'd exploded or burned, or gone and hit the silk . . . if there'd been Kraut and onions à la king all over my shiny plexiglas, we would've had us an argument. But, gentlemen, lacking such criteria?"

"Aw, *c'mon!*" Cohn protested.

"Come on yourself, knucklehead!" Patecki rasped at him. "You *see* that mother buy the farm? Didja?"

"Well, no . . ."

"No more did I, so I rest my case. Like the Captain says, no evidence, no cigar."

"Don't nobody waste no time askin' me." Sergeant Smithson was laughing. "I slept through it all."

It was all to do with the swastika.

Under 'Big Apples'' cockpit windows there now reposed twenty four bomb symbols which, soon, would rise to twenty five. Sergeant Cohn wanted us to add the swastika that would celebrate an enemy aircraft destroyed in combat. The single flaw in Cohn's argument was that the coveted kill could not be confirmed. An uncertain trail of vapor, pieces seen flying off the airframe, were not enough.

We loved the idea of it; a swastika would really be something to write home about. We were with Cohn all the way in our hearts: had there been the smallest chance of pulling it off . . .

He mused, disconsolate, "well, what about a probable? Or a damaged? We sure as hell *damaged* that scheisskopf."

"But that still wouldn't get us no swastika," Andy Devine declared. "Only a confirmed kill gets a swastika."

Cohn wore a sulky look. "Put the Goddam thing up, anyway. We're doin' it for ourselves, aren't we?"

Stuck in Senlis, we were denied the artistic talents of Technical Corporal Flaherty. Instead, following each completed mission, we would daub on our own crude bomb symbol, superstition keeping us on our toes: it was vital in our eyes that the tally remained right up to date. Delay was viewed collectively as pushing luck, and Providence never missed an opening.

We took the vote on the Messerschmitt, coming down an unwilling five to one against putting in for a kill, reporting, instead, a One-Ten damaged in combat. Which was allowed without further comment. But no swastika.

The twenty fifth mission went into the history books. In all, that one had cost the Ninth A.F. three B-26s, a Spitfire, a Mustang and a Thunderbolt. 'Big Apples' had brought us through once again, and now there were ten left to fly. So that, while taking care to rock no boats, we could begin to consider the still-remote prospect or an end in sight?

*

The twenty sixth was an easy one, out and back in ninety minutes, hitting Tilburg, across the border in Holland. Everything hunky-dory until we were back on the ground, completing the landing roll-out. When, for the first time, I damaged an airplane.

With all three wheels on the ground, moving ahead, slowing, I pressed lightly on the toe brakes.

'Big Apples' responded immediately with a violent lurch to the right, and the screech of tormented rubber on steel matting . . .

The aircraft's brakes were activated by pressure applied to the tips of the rudder pedals. Such pressure must be applied lightly and evenly to both pedals to hold the airplane straight on the runway. Unequal pressure, or a brake failure on one side, would bring about an ugly and often damaging movement called a ground loop.

I felt the right brake grip, but the left remained slack and unresponsive, the pedal limp under my foot. At once, pivoting on the single effective brake, 'Big Apples' ground looped viciously.

The PSP strip was narrow, and we shot straight off the edge, plowing fast into the muddy infield, the main landing gear sinking to the hubs, the struts and oleos loudly protesting the imposition of intolerable stresses.

Liquid mud went flying, showering and spattering across the windshield to blind me. From somewhere else, a world of which we had ceased to be a part, I heard the full-power bellow of engines as the Marauder following us in on final approach poured on the coal and went around for another attempt.

The off-runway area of what had been farmland until very recently was soft, rough, and criss-crossed with unrolled dips and hummocks. The nosewheel struck one of these, and its leg, never designed to withstand such abuse, collapsed at once. The sharp snapping from the shattered plexiglas nose cone was accompanied by the slamming shock of the idling propellers digging into the mud, killing both engines, and emitting a whole new series of expensive-sounding noises.

'Big Apples' came to an abject halt, and stood on her nose.

Everything was very still, and I could hear clearly the ping and crackle of cooling and contracting engines, and the soft moan of wind, forlorn and lonely, around the cockpit windows. A sudden draft blew up the crawlway from the broken nose, bearing the rise and fall of the sirens on the approaching emergency vehicles. We hung in our harnesses at a steep, unnatural angle.

I was okay, not even bruised, and busied myself, running through the crash-landing drill, snapping off electrical switches, fuel booster pumps, radios, magnetos, stopping the flow to the hot engines, the sources of spark to induce fire and explosion.

The sirens were loud outside: I caught glimpses of the fire truck and ambulance, of the hurrying figures of men, as jets of fire-preventive foam smothered both engines, and further obscured the mud-encrusted windshield. The shriek of tires came then as another B-26 touched down with greater success, and I felt some consolation in the knowledge that I had not blocked the landing area.

With the intercom switched off, I must yell down the fuselage, "you guys . . . call in *now!*"

Hearing with huge relief all their voices: Smithson, Patecki, Cohn, Andy Devine . . . even some shaky laughter, the note of shocked incredulity, the undisguised delight to be drawn from having survived . . . again.

Sergeant Patecki, suspended twenty feet up in the high-canted tail, wondering, "hey! We landed yet?"

And O'Connor, emerging gingerly from the crushed wreckage of his nose compartment, supplying—as always—the last word. "Looks like we're gonna have to brush up on the old technique, kid."

*

Grounded once more.

'Big Apples' towed from the field, humiliatingly tail first, and away to the dispersal area.

There would be no D.F.C. or Air Medal for *this* one, and I faced the strain of waiting—as bad as for any mission—for the inspection report, wondering if 'Big Apples' would merit fresh repairs this time, or be quietly written off, condemned to the dump, stripped for usable parts, the gutted carcase left for the local French children and their endless war games. Waiting for the board of enquiry to sift through the evidence which would blame or exonerate me.

I was like the repentant murderer impelled to re-visit the scene, wandering out to stand, disconsolate and beyond comforting, before our broken airplane. Propped on heavy jacks under her wing roots and tail, the buckled nose gaping in an 'O' that was like an expression of frozen shock and pain. One nosewheel door gone, the other twisted beyond repair, hanging by a hinge. The mushroom head of our brand-new radio compass housing missing. The cowlings stripped away to expose both engines. Both propellers, their blades bent beyond recovery, off on one side, abandoned.

Work platforms stood before the engines; a master sergeant crew chief, carefully expressionless, called down, "you the pilot, Lieutenant?"

"For my sins . . ."

"Well, you oughtta know it ain't all doom an' gloom." His grin seemed sympathetic.

"Tell me about it. I need some good news."

"We micro'd both shafts," he reported, tapping a wrench against an engine casing. "An' they're still legal." He chewed thoughtfully for a moment on the thick, soggy butt of a cigar. "Which means, for a start, the engines stay."

He enquired politely about my claimed brake failure and, as much to convince myself as the master sergeant, I ran through it again for him. And would he, with his trained technical mind, latch on at once to whatever the stupid mistake was that I had made, but failed to recognize for myself?

He offered instead, "well, you know sir, it happens all right. More often than you might think." That sounded marginally encouraging, a straw at which to grasp. "We'll be checkin' out the hydraulics, an' if they're haywire like you say, we'll find out an' let you know."

And if there is nothing haywire, I thought, I'll get to know that, too.

TWENTY ONE

"Lieutenant, maybe you'd care to take a look-see at this?" Major Mallalieu invited in the wire-twanging accents of Texas. He handed over a small brass fitting. "You'll he pleased to know, I'm sure, that little doohickus gets you off'n the hook." I took the scrap of metal, like an item to be found in any dime store. Oily to the touch and with the sweet reek of hydraulic fluid. "Go on, you can keep it," Major Mallalieu told me affably. "Wear it up there with your dog tags and your Air Medal . . . a real live hair-loom." He was having fun, but was that at my expense? And what, exactly, did he mean by 'off the hook'? "You got any notion what that thing is?"

"Looks like a hydraulic valve, Major."

"Right first time. Looks like, and is. And, more to the point, *your* hydraulic valve. Designed to help actuate your left brake. Which, somehow, it never got around to doin' on that occasion."

Two more days of strained and fretful silence had followed my talk with the master sergeant. All that time keyed-up for the peremptory summons before an unsmiling board of vengeful investigating officers. Instead of which, a corporal had appeared: Major Mallalieu would 'appreciate it no end' if I would 'stop by the office'. Major Mallalieu, easy-going, Texan-expansive, wearing the wings of a lead bombardier. One of Us . . .

"All yours with the compliments an' best wishes o' Master Sergeant Ulvaan," he was telling me. "With his promise also to install a replacement that'll work next time and the time after."

The tiny, cheap valve had caused the brake failure and the resulting thousands of dollars in structural damage, and I thought of the legend of the horse, the battle, the kingdom lost . . . and all for a nail. Now it was a valve which had worked without fail and perfectly until one time it had not. And then the hydraulic fluid could not flow, and the brake became ineffective . . .

"The machine this time, not the man, takes the rap," Major Mallalieu said.

I exclaimed, heartfelt, "Jesus!"

"I know the feelin' real well."

"So . . . what now, Major?"

"What's up?" He grinned. "You lookin' for another medal, boy?"

I laughed and shook my head. "What you said then about a new valve. Does that mean the airplane's worth saving?"

"Would we waste our precious valves if she wasn't?"

'Big Apples' would be made borderline airworthy at Senlis, sufficient for the limping ferry flight back to England and a fresh spell in the Tiverell Lacey heavy maintenance hangar. First, though, more days of heel-kicking to live through as we waited for the arrival of the vital parts.

"I've heard war defined as two percent mind-numbing terror." O'Connor looked up at me from his bunk, and yawned. "And ninety eight percent crushing boredom. I can only agree, and confess to the crying need to be terrified some more." His point made, he rolled over for his afternoon nap.

At the end of that week, a C-47 flew in from Warrington with a load of gleaming new propellers, ring cowls, landing gear doors, a new nosewheel leg, and sundry other necessary pieces. Three more days, we learned, and we could fly away.

*

'Dearest Heather,

'It is no exaggeration to state that these two weeks have been the longest and drabbest of my life. Far from you, and unable even to phone. Pure PURGATORY!

'At such times I get the feeling that the metabolism must slow, leaving the mind racing on at its usual speed, fretting without let-up over inconsequential matters that assume almost monstrous proportions.

'Those who know such things claim that the harvest mouse has an average lifespan of six months if the hawk or the owl don't get there first. But that six months to a harvest mouse would feel like our seventy allotted years. I think I know now how it must be for the mouse. At the rate of six months to seventy years, these two weeks equate with about seven years away from you!

'Now, however, an ending is in sight, albeit one of my own chance devising. I will keep the gory details until we meet, they should be good for a few laughs over a few pints. Suffice it for now that we have had some technical problems, all serious enough to bring me flying back to you.

'I cannot put into words just how much I am looking forward to the opportunity to enjoy YOU once more. Talk of the harvest mouse reminds me of harvest time, and dare I ask how it goes in your neck of the woods? Do the welcoming stooks—like little straw cottages—stand tall now in the Essex fields? Cannot wait to see them for myself, and, maybe, to try some out for size?!

'Must finish in a hurry. There is a Dakota running up outside on flight plan to England, and the pilot has promised to mail this the moment he lands. With luck you will have it tomorrow or the next day. With me soon after, hot and breathless on its heels . . . '

*

The word came that we were losing Sergeant Smithson from the crew.

Since the wounding of Deeks at Eindhoven, 'Big Apples'

had been flying one gunner short, and, with scant hope of a replacement, Smithson had become more of a spare hand: the dwindling German fighter opposition, and the presence of numerous escorts, left little need for waist gunners. Smithson declared himself inconsolable over having to leave us, although not averse to the notion of being of use once more. He was to be given the top turret on 'Hound Dog Howlin" a ship and crew with eighteen missions completed. Replacing the regular gunner who was in hospital with a ruptured appendix. The sick man would not be fit for duty for some time to come; Smithson would finish his own tour with the new crew. "After which . . ." He was laughing. "Some other poor sucker can help them finish *their* missions . . ." His face fell then. "But I'll tell you guys this . . . it ain't gonna be the same without ya."

"On the strength of such honesty and raw emotion," O'Connor decreed. "And seein' how time hangs heavy right now, I'd say a party is called for."

*

There was a suitable café in Senlis, on the cobbled square where the cathedral stood.

The proprietor succeeded in extracting some meaning from my rusty prep school French, spreading apologetic hands: due to grave shortages, I must understand . . . an elaborate meal? A small bit difficult, perhaps. His shoulders rose to his ears in a mighty Gallic shrug. "*Vraiment et malheureusement impossible, mon colonel.*" But—he brightened—fine wine was in abundance . . . '*les sâles Boches*', even after four years, had not managed to get their pig hands on it all. Yes, there would be wine . . . was this not France? And also beer. Unfortunately (again) . . . "*le whiskee, mon génèral, n' a pas beaucoup . . . un morçeau seulement, et évidement très cher . . .*"

"No end of wine and beer," I reported back to the others. "Shy on Scotch, though, and beaucoup pricey."

"Well, it's a start." O'Connor enquired, "food-wise?"

"Soup, bread, cheese, some ham . . . maybe some chicken. He'll see what he can do. Plenty of salad and dressing."

"Tell the ol' guy," Andy Devine enthused. "The Plainsman Grill couldn't do no better."

"Where in hell's that?" O'Connor wondered.

"Finest beanery in Enid, Oklahoma!"

"Like I said," O'Connor murmured to no one in particular. "Where in hell . . ."

*

The late summer evening was warm enough for sitting outside on the square, overhearing Bach being played on the cathedral organ; German music which transcended bitterness and hatred, the deep-seared memories of years of brutal occupation.

The café proprietor had laid on a good spread, and the party should have been a success, but a glum sense of loss weighed upon us.

"At least, as a *wake* it's not so bad," O'Connor commented, and smiled ruefully. "Which, given our present sad circumstances, seems fitting."

Sergeant Smithson reiterated his unhappiness at leaving us.

"I say it ain't God damn' right," Sergeant Patecki told him forcefully. "Them bastards never oughtta screw around with a top-notch crew like us." He did not specify just who 'them bastards' might be; the shared and unspoken understanding was that he referred to the much-maligned brass. He patted Smithson's knee consolingly. "Ol' buddy, you been shafted."

His words gave me comfort, still smarting as I was over the humiliation of the crash-landing. True that the failed valve placed me in the clear, but I was hungry for more. The use of 'us' and 'top-notch' could fill my need very well, especially when it was Patecki—chronically difficult to please—who uttered the words and included me without question in that select number.

*

The mood of Major Delaney was less generous or forgiving. "Lieutenant Pilgrim, this is getting to be a habit, it seems. Your aircraft out of service *again*. A crew unemployed."

"May I remind the Major that last time was the Eindhoven mission, with the cause attributable to enemy action?"

"And this time?" His brows arched quizzically.

"It's there in the report, sir. A clear case of mechanical failure . . . signed out by Major Mallalieu at Senlis."

Delaney's lips compressed. "Well frankly, between ourselves, I'm inclined to suggest the hell with the report." I offered no reply. "This Major Mallalieu springing to your defense."

"There was nothing to defend. The investigating officers didn't even want to talk to me."

"And Major Mallalieu has wings?" The voice dripped acid. "Or so I'm reliably informed."

I stared hard at the place above Major Delaney's left breast pocket where wings would never be. "That's right, sir. A lead bombardier on B-Twenty Fours. Two tours . . . a D.F.C. and Air Medal."

"And how you fly-boys stick together, eh?" He watched me with disappointed eyes, seeking a scapegoat, finding none. "All the same, Lieutenant, this is a considerable inconvenience to all concerned."

And, tough shitski, I thought. "I'm sure of it, sir. But the aircraft will soon be serviceable again. We have the assurances of . . ."

"I don't give a rat's ass for *anyone's* assurances!" His hand slapped down hard on the desk. "We're trying to win a war here. Do you ever stop to consider that?"

"All the time, Major. And never more so than when we're cruising down Flak Alley." He searched my face for evidence of calculated insubordination, then let it drop.

"*Full* participation, Lieutenant. And that means you."

"We're perfectly ready," I answered coldly. "To participate in every way, just as we've been doing." I would have loved to suggest to him that we were ready to accept his participation as well . . .

invite him to put his money where his mouth was. "If the Major can lay on a stop-gap airplane?"

"You know damned well there's none to be had!" Bored with his ranting, I gave a shrug, and he glared. "We're already running through planes and crews like there's no tomorrow."

And what would be the response of desk-tied Major Delaney were I to draw to his attention that, more often than not, I was right there when and where those losses occurred? That, on more than one occasion, I had been uncomfortably close to becoming such a loss myself . . . as the countering possibility presented itself that Major Delaney might truly agonize over downed aircraft and dead crews, the endless, seemingly insurmountable difficulties incurred in trying to fill the gaps, meet the ordered quotas. Maybe, in his own hard-nosed way, he did feel for us, conscious always of his disdained outsider status . . .

He, of course, would be viewed in a quite different light from the more exalted levels of command. From way up there one saw only the over-worked and down-trodden major, the middle level manager taking the flak from all directions; the possibly ineffectual operations officer who kept on having problems with the business of making ends meet. To our remote and irascible commanders he was someone placed just *so*, to be leaned on, cajoled, threatened. It might have been easier for us all to respond to him with sympathy had he not, in turn, leaned, cajoled and threatened.

"I may only indent," he informed me frostily. "For replacement aircraft to cover combat losses, or for those written off beyond repair. Even then, there's no guarantee of getting what's asked for. An aircraft down in the repair hangar is just so much dead weight, and about as much use as tits on a bull. Likewise a decked crew!" He gave a disconsolate sigh. "That God *damned* crash landing!" I braced for the next round of his tirade, but he appeared to have run out of steam, saying only, "yeah, I know . . . I *know* . . . no one's to blame. Just one of those things . . . shitty luck . . . and I shouldn't take it out of your hide. But it makes me hopping mad, and then I call you in here to do just that, and . . ." He held up his clean, manicured hands in final defeat. "That's wrong."

As an apology it was not bad.

*

Heather and I sat together in the Sunday Roast, and I said, "I had a run-in with an old friend of yours today. Major Delaney?" She looked puzzled until I reminded her, "the Squadron dance . . . the one who greeted you at the door."

"I remember." She was nodding in a distracted way. "He told me I looked waif-like." She wondered, "do you mean an argument? But isn't he your senior officer?"

"And that sort of thing," I suggested playfully. "Is simply not done in polite military society?" She gave me a brief level stare, but did not speak. "Sorry about that, but he was doing his usual griping, looking for a mug . . . like me . . . to pin some blame on. And I wouldn't let him."

"Blame for what?"

"What I hinted at in my last letter."

"Oh, that." The look I was given then could be described most charitably as cool. She was being odd again, and, no doubt about it, the oddness was aimed straight at me, although I could not think why. "You said you didn't want to write of it."

"I had a crash-landing in France, and bent the airplane pretty badly . . ." *That*, I saw, had recaptured her interest. Which vied with, but did not quite dispel, the cold-shoulder treatment. To focus her attention on me, I told the full story, holding out the failed valve for her to see. "A trophy."

She examined it. "Funny smell. Like nail polish."

"That's hydraulic fluid . . . the stuff that makes the brakes work," I said. "And it's the reason for the dust-up with Delaney. He questioned the genuineness of the equipment failure, but that little valve was the proof needed, and he got sore about it." I dismissed Major Delaney with a gesture. "He's a jerk."

"I found him charming," Heather said.

That sounded cutting, and it got my back up. "Well, there's this difference, you see? He never makes a big play for me when I come through a door, and we don't dance together."

There was not a thing that was charitable to be said for the look I received that time. "I suppose you feel some pressing need to say things like that?"

"Yeah . . . maybe I do." I frowned at her. "Look, Heather . . . if you've got something on your mind, let's hear it."

But she insisted then that I was (as usual) imagining things, and we sat in stiff silence for some time, each waiting for the other to weaken.

I weakened. "You must know how much I've been looking forward to seeing you again."

She shrugged apparent indifference. "Have you really?"

"I said as much in my letters . . ." Her expression in response made it clear that mention of the letters had been a tactical error. "You were all I thought of while I was away. Is there anything wrong with that?"

Her reply was to come swiftly to her feet. "Could we go now, please?" The pub was filling, and growing noisy. "There are some things that need saying, and, if you don't mind, I'd prefer to be somewhere where we won't be disturbed."

I said that I did not mind, and wondered if her behavior was part of the game that women were said to enjoy playing . . . the so-called 'battle of the sexes'. During the course of which the hapless male was left to dangle . . . and to try harder. As we steered through the crowd toward the door, Heather glanced back. "We really *do* need to talk, you know."

*

We followed the lane that led toward the horticultural station, walking on in near-silence, broken only by the infrequent trivial remark. We passed by a field where the harvesters were working late: an old-fashioned corn binder circling behind a pair of draft horses; Land Girls and men stooking the sheaves.

Heather pointed suddenly. "Let's go in there."

It was an adjacent field that had been cut already, the stooks in orderly rows. And I thought at once of . . . the *wheatfield!* It was all explained then, her snappish tension, her withdrawal from me: she had been planning the whole thing, steeling herself to take the initiative, yet worried and nervous about what she did.

I scuffed along happily behind her, thinking of how typical this was of Heather; the oblique approach, unpredictable, motives carefully concealed: I claimed to know her, and should have *guessed*. But, as ever, without effort, she had gulled me.

We walked past the final row of stooks, moving on toward the field's edge, a ditch, a fence, a gnarled elm. Beneath which she chose to sit, and I took my place at her side, and thought, under a tree? Well, why not . . . ?

I took her hand, and she said quickly, "Denney, listen . . ." The sharpness in her voice brought fresh unease.

"What is it, baby?"

"Two things . . ." She was gazing out across the darkening field. "The first is . . . I'm not pregnant."

"Oh . . ." There was an immediate stab of regret and disappointment. I waited.

"Silly of me even to think it." She faced me. "Does that disappoint you?"

"Do you want the truth?"

"Yes. Always."

"Okay then, it does. You asked me that before, as a hypothetical question. Now it's for real, and the answer remains the same. I'd pictured it, and how great it would be, and kind of hoped." Speaking, I thought of how Heather, not carrying our child, would have even less reason to commit herself; so much easier from now on to duck and dive. "Well . . ." I did not try to hide dejection. "You're spared all the problems now."

"Spared, yes." She was smiling faintly. "Ten days ago, right on time."

"What . . . ?"

"My period, of course." The bluntness startled me: it was

not something that got discussed between the sexes. "Although, this time, it felt more like losing a baby."

I kissed her hand. "Heather, I'm so sorry."

"Then you needn't be. No harm done." She withdrew her hand. "Much more than that, it was your letters which hurt me. That, by the way, is the second thing."

I watched her, mystified: what could have been wrong with those innocuous scribblings from France, other than the fact that they *were* innocuous? I had gone out of my way to be careful . . .

"Writing of loving me," Heather went on. "And of the possible baby, and of marriage."

Lost and baffled, I began, "I knew how you felt about things . . ."

"You knew *nothing!*" She turned on me fiercely. "You've said you love me, and I made it clear to you how happy I would have been to have our baby. But . . . *feelings?*" She drew a shuddering breath. "When you spoke of marriage, and standing by me, I was touched . . . I almost cried right there. But I didn't . . . and I didn't answer. Because I wanted time first in which to think it through. Without having you there, tempting me, weakening me. It seemed almost a Godsend then, your being sent off to France," she said. "Because that gave me the opportunity to work things out. No outside influences, you or Mum. No busybody relations telling me what a marvelous catch you were . . . or that you were just another Yank wanting only one thing." A twist of the mouth then might have been a smile. "Which I was glad to give, anyway."

"Yes," I said.

"You've been gone for two weeks, and I've had my thinking cap on, and I wondered if it might be the same with you? I wanted to be with you, and to go to New York, and meet your mother, then see how things went from there . . ." She faltered, and turned her face aside. "Then your letters started coming, and ruined everything."

"For God's sake, *how?*" I was aghast.

"You made a rotten joke of it," she accused. "Sounding for all the world as if you didn't care."

"That's crazy. Of course I care, more than anything." I pleaded with her. "Heather, this is obviously a misunderstanding, and on both sides. I'd never do anything like that to you . . ."

"Wait . . . please." She opened her purse, and produced the small packet of my letters. "Show me where I'm wrong, and what it is that I don't understand. I'd really like to know."

In the dregs of daylight, she read them back to me, and she was right . . . they sounded as she had claimed, flippant, forced, trite, banal, insensitive. Most certainly when she read them like that, dismissively and with scorn. Writing with the desire only to ease her mind, I had, instead, managed to sound cheap. That belated realization made me abject. "Yes . . . that approach stinks. I can see it now. But I didn't then, truly. They were never intended to slight you. I wanted to tread lightly, and ease off the pressure on you. Instead, as I see now, I managed to screw up completely." Tentatively, I touched her shoulder, and she turned again to look at me. "Please try to see that. I spoke of marriage in London, but it seemed you weren't keen on the idea then . . ." She gave a small nod. "So, I decided it was best to back off, play it low key. But that's all, and it's as I've said, a misunderstanding." I insisted, "I've thought of you every minute while I was away." That earned me another searching look. "I'd even wondered if you might send me a Dear John."

"A what?" She shook her head.

"It's the kind of letter a guy gets when he's overseas. From his girl back home. Which begins 'Dear John, I don't know how to tell you this, but'." I forced a laugh.

"I see." She began to smile. "But I never thought of writing you one of those."

"Heather, I *am* sorry," I repeated then. "But I'd never demean you, or us."

She hesitated, then agreed, "no."

It was almost dark. The corn binder had been unhitched in the nearby field. The Land Girls and farm hands with their horses had departed in a burst of fading calls, laughter and wobbling bike lamps in the lane. Leaving us alone together with the night sounds, with the high, muttering drone of Lancasters heading out to Germany.

Seeking a neutral topic, I ventured, "I don't know how they can do that night after night. It's grim enough doing it in daytime."

Heather raised her head, following the sounds. "I was thinking then that that might have been you. We would have been parting on a quarrel, and that would've been awful." She added almost inaudibly, "and, of course, I'm terribly sorry as well."

I touched her hand. "Would this be a good moment for kissing and making up?"

She turned back to me at once, without a word, and it was as warm and tender, as giving, as ever it had been in the past. She murmured, "are we friends again?"

"Isn't that what I should be asking?"

"Always *friends* . . ." The word, and its emphasis, registered depressingly. "No matter how much you succeed in infuriating me." With that, by way of compensation, went an up-to-the-eyes smile.

I echoed, "always." Ready, willing and able to yield ground and ignore feelings of disappointment. If, by doing so, the status quo could be restored.

I leaned down to place my lips against the soft swell of her breast above the low line of her summer dress, to explore with my tongue those sweet known contours, hearing her sigh in response, feeling the small movements of her body against me. It was quite dark, and the farm people were long gone. No one need find us, no one need know. Warmth rose from her, and my encouraged hand moved down . . .

She went rigid in my arms. "Denney . . . *no!*" I could feel her trembling. "I'm sorry . . . I can't."

Embarrassment burned my face like the heat of a hard slap. Still holding her, I felt like a shabby molester.

She edged away from me, sitting up with her arms locked about her drawn-up knees. "Now it's my turn to beg forgiveness and understanding."

It took an effort to say, "no . . . I was being too pushy."

"Not that."

"Then what . . . *tell* me." I offered for her, "you're upset still, on edge, and I don't want that. But your moods switch so fast, and I get left behind." I appealed, "Heather, I'll go along willingly with just about anything you say, or want, if only you'll put me in the picture." She inclined her head in what seemed like agreement. "Is it still your . . ." I began to ask, and could not finish.

"My period, you mean?" She picked up on my hesitation with brutal frankness. "You can speak of it, you know. It's not taboo."

I retorted, "nor is it easy."

"Not an acceptable topic for polite tea-table conversation in a swish Manhattan penthouse?"

It was like a repeat of the moment in Hyde Park, a sudden, sharp feeling of dislike. "That was hardly called-for, or necessary."

She said, sounding weary, or bored, "you can be so incredibly pompous."

I knew that, and needed no lecture from her. "Call it my defense mechanism. We all have our little oddball ways, Heather. You could allow me that one."

Seconds passed before she acknowledged, "that, too, was uncalled-for, but probably well-deserved."

A capitulation could always disarm me in turn. "Although you're right . . . I *am* pompous."

"And in answer to your half-question," Heather said. "No, it's not my unmentionable. That was over days ago."

"Fine. But I'm no expert." I asked, "so why the sudden brush-off?"

"It's just that I don't think we should . . . not here and now. That's all."

"It may be all to you, but it's still a hell of a let-down," I grumbled, adding, "sorry again, but that needed saying."

She shifted fitfully, making the long grass rustle. A small current of air stirred the leaves above us. "But the thing is, Denney, you must try and see how very lucky we've been."

"Lucky . . ."

"*Yes!* All those mad risks we took, yet we still got away with it. I suppose I find a sort of meaning in that."

"Like . . . you've been warned? Don't pull the same stunt again or else?"

"Something of that nature, perhaps."

"So, how is it that you would have liked a baby?"

"Denney, that was *then*. And yes, I would have if it had been the case, but now it isn't. Then, it was exciting, like both fingers up to the doodlebugs in the night. And, really, we didn't deserve to get off." She added in a low voice, "from either situation."

"Are you telling me now that we'll never . . ."

"All I'm saying is that we must be careful. Which, before, we were not."

As a piece of reasoning, it seemed almost callous; the act of passion and love drawn to its conclusion, then filed away as a cold sexual exercise from which a salutary lesson could be drawn. The kind of shopworn exercise that might be expected to begin with the obligatory visit to the prophylactic station before setting out. Being careful before seeking out a hooker, or a Gladys Gibbons. For a reckless and cruel moment then, I would have liked to suggest that comparison to Heather.

She admitted haltingly, "for days . . . I haven't felt like . . ."

"Was that because of my letters?"

"In part. They did leave me feeling a bit drained." She shot me a glance. "Which is not the way I want to feel with you, but . . ."

She begged me once more for time, and for my continuing patience, then floored me when she wanted to know, "I don't suppose you came . . . you know . . . *prepared?*"

I let the shocked moment pass before replying—pompously—that, no, I had not. That, with her, while ever hopeful, I did not presume to plan such things in advance.

My Puritan, if he was listening then, might have approved.

TWENTY TWO

FLIGHT LOG.
DATE: 8/21/44.
AIRCRAFT TYPE: Stinson L-5.
NO. or REG.: 40-9912.
PILOT-IN-COMMAND: Self.
SECOND PILOT: Nil.
CREW: Nil.
FLIGHT ROUTE: T.L.-Local-T.L.
FLIGHT HOURS: 1.25.
HOURS VISUAL: 1.25.
HOURS INSTRUMENT: Nil.
HOURS NIGHT: Nil.
OBSERVATIONS: Twice in one day humbled—by an airplane,
and a girl!

*

"Permit me to hazard a guess," Captain O'Connor mused.
"You are confused, somewhat distraught, and uncertain at this
precise moment which is your ass, and which your elbow. You
are not a happy person."

I had explained to him, also to Andy Devine, recumbent
upon his dingy bunk on the far side of the Quonset's center aisle,
the reason for the latest summons to the office of Major Delaney.
Whose oak leaf rank insignia had switched, overnight it appeared,
from gold to silver. Which meant that Major Delaney had become
a lieutenant colonel, a fact which caused me to re-consider my
earlier charitable thoughts about down-trodden majors.

He informed me without preamble that I was being returned

to immediate flight status, placed in command of the Squadron's diminutive Stinson L-5 liaison plane.

"Gopher duties, dear boy." A happy smirk sat square on brand-new Colonel Delaney's smoothly-shaven and powdered face. "Good for what ails one."

I was no stranger to that derisive term; had employed it myself many times. The pilots assigned to the L-5 were winged messenger boys, although no demi-god Mercurys. Guys whose duty it was to 'gopher' things like the mail and papers, and to transport free-loading passengers (one at a time in the two-seat puddle-jumping Stinson).

As with courier work, gopher flights did not count as missions.

Pondering my news, O'Connor affected a look of concern. "Does this signify that the rift between us shall be permanent?"

"Only until we're operational again. Delaney gets nervous about idle hands . . . mine in particular."

"Aw, shucks!" O'Connor sighed. "And here was me hopin'."

I showed him my back, and fished in my locker for my headset and mike.

Andy Devine enquired mildly, "off aviatin', then?"

"Our brave new light colonel has commanded me to check myself out on the beast."

"Whaddya say we all come down an' cheer from the bleachers?"

"Anyone who's interested," I told Andy. "I've got a spare seat going." He laughed, and wriggled his way deeper into his fusty blankets.

"Thank you kindly, Ma'am," O'Connor murmured. "But us chickens is eschewin' all hair-raisin' activities hereabouts." The two of them surveyed me mirthfully. "The sedentary life becomes all too easily an ingrained habit."

I showed them the finger, and headed for the door.

Andy called after me, "have fun, y'hear?"

"Just follow the Yellow Brick Road, son," O'Connor advised. "All it takes is guts and endless luck."

*

The Stinson was runty, to my mind, woefully under-powered, and was claimed by those who knew it well to be an inveterate ground lover. A thoroughly demeaning mount for a self-proclaimed hotshot B-26 jockey, and I surveyed it with no enthusiasm, although considerable disdain.

It possessed one small putt-putt engine which was started by a mechanic hand-swinging the propeller; the time-honored Wright Brothers ritual of "Switches off . . . throttle set . . . brakes set . . . switches on . . . CONTACT!" The mechanic would then heave and, in theory, the motor would fire up.

Airborne, however, the tiny airplane surprised me by proving stable, nimble and, as I discovered, real fun to play with.

Apart from the fact that it could get itself off the ground and fly, the Stinson bore no discernible resemblance to the B-26, a machine that required unfailing close and critical attention. Much in 'Big Apples' and her sister ships could, and would, go dramatically wrong; failing engines, brakes, landing gear, the list was long and exhausting. Bomb bay doors could jam, bomb releases decline to release, power-operated turrets find themselves without power at the most nerve-racking moments. There also, and always, were the whims and foibles of one's fellow crew members to reckon with, bringing about frequently the feeling less of flying than of struggling to prop up an overweight, floundering corporation in chaos and terminal decline.

Within the tiny greenhouse cabin of the L-5, all was peaceful solitude and simplicity; simply wind the rubber band up tight and go.

Beginning with the obligatory series of touch-and-go landings to get the feel of the thing off the ground and on it. Imbued with my long-established B-26 habits, I made the first approach much too fast, finding thereby that the little machine refused to stop flying as I sat there watching musingly the runway drifting by twenty feet below my wheels.

A Marauder took up every grudged inch of the Tiverell Lacey strip to get itself down and halted. The Stinson could have made half a dozen landings in series, and still had space to spare. It could, I was coming to believe, have perched on a twig.

My third attempt to return to earth was more successful: I had merely to accept that the L-5 would flutter on at speeds at which any self-respecting Marauder would fall out of the sky.

Final approach, half a mile out with three hundred feet showing on the primitive altimeter. Close the throttle, hearing the engine die away to a whisper, seeing the yellow wooden blades of the stumpy propeller ticking over as the strip floated up to meet me. Reset the stabilizer, then, at fifty feet, bring the stick back a little to flatten the glide. Keep coming back and . . . a mite too far so that the tailwheel hits first, then the main landing gear . . . the squelch of rubber, then bunny-hopping embarrassingly along the ground, imagining the many unseen critical and amused eyes observing my performance. Not a landing to boast of, but at least moderately under control. Any landing that you could walk away from, it was drummed into you, was a good landing.

I climbed away from it all the way to five thousand feet which, with my Singer sewing machine motor, seemed to take a very long time. Up there, I practiced stalls, steep turns, and a few spins and recoveries. The Stinson would loop after a fashion, chandelle pleasingly, and perform a modest stall turn. It declined to roll for me, and I did not insist: it knew its limitations better than I. With that, it was time to go home, primed and ready for duty. The new Squadron gopher.

Up ahead a few miles, Tiverell Lacey dozed peaceably in the afternoon light, and I could see the Granger house. And, hey . . . I thought. Why not? Time to wake up Tiverell Lazy with a little old-fashioned, 1920s-style barnstorming. Pull a few stunts above the rooftops to win some attention, then land in a nearby field—the fearless birdman—to await the arrival of the rustics, clutching their hoarded and rumpled dollar bills, all looking for five-minute hops.

"Hey . . . will ya show me a power dive, Mister . . . ?"

"Will ya loop th' loop, Mister . . . ?"

"Whut happens if ya loop th' loop, an' ol' Abner here falls out, Mister . . . ?"

Maybe not quite like that, I reflected, smiling, but somewhere close to it.

It was against all the rules in a military airplane, and I would get it in the neck if I were found out. To quote Margot Granger quoting the sleek public relations officer, they would lower the boom on me, and my eyes would really water. But, so what, we all did it whenever an opportunity presented itself. As long as I'm careful, and fly right, I warned myself.

I began a gliding descent to build up airspeed, lining up the Stinson's little pug nose on the distant gabled roof beyond the poplars that marked the garden's boundary.

Speed up in the dive to a ludicrous one hundred flat out. Level off at fifty feet with a touch of rudder to re-align myself. The airplane's response is not exactly the stuff to stir the blood, but it will have to do, and fifty feet will be ample to clear the roof, then nose up steeply into the classic chandelle as the flying circus hits town . . .

A mile to go as I fly over a field of stooks, a fence and ditch, a tall old elm tree . . . remembering the bickering and making up, then, seconds later, another rejection . . . "I can't."

Now, in the field, there stands a half-laden flatbed trailer, and Land Girls with pitch forks are breaking down the stooks, loading the sheaves. Stopping work to follow my underwhelming approach, waving bare golden arms, teeth alight in brown faces as the tractor driver cranes round in his seat. Wagging my wings at them, and thinking with sorrow of the field cleared and empty by sunset. Heather and I would never . . . not there . . .

I pulled off my chandelle above the poplars, glancing back to find the garden empty. Which made me go for broke then, shoving the nose back down to swoop once more over the roof.

Heather and Margot emerged from the house as I made my third pass, Margot waving dutifully as Heather stood motionless, peering up, and even at the distance and in that split second, I felt her cold disapproval of my antics.

Stung, I kicked the Stinson round and down, passing above

their heads with one wingtip perilously close to a tall chimney. But, as Margot waved on, Heather would not acknowledge me.

I climbed away, heading for the base, feeling foolish and ashamed of my childish pique. I glanced back unhappily hoping for a sign of some kind: the small receding figure of Margot stood on the lawn still, but Heather had vanished.

*

Gopher flying consisted in the main of short hops to neighboring air bases, carrying people who sought flights on various pretexts in order to save themselves from trains, jeep rides or the backs of trucks. On one such flight, I conveyed a grimly-silent Lieutenant Colonel Delaney to Bomb Group H.Q.

An hour after I brought him back, looking more glum than before, flight crews were summoned to the ops shack to be told of the Command decision to increase the number of missions we must fly to forty.

The C.O. was up on the dais to spread the word, flanked there by Lieutenant Colonels Friend and Delaney.

"I won't try to feed you fellows with horseshit . . ." There was some uneasy laughter: even if the news was awful, the C.O. was well-liked, a senior hand who would not hesitate to leave his desk and fly missions with us. "I'm informed that it's a question of economics. You know for yourselves how we stand at present . . ." He turned away to the giant wall map of Western Europe with the Allied advance line picked out across it with pinned white tape. "We're being saddled with the extra trips to support the up-and-coming end run on the Rhine. There's a lot of shit road still to travel, and we know that Jerry will make us pay for every mile." He gazed down at us, looking troubled. "We're having difficulty getting hold of the replacement personnel and aircraft we need. I'm sorry, but that's how it is, and how it's likely to remain for some time to come." There could be no debate, and no appeal; it would be so, and the Colonel told us why. "Because of heavy crew losses in all theatres, not just the

E.T.O., it's taking Training Command longer to make up the numbers. So, until they can, *we* get to fly more." He faced our concerted dismay. "I'll spare you the usual platitudes and soft soap about five more missions being not that many. Five are too God damned many, and who'd know that better than you?"

The uncompromising words made each of us freshly aware of how our lives were in hock, held under the inviolable terms of a contract, all clauses of which were dictated by the United States Government. Which claimed also the privilege of writing in fresh clauses whenever a need was felt.

"It's a bum deal." The Colonel simplified our shared thinking. "One more among so many. But, maybe . . ." He wore a mirthless smile. "They've worked it out that we might not notice. Caught up as we are in the biggest bum deal of all . . . the war."

The new ruling would not apply to everyone. Those crews with less than five missions remaining from their original tours were to be exempted. Even the don't-give-a-shit brass retained enough sensitivity apparently to realize that pulling such a stunt on those men would be too much. Whereas I, selfish, angry and embittered, begrudged them this concession. The hell with *that*; what about those with only six left to go, or ten, twenty, a full tour, even? Did we not also have feelings, and deep, indelible fears? We faced the same chances of death and maiming and insanity: more so, twisted reason could claim, than the short-timers. Not one flying man could bank on escaping until the very last landing had been made.

All I could see, feeling angry enough to weep, was that with twenty six missions completed, and down to single numbers on the original deal, five more tacked on arbitrarily was the most cruel blow, a grim second mortgage on life and limb. Envying them, I could also hate the spared crews, even those for whom the sparing would prove meaningless in the end. The ones who would go out and die anyway. Scared and furious, I could not appreciate their position, nor feel the slightest generosity of spirit toward them.

The accusatory thought was nagging at me . . . if *only*. If only we had not been stuck on the ground after Eindhoven, or had not taken the furlough, with the bittersweet weekend in London. If *only* 'Big Apples' and her lousy brakes had not failed at Senlis! *Then* we, too, would be numbered within the charmed circle. And I could think of its present fortunates with more kindness and charity.

*

O'Connor topped off his glass, and emptied the remainder from the beer bottle into mine. We drank in silence, drinking for the sake of drinking; there could be no celebratory grounds for doing so.

My contribution that day to the war aims of my country had been to fly the Stinson forty miles to an air base in Kent, there to collect a stranded Bomb Group chaplain. Whom I would fly on elsewhere in the morning. Until undertaking that vital assignment on the road to victory, I was free to drink moodily with O'Connor, killing time until I could keep my planned date with Heather. Who had managed to borrow the smart bike again: we would ride out to Tiverell End where the village pub served an evening meal.

An advantage of gopher flying, in addition to its relative safety, was that it kept me at home with my evenings free, which meant, in turn, that we could meet regularly. Meetings which I would not have missed, the fact notwithstanding that, of late, much of the sparkle had gone out of our relationship: something that had slipped from the grasp, impossible to retain . . .

I had quizzed Heather on the buzz job over her house.

"I thought it was rather foolish," she informed me coolly. "And almost certainly dangerous."

I held back annoyance on a tight leash. "Was that why you wouldn't wave?"

"I saw no reason to encourage you," she said, and brought the subject to an abrupt close.

Still puzzled and sore, I was remembering that exchange now.

As O'Connor, uncharacteristically glum, began once more to grumble about the extra missions, and demanded to know the state of 'Big Apples'. "Heard anything from the hangar yet?"

"Day after tomorrow . . . that's what they're saying."

He swore softly. "How long do those deadbeats *need*, for Christ's sake?"

"What's up?" I wondered sourly. "Can't you wait to get started on what's now our last *fourteen* missions?"

"No I God damn well can't!" I received a frosty stare. "If you want the truth, I'm hoping they'll fly our butts off. Two a day, if they want, or more . . . each day and every day, and never mind. So's we can just make it through and get the hell out of here before some jackass gets it into his little pointed head to hit us with a few more."

"They couldn't do that, surely?" The bare suggestion of it could leave me shaken. "Holy shit . . . there'd be a mutiny!"

"You wanna bet on that? Who's gonna lead it . . . me . . . you?" He drank some beer and belched. "Bullshit's my response to that pipe-dream. Now that they've seen how easily we knuckle under, what's to prevent the bastards putting the jacks under our tours any time they feel the urge? Five missions . . . and five more. Then *another* five . . ."

"You can't really believe that . . ."

"I can believe anything that's crappy and disgusting about the upper and far-rearward strata of the A.A.F."

I protested weakly, "but it'd be inhuman."

"So's war inhuman, right? Either that or *very* human." He advised me coldly, "time to re-think your arguments, kid. This little slug-fest we're caught up in has to be ended somehow. If it takes inhuman methods, then so what? Tough titty. Fifty missions . . . a hundred? Well, why the hell not? The dimwits who get to fly them won't squawk." He shook a finger under my nose. "So you go tell those dumbbells in Maintenance we want our airplane back tooty-sweetie. Then, by Jesus, watch how we'll fly . . ." He laughed harshly. "Fourteen missions over an' done by next weekend . . . whaddya say, Mister Rickenbacker? Before

Group can get any more bright ideas about the most effective utilization of available resources." He mused, "you realize, son . . . when, *if*, I complete this tour, I'll have flown sixty five sonofabitching missions in the E.T.O.? So do, please, spare me your wailings about matters inhuman!"

*

A warm August evening that was custom-made for biking the five easy miles to Tiverell End. Where, at the pub, they could supply cold ham and beetroot salad, and sweet, dark pickle. We ate and watched the local darts team displaying their skills.

"They make it look so easy," I said. "Someone calls a number, and straightaway there it is."

Heather replied absently, "it takes practice."

"They'd make top-notch bombardiers . . ." With difficulty I kept up the light-hearted approach: she was being odd again, and that was the best word for it. "Many things take practice . . . and patience." I took her hand, and she let it rest, cold and unmoving, in mine. "Heather . . . what's happening to us? Can't you tell me . . . talk to me?"

"I don't know." Her immediate acceptance that things were not right caught me off-balance, which, with Heather, was par for the course. I had been expecting more evasion, but she seldom gave what was expected of her. "But I assure you that I haven't wanted it so."

Her off-hand manner brought my sharp retort, "and you can bet your sweet life *I* haven't, either!" To an approving murmur, an old man planted his dart dead center in the treble twenty. Heather sat on, unmoving. "Don't tell me you're still sore about those stupid letters?"

She shrugged peevishly. "We've been over that already."

"So *what*, then? I'm sorry if this annoys you, but it all stems from my never knowing where I stand with you, or even *if* I stand."

"We've made lots of war films . . . home front stuff, you

know?" Her mystifying reply made me think, at first, that she was avoiding what she saw as another challenge from me. "About all those left behind when the men go off to fight. Women smiling through tears . . . the long-drawn goodbyes at railway stations . . . all those agonized faces." I nodded, still not getting it. "Anna Neagle and Phyllis Calvert and Flora Robson . . ." I spotted the ghost of a smile. "You've probably never heard of them."

"So educate me. I'm willing." I listened with care, trying to gage this new mood.

"The famous stiff upper lip proudly on display all over the show," she went on, and her eyes were distant, well away from me. "Every line and gesture so studied and predictable. Always able to guess what's coming next."

"Hollywood's good at that, too."

"Until the moment came . . ." She turned to look at me. "When, actually, you saw and heard those exact things at stations. At Liverpool Street when Mum and I would go up to Town together. Servicemen and wives and girls and mothers. So that you'd wonder if the film studios had an arrangement with the London and North Eastern Railway to shoot their sob scenes on location there."

I offered a hesitant smile. "What's that line about truth being stranger than fiction?"

"You certainly found out there where the fiction came from," Heather said. "Some tricks of light and camera, and getting the leading characters suitably tarted-up. Then sit back and listen to the weeping in the one-and-nines. Hackney and cliché rooted in hackneyed, cliché'd reality . . ." I saw that her eyes were damp. "Although isn't that what the hackneyed and cliché'd are, really? Simple human events re-worked and flogged to death . . . all from the same old tatty script entitled reality." She sniffed then, but restrained the tears. "I'm not saying this awfully well."

"No. It's making sense."

She nodded thanks. "You realize then that the same things must be happening all over the world, and on all sides. All that worn-out pain and anguish . . . but nonetheless real." She paused, then ran on swiftly, like someone taking the plunge at the deep end. "And that may be our problem, or, at least, mine. That I'm trying to steer clear of hackneyed repetition. Or, more probably, like a bloody coward, always running away."

"Tim?" I asked, and Heather bowed her head in agreement. "I guess I've always known he was still there somewhere."

She insisted, "Denney, it's not you."

It did seem then that I was seeing the light finally: the brutal, unarguable fact that Heather had suffered loss, a father to borderline insanity, a fiancé to violent and pointless death. She had handled those, her mother believed, with stoicism. Until now, this moment when the first cracks appeared to reveal the depths of her inner doubt, the entrenched fears that made her skittish and beyond predicting. Like a whipped animal that wanted still to trust, but could not, quite . . . yet.

TWENTY THREE

A fresh mug had been commanded to take over my place. I had landed the Stinson for the last time, and was retrieving my map case and headset when the detested voice from the past announced, "well, *hey* . . . I see you found your niche."

I turned, stiff-faced. "Hello, Azevedo."

He was a captain now. But then, on the B-26 graduating course in Texas, he had been an old hand already, a former senior pilot with a California-based airline. The ideal man, following completion of the training program to accept an immediate instructor's appointment at a comfortable Stateside base. A shame that such an outstanding airman should have to be a total prick with it.

From the look of him, he had kept himself in shape; still playing squash and handball, I guessed, and his murderous game of table tennis. There was, too, the boxing background, a promising middleweight contender who had made it through to the Golden Gloves quarter-final.

Boxing had not marred his looks; no scarred brows or flattened nose, no cauliflower ears. His skin was smooth and, as ever, overlaid by a deep tan. He affected still the thin, melodramatic 'Smilin' Jack' moustache that had irked us, his fellow students, at the advanced training base. Which he stroked often with a forefinger.

Within a group of excitable young men, each one tied up in a world war, all of whom had far too much to say concerning just about everything, Azevedo stood out as the supreme authority on the favored subject of . . . himself. The bantering and self-satisfied note on which he renewed our acquaintance after so many months suggested that he had not changed.

I closed and latched the Stinson's side hatch, then gave him a great big smile. "And they managed to drag you away from your safe hole. Bitching and bellyaching, no doubt?"

But my ponderous irony produced no visible effect: insult had always bounced straight off that armadillo hide.

"They said I'd find you here." He grinned a no-hard-feelings grin. "Seen you landin', an' had to mosey on down an' give an old buddy the glad hand."

Only Azevedo could imagine that we were ever buddies, old or new.

*

Evening, dateless and disconsolate, nursing a flattening beer on my own in the Officers' Club as Azevedo sounded off at the center of an attentive circle. I listened, smirking, allowing that, with that mouth of his, he could always pull a crowd. Was that not how the old-time patent medicine and snake-oil salesmen got to be millionaires and Powers in the land?

He was 'hangar-flying', both hands held side by side in tight formation and flattened to represent airplanes performing intricate maneuvers. I told myself, with the benefit of personal knowledge, that those rapt listeners would soon learn. But let it be the hard way, suffering Azevedo undiluted. As once, in Texas, it had been for me and others.

The interminable tall stories of pre-war civil flying, the tricky routes and lousy weather, carrying the mail in open cockpits with chronically unreliable en route navigation aids. What had infuriated and frustrated us was that the stories were largely true. Once one saw through the embellishments, with Azevedo front and center, larger than life, and got down to the substance.

With a little luck, I thought, it would be different here. With the Germans ever ready, willing and able to cut him down to size. They, for sure, would not be bamboozled by his thousands of hours accumulated on Douglas DC-2s, Boeing 247s and Ford Tri-motors.

Massacred at Falaise, kicked out of Paris and Brussels, threatened on their own doorstep, the Germans went implacably on with the business of causing us grief and hurt. They would, I decided happily, find ways to fix Azevedo's wagon for him . . .

Completing his latest saga, Azevedo flew his hands down to a smooth landing on the tabletop, announcing with that same maddening self-confidence, "and that's how I see it, fellas. Clear-cut and simple."

Corliss, the navigator in 'Sloppy Joe', an old hand with thirty one missions logged, wondered in dry tones, "how exactly do you figure that, Captain?"

The irony was lost on Azevedo who smiled a smile that asked how anyone could overlook so obvious a point. "Why, now me and my boys are over here, we're gonna get this local conflict wrapped up PDQ, and move on to bigger things." His loud, confident laughter filled the room.

*

With 'Big Apples' back on the line, we flew two missions in quick succession, both costly.

Again to Antwerp where, now, our armies were besieging the city, although, from their response to us, the Germans might not have known of that, or cared if they did; so deeply dug-in and determined, their flak as deadly-accurate as ever. By fire, explosion, ditching and crash-landing, damaged beyond repair, Antwerp cost the group fourteen aircraft and twenty one men killed, wounded or missing.

Riding the truck in from the hardstand with the fresh memories of battle and murder hot and raw behind our eyes, we listened, numbed, as O'Connor mused aloud, "the flood of replacements, bodies and machinery reduced to a poor trickle, they tell us? So what say, comrades, to an imminent an' cryin' need for forty *five* missions?"

From Antwerp, 'Big Apples' returned without damage, as did Azevedo's newly-christened 'Bomb Boogie'. Technical

Corporal Flaherty—recently promoted to buck sergeant—stenciled on Azevedo's first bomb symbol.

*

The Squadron landed without incident at the designated forward strip close to Brussels, refueled, loaded up with bombs and, after briefing, flew on to the target, a large, well-camouflaged chemical complex hidden away deep in the forests of the High Taunus to the east of Limberg. We went, encouraged and comforted by stern warnings of a target area ringed with flak guns, all manned by veteran Luftwaffe troops, and that we could almost certainly expect to meet fighters. The escorting P-51s would join up with us over Vervier for what was to be a low-level attack with some hairy hill flying thrown in to make life interesting. A round trip of three hundred and fifty miles: the more fortunate among us could expect to be back on the ground in two hours. We/they would refuel once more, eat lunch and fly away home.

O'Connor rolled his eyes at me, an expression of I've-heard-it-all-before. "Just like bankers' hours, huh, son?"

The briefers had got the flak summary exactly right. On the long approach leg, and, already, three B-26s were hit or burning, one plunging straight into the forest, its point of impact marked by dark smoke staining the clear sky.

Because of its being an on-the-deck run, and with the rugged terrain involved, there could be no mathematically-pure straight approach to the point of release; instead, we wove in and out of steep valleys, and dodged around hilltops where jutting outcrops of black rock reached out to snare the wingtips. When I was not booting rudder to skid 'Big Apples' around some obstacle, I would be hauling back hard to drag us up and over the succession of peaks and ridges, exulting in speed and nimbleness, in the dramatic, varied landscape flashing by just below.

From the Rhine and on across the North Eifel, then the Hohe Eifel, skirting the Westerwald before flying into the Taunus region, with Andy Devine at my shoulder calling off the visible check-points from his eight miles to the inch strip map, giggling, happy as a kid, yelling, "way to GO, Skip . . . way to Goddam GO-O-O!" each time I was forced to stand 'Big Apples' on one wing, racking her around some new in-path hazard.

From over Andernach we could see the smoke of Bonn in the northern distance: on then by Limberg on the banks of the Lahn River, almost to Wetzler and Gneissen. The final hurtling ten miles when Andy could fold up his map as we were guided to the spot by the smoke and dust legacy of the early arrivals.

Plunging in through the flak ring, and, at once, there it was; the old slow motion effect as every clearing and hillside and dark forest hollow flamed at us with their batteries of quick-firing guns, the bursts shredding the sky, the close, ugly crack of shells all-too audible over the engines. Tracers rising in slow arcs, casual-seeming, beguiling, until, suddenly, close-to, they turned mean, zeroing in to whiplash across the wings. Once more the heavy hail rattle of hot steel scraps against thin duralumin skin.

So very glad then of this swift, sneak approach through the treetops which kept the defending guns fully-depressed and, thus, at an (alleged) disadvantage. We sailed through without harm, and O'Connor hit the switch on time. 'Big Apples' did her wild horse buck as the bombs fell free into the smoke and flame below, and I turned hard away, a wingtip almost in the treetops, yanking back on the control column, feeling the blood-draining tug of 'G'. A flying visit to Germany.

As promised, we learned later, there had been fighters, and the Mustangs, there for the face-off, had intercepted and kept them off us while knocking down four, a 109, a Focke-Wulf and two of the hot new Henschels. Marauder losses were seven, six to the High Taunus flak, one with collapsed landing gear on the home runway.

And, on his second mission, Azevedo shot down a German plane!

*

"That dirty, lucky son of a *bitch*!" I shook my head in despair and disbelief.

"Now there's the kinda yo-yo," Andy Devine affirmed. "That'd fall dead-drunk in the privy, an' find the Russian Crown jewels."

We had listened, muttering and resentful—recalling with pain our own near-miss with the Messerschmitt 110—at the debriefing as Azevedo, with infuriating casualness, lodged his claim. Tasting added gall when the kill was confirmed by the entire crew of 'Ground Hog' who had been flying nearby.

Heading for home flat out on the deck, 'Bomb Boogie' and 'Ground Hog' had stumbled straight on to the Luftwaffe airfield with its camouflaged hangars and lines of mottle-painted aircraft parked out. A triangle of concrete runways: on one of them a machine taking off.

Lieutenant Colonel Friend demanded crisply, "aircraft type?"

"A Dornier, Colonel." Azevedo was cool, self-possessed, looking faintly amused. "A Seventeen or a Two-Fifteen. Medium aspect-ratio wings, slightly tapered . . . pencil fuselage." Sounding like an aircraft recognition lecture. "Twin fins, twin radials, main gear and tailwheel."

Lieutenant Colonel Friend jotted things down. "Then what happened?"

Nauseatingly off-hand, Azevedo related it. The Dornier had been completing its take-off run, tail up, about to break ground, as 'Bomb Boogie' flew over the field. "Couldn't say for sure if he seen us . . ." Annaka, the bombardier, had got in the first shots with his nose fifty-caliber, scoring hits, seeing fragments knocked off the enemy airplane. Then the dorsal gunner, Sergeant Callison, was given his opportunity . . .

"His left engine took fire," Azevedo reported. "A wing dropped, and he spun into the deck." He smiled and gently stroked his moustache.

Almost sick with jealousy, we sought for ways in which to diminish the achievement: it had been purest chance, and nothing but a sitting duck, anyway. An old, obsolete bomber on some training hop as like as not; a poor, green dumbbell crew caught napping during take-off, the most vulnerable moment of flight. Only . . . for Christ's sakes . . . why *Azevedo*?

Providence, for ever dependable, was against us when the pilot and bombardier in 'Ground Hog' confirmed that there had been Lichtenstein tracking radar antennae mounted on the Dornier's nose. Not, then, a clapped-out has-been full of greenhorns but, instead, an experienced hardcore crew. Radar spelt night fighter, a role in which the Luftwaffe's redundant medium bombers were proving newly-deadly. Of minor importance now that the Dornier had been caught with its pants down. What counted was that 'Bomb Boogie's' guns had scored one of the feared and hated scourges of the night-flying R.A.F.

The most hurtful knowledge for us was that Bigmouth Azevedo could now paint up a swastika under his cockpit window, the only one in the Squadron, and one of just three in the entire Bomb Group.

It got right under the skin of all but O'Connor, who claimed to find it funny. We had received our timely and well-deserved comeuppance, he declared with great righteousness. For being such a bunch of sore losers.

*

The Sunday Roast was packed out on the evening of the High Taunus mission, with all talk centering on Azevedo and 'his' Dornier.

With her appetite for news seemingly insatiable, Heather plied me with question after question, her eyes wide and intent. It made no difference to her that I was not there to witness what had taken place: I had been on the same mission, therefore I must know it all.

"For Pete's sake, it was only his second mission . . . he hasn't even got his feet wet," I told her sullenly. "And, anyway, the Kraut was a lousy sitting duck."

"Do I detect . . ." Her eyes were bright with mischief. "A bad case of the green-eyed monster?" I gave her what was meant to be a crushing look, and she said, "you don't seem to like him much."

"About as much as you like Gladys Gibbons."

She nodded, accepting the point. "But why? What has he done to you?"

I made the attempt to explain how it had been back in Texas, and knowing Azevedo there, and my abiding dislike for the man's conceit and bombast, and tried also to excuse my unreasonable attitude. "It wasn't just me . . . he riled up everyone on the base."

"All right. Fair enough," Heather said.

"It's bad enough having him shoot down a Jerry," I admitted. "But then being made to sit there and listen to his phony-baloney modesty, and making out like there was nothing to it . . ." Forgetting in my irritation how we, too, had disparaged it . . .

There was some hollering from down the bar, and a small commotion around the entrance: I looked, and there was Azevedo standing in the doorway, grinning around, his clasped hands held aloft. The not-quite Golden Gloves champion, I thought, glowering. "Well . . . talk of the devil."

Heather looked up. "Is *that* him?"

"Feast your eyes on the Latin lover." She was studying him critically. "All this stupid hoo-haw for an old bomber that hadn't even got off the ground . . ." And forget about the fact that that old bomber would never again stalk and kill the midnight Lancasters and Halifaxes.

"Everyone does seem to be making rather a fuss about it," Heather agreed thoughtfully, and irritated me again by adding, "he's quite good-looking."

"In a greaseball kind of way."

"Now, now . . ." Smilingly she wagged a finger. "*Nas*-ty."

"Where he's concerned, I get to feel nasty. He's a first class pain in the ass."

Heather had stopped smiling. "You're more foul-mouthed than I seem to remember."

"Blame the Army." I was in no mood to be conciliatory.

"No, blame yourself," she told me sharply. "Someone like you shouldn't be influenced."

I said nothing, and watched Azevedo holding court, flying his flattened hands, everyone crowding in, silent and attentive as he told it *his* way . . . "I lined us up, telling my guys to hold off until I gave them the nod . . . the old whites of the eyes thing, huh? And then . . ." The flying hands clapped together. "Bingo!"

I said, not quite under my breath, "you lying bastard."

"And how do you know that?" Heather gave me a level stare. "You told me you were nowhere near."

"I *was* at the debriefing, though. It wasn't quite the same story then. What happened was they lucked in, and that's the beginning, middle and end of it right there." I returned Heather's unfriendly stare. "If you want it on the level, the way it'll show up on the official report, it was Azevedo's bombardier and top gunner who nailed the Jerry. Before Mister Wise-Guy found time to scratch his butt." Heather frowned her annoyance at my crude, and willful, choice of phrase, and, for once, I did not give a hoot about what she thought. "The prick had to come clean there."

"Do you feel a need to talk to me like that, Denney? Because, if so, I'd rather you inflicted it on someone else."

I wondered then . . . whose side is she on? With that well-developed intuition of hers, could she not understand how this affected me? Okay, point taken, my language was a little rough, maybe, and that was to be regretted once I had cooled down. But always, at other times, she had grasped the full meaning in the things I said and thought . . .

She was saying in a low, urgent tone, "it looks as though you'll be able to make your feelings known to the man himself."

Azevedo strode across the room to us, beaming. "Hey there! A friendly face!"

"Oh, I wouldn't say that," I began as Heather nudged me. "You seem to be doing all right for friends. You don't need any help from us."

But all his attention was on Heather. "Well, hel-LO!"

She nodded at him, half-smiling, and I wanted to bawl her

out then for her betrayal, and never mind who heard me. He turned to wink at me. "Whaddya know, you sly dog, you? What's this you're hoggin' to yourself?" Not waiting to be asked, he squeezed himself a place at Heather's side.

"We're having a private conversation, if you don't mind . . ."

But Heather had moved up for him. "Don't let me stop you." He sat closer to her than I cared for, giving her his full attention. "Now, tell me *all* about *you.*" She glanced a question at me and, at once, I caved in, making unwilling introductions.

"Miss Heather." He bowed over her hand ceremoniously. "A fair English rose."

"Oh, come *on* . . ." But she was laughing. "That's a bit thick . . . even for a Yank."

"Then you must try and forgive me." Azevedo was unfazed. "But you're the first true-blue English lady I've had the pleasure of meeting." He acted out the Southern plantation gentleman role for her, smiling, confiding, displaying flawless teeth. "Just a new arrival shakin' down."

"Then you won't be familiar yet . . ." Heather was at her sweetest. "With an English response . . . forgive the pun . . . to such flowery phrases?"

Azevedo kept right on smiling. "Which is, Ma'am?"

"Pull the other one," Heather said.

Now I could have hugged her; she had his measure in the first few seconds!

He took it well, playing up to her, choosing a more self-effacing line about being so glad to be in England at last: he would have hated to miss this. A Johnny-come-lately, he might have been overseas much sooner, but . . . I was favored with a sidelong glance. "Like good old Denney here. Who, I'm told, has nigh on finished his tour?"

"Yes he has." Heather's smile for me was proud, and pleasingly possessive.

Azevedo asked me, "how many you got in now?"

"Twenty eight."

"My! Only twelve to go, then?"

"And you only thirty eight," I said.

It was Heather's nails warning me this time, digging into the back of my hand.

"That's right. And you'll finish up and go on home." He looked rueful. "And here I'll be, still sloggin' away . . ." He turned his fixed smile upon Heather once more. "But gettin' to know people . . . makin' friends." I could not credit this: here, right before me, Azevedo was muscling in, making this blatant play for my girl! Until then, where he was concerned, it had been simple dislike. Now I hated his guts!

Heather was looking at me. "You've gone quiet."

"Well." I stared hard at Azevedo. "Someone needs to."

"Hey . . . who's the sorehead?" He threw a playful punch in my direction. "What happened to the Denney Pilgrim I used to know?" He told Heather, sounding regretful, "back in Texas, we were old formation buddies."

I saw the question, and the reproach, in Heather's eyes, and could come up with no worthwhile defense or justification of myself for her. As Azevedo, sensing an advantage, moved in to claim the field. While she, instead of being with *me*, sat there, smiling at him, lapping up his bullshit.

He stayed put, and our once-quiet corner became the focus of attention as a succession of latecomers arrived to congratulate him, and ask about the Dornier, and he preened, and Heather listened to him as, once, she had listened to me. While I, eclipsed and forgotten, was left to reflect sadly upon the gullibility of others less well-informed, and to wonder how she, of all people, could swallow this garbage?

Until, sick of it, and of her, I demanded abruptly, "okay with you if we go?"

Her eyes searched mine. "If you want to."

"You *bet* I do!"

Azevedo looked up, smiling a question. "You guys aren't leaving?"

"You catch on quick," I said.

"*Now* what's eating you?" He implored Heather, "come on, stick around. The night's young."

"Thank you." She shook her head. "But I don't think so, not this time." Or *any* time, I thought.

"That's too bad." He feigned bewilderment. "Hope it's nothing I've said?"

I went for broke then. "Thing is, Captain . . . we need to get out of here fast. Before the crap rises past our knees."

I said it loudly enough to be overheard, and someone, somewhere, laughed out loud, and I began to hope then that I was not alone in getting Azevedo's measure.

*

It was raining, and I helped Heather into her mac, and stood in the cold drizzle waiting as she buttoned and belted it. Preparing myself, clearing the decks for the coming broadside. But all she did was take my arm, falling into step with me, giving me the unexpected opportunity to get in the first shot, a defensive one. "Do I get my marching orders?"

"Should you get them?"

"I guess I've upset you."

"And *I* guess you have. Now, knowing that, do you feel any better for all the rotten things you said?"

"You want the truth as usual?" When she made no reply, I told her, "then yes, I do. Because someone needed to put that jerk in his place."

"You wouldn't deny, though, that you were perfectly beastly?"

Her tone stayed light, almost jocular, and I felt encouraged. "I wouldn't for a second. But he's had it coming."

I could recognize, however, that it had been pointless, and quintessentially unfair. I had a big bee in my bonnet about Azevedo, but the truth was that the creep had never harmed me personally. His seeming play for Heather existed probably only in my imagination, stemming from a mind geared up with intent to dislike, and no questions asked. He might flirt with her, and drop his unsubtle hints, and I did not have to like it. Yet it was not unreasonable that he should try his luck. If I chose to pick fights with everyone desiring to make time with Heather I would probably need to take on half the air base.

I asked her, needing to know, "so where do I stand with you now?" Beneath the studiedly off-hand manner, I waited with deepening anxiety for the break I did not deserve.

We had halted at the corner of Heather's road which was very dark and dripping with rain. She reached out and pulled me close. "You really should, you know. Get your marching orders."

"Accepted . . ."

"Then I suppose that's something . . . a little hope remaining for you yet." I could hear the laughter—no doubt about it—in her voice. She was fiddling with a button on my trench coat.

I warned, "you'll pull it off, and I'm not worth a damn with a needle and cotton."

"I'd probably sew it back on for you." The laughter broke out into the open. "For old times' sake."

Hope was re-kindled sufficiently for me to venture a joke. "Would you still do my darning, and take in my laundry?"

She twisted the button some more. "You never know . . . I might even warm your bed."

Humbled, I confessed, "I know I don't deserve it."

"You really were . . ." Heather peered into my face. "A bit of a B."

"Well, maybe."

"Simply to establish my point in this debate, and to cheer you up at the same time," she said then. "Now that I've met him, I admit that he's somewhat hard to take, other than in quite small doses. At the same time, I'm sure he's harmless, a good-natured blowhard." She insisted, "and no one for *you* to fret over." She leaned forward, grinning, to kiss me briefly. "Yank-bumptious, of course, but that's what we've come to expect, and you never let us down there." I could mix in my own chagrined laughter with hers then. "He's quite fun in his way, I suppose, but of no importance whatever to me."

TWENTY FOUR

FLIGHT LOG.
DATE: 9/20/44.
AIRCRAFT TYPE: B-26C.
NO. or REG: 43-2693.
PILOT-IN-COMMAND: Self.
SECOND PILOT: Nil.
CREW: O'Connor, Devine, Cohn, Patecki.
FLIGHT ROUTE: Brussels-Bocholt-Brussels.
FLIGHT HOURS: 1.35.
HOURS VISUAL: 0.20.
HOURS INSTRUMENT: 1.15.
HOURS NIGHT: Nil.
OBSERVATIONS: Arnhem (Market Garden) support mission.
Weather poor: target partly-obscured at low level. Overall bombing
results inconclusive.

"Listen up everyone." Lieutenant Colonel Friend rapped the lectern. "This is the drift."

Hearing from him what we knew already: that British, American and Polish paratroops had been dropped into Holland behind German lines to seize and hold the Rhine bridges at Grave, Nijmegen and Arnhem.

At first, with everyone betting happily on the continuance of our long winning streak, it had been like D-Day all over again: that same, heady, electric thrill, only more so because this was not a French beach, but Germany proper. Honest-to-God bridges across the honest-to-God Rhine!

Lieutenant Colonel Friend poked the wall map with his pointer. "Now, Nijmegen and Grave are in the bag already, both bridges sewn up . . ." The bellicose jargon tumbled from his lips as the pointer slid away to the north. "At Arnhem, though, we've stepped in some temporary shit, and a little extra help's needed. Which the Ninth Air Force *will* provide . . ."

He filled in the details in clipped, fearless little sentences: British airborne men cut off and surrounded at the Arnhem bridge: re-supply by air falling short, all that parachuted ammunition, fuel and food drifting unchecked into the nearby German positions. The paratroopers, taking heavy losses, unable to hang on for much longer.

"We're getting good intelligence from the Dutch underground of Kraut reinforcements massing here and here . . ." The pointer stabbed twice. "Emmerich and Bocholt." We, we learned, were to hit Bocholt. "While the R.A.F. go after Emmerich with their fast Mosquitoes."

We would all fly from Tiverell Lacey to the same forward airfield near Brussels, making that our base of operations for as long as air support missions were called-for.

"Twelve to go, pardner," O'Connor reminded me in a soft aside. "Finish the old tour this way? One fell swoop?"

The prospect could stimulate, although it would mean another prolonged period away from Heather. "Could be."

"It's all short-haul stuff," he pointed out. "Couple o' hundred miles at most on each trip, there and back. Nothing to prevent us flying three trips a day at that rate."

"Yeah . . . real nice." Yet I could not quite match O'Connor's cheery optimism, mindful always of pitch-queering factors like weather, mechanical hitches and other unanticipated snafus. The memories of Senlis hovered. "Let's not count on it, though."

Crews were to fly independently to Brussels, load up there, obtain target briefings, then head out to Bocholt as a Group. Lieutenant Colonel Friend passed us on to Major Ambruster, the trusty weatherman.

Who spoke of low pressure moving in from the Atlantic, bringing rain and high winds, with overcast conditions down to the deck in places. "Sadly, gentlemen, by the time you get there, right bang-smack in the area where you'll be doing your stuff. I wish to hell I could do better for you . . ." Major Ambruster was of that breed of meteorologist who took his weather—and the blame for it—personally. The package he offered with evident regret consisted of near-gale conditions, squalls, cloud masses topping at or above fifteen thousand feet, with their bases below a thousand. For good measure, he tacked on heavy turbulence and zero visibility in widespread and frequent squalls.

Andy Devine was grinning round at me. "All this and low-level, too?" He rolled his eyes heavenward, and, as Major Ambruster went over his maps, circling the giant air mass and crammed-in isobars, murmured, "I tell ya, Skip, them poor God damn' paratroopers ain't the only ones gonna take a shit-kickin'."

*

En route to Brussels we were given liberal foretaste of what would be our lot later over Brabant and Campine, and Westphalia where Bocholt lay at the edge of the Teutoburger Wald.

Twenty minutes airborne, over the North Sea at wavetop level, on track to landfall at Ostend, discovering the physical realities of those complex, jumbled symbols on the weather map: at first a deepening slaty darkness that erased the visible horizon, then the cloudbase sliding down into the sea like snow coming off a roof. While, on the water, scant feet below the wings, the long streaming tracks of wind-driven waves ran whitely on. Turbulence slammed into 'Big Apples' like angry fists, sending her staggering as I struggled to hold us level and on course, flying then into the first rolling banks of fog that touched the surface like spectral fingers, more of it, and thicker, as we pushed our way into the weather system, until I was flying entirely on instruments at an estimated fifty feet above the sea. In theory, it should have been safe enough: the sea's level was a constant . . . with our altimeters set at the correct barometric pressure it would have been pretty hard to go wrong. In practice, it was utterly crazy and self-destructive to continue so, penetrating deeper into the low pressure area which produced a constant barometer drop, placing the altimeter—itself a barometer governed by atmospheric pressure—hopelessly in error as we flew blindly, with no way, lacking radio contact, to have the error corrected.

To that must be added the factor of our rapid approach to the Belgian coast where there were tidal sands and dunes, with pancake-flat Flanders beyond. Where, also, there would be buildings—hard, immovable obstacles to our progress—strung along the Ostend waterfront, and high dockside cranes filling the port. Inland, if *those* did not nail us, we would encounter, with possibly fatal suddenness, trees, radio masts, powerlines, silos and tall barns . . .

Fifty feet of altitude, it was now clear, would not suffice. On the intercom, I informed the others, "we're heading up." I went to climbing power, re-trimming: not too high . . . enough, though, to provide a safety margin. A thousand feet to hold us well clear of sudden and unpleasant surprises.

I told Andy Devine, "what I'd like about now is a tight estimate on reaching the coast."

"'Kay."

As edginess crept up anew, I demanded, "got any idea where we were when we entered cloud?"

"Holy Christ!" He stared at me, aggrieved. "We're only a half-hour out. Even I couldn't get us lost that fast!" He went back, muttering, to his slide rule and pencil, then looked up at me again, challenging me. " '*Course* I know. I got the wind speeds and direction, enough allowance made for drift . . . what the hell more d'you want from me?"

I grimaced apology. "It's getting so that I don't trust anybody any more."

"That ain't so good, ol'-timer. Y'oughtta talk to someone about that . . . you really did." His diagnosis of my problems delivered, he promised, "see what I can come up with."

"And a revised heading for Brussels, please."

"Sure thing."

I dialed across the radio band, searching for some kind of contact. We were flying independently, neither waiting, nor waited for. Several other aircraft were already in the soup up ahead of us; the first should have crossed the Belgian shore by this time. I scoured the set in the hope of some re-assuring words about improving weather: someone up ahead might just think to send back a pilot report, or maybe a clued-up ground controller alerted to incoming traffic would seize the initiative and broadcast an up-to-the-minute altimeter setting. But there was only intermittent static to reward my quest, and the gainy hiss of carrier wave. No one was giving anything away.

Andy came back to touch my sleeve. "Way I figure it, we'll hit Belgium in five minutes flat."

"Not literally, I hope?"

"That part's up to you." He smiled fleetingly, then became businesslike. "For Brussels, you'll be needing a heading of zero-seven-seven, which takes in the known wind-drift corrections." At once, obedient, I flew the instruments around on to the new heading. "Now you're cookin'," Andy approved.

*

As he had on the Cobra mission in July, Andy came up trumps; our good fortune and the element of coincidence seeming almost staged as a few breaks appeared in the overcast to reveal a strip of gleaming sand edged by gray, cold-looking surf. Buildings swam into view, all safely below now. Seen, too, the well-justified satisfaction in Andy's smile. "Ostend on the nose . . . right where she's meant to be." He reached out to tap a finger against the glass face of the directional gyro compass. "Hold that heading for now, and we're fat. On the deck, Brussels, twenty minutes."

More breaks appearing to reveal the flat green earth in a livid light, enabling us to pinpoint our position. A town off the right wing was Turhout, Andy claimed, and he pointed out Ghent. "Just an itsy-bitsy ways north o' track. Bring her right two degrees," he advised. Another town came into view. "Aalst," Andy confirmed. "We'll have Brussels in sight any moment."

The cloud spaces widened further, leaving more clear air below.

From a slow and gentle let-down, I found that I still had five hundred feet to call my own as we dropped below the gray bases. Northward, though, toward distant Bocholt, the sky threatened sullenly, the horizon obscured by the whitish drifts of wind-teased rain. A few miles ahead, Brussels spread itself out across the plain, with the open green expanse of the landing ground visible.

"Now, ain't that somethin'?" Andy wondered.

"Nice work. Thanks a lot, Andy."

"Betcha," he said. "An' my name's Steve."

I laughed.

Four B-26s were parked out on the ground, and a fifth was on final approach, touching down as we entered the traffic pattern. I followed it in.

On the ground, I reset the altimeter, discovering that, in the hour since leaving England, the bottom had fallen out of the barometer. Judging from that ugly sky over toward Germany, things were likely, and soon, to get worse.

*

Flying out of Brussels in a gusting squall, then back into cloud, and blind again, at four hundred feet. I took 'Big Apples' to a thousand as an ongoing safeguard against ground obstacles, leveling off as we flew into the squall-line turbulence which made the instruments run amok, each with a mind and will of its own against which I must fight, sweating, to keep them centered.

Until we left the squall behind for more quiet air, and I could sit back and begin to chew over the problems still lying before me. Such as what to expect when, or if, we found the target. The weather system was tracking northward, and moving fast: would it have reached Bocholt before us to obscure the mission's objectives, or might we hope for a repeat of the brief pre-frontal clearing that had attended the Brussels arrival two hours before?

Bocholt was to be another low-level strike which would necessitate a hazardous instrument descent from an already low altitude, inching earthward without the assistance of radio navigation facilities, and no knowledge of where the ground might lie relative to the cloud base, or if the two might merge in impenetrable fog. A situation akin to dipping one's foot into an invisible pool.

Considering these very real possibilities, I began then, cravenly, to consider also the matter of aborting my own minor part in this adventure: it could seem the proper and sensible thing to do under these conditions. Just be smart, that insidious voice in my head urged. Call quits and turn around now because to fly on like this into the unknown was insane.

What stayed my hand then was knowing that, somewhere out there in the bomber stream flew the head honcho, a mildly-spoken lieutenant-colonel from Florida with an admirable track record for handling tight situations. Only he could make that decision and issue the appropriate order to all; any initiative of my own would earn no plaudits. Instead, then, holding a course and altitude which made me more uncomfortable with every minute flown, I listened on the command frequency as, once before, I had listened on the way to St. Lô. For the voice telling us to scrub, turn around, head for home. Much as I willed it, though, the colonel did not speak.

*

In his place an unknown voice filled with relief and excitement, "hey . . . I'm in the clear!" Followed at once by the more formal reporting, "Command from 'Zero-Four . . . advise attempted let-down, and am below cloud at six hundred feet indicated. Approximately two hundred feet of clearance above ground, over."

The colonel responding, "roger, Zero-Four . . . state your known position if possible."

"We have a town in sight to the east . . . stand by one." A pause. "The town is Venlo . . . Victor, Easy, Nan, Love, Oboe. Forty miles from target."

"Check that, Zero-Four. Give us a pirep on your weather."

"Zero-Four, roger . . . cloud base is holding. Forward visibility estimated two miles. Moderate turbulence. Further estimate headwinds at three-zero knots, over."

I mulled over the salient points of this eavesdropped information: headwinds slowing us for a late arrival on target, while, beyond the reported two-mile limit of visibility could await the ambush of another dropping cloud base. Letting down from our position, still not fixed, if 'Big Apples' had not found clear air with the altimeter reading five hundred feet, then matters would be starting to get tense. But the pilot of Zero-Four had taken his chances, and made it down . . .

The colonel appeared to have been thinking along similar lines as he issued orders for a precautionary collective descent at two hundred feet per minute to no lower than five hundred feet indicated on altimeters. If, at that height, a pilot found himself still lost in cloud, he was to climb to no less than a thousand, and await instructions. "No hard contacts, gentlemen, no near-encounters. If in doubt, feel free to sing out . . ."

As a descent procedure for massed aircraft flying in close proximity without vision, it was stuff to whiten the hair, although in an environment made hostile by men and nature about the best anyone could come up with.

As can occur in times of extreme fright and stress, there was a moment of mad hilarity then as I thought of asking O'Connor, down in the nose, the lowest point of the airplane, if he could contrive to dangle his legs outside and wait as I made the let-down. "And the moment you find yourself running on the ground, let me know!"

More turbulence shook the airframe as we went down, the bumps feeling horribly like collisions, my heart freezing over each time at what I imagined to be the instant of disintegration.

Lost in clinging vapor, out of sight of one another, separated by miles or yards, or not at all, we inched on downward. I concentrated my mind hard on holding the ordered two hundred feet per minute, following the array of dancing needles before me as the gloom deepened outside, and heavy rain hissed audibly across the windshield panels. The altimeter dropped past seven hundred feet, and went on unwinding . . . one more minute and we would hit the ordered minimum. Feeling very unhappy, I risked a glance outside . . . and found nothing but endless gray blankness.

Another heavy bump caught us, the instruments faithfully recording the resulting confusion: a dropping wing reflected on the artificial horizon, the gyro compass swinging away from the assigned heading as the altimeter clawed back an unwanted fifty feet of height. As 'Big Apples' bobbed like a cork in a mill race, I battled and cursed the fractious gages, and cursing aloud helped a little to keep panic bottled up.

And more calls were coming in to verify the claims of Zero-Four as machine after machine dropped out of cloud. While my own altimeter seemed to shout at me, demanding to know why we, too, were not getting the breaks.

Instead of clear air, we hit another squall, and my nerve went. I grabbed for the throttles to pour on power and climb us out of there . . . as the light outside switched from stone gray to a bilious green, and O'Connor was yelling on the intercom, "hold it! . . . HOLD it! . . . we got contact!"

"How far?" Already I was applying power, easing us back into level flight.

"Not far enough! Get any closer and we'll be taxiing!"

At that perilous distance from the earth the reason for the strange green light became clear; the reflection of land, green fields and woods, from the ground-hugging cloud base. We saw it now, the whole patchwork mosaic of it hurtling by, seeming no more than inches away.

The squall line spat us out, and then I could spin off fifty feet more to keep us just under the cloud as we hurtled across the swayback roofs of a nameless village where people stood unmoving in the puddled main street, watching us go by. A Dutch village? German? And I shivered, thinking of how very close we had come to flying blind into that village, seeing with horrible clarity the cataclysm of blazing fuel and a ton and a half of high explosive. I tried to swallow, and my parched throat would not allow it.

Almost at once we came upon, and followed, the beautiful, wide four-lane highway that curved away into dimness: at the briefing, we had been advised to look out for that and follow it and let it lead us to the objective. On the frequency, then, the first target calls were coming in, and I began the long run-in down that magnificent road, taking its curves with light flicks of aileron; like driving a good, fast car on the Taconic State Parkway . . .

Until, filling the westbound lanes, a dark mass hardens into a long, long military column halted there. With blazing gaps torn in it, and shattered machines, flame and wind-whipped smoke, fire-dappled mushroom bomb-bursts sprouting, reminding brutally of the scenes of July and Falaise, of another road, more narrow, more dusty. Repeating in the wet cold along a beautifully-precise German autobahn.

We go in then with the other Marauders around us, olive-drab phantoms soaring and dipping, then the old skip and bounce as O'Connor salvoes the load amongst the enemy moving up on Arnhem.

Wondering, mystified, as we climb away, where the Germans *get* all that stuff? They are said to be whipped, their industry, their country, lying in ruins. So, just how come?

Gaining altitude, chased by the shockwaves from our own bombs as Sergeant Patecki reports from his rearward grandstand position that we have succeeded in bombing empty fields beside the highway. "Although I reckon we may have shook up their morale some."

*

An easier return to Brussels, if not exactly a triumphant one, with the wind on our tail, driving us on. Landing in thick drizzle and mist, rattling in dejectedly over the slippery PSP.

The Group had suffered no losses at Bocholt. No one on

our side got hurt, yet no one among us saw cause for celebration. At the de-briefing, we told it as it was, disconsolate, grimly certain that we had failed the encircled soldiers. Yet, given the abysmal flight conditions, a small wonder that we had bombed at all.

Despondency gripped each crew: we liked to think of ourselves as professionals, good at the job; now Bocholt pointed out the considerable error in such reasoning. Our shared mood was not lightened by more intelligence filtering in from the Dutch underground. Speaking of damage done, but not enough of it. The Germans, thrusting aside ruthlessly the bodies of men and the broken equipment that could serve them no more, had reformed swiftly and were spearheading their resumed way westward along the splendid white road.

*

We hung about, glum and restless, awaiting further orders to strike, no longer caring about the continuing awful weather. It was bad enough to have failed, but when failure spelled ruin for men who had counted on us . . . We sat in Brussels, facing no danger, while they . . .

And kept on sitting, helpless and grounded, as the Atlantic low pressure system took over and dug in: it appeared to us that the two-timing weather had passed judgement on the efforts of both sides, and, finding us lacking, turned to favor the more successful.

Cloud and fog and rain and wind socked in the field, and the useless aircraft sat there, silent and dripping. As the armored column, largely intact, went upon its way, and time ran out for the survivors at the Arnhem bridge.

*

With only that one mission to show for our efforts, it was an ill-humored return to Tiverell Lacey, and so much for O'Connor's empty dreams of a swift completion.

The gloom of Arnhem would not leave us. Psyched-up to winning, we took set-backs with ill-grace; the adolescent thought shared—sometimes aloud—that the Germans did not fight fair. Did they not know they were beaten, that it was time to see reason and throw in the towel? Had no one got round to telling them that yet?

Our problem was that, since the Normandy break-out, Falaise, then the rapid drive on to Paris and Brussels, we had grown complacent, convinced of our innate superiority over our enemy. We had had it too good, and that made us forget humility, and the ways in which to deal with the still-inevitable off-days.

Which, in turn, made us querulous and self-pitying. Unlike the phlegmatic British who had known bad times galore, learning to take them in their stride along with the harsh lessons they taught. For us, feeling bound to win, that went against the grain: following Arnhem we sulked, complaining about the rampaging Germans who, as we saw it, had forfeited the right to rampage any more.

*

For the Squadron, on the heels of Arnhem, there came a prolonged lull that was never to be explained.

While other outfits flew daily, and suffered losses, we sat around on the ground, and bitched. Far from accepting what should have been a welcome hiatus, the shared tendency was to view it as a silent censure of our poor showing at Bocholt: we were no longer good enough, not fit to be used. Nothing was said, ever, and we continued to rise each day, and lie down at its end, keyed-up for the flying that no one wanted us to do. September drifted into October, and the call for our services came seldom. Which frustrated everyone, inducing peevishness and complaint to the point where we longed to do those things we loathed doing.

We did fly . . . a little.

Mission Thirty, via Brussels, to bomb Bergisch-Gladbach.

Where 'Big Apples' was staggered by a very near miss that
knocked out the radios and started an electrical fire which Andy
managed to put out with the carbon-tet extinguisher. Sergeant
Cohn received a slight splinter wound in the back of his hand,
and went off, pale and proud, in the meat wagon. He returned
to us two hours later with his clean bandage and his Purple Heart.

More days of idleness followed until they squeezed out
Number 31, a milk-run to Groningen in North Holland.

Two more weeks then of kicking around before being let off
the leash for the run to Wilhelmshaven, our longest trip to date
from England, with horrible, exquisitely-precise flak, and fighters
pressing their attacks right through it with insane bravery,
succeeding too well in spite of being massacred by the Little
Friends. Nine Marauders gone, and three P-51s. Two of the
Marauders were Tiverell Lacey airplanes, and one was 'Hound
Dog Howlin''. To which Sergeant Smithson had transferred at
Senlis. Smithson, for ever one of us although absent, was our
first fatality.

Until, walking back to the Quonset with the news of personal
loss heavy in our hearts, Andy Devine exclaimed, "Jesus Christ-
on-a-crutch . . . *look*!"

Smithson approached us slowly, grinning and sheepish. "'S
okay . . . I ain't no spook. I missed out by one mission."

The Groningen milk-run had been his last: he had flown
more in 'Hound Dog Howlin'' than we had of late. Enough to
qualify him for the thirty-plus amnesty. Smithson returned from
Groningen with his tour completed, to begin waiting for orders
shipping him out.

"Jim . . . ?" Subdued for once, O'Connor asked, "you've
heard?"

"Sure, Captain." Smithson nodded soberly. "I seen how many
come back, and who." He wanted to know how it had been.

"A One-Oh-Nine," I told him. "Blew them out of the sky."

"No 'chutes?"

"Not a one we saw," Sergeant Patecki admitted.

"Sorry as hell, Jim," O'Connor said.

Smithson turned to stare out over the airfield. "I feel real shitty about my replacement. Fresh in from the States . . . I'd just checked him out on the turret. That was his first God damn' trip . . ." He smiled round at us sadly. "Sure happy you fellas made it, though." But his eyes were not happy, and held only unanswerable questions.

We were unharmed, undamaged, and I thought of Heather's spell. Still working?

Another fortunate one was Azevedo's 'Bomb Boogie'. Now, beside the proudly-emblazoned swastika stood a row of five bomb symbols. Azevedo had been with us at Bocholt, claiming hits on the German column which were confirmed, flying with unruffled skill through the foul weather. Wondering, loftily amused, what it was we were griping about. "You guys call yourselves *airmen*, don't you? That kind of thing's what the air's all about."

With all his airline instrument hours, he was, certainly, the acknowledged weather flying expert. Even allowing for that, we did not have to like the way he crowed his expertise at us while belittling our own. Although, on the positive side, all that crowing gave us more substantial grounds for disliking him.

More flightless days passed drably by as October gave way in turn to November. The leaves of long summer came down, scattered by the winds which picked up to usher in more storms, a dismal series of Atlantic lows apparently without end. The occasional mission would be called, and we would go out and fly it in the wet, and come back to brood over fresh losses, and sit around some more. That, or as took place with increasing frequency, the mission would be recalled en route, or scrubbed as we waited on the ground, hyped-up to go. These, notwithstanding the hard work and fraying nerves involved, did not count toward the longed-for and ever-illusive total.

*

It should have been a blessing, this gift of free time to be spent with Heather. Heather, though—it was becoming painfully apparent—was rather less than enthusiastic about passing time with me.

It reached the point where, when I telephoned her to make a date, I would do so expecting her to cry off. Most reasons could not be argued; the dreadful weather, a bad day at work, the old faithful stand-by about washing her hair. Fair enough, bar the fact that, now, there seemed to be more cryings-off than meetings, something that I brought up on one of the occasions when we were together.

It was another rainy night, gusty and raw with the east wind cutting in from the North Sea. She had hurried damply into the pub, muffled to the ears in her mac, and visibly irritable. "I must be quite mad, coming out in this . . ."

I remembered the Great Storm then, soon after the Invasion, a time when everything for us had been bright and new; the pub, and an evening no less foul. She had not minded coming out in *that*.

I tried a smile, and showed concern. "Let me take your coat."

She preferred to keep it on. "I can't stay . . . sorry."

"Well, fine . . ." Only it was not one bit fine. I wanted to beg her to remain with me, to blurt out that I needed her around, that I loved her, and did she not know that? To demand of her, *why* this iceberg treatment. I managed, "has anything happened?"

"What should have *happened*?"

"I was wondering about the big hurry to get away when you've only just got here."

She dropped her gaze, biting her lip. "I really *am* sorry. It's nothing, really . . . just a grisly bloody day, nothing going right, and it's made me tired and cranky." Her smile was strained. "And thoroughly rotten company."

"That doesn't matter to me. I'm happy to see you, regardless."

"Then all I can say is, you're easily pleased!" Her voice grated in sudden exasperation, then she was quickly contrite. "Oh, God . . . how *can* you put up with me, Denney?" She lifted a hand as though to touch my face, then withdrew it. "I thought . . . a drink, and say hello?"

"Hello," I said.

"After which I do feel an early night is called for to improve my currently nasty frame of mind."

"Couldn't you relax for a while first, now that you've made the effort? Fifteen minutes? Would that be too much?"

Fifteen minutes, then, Heather conceded, might be all right.

Grateful for this crumb, I went to get our drinks, and wondered, newly-baffled, what could have gone sour this time? And—with resentment—for fifteen lousy minutes I could have spared myself the draughty and uncomfortable truck ride to the village . . .

I set down her drink. "Can't you at least tell me what's wrong?"

"What's wrong, what's this . . . what's *that*!" The brief truce ended as she snapped at me once more. "You're always asking me things like that!"

No less exasperated, I fired back, "you give me cause to these days."

She stared at me with hostility. "I've *said*, haven't I?"

"Heather, you've said many things. And, sometimes, when I try to tally them up, they seem to conflict."

"Oh? Like what, for instance?"

I paused then, right at the brink of a full and thorough airing of accumulating grievance. "I keep remembering London."

"And I remember it, too. What *of* it?"

"How can you ask me that? It was an unforgettable experience . . ."

"You've said that before, too." But her voice had softened a little.

"Because it bears repetition. A time when I knew a closeness with you such as I've never known or imagined. Something that, it's true to say, changed my life. Only . . ." I paused again.

A second or two passed, and Heather prompted, "only?"

"I wonder why you seem to be trying to spoil it all?"

The anticipated explosion did not come: she replied quietly that she did not want to see me upset or unhappy, but that, once again, I should try to understand. She was going through . . . she gave a little embarrassed laugh . . . something of an emotional turmoil. "Forgive me for whining."

I offered, "a little whine never did anyone any harm."

Her mouth quirked. "I think you'll find that's *wine*."

I pressed then, "do you know what's causing it?"

Without any hesitation, she came straight out with it. "Being too close to you? When you do what you do."

"But the war will be over soon. Jerry's almost had it, and . . ."

"I *know* that! And, when it is, everything in the garden will be lovely. But before the time comes, people are still going to die, and get hurt, and be bereaved."

The point, beyond argument, was that I stood in line for any, or all, of that; the road that Tim had gone down already. I feigned a grin for her. "What happened to our spell?"

Heather shrugged tiredly. "Perhaps I forgot."

"But that's not allowed. You're on a contract with no escape clauses." I wondered lightly, "or doesn't the policy cover added missions?"

She answered pettishly, "oh, it's just me being a pain, and looking for opportunities to grizzle." I tried to put a comforting arm around her, but she shook her head and edged away. "I'm being a silly cow, and don't deserve coddling." She looked back at me, and grimaced. "There! That's my lapse, and I feel wretched about it, and an utter B.F. So would you mind awfully if I left now?"

"I mind like hell, but you know best."

"Thank you for understanding."

But I was wishing emptily still that I *could* understand. "Tell me when I can see you again."

"Would you give me a little time, please? Just to get over the morbs."

"All the time you need . . ." She was her father's daughter, and perhaps prone to those same bouts of depression which had disrupted his life. This I must accept, and try to live with.

"I know I'm not being at all rational," Heather said in apology. "And when I'm with you, I should at least make the attempt."

I offered no answer, thinking that it was not the break between us in *time* that mattered; time, whether long or short, always passed . . . in time. What nagged at me now was my deepening conviction that there was more to this than Heather chose to reveal, and which presaged greater pain to come.

"Keep on phoning me," she said. "And telling me all your news, and how you're getting along . . ." For news, I thought with regret, substitute missions. It did seem that emotional turmoil could not manage to dull her enthusiasm for those.

She kissed me, and was gone, not looking back. She needed time . . . so why could I not take that declared need at face value instead of viewing it as a first oblique warning that that time might be for ever? Margot Granger's words returned to pick at my mind: Heather could hurt me while not wanting to. And, for that, I should be prepared. What eluded me still, though, was *why*.

TWENTY FIVE

Overnight it turned to winter, and all the good memories of summer were purged by gales and rain and bitter sleet.

The flying lull went on, with the dire weather conditions an added factor to keep us on the ground, the pressure lows tramping in in heavy-footed succession, like soaked gray armies. Now, the light burned inside the air base buildings at noon while our aircraft lay out on their hardstands, glumly silent and rain-gleaming, their engines, cockpits and gun positions shrouded, incapable, it seemed, of flight.

Still perversely eager to be aloft once more, we pestered Major Ambruster out in his weather shack, peering over his charts, loudly critical of his carefully-worked synopses, studying in dejection the closed-in isobars of storm after storm.

He answered our querulous and ill-informed questions with enduring kindness and patience, voicing no objection to the procession of bad-tempered airmen passing through his cramped, teletype-clattering domain. "Come on over any time. You know me . . ." A little indulgent chuckle. "I enjoy talking about the weather."

With thirty four missions behind us, we were now the second senior crew on the base. Only 'Mean an' Ugly' was ahead with thirty seven, and Boyard, Zweng, Coles, Middlehouse and Partridge were no less keen than we to get airborne, and have done with it.

With only those six missions remaining, much as we feared them, still we ached to fly them, and railed with helpless fury against the God-awful conditions, the top-level plotters and planners who gave the impression of having turned their backs upon us with deliberate malice. For ever waiting, we paced back and forth under the weeping skies in a nerve-stretching stew of boredom, frustration and scared anticipation. Destined for all time, it did appear, to lie one mission short of the magic reprieving mark of five or less to go.

A different story for more junior crews, many of whom had still half a tour or more to fly. For them, the ongoing respite was a blessing, a Godsent time for hanging out, shooting pool or craps, bumming rides to the village to sit around and drink beer. A spell of inactivity could help to raise their uncertain hopes.

Time was passing, and the war's end was almost within grasp; ergo, if they could manage to sit tight for long enough . . .

When, however, only six were left to be flown, such thinking was misplaced and potentially hazardous, the means whereby necessary will and vigilance could be undermined, heightening the extreme risks attendant upon falling into a collective state of mental idleness.

While the threat of further increases in the number of missions might have receded following an upsurge in the flow of replacement aircraft and crews, we could not be certain, and did all that we could to tread lightly in our desire to be overlooked should that happen again.

An increase now would find us, by one miserable mission, outside the privileged number of those not affected. With not six, then, but *eleven* to go, or even more. And O'Connor, who, since the Arnhem debâcle, appeared to have forsaken all hopes of completing the tour in one go, could contemplate the unalluring expectation of (maybe) completing seventy in the E.T.O.

O'Connor, with a current total of fifty nine flown in total, had taken on the aura of a patriarch. Andy Devine, Cohn, Patecki and I considered ourselves to be pretty salty as well. Since that beginning in May, so many had come and gone, killed, wounded, prisoners or, simply and almost anti-climactically, completed. For us, still in place and fretting, there was the feeling at times of living in another era long gone. In a place too well-known, but peopled now by strangers.

Like our now battered and shabby airplane, we had all aged

visibly, although among ourselves, the process was not always discernible. Until the sudden glimpse of someone's face in a flecked shaving mirror, the shocked awareness, still doubting . . . is that *me*?

*

The war on the ground was, like ourselves, finding itself bogged down by weather. On the Rhine, in Italy and East Prussia and Poland. Barring an unlikely German collapse within the next few weeks, or a more successful attempt on Hitler's life than the von Stauffenberg fiasco of July, followed by some quick deal worked out with Der Führer's successors, it must now be 1945, probably the spring, before the final halt would be called.

On the heels of the rapid successes of Nomandy, Brittany, Paris and Belgium, it had been tempting to think in terms of an imminent ending. Using the rate of advance from July to September as a yardstick, by November we should have been encircling Berlin and back-slapping with the Russians. It was not working out in quite that way.

We were hearing frequently and dispiritingly of failing bombing strategies. That, the incalculable damage done to it, notwithstanding, Germany's manufacturing output was actually on the increase. With their plants collapsed into ruin, still they contrived to build tanks and guns and aircraft: their Messerschmitt 262 jet fighter outclassed anything that we could put up against it; American and British operational jets, while promised, were still barely off the drawing board. They were producing the fuel to power the machines, including the specialist mixtures required for the V-1s and the V-2 rockets.

Now, the word making the rounds was that, for the time being, where Jerry was concerned, it might be more advisable to shelve the earlier happy slogans that had trumpeted the 'desperate measures', 'last-ditch stands' and 'imminent final demise' of the Third Reich.

Despite the vow of the British Air Marshal Harris to crush it completely, German morale remained good. The strategic roles had been reversed; Germany found herself where Britain had been in 1940, alone and isolated, awaiting invasion and the boots of hostile armies trampling the land. And every German, it was being said, looked forward keenly to an apocalyptic face off with the world.

Within the confines of the Tiverell Lacey air base, the stories were received with mixed feelings and conflicting fears. Those of us with a few missions still outstanding were more than ever conscious of our extreme vulnerability; a war in its last gasp could still kill you so easily.

While, for the crews farther down the ladder, a fresh fear was emerging: of having the European war reach its conclusion, and being compelled then to fly off the balance of a tour against Japan. Which very few expected realistically to survive.

From my own personal level, it was not difficult to draw uncomfortable comparison between the uncertain state of international hostilities, and my now steadily deteriorating relations with Heather.

In the country of the Ardennes, the Hürtgen Forest, in the Eifel and the Saar, the war was locked in tight by the winter freeze. And, Heather's denials aside, all that we seemed to share now was iciness.

While, close by in the wings, Azevedo hovered.

*

There were few places in winter other than the village pubs where Heather and I could be together. The bitter weather ruled out biking. There were the country busses to take us to nearby towns and villages, but in Colchester, Chelmsford, Manningtree or Ipswich only the cold, wet streets awaited us, the blackout, glum drinking places and grubby cinemas.

With time hanging heavy, we settled into a torpor of semi-hibernation, our chosen burrow the familiar Sunday Roast. There, too, however, would be Azevedo who never passed up on an opportunity to make his way over, oozing compliments, forcing conversations which Heather showed every sign of *enjoying*.

Increasingly impatient with what she saw as my intransigent attitude, she would quiz me sharply, and, no less sharply, I would remind her that my response to Azevedo was a carbon copy of her expressed feelings for Gladys Gibbons. Pious and pompous, I pointed out also my unquestioning acceptance of her particular antipathy. Could she not, then, respond in kind?

She gave the impression often that she flirted with Azevedo with the express intent of making me squirm. Certainly, with him around, I would find myself relegated to Position Three in the three's-a-crowd scenario, and would be gnawed to the bone by jealousy, detesting him, mad as hell with her. It would have been nice then, and great fun, to haul out a G.I. .45 automatic pistol, and blast the son of a bitch!

I pictured it with relish: Azevedo gasping out his life, bleeding all over the pub floor. And then I would give Heather a sound talking-to about her flirty-flirty wayward ways before the M.P.s arrived to haul me off . . .

Yet, when I voiced my suspicions aloud in protest, I faced furious denial. "What do you think I *am*?"

It was well after dark, and I was walking Heather home through the drizzle. We had spent a tense hour at the pub, forty minutes of which had included Azevedo's unsought (by me) company. Until he was called away to compete in a darts match. By which time the evening was ruined. Made worse when, as we left, he called after Heather, "stay beautiful for me, babe." And she smiled back at him—simpered, I thought savagely—and I longed once more for that .45: I would have used it on him then . . . I *would*!

Heather informed me cuttingly, "someone should make a record of you when you're playing your sulky, spoiled brat role. You'd be amazed by the way you sound, and appalled, too, one would hope."

"Oh, *would* one?" I jeered back. "And I'm supposed to sit there like a good boy, giving no offense, while that two-bit, phony prick shovels his crap . . . is that it?"

"Kindly don't speak to me like that!"

Wretchedness and rage made me careless of possible consequences. "And, maybe, while I'm getting recorded, someone else should take your picture!"

"Oh, really . . ."

"Yes, *really*. The way you sit there, lapping up his bullshit!"

I waited then with my boats and bridges well-burned. Now, assuredly, she would flounce off, leaving me cold, and for good. But Heather rarely did what was expected of her. "This is so sad, you poor, lost boy." And her taunt speared me right through, not least because she was right. "So pathetic and jealous, and why? For what? Do you honestly believe that I don't see through him? When he's even more transparent than you? And, if you must know, he's also not at all my type."

"No one would think that from the way you moon around him." Despair inflamed my reckless mood further. "You're like someone besotted, and, yes, I *am* good and damned jealous, and *no*, I don't understand any of it." I added, "that's what you're always asking for, Heather . . . my understanding. Well, so help me, I've tried, but it's just not working . . . at least where he's concerned."

"You've made up your mind, without any grounds, that I'm gulled by him," she retorted. "But that's you, and you only. All it is with me is politeness and good manners. He speaks to me, and, *politely*, I listen. I don't always agree with what he has to say, and, yes, I do find him impossibly bumptious and self-opinionated. But still, as I said before, a mere harmless blowhard."

"Yet you know I can't stand him." Churlishly I concealed from Heather the pleasure and relief that her words brought to me.

"You have made that rather clear, I agree." She watched me with returned amusement.

And, of course, I was out-classed hopelessly in any argument or debate with her; I needed to be older and a whole lot smarter to offer any kind of worthwhile contest. All I had right then was the same old threadbare excuse. "Disliking Azevedo goes back a long way."

"So you've said . . ."

"And so I say *again*!" It was possible to get quite upset when an adversary was always so reasonable, and logical, and right. "That bastard keeps on muscling-in, and he's too damned thick-skinned to recognize your politeness as just that. He'll see it every time as encouragement . . ." I jeered bitterly, "old formation buddies, my ass! We were never buddies, and he knows it. But he trots that out as a cock-eyed ploy to win your favor and make time with you."

"Perhaps he does . . . I couldn't say." I would have taken an oath there and then that there was satisfaction in the acknowledgement. "Which still doesn't suggest that he'll get anywhere with me. Nor that because he says all those boastful, but rather funny, things, I'm going to turn round and snap his head off." She concluded frostily, "I would have thought . . . mistakenly, it appears . . . that you'd know me better by now."

"Well, it seems I don't. Sorry to keep on disappointing you, but you're still a mystery to me, and even more so since London." I appealed to her, "all I'm asking is that things should be clear between us. And then that jerk comes along, and you start acting interested . . ."

"Polite," Heather corrected me. "And *looking* interested. That's the difference."

"Okay, so now I know. But I didn't, and I couldn't stop myself thinking the worst."

"Denney, can we end this pointless discussion, please?" Heather asked wearily. "And try to forget it ever happened?"

But I could not, not yet. "And where does that leave me?"

"At this moment, I really couldn't say." She spoke without inflection, and I saw in the dimness the way she watched me. "You're not someone I know awfully well tonight, or, I'm afraid, like very much." The words were like a kick in the stomach. "So, let's stop it now, and see how we feel in the morning."

"I'll feel lousy. I can promise you that now."

"Me, too, I expect," she admitted. Her hand came out to touch mine. "Call me if you want to. When you've stopped being a bear." The hand squeezed once, and I hoped that we might kiss. But she turned from me, and the opportunity, again, was lost.

TWENTY SIX

Well into December the mystifying lull went on, and we went on bemoaning it. At times, then, I would remember O'Connor's wry definition of war, its ratio of boredom to terror. Now I, too, found myself yearning for some terror.

Out of the blue then came two missions in two days, both of them trouble-free and flown in bright, clear weather; first to Aachen, then Cloppenberg, each with its now customary stop-over at Brussels. Eventful because, being Numbers 35 and 36, they got us at last over what everyone had come to refer to as the 'Amnesty Hump'. Now, we reasoned, should some bright spark take it upon himself to up the missions once more, we, at least, should be home and dry.

Among the many negative psychological effects of the now weeks-long lull, was a growing suspicion, shared by all, of 'things cooking'. Our Squadron appeared to be the only one in the 9th A.F.—that we knew of—to be spared continuous combat flying. That, we all felt, must possess some significant, and sinister, meaning. The nameless, faceless 'They' were holding us back for something that would be 'way out of the ordinary. Which, when revealed, would prove itself unpleasant.

*

Even so, with Cloppenberg and the Hump behind us, we felt the natural uplifting of spirits that came with that reality. *Now*, we crowed happily, *let* the bastards jack up their stupid numbers all they liked; we at least were fireproof. In our noisy triumphalism we spared not a thought for those who might be less-fortunate should events take that threatened turn. O'Connor, disdaining Providence, went so far as to suggest that we might down a few celebratory beers at the Officers' Club. This on an evening that I was planning to spend with Heather.

Since our most recent bout of wrangling over Azevedo, a truce of sorts had been agreed. While this left us wary of each other to some extent, I was still eager to be with her at every opportunity, and to find ways to make up lost ground. Compared with that, bachelor beer-drinking with O'Connor and Andy Devine remained well back among the also-rans. I asked for a rain check.

"Headin' out to see your gal?" Andy winked. "What hopes we got against that kind o' competition?"

"You read me like a book," I confessed.

"Also loud an' clear, kid." O'Connor wagged ironic brows.

"I'll give her a call," I said. "And if it's no dice for any reason, then I'll come back here and get stiff with you guys."

Andy guffawed. "You gonna get *stiff*, brother, best you don't waste it on the likes of us . . ."

I hung up the phone, smiling: Heather was free and, yes, we would meet. "You can tell me all about the latest milk-run. And about the joys of being over the dreaded Hump."

*

The phone call induced a euphoric state which lasted through showering and changing into Class 'A's, then through the lift to the village in a timely six-by. It stayed with me right up to the moment when I stepped inside the Sunday Roast. Where, in an instant, it withered and died, supplanted by shock, disbelief and hot, blinding anger.

Heather was there, seated at ease in our favorite corner, although it did appear, this time, not waiting for me. Azevedo was with her, parked in my place, his face close to hers. Talking, as ever, a blue streak.

She looked up then, saw me, and her hand came up to wave: I felt a pang that was stronger momentarily than hate and rage as

I saw how lovely she was with her flushed cheeks and bright, alert eyes.

Azevedo had not noticed me there.

I pushed rudely, not caring, through the crowded drinkers, ignoring someone unseen who called out, "hey, you . . ." Passing by Bob Reeves, the landlord, who offered a greeting to which I paid no heed. Seeing only Heather watching me, looking stricken now. I demanded, "I guess you've got some kind of reason, and maybe an explanation?"

"If you're willing to listen calmly and sensibly, then yes."

Azevedo looked up at me, his expression guarded, one finger caressing his moustache. "Hey, fella . . . how they hangin'?" He grinned. "Me an' Miss Heather here . . ."

"Can it," I told him.

His face darkened. "Now just a God damned minute . . . !"

"Shut the hell UP!" I did not care who overheard me, nor what anyone thought of it. "You read me . . . *Captain?*"

Heather began, "Denney . . ." I turned to glare at her, and she fell silent. The pub was very still. No one spoke; no one wished to miss any of this. And then someone came hurrying down the bar, easygoing Bob Reeves, always kindly toward Heather and me. "Not in here, gentlemen, if you please!" His gaze was cold and level as he informed me, "not the young lady's fault, sir."

I thanked him, and insisted that it was okay. "If we have to, we'll move it out in the street . . ." Thinking wildly, SCREW his being a captain, *and* the Golden Gloves quarter-final . . .

"There's no need for any of that, inside or out," Bob Reeves said severely.

It was Heather who assured him, "there won't be any trouble, Mister Reeves." And, to Azevedo. "I think you should leave now."

His eyes shifted between us, and I thought he might contest the point, but he came to his feet. "Don't go getting steamed-up, Lieutenant."

"Where you're concerned, jerk . . . and you'd be smart to keep this in mind," I snapped at him. "Heather's off-limits . . . now and always . . ."

"Denney, stop it!" Heather ordered sharply.

And Bob Reeves warned, "now then . . ."

Azevedo stared at me, shaking his head regretfully. "A little friendly advice, fella . . . grow up."

"Just blow!" We bristled at each other.

"Please sit down," Heather said to me.

And I sat, fuming, as Azevedo moved over to the public bar to join a group of pilots. I saw them glancing curiously in our direction, and heard Azevedo's laughter as, in a low, furious voice, Heather said, "it's over now. All right . . . understood? *Over!*"

"It had damned well better be." I watched Azevedo, and he watched me, and it was out in the open, good, honest, mutual hating . . .

"Let me," Heather said tautly. "Make one or two things perfectly clear."

I looked at her, thinking, here it comes. No one was watching us now. Bob Reeves had moved away to serve some customers. She had me to herself, with both barrels loaded. "Go ahead. Let's hear them."

She said flatly, "I'm over twenty one. Old enough to vote, hang, drink, marry without my parents' consent, and to choose freely with whom I want to speak . . ."

"So you *did* want to . . . ?"

"Would you mind?" She raised a hand. "I'm not finished." And went implacably on, "also where and when I want to. Likewise to decide for myself whether or not I'm what you choose to call off-limits." I could only nod agreement. "You got away with that only because I didn't want a worse scene than the one we had." Heather was a hostile stranger. "But I'm not your chattel, and I'm not in purdah."

"Look," I began. "I'm sorry about *that* . . ."

"You're always sorry, and always when it's too late." She looked me up and down. "Well, we have another of our so-called quaint Limey expressions to cover that . . . 'don't be sorry, be careful'." I gave another defeated nod, and she added musingly, "I'd say he had a point there, wouldn't you? About growing up . . . ?" She was shaking her head. "Denney, what's happening to you?"

"You mean you really don't know?"

"Would I ask?"

"We had a date, in case you'd forgotten. I was looking forward to it, and even imagined that you might be." She dropped her gaze at that. "I've never thought of you as a chattel. Only as the girl who walked into my life and turned it upside down." With that stated, I was not ready to yield everything, not ready to crawl. "About Azevedo, though, I know I'm not wrong. I can be sullen, and childish . . . okay, accepted. But I'm not a fool, Heather, and sometimes I get it right. Like now . . . with him, and you."

She looked up, hard-eyed. "I'm letting him get off with me, is that it? Encouraging him?"

"Not at all . . ." But I had been thinking that exactly. "Even so, he's trying his damnedest with you, and has been from the start."

"He's had no support from me, ever."

"I believe that," I lied. "I heard Bob Reeves say it wasn't your fault. But the Azevedos of this world need no inducements, or anyone to give them the go-ahead. They just charge in, and the hell with what anyone else says or thinks."

"Calm down," she urged me, and looked quickly around, but no single eye was on us. Azevedo, in gesticulating conversation, had his back turned. "Won't you try to be fair?"

"What's with fair?"

"The things we were discussing when you came steaming in."

"Yes? What about them . . . what were they?"

"At first . . . not that it's really anything to do with you . . . it was generalities. Small-talk."

"Oh, I'm sure . . . at *first*."

"And then, yes, he did ask me to go out with him."

"And you said?" I added bitingly, "*if*, of course, that's anything to do with me?"

"I said . . . thank you very much for asking, and most grateful for the thought," Heather told me coolly. "But that I was going out with you, and preferred to leave it like that." She asked, "will that do, or do you want to hear more?"

"Is there more?"

"If you will insist on punishing yourself."

"Why not? Let's go the distance."

"*Then* he said . . ." Her gray eyes appraised me. "That he was sorry, and hoped that he hadn't given offence, and offered his considered opinion that you were . . . the expression he used was . . . 'a lucky stiff'. And that he hoped you were aware of that."

And I could no longer meet that level gaze. "So, once again, I got it all wrong."

"You did, you know. You really did."

I took her hand then, our first contact. "I'm grateful for all you've told me. You see, it really *is* important for me to know."

"Why do you worry so much? Can't you trust?"

"I'm the worrying kind." I extended a tentative peace offering. "I did notice that he was doing all the talking."

"Isn't that his way? As you keep telling me?"

I took the barb as my due. "What was it? Heavy persuasion?"

"A little. Until I made things clear."

I pressed, "such as?"

"God!" Her brow creased in fresh irritation. "You really don't give up, do you?"

"Once I get my teeth in . . ." I found a smile somewhere. "Sorry."

She relented. "He aired his reasons why I should go out with him. It would be fun. He would show me a good time. He feels drawn to me, etcetera, etcetera. As already explained, I was not persuaded."

"I have to say I'm glad."

"And in the midst of not being persuaded, in bursts you, ticking like one of your own bombs."

"Ours don't usually tick, but never mind."

She began to smile, "And the rest we know."

*

I walked Heather home, and we talked for a while outside her home, or, to be more exact, *she* talked. Listing the numerous faults that she observed in me, and what I needed to do about them. I must worry less, and not be so doubting and needlessly, foolishly jealous. There must be no repeats, please, of what had taken place that evening. She had to go on living here, and American officers squabbling over her in public did nothing to enhance her standing within the community. One Gladys Gibbons was more than enough, thank you . . . And then, with no warning, she began to laugh aloud, making it all sound like a big joke. Which, of course, it was not.

I accepted without demur what she said, and acceptance lasted all the way back to the base. Only when I lay on my bunk, thinking, did the tide of doubt and anger come flooding back.

Not that I doubted Heather: Heather's word was her bond.

But . . . Azevedo? She might kid herself that she had put him in his place, and accepted as true the kindly-sounding words he offered about herself and me. He, though, would not see it as she did, but, instead, would imagine a subtle feminine artifice; Heather's come-hither challenge to his manliness and persistence, a persistence strengthened now by the thought of getting back at me.

He, I *knew*, would view Heather's refusal as a good move in a continuing game of wits: first his, then hers, then sit back to contemplate the board, considering what should come next . . .

The game would provide now the spice of added excitement as he pondered the presence of a third, rogue player . . . me. I had made my heavy, threatening move, and he would go all out for even-steven, then on to seize the advantage if he could. My angry and reckless move had tipped my hand, and from here on, between us, it was to be bare knuckle. And Azevedo, whatever his faults, would not be the one to back away from confrontation.

TWENTY SEVEN

I had been in England for eight months, had flown thirty six missions out of a (revised) total of forty; a period of time during which I had been exalted, thrilled, appalled and for ever terrified by what I did for a living, and the many ugly consequences of that. On the more positive and practical side, I was a much better pilot, my reflexes fine-honed to the majority of events to be encountered while flying a medium bomber in a vicious shooting war.

I had come to this place, and to all of that, a callow, self-opinionated and priggish youth, hampered by the too-easily pricked bubble of my self-esteem, and had learned—because I must—how to live reasonably and amicably under conditions which, once, I would have found intolerable.

With a young Englishwoman who, frequently, could delight and infuriate me at one and the same time, I had discovered the heights, and the counter-balancing depths, of what I could see as true love.

With all that—and in spite of Azevedo's jibe, and Heather's ready concurrence with it—I felt that I *had* grown up. Could it be possible to know all that I had known, and not do so?

Now, it was coming up to Christmas of 1944, a Christmas that would be my first away from home. To be spent on a sleet-swept English airfield, or at some bare and cheerless forward combat strip. Because this new festive season would bring no halt to war.

Back at Christmas of 1942 and '43, I had not stopped to consider the likelihood of finding myself in such a situation. True that that strong possibility did exist, but later, sometime . . . and maybe. To coin a piece of popular vernacular, not yet awhiles.

In '42 I was freshly-commissioned and very conscious of my gleaming gold second lieutenant's bars, my bright new wings. With a whole week of furlough to call my own, and anticipating the seasonal pleasures and comforts of Sutton Place. With mother and her friends, and her friends' biddable daughters; front and center stage for the Happy Warrior fresh from the thrills and spills of the advanced training base. Scott Fitzgerald all over again a quarter century on.

Christmas of '43 had been a more subdued occasion following two chastening years of set-backs, defeats, heavy casualties and hard going.

By then all sides were groggy, content to ease up and leave the grueling winter war to the Russians and their deep-frozen battlefields at Stalingrad and Kursk. Russians were showing all the signs of thriving on that kind of thing.

Christmas, a year—and many lifetimes—ago. Approaching graduation on the B-26 course, the base winding down for the holiday, and lucky enough to score myself a four-day pass *and* a round trip in a Marauder to La Guardia Field. Only a few friends and relatives calling in at Mother's penthouse, and the bachelor girls thinner on the ground, many gone away to the WAACS and WAVES.

Now, one more year melted away with December scheduled as just another month of pain and loss, which seemed, *still*, to be passing our Squadron by. So that we could speculate hopefully on our chances of a Christmas Day stand-down, even, maybe, an All-American Squadron drunk on Christmas Eve.

Whereas I wondered how much, if anything, I might hope to see of Heather over the holiday; might there be some small chance that I—the foreign soldier far from home—could be offered traditional hospitality at the Granger fireside?

Fond hopes and elusive fantasies, with no way to know that they would never be.

*

O'Connor leaned through the open door as I plied the razor in the draughty communal bathroom. "Prettyin' up for the big social whirl?" The languid Virginia drawl was much in evidence, which, usually, was not too good a sign. "If you is, ol' friend, then it's my sad an' bounden duty to inform you you ain't."

I stared at him, and the old dread grumbled into wakefulness after its long rest.

"Now what's happening?"

"Seems I'm pre-destined to be the bringer o' bad news, but looks like we went an' stepped in it again . . . an' deep this time." He stood there, shaking his head in utter weariness. "With the dumb clucks we got runnin' things at Su-PREME Headquarters Allied Expeditionary Forces, wouldn't surprise me one whit if, between us, we still managed to lose this God damned war."

*

It had been known for days that the German Fifth Panzer Army was on the move, taking up new positions at Prun on the Luxembourg border. While the Sixth Panzers maneuvered to take over the Fifth's old ground. Until, on December 16, along a forty mile front, both armies attacked westward together in the opening moves of the Battle of the Ardennes. The Bulge.

Once again, the stubborn Germans declined to follow the agenda we had set for them: a 'defeated' army striking brilliantly, lightning-swift, to smash its way through all opposition and catch us unprepared. Bad enough to do such things when those in the know had declared already that they could not; worse still to do them at Christmas!

They had picked out their best routes, and gaged precisely the strength of force ranged against them, over-running thinly-held positions like a tidal wave, routing a newly-arrived U.S. division at Malmédy, then, by swift flanking attack, taking out an armored unit, our troops forced back or encircled, with Corps and Army headquarters driven to ignominious flight.

The ensuing confusion and not infrequent panic were

exacerbated by the German tactic of sending fleets of V-l flying bombs into the crumbling lines as their paratroopers landed to the rear to snipe at our retreating columns. They dressed themselves in American uniforms, and made use of captured jeeps, trucks, half-tracks and tanks, so that beleaguered men, seeing them coming, imagining relief at hand, held their fire . . . and were slaughtered wholesale by those they imagined to be their friends. Up on the front line it came to be that no soldier could quite trust the man in the next foxhole, or expect to *be* trusted.

As communications collapsed, no one among the top brass, right up to Supreme Headquarters, knew what was going on. And the Supreme Commander was away, attending his chauffeur's wedding!

By December 17 it was acknowledged that Allied forces no longer controlled the situation in the Ardennes. As at Arnhem, weeks before, the Germans were holding the good cards, winning every hand with what looked like ridiculous ease.

*

"Now, men . . ." Lieutenant Colonel Friend appeared to get a kick out of referring to us as 'men'.

To Major Ambruster, our urbane and unflappable weather wizard, we were 'gentlemen' always, and Lieutenant Colonel Delaney enjoyed calling us 'chaps'. O'Connor believed that Lieutenant Colonel Friend had allowed himself to be influenced by too many John Wayne movies.

The colonel announced, "the Krauts have let go a haymaker and, by chance, connected. So we're temporarily in a corner, but holding on in the clinch. It's up to the seconds now to get our man shaped-up to hand out the sure-fire K.O."

The overheated room filled with restless and embarrassed muttering. Until, "*God* bless America!" O'Connor's strident tones boomed over our heads. "We're a lead pipe cinch to win!"

The ops shack rocked with laughter, but even irony as weighty as that was lost upon the unresponsive head of Lieutenant Colonel

Friend. "That's the attitude to take, men . . . *right*! That's how we'll make the last few yards for a touch-down!"

"Well, at least . . ." O'Connor sounded resigned. "We've managed to switch from the prize-fight analogy."

"Fine . . . fine, but that's enough now." Lieutenant Colonel Friend gazed about, firm-jawed and resolute. "Back to business."

As at Arnhem, we would fly support missions, their purpose to assist the Ardennes defense by cutting off the Germans' supply lines, starving them of fuel, ammunition and transport. We considered the reference to Arnhem an unfortunate one. At Arnhem, we had failed.

Not all the news was dire, Lieutenant Colonel Friend assured us. A number of sectors were holding, while surrounded units dug themselves in to harass the enemy from the rear. Stavelot had been lost, but Bastogne, although encircled, remained rock-solid, and was being supplied by air-drop. Patton's Third Army had been diverted from its eastward drive, and was heading to the rescue. It was, Lieutenant Colonel Friend vowed, only a matter of time. The medium bombers and fighter-bombers were to buy that time.

We were returning at once to Belgium, and would make our base at a fresh forward strip at Chiny on the Semois River. Where we would be only minutes distant from our targets, able to fly a continuous shuttle.

Lieutenant Colonel Friend offered comforting words on the subject of flak. "It's sure to be light. Everything Jerry's got is going into the ground battle. They've nothing to throw at us in the air but small-arms."

We had heard that too often before, although, this time maybe, considering how tight things were for the attacking Panzers, we might allow ourselves some small hope . . . ?

"Hey, now . . ." O'Connor nudged me gleefully. "Whaddya say *this* time round? We gettin' another kick at the cat? Back an' forth we go, an' every few minutes another mission chalked up? Jesus Christ, kid, if we start out early enough in the morning, we could have our tour finished in time for lunch!"

He was back on that hopeful kick for the first time since Arnhem, and, much as I would have wished to, I could not yet bring myself to share his optimism. It was left to Major Ambruster to drop the first hypothetical fly in the soothing ointment of O'Connor's hopes.

"I hate to play devil's advocate, but if we're to achieve results, we're going to have to get moving fast. Because, as per, the weather shows few signs of playing ball." He swept his hand across the map. "High pressure's calling the shots, giving us fine, cold conditions . . ." The hand edged down into France. "But down here, there's a tricky brew in the making . . ."

*

The afternoon was well-advanced by the time we had all landed at Chiny, with frozen dusk dropping over the winter-dead landscape. Clear, with not a breath of wind, the crisp air searing the lungs as we climbed down from the aircraft. Nothing whatever in that crystal atmosphere to lend credence to Major Ambruster's pessimistic prognosis. For once, the old magic had let him down, and he was wrong: flying conditions were ideal, and, in that still calm, we could hear clearly the steady thud of the artillery a few miles to the east.

It was too late that day to fly missions, and the airmen trooped off to eat and get some sleep, ready for the dawn start, leaving the line crews to swarm over our airplanes with their fuel hoses and oil drums, hoisting bombs into deep bellies.

*

Pitch dark still when the lights snapped on in the Quonset, and a grinning sergeant informed us, "sorry as all get-out, gents, but missions is scrubbed." He was assailed by a barrage of peevish enquiry, and waited patiently, saying nothing, until we settled down. "The answers youse lookin' for's all outside." The grin stretched. "Wrap up warm 'fore youse head out. Colder'n a whore's heart out there."

Everyone lay back, griping and listening to the drumming guns which were sounding oddly-muffled. Some men shambled out into the pre-dawn blackness, yelping shrilly about the cold. A muffled figure returned, shaking his head, to report, "Woxof."

An irate voice yelled back, "whaddya talkin' . . . Woxof?"

"I gotta spell it out for you, dummy?" The bearer of the news sounded irritable. "Woxof is *Woxof*, for Chrissakes!"

W-O-X-O-F . . . the meteorologist's acronym for 'Weather Obscured, Visibility Zero in Fog'.

"An' I'm tellin' you, brother, that means *obscured*," our informant declared with force. "You don't believe me, then get your sorry ass outside and see!"

The fog lay over the land like an iced blanket, coating the few squalid base buildings with heavy frost. Visibility was less than fifty yards, and we were the ones in the wrong, not Major Ambruster. He, as always, had provided ample and accurate warning: mid-winter high pressure over continental Europe with the strong risk of blinding freezing fog.

It mattered not that, only a few hundred feet overhead, the air would be clear of fog and brilliantly starlit. On the ground, we were without sight, and firmly stuck. Even if we attempted instrument take-off's, it would be impossible to locate a target, or to get ourselves safely down afterwards. And Major Ambruster had provided additional warning that the fog would be widespread, leaving us with nowhere else nearby to go.

It was Arnhem all over again, the fickle, two-timing weather coming down against us. And how the Germans would be loving this. The bastards had probably arranged it!

"No-good, God damned whoring son of a bitch!" someone was swearing bitterly and futilely. "Can someone . . . *anyone* . . . say to me when it's *us* that gets the breaks?"

*

At mid-morning, as if relenting, the fog lifted grudgingly above the trees, and the sun burned some sizeable holes. Horizontal visibility increased to a mile.

Everyone raced to the briefing as ground crew chiefs warmed the engines and saw that the wings and tail surfaces were swept clean of lift-destroying frost. The briefing was straightforward: go in low against a German motorized column halted on the highway between Neufchateau and Bastogne. Follow the highway, seek it out, find it, hit it. Flying time to target an estimated seven minutes.

The B-26s went booming off nose to tail, each rocking and sliding in the slipstream of the one preceding, scrambling into the misty air, heading out into the gray north-east as O'Connor crouched, chuckling, over the Rube Goldberg bombsight. "Swear I never thought I'd see the day when departure point and I.P. were one and the same!"

But the fog hung on, never quite giving up, trailing vapor tentacles through the treetops; at dusk it would regain the upper hand. Very little to be seen below, and I flew the compass heading with Andy Devine beside me, poring over his strip map, picking out the rare landmarks. He offered worriedly, "be hard-put to make more'n one trip, two at the most, before she socks in again."

I nodded agreement, but even two missions would put thirty eight in the bag, leaving the final two to go. Tomorrow, with luck, another quick break, and two more? After which the fog could move in for good if it wanted. We would go home on the subway!

I thought with envy of 'Mean an' Ugly' out there with us in the bomber stream: for Boyard and the others on board, this was it. Get back from it safe and their Stateside tickets were ready and paid for.

In the end, the weather split matters fifty-fifty between both sides: the fog broken just enough for target identification, yet not enough to deny the Germans a measure of concealment.

There were sufficient visible landmarks for us to take up positions for the run-in, then, right on time and in place, there was the highway, first a wide, shallow bend, then a straight stretch . . . and there they were, sitting there, waiting! The entire column stationary; a long line of soft-top trucks with half-tracks and armored cars interspersed among them. More fog was closing in, but damage had been done already, big fires blazing, the black smoke of burning fuel rising vertically in frozen, unmoving air. Fires and smoke to provide us with vital target markers as more fog gaps revealed the column's armored spearhead . . . many tanks, Mark IVs, and the slab-like, long-gunned hulls of Tigers.

We made our run on one especially large fire. "Fix on that," O'Connor commanded. "And we'll be straight down the middle of the road. Even if we don't see a thing, we'll score."

"Roger," I said.

"Keep 'er steady, son."

I did it for him because, for once, it was easy: with all that smoke flagging us in, how could we miss. Plus the blessed fact of no distracting flak: the Germans appeared to have buttoned-up inside their steel hulls, or high-tailed it sensibly into the roadside woods, making no attempt to defend themselves, the sky empty of their fighters, making it feel like an old-style Texas training mission . . .

O'Connor released at two hundred feet, yelling at me to, "climb her out *steep!*" I lifted 'Big Apples' from the cauldron with the stick right back and throttles open to full take-off power, picking up a zooming thousand feet of clearance almost before the bombs were down. Hearing Sergeant Patecki whooping on the intercom, "oh, SHIT! Dunno what we nailed, but we sure nailed it!" There had been the initial surge and ripple of the detonations. "Then some Goddam ol' thing went an' blew its cork . . . like ammo, maybe, or a tank. Whatever, it's screwed *their* plans for a foggy Friday!"

A few minutes saw us back at Chiny with thirty seven missions well in hand. By then, though, a thin, high overcast was spreading up from the south, killing the sun's meager warmth, and more fog was swirling in as we circled for the approach. We would fly no more that day, and my thoughts turned once more, with anxiety, to tomorrow?

*

We taxied in past the solitary B-26 standing forlorn and alone at the edge of the strip, its nose buckled, the plexiglas dome smashed, both propellers bent. The mirror image of 'Big Apples' at Senlis.

"Well, *whaddya* know?" O'Connor sounded pleasantly surprised. "If it ain't 'Bomb Boogie'. Could it be that Senhor Bigmouth went an' laid an egg?"

It had been an exploding tire in the middle of the take-off run, the aircraft out of control, swerving violently, at high speed, off the strip, collapsing the nosewheel. We knew about that. We had been down that route.

Amongst the crew, some cuts and bruises, a broken nose, and Azevedo had a fractured arm, which meant a flight back to England as soon as the weather permitted. News that I greeted with dismay: his arm could be treated without difficulty at the base hospital; Azevedo would be grounded but ambulatory, free to roam at will, to drop down to the village and drink beer all day, and play one-handed darts. Free to spend time with Heather, with me far away, unable to queer his pitch. His move, and a good one.

Thus ended December 17, forty first anniversary of the Wright Brothers' flight from Kill Devil Hill. Despite all those years, and the phenomenal strides made since then in aviation, it did seem, on this red-letter day, that we had achieved little more in the air than they had.

*

The fog granted no favors on the following day. Crews hung about, dressed and ready and bitching, impatient to go, but it did not lift, and, at three in the afternoon, the order came to stand down. The only ones with grounds for celebration were the men from 'Mean an' Ugly' for whom it was all over.

We listened with increasing anxiety to the news stories put out by the B.B.C. and our own Armed Forces Network, hearing that the Germans had committed two hundred and fifty thousand men and two thousand tanks to their Ardennes campaign. Their aim, it was stated, was to re-capture Antwerp, driving a wedge between the Allied armies with a view to making us change our minds about unconditional surrender, and look more favorably upon a negotiated peace. After which Germany, with Der Führer still at the helm, would become our pal, and we would all gang up to kick the Russians back to where they came from.

The radio broadcast also the atrocity stories, which alarmed us, and made us mad, and vengeful. Of how S.S. troops were taking no prisoners: ugly reports being confirmed of a massacre of American captives in a field near Malmédy; of Allied wounded left behind being shot where they lay. The bulletins went on to define the battlefield situation as 'fluid', a word that translated with ease into 'snafu', 'screw-up'.

*

December 19, then 20, ticked by with reports of the Germans still advancing, keeping up the pressure; information supported by the constant thud of guns edging closer, becoming louder, out there somewhere in the fog. Stranded, we began to hear also of contingency plans. In case the enemy should overrun Chiny.

Being captured on the ground was an event that none of us had ever taken seriously until then. One thing to be shot down and taken prisoner, quite another to find ourselves rounded up, hands in the air, beside our useless airplanes. If, by then, the Germans were back in the mood to spare their captives?

On December 21, with the artillery sounds too close for anyone's peace of mind, preparations to destroy the aircraft were being completed, and for everyone to pile aboard whatever transport could be found, and, ignominiously, to bug out. And would the ordinary dogfaces fighting in the mud and snow allow the high and mighty A.A.F. to live that one down?

Right up to Christmas Eve, though, that was in the cards for us, as, worryingly nearby, the attackers reached their farthest point of advance at Dinant. And there, in the most literal sense, ran out of gas.

On Christmas morning an American thrust from the north turned them back.

And the weather, dependably treacherous on whim in its dealings with either side, switched allegiance once more, the fog clearing away in the night to leave the skies of morning bright blue and cloudless, the conditions in which we could fly and fly.

The Marauders went out from Chiny to accompany the Typhoons and Thunderbolts and Mitchells and Mosquitoes and Fortresses and Liberators converging on the Ardennes sector from bases in Belgium, Holland, France and England, and the radio announcers exulted over the figures: five thousand aircraft to blast the German lines out of existence, and destroy their supply columns and communications. A quarter million men and two thousand tanks—even when out of gas—took a lot of killing.

From each mission the jubilant crews returned yelling that it was Normandy again, another Falaise, with the added satisfaction of having it take place in the Germans' very own corner of the world.

American units surrounded and cut off until they found their roles reversed. No longer beleaguered, freshly supplied, they became a sizeable force in the enemy's rear to block attempts at an orderly withdrawal.

Through all the heady days of changing fortunes, as New Year 1945 approached, 'Big Apples' did not fly once.

*

We attended the Boxing Day briefing, then trooped out to the airplane, strapped in and sat waiting for the start-up flare. When it rose, I hit the switches, first the left engine, then the right. The left fired readily, blowing smoke, the propeller blades blurring as the instrument needles jumped into place.

The right engine then: primer, fuel booster, mixture, starter . . . the prop blades groaning over slowly, awaiting the life-giving kick from the magnetos. The first ignition cough, and more clouding blue oil smoke. Followed by sudden and unexpected ugly sounds that transmitted a bone-shaking shudder through the airframe. The right hand propeller stopped turning, locked solid.

*

'Big Apples' had swallowed a pot.

A piston in a tired and over-stressed engine which had been standing idle for days in temperatures low enough to render metal fragile and brittle. The sudden shock of movement, the first mixing of fuel and air in the cylinder, then the too-great pressure on an ailing piston as it stroked downward to compress super-heated gases into raw power. All too much to take, the piston disintegrating inside the cylinder, freezing the engine . . . and we did not fly that day, or again in the great Ardennes battle.

"I tell you, it's a chickenshit *conspiracy!*" Andy Devine sounded close to tears as he sprawled on his bunk, furiously cracking his knuckles. I wished that he would not do that; it was setting my teeth on edge. "That miserable, lousy, stinkin' pile o' crap!"

We others rose at once to the defense of our airplane. "Son, you can't blame a machine for bein' a machine," O'Connor pointed out. "They get their off days as well."

"Yeah, well maybe so . . ." Andy conceded the point grudgingly. "All the same, she's got one shit sense of timin'. *Four* missions . . . we shoulda cleaned up in a single day, God damn it! Instead, we frig a whole week away, and *then* what do we end up with?" No one responded to that rhetorical question, we all knew. "If that ain't gettin' shafted by the fickle finger o' fate, then I dunno what is!"

A swallowed pot would mean one more in a growing series of engine changes. There were no spare engines at Chiny, nor the men qualified to install them. Engine and men must be flown in, and would not be while Chiny lay at risk still in the forward zone.

'Big Apples' sat out forlornly on the line with 'Bomb Boogie' for company, frost-bound and silent, her crew once more unemployed, watching with helpless envy as the scores of other crews rose by up to four missions a day. Suffering the ultimate mortification of having juniors catch up, then overtake us, two crews going on to completion while we sat around and twiddled our thumbs.

"I *ask* you," Andy Devine appealed, looking about fruitlessly for someone or something to blame. "Where's the God damn' justice?"

*

The other Squadron aircraft flew back to England on January 2, taking 'Bomb Boogie's' stranded crew members with them.

We remained at Chiny. When—*when*—our replacement engine arrived, we were assured that it would be installed and tested inside a day. Then we, too, might leave.

On the battlefront our armies were advancing once more, gathering momentum as they drove deeper into Germany. The two Panzer divisions had performed miracles, and come perilously close to breaking our line. Close, though, did not count. That was all over now as the artillery sounds grew fainter, moving away to the east. And, on January 4, a C-47 landed.

"Well, heavens to Betsy an' woe is me," O'Connor cooed. "Does that mean it's safe around here now?"

Men worked to rig lifting gear and off-load the new engine. We stood and watched, criticizing and finding fault as they labored in the frigid air, intolerant of the smallest hitch or delay, begrudging the numbed, cursing mechanics their snatched smoke breaks, and the chance to huddle for a few minutes around the coke stove in the operations shack.

TWENTY EIGHT

There was discernible irony in the manner in which Sergeant Flaherty painted on the single bomb symbol that represented our contribution to the Ardennes conflict. "Just th' one, huh?" he had acknowledged our depressing achievement. His grin clashed with the sympathetic tone. "Well, every little helps. All adds up, you know."

There had been significant changes at Tiverell Lacey during our enforced and prolonged absence. All the completed crews had left, one more bitter pill to be choked down. 'Mean an' Ugly', the veteran of many missions dating back to 1943, was being prepared for the flight back to the United States where she would be placed on display at an Army Air Forces museum.

We listened to the scant information available on the fate of Glenn Miller, gone missing on a flight from England to Paris. His Norseman liaison aircraft had flown out blind into the same dense fog that smothered the battlefields, and was not seen again.

*

The phone rang on emptily inside Heather's house, and I waited, willing a response that would not come.

I put down the receiver, and decided . . . take a chance. Grab a ride to the village, then walk to the house. By that time, someone might be there . . .

But the place lay in darkness, silent, and no one appeared in answer to my tentative knock. Not satisfied, I wandered around to the conservatory where, in the glow from a young moon, I made out the remembered shapes of the white cane furniture, the plants in their pots, the same glass-topped table from which we had taken tea. A book lay open on the table, while, on one chair, a pale garment was draped. Heather's mac? I peered within like a wistful voyeur.

Heather had not been expecting me, and probably thought that I was still stuck in Belgium. No reason for her to be sitting at home awaiting the warrior's return. It would have been pleasant, though, if she had been.

Now, of course, I would go away from there, and try the telephone again later. She would be at home, and would answer my ring; everything would be explained. I would extend my belated Christmas greetings, and throw in a Happy New Year: so sorry I could not manage it on time, but, about then, I was expecting to be shot by the S.S.

There was no justifiable reason why I should try the conservatory door; or why, when I did, that it should be, surprisingly, unlocked. Even then, I had no true excuse for opening it, and my hesitant "hello?" was a poor subterfuge, the prelude to my explanation—should someone appear suddenly to confront me—that I was just double-checking. When no one did show up, although I told myself that I would not enter, I was stepping inside, driven by an empty longing for contact of some kind.

The air was still and cold and filled with the mingling scents of green vegetation and nurtured earth, with the overriding tang of coffee. And another, familiar waft of . . . Heather's cologne.

I picked up the draped garment; I had been right, it was her white mac. Furtive and ashamed, I trolled through the pockets, finding her handkerchief in one, and the tiny bottle of hoarded cologne. I withdrew the stopper and breathed deeply of the fragrance that hung about her always, an illusory way in which to draw her close.

I wondered then about keeping the handkerchief, a sop to disappointment, and put the idea out of my head: I could not let myself sink to petty theft. I returned it, but did permit myself the small indulgence of a smear of the cologne on my fingertips before leaving, closing the door, walking away with the sweetness of her in my nostrils.

*

The Sunday Roast was jam-packed and, at first, I did not see her. Seated in our corner with Azevedo, laughing at something he was saying to her. Azevedo with his broken arm in plaster, the wounded hero. Exactly as I had pictured it. I watched them there, feeling the chill tightness in my chest, until I had to look away, only to meet the troubled gaze of Bob Reeves from his nightly place of duty behind the bar. Who grimaced regretful concern at me. Bob, this time, could have no excuses to offer for Heather.

The pain eased a little, and cleared my head to a state of drab acceptance: I knew then that I had been expecting this, or something like it, for some time. Even this late in the game, though, I still could not figure out why it should be.

I saw the wary question in Bob Reeves' eyes, and shook my head: no, Bob, I shan't cause a scene or pick a fight. After all, with the cards out on the table now, what would be the point of that? Thinking of that could induce the wry awareness that I must be growing up fast. Heather would be proud of me. If Heather knew, or cared . . .

I walked through the bitter January night, the entire three-mile stretch back to base. Vehicles passed, and I was offered rides which I turned down, waving them on, making labored wisecracks about having begun a health kick. Wanting to walk, because that allowed me the solitude I must have, the time needed for going over the pictures in my mind: Heather with *me* in that corner, listening and laughing in that self-same way at the foolish and bombastic things I said. Watching me with calm and attentive gray eyes that could not, would not, deceive.

I marched through the darkness and the iron frost with the scent of her cologne on my fingers, weeping and unable to stop it, the hot tears turning icy on my face.

*

Unfailingly perceptive, O'Connor wanted to know what it was all about, and would not be deterred by my sullen attempts to evade interrogation. "Well, now . . . just give me three guesses."

"Sure, go on . . . *guess*," I told him pettishly.

"Woman trouble, woman trouble and woman trouble," he said at once. "Heather, Heather and Heather."

I tried to joke. "That's six guesses."

"Let's call them inter-related."

I talked to him then, a friend in need, *wanting* to, busting to get it said, the flood-gates buckling under intolerable pressures, undermined further by O'Connor's quiet sympathy. Until I reached an end of sorts. "Something you said that night at the Savoy. Talking of Jeanne." He gave a guarded nod. "That you hoped I'd be as lucky, woman-wise, as you."

"It's *that* bad, is it?"

"As bad as it gets."

I tried to explain how, since London, it had gone downhill with Heather. And had hit rock bottom tonight.

"Son, so many people keep tellin' me from rock bottom there's no way left but up."

I shook my head, unable or unwilling to accept encouragement. "Not this time. I don't think so."

O'Connor looked reflective. "What a hell of a shame it was only his arm got broken." He patted my shoulder. "What we need now, we band of brothers, is a long shot."

"What long shot?"

His answer was typically oblique and unrevealing. "As per, it would seem that I have one or two left in store. Held back for that good, old rainy day." He winked. "Which does seem to be upon us now."

*

"Lieutenant, you got an incoming call over at Headquarters." The corporal looked down at me, flopped on my bunk.

"What call would that be?" Instinctively, I pictured an irate Lieutenant Colonel Delaney with some fresh gripe.

"Couldn't say, sir. But they're holding the line, so you better make a move."

Or, just possibly, it could be Heather, feeling the need to make an urgent call? Someone—Bob Reeves, perhaps—giving her the word, so that, now, she was feeling a need to explain herself, to set the record straight. I'll listen, I promised Heather silently. You'll get a full hearing. And, if I *am* wrong, then I will humbly beg your pardon.

*

"Denney, darling . . ." My mother's voice coming to me through what sounded like heavy surf. "I simply had to find out how you are."

"Well, okay, fine . . . no strain." But she had caught me out completely, and I could come up with nothing worthwhile to say. I fell back on flippancy. "Who are you blackmailing?"

"What was that, dear . . . ?" She came through the breakers distantly. "Something about . . . was it *blackmail*?" She sounded a little put out.

"A silly joke, Mother . . . skip it. I was only wondering how you managed to swing a trans-Atlantic call in wartime. When F.D.R. and Stalin and Churchill have to get in line."

"Oh, there are always ways." I heard her conspiratorial laugh from beyond the ocean. "I did try at Christmas, but I was told you were out somewhere . . ." A note of reproach pierced the surf.

"That's one way of putting it, I guess. Although maybe you've heard by now . . . on the radio?"

"Radio . . . ?" She seemed puzzled, and that was how much, I thought, the Ardennes offensive had meant to the folks at home. Something that you could not seem to recall.

"There was some trouble with the Germans over Christmas, Mother. It kept us busy for a few days."

"But you're all right, aren't you?"

"Couldn't be better . . ." Heather's attentive face smiled into the loathed one of Azevedo, and my cheery words turned to ashes.

She informed me, "I've sent off your Christmas package, although I can't say when you'll get it. Everyone here is using the war as a convenient excuse for slovenliness."

"Thanks. I'll look forward to it whenever . . ." Thirty five hundred miles of open sea between us: all the string-pulling and finagling she must have gone through to get this call cleared, and all we had to share were banalities. "And I've cabled you some money," she said.

"Money . . . ?"

"It's only a small sum, so please don't get all stiff and proud again, dear. As you did beforehand when I . . ."

"Mother . . ."

"A little extra for you at Christmas . . . this one time," she insisted. "Because you couldn't be here with us. Two hundred and fifty dollars being held for you at our London embassy. You'll be able to collect it there."

"Two-*fifty*? Hey, that's swell!"

"I'm so glad it pleases you. Christmas and New Year, that special time for us all . . ." Her voice was swamped for a moment by a heavy wave. " . . . a little party for all your friends in the airplane."

Only Mother could make O'Connor et al. sound like my fellow-sufferers of long ago at the detested Connecticut prep school. "We'll have that party," I told her with warmth. "And all thanks to you."

She directed, ever helpful, "you must choose somewhere tasteful . . . in London, perhaps? London's a wonderful place, you know." She had never been to London.

"Tasteful as they come," I vowed, and tried without success to ignore the pain-filled memories: carpeted passageways, an ivory-colored door trimmed with gold . . . steam clouds pouring through a bathroom door . . . "London, war or no war, is really tasteful."

It was planned out already in my mind: a monumental drunk

to obliterate all sorrows, all memories, every-damned-thing, in good, dependable one hundred-proof. Two hundred and fifty bucks would pay for a respectable, and tasteful, level of obliteration . . .

"Are you there, dear?" my mother called through the surf.

"Sorry." And would the strain in my answering laugh be apparent to her across the miles? "I was just gloating over that money." Words in passing, like those of strangers on a train. I asked again, filling our precious and irreplaceable time with inanities, how she had managed to get an overseas call put through.

"Oh, it was the office . . ." My father's old law firm would be for ever 'the office', an airy—and erring—presumption of proprietorial right. "They have a vast amount of contract war work now, and they're highly thought-of in Washington, as you would expect. So that when I suggested it to Mister de Villiers, why, he went ahead and arranged everything . . ." Her contented and well-fed laughter flowed across the sea to me.

I thought, smiling, of old Jeb de Villiers; living caricature of the shrewd, winking, nose-tapping litigator, thickly armored against the decades of rebuke passed down from the bench. Who knew the right strings to pull, the best arms to twist. In his dusty, law-book respect for his dead partner's widow.

"He located you without difficulty," my mother explained, adding on an aggrieved note, "although it does seem that I'm not permitted to know exactly where you are."

"No big deal, Mother. Uncle Jeb tracked me down, and now we're talking. Isn't that enough?"

Never one to miss the smallest opening, she got back at me with a timely reproach. "Darling boy, apart from the fact that he is not blood kin of ours, I don't think it's entirely respectful to refer to one of Mister de Villiers' stature as 'Uncle Jeb'." I let it pass, casting about for a more neutral topic, and was forestalled once more by her enquiry, deceptively-casual, about, "this delightful-sounding and interesting young woman of yours?"

Of course I had mentioned Heather in my letters, and my mother's replies had been noncommittal. Now, like someone backed into a corner, I evaded, stammering awkward response: everything was fine . . . good . . . just hunky-dory, and thanks. And then, more achingly truthful, "she's hardly *mine*, you know." Telling of friendship, and of how we were shunning commitment or heavy involvement. A claim that, at that moment, sounded wildly optimistic.

My mother expressed her relief and pleasure over our sensible behavior: we were 'being smart'. Unlike so many foolish young people in this war. Who, following unseemly haste, were certainly repenting now at leisure. A vision took shape before me . . . Gladys Gibbons on the Savoy dance floor with her skirts flying: now *there* was repentance for you . . .

I was almost glad when the operator—in an uncompromising Bronx voice—warned that time was up. My mind, still skittering, evolved images of her: old, young . . . caring or bored? Concerned there at her switchboard for the feelings of a mother and son separated by war, or chewing listless gum as she eavesdropped on our final hasty good wishes and goodbyes and thanks a lot for callings. Until she pulled the plug on us.

I hung up, thinking with sadness of all the things left unsaid. Looking at my watch then, and subtracting the time zones: for my mother, ten forty three in the morning, Eastern Standard Time. She would be seated by her ivory telephone: mere *white* phones, she felt strongly, were evidence of upstarts and the *nouveau riche*. With her, too, almost certainly, would be her mid-morning pot of Sanka. Sanka, it was claimed in the advertisements, did not fray the nerves like other, lesser coffees.

*

I was writing the obligatory thank-you letter . . . for the call, the Christmas package on its way (if some enterprising U-boat had not already nailed it), for the money, when O'Connor appeared, beaming and rubbing his hands in a satisfied way. "Kid, we're hittin' the bricks."

"Yeah . . . *right*." I glanced up, skeptical. "How's that exactly?"

He sighed, and perched himself on my bunk. "That's what I love so much about you . . . your immediate and unfettered enthusiasm." He leaned forward to confide. "We, *Herr Leutnant*, have scored again. *Jawohl!*"

"That's nice," I said. "You must tell me about it sometime."

"Hey there, Sourpuss . . ." He wagged a finger at me. "Now, you sit up straight and brace yourself for the all-important question. Which is . . . what would you say to the idea of a forty eight-hour pass?"

"Would 'whoop-ee' do?" I wondered, "*if* it's for real?"

"The absolute ding-dang McCoy . . . o ye of little faith."

"Okay to enquire at whose head you pointed your forty five for something like that?"

"Suffice it that I was owed a favor." O'Connor added, "now I ain't."

"Then thanks, Buzz. Jesus . . . I could really use something like that."

"Ho-ho-HOLD it . . . let's not get ourselves carried away. This-here's not entirely altruistic, you know. On that small matter of favors, it's you in the hot seat now."

"Suits me. And I may just have the best way to square the deal. Although we'd need to go to London for that."

"London *was* kind of envisioned."

"Grosvenor Square?"

"A highly salubrious region of the great metrollops," he agreed, eyeing me. "Now, may one enquire as to why?"

"The U.S. embassy." I smirked at him. "Where there awaits at this very moment a banker's draft for two hundred and fifty beautiful smackers made out to yours truly. To help finance the expedition."

"That may serve in some small measure," O'Connor observed judiciously. "To lessen your already crippling indebtedness to me."

TWENTY NINE

On request, I displayed my I.D., and was asked to sign a paper, upon which the bank draft was handed over. An embassy official remarked that I now possessed funds for the purchase of much red paint to spread around town.

It was Saturday afternoon, and the banks were closed: no one at the embassy could cash the draft. The official thought about it. "Hold tight, Lieutenant. Let me make a call."

O'Connor and I waited, listening as the obliging official outlined the situation. "A Lieutenant Pilgrim from the Air Corps . . . yes. Sure, we'll vouch for him." He winked across at us, and O'Connor, not to be outdone, winked back. "You've just made this young officer's weekend," the official declared then.

O'Connor mouthed at me, "*and* this young officer's!"

We were to present ourselves without delay at the London Post Exchange and ask for a Mr. David R. Speissmann who would be pleased to accommodate us.

The Marine guards saluted as we left the embassy, and one held the door open. O'Connor thanked him, and wondered mildly, "I guess London's better duty to pull than Guadalcanal, huh?"

"I wouldn't know, Captain." The Marine's fixed expression did not relax. "We took Guadalcanal in 'forty three. We're back in the Philippines now."

"Well, whatever next?" O'Connor shook his head in wonderment. "Where have I *been* all this time?"

A cab delivered us to the PX where Mr. Speissmann counted out sixty two pounds and ten shillings, the healthy equivalent of two hundred and fifty U.S. dollars. I picked up the bundle of

416

fivers and single notes, and thought with a fresh pang of Heather, of afternoon tea and a silly spat over money . . .

In another cab, O'Connor leaned back with a sigh of contentment as London flowed and rumbled around us. "I got this feeling in my water, kid . . . the wind's set fair for the weekend." He chuckled. "If you'll permit the mixing of a few metaphors?" He went on dreamily, "how 'bout that? Sixty two quids and ten bobs. Coupled with what you had in your poke when we hit town?"

"A little over twenty," I said.

"To which add my humble thirty." He looked pleased. "Adding up to a combined pot of rather better than a C-note in big, bold sterling currency. We're loaded, bubber. Let's go!"

*

On the Town with money to spend, indulging ourselves in what the British termed fondly a pub crawl. We rode numerous cabs across a wide area of central London, and remembered to eat lunch somewhere, and drink some more with that. After the meal, we resumed our seeking out and exploration of public houses until they all shut their doors at the same time, and threw us out on the street. By then, feeling no pain, we pondered our forthcoming moves on a grimy corner in Shepherd Market, where two tough-looking hookers with not a smile to share between them offered us a fun time.

O'Connor swayed, benign and expansive, before their hard eyes. "Ah, me . . . the sporting ladies of Merry England . . ."

The tarts exchanged scathing looks. "Pissed," said one. "As arse'oles."

"Yanks," the other said. Which explained everything.

"Bit bomb-'appy, I 'spect." The first tart displayed carious teeth in a rictus grin. "Are you bomb-'appy then, darlin's?"

"Always deliriously happy about bombs," O'Connor assured her. "In all their shapes, sizes and degrees of explosive potential . . ."

The tarts laughed, and the second one said, "sounds like some punters I've known."

"Now, to some . . ." O'Connor was in the mood to lecture upon his specialist subject. "Bombs are but bombs. While to others, like ourselves, they are meat and drink, our daily bread, music and dance, also poetry in downward motion . . . the very stuff of life and death . . . *that* dependent upon which end you happen to be on . . ." He bent his head reverently. "Now, *mesdames*, a single, humble request . . ."

"No free shags," one tart warned.

The other confirmed, "we're not the bloody Red Cross, you know."

"An' we don't give a twopenny stuff for Allied solidarity, neither," the first finished.

O'Connor appealed to me, "aren't they splendid? Like Abbott and Costello." He appeared all set to continue the debate at length.

"Well? You want it or not?" the first tart demanded with aggression. "We 'aven't got all day for fartin' about."

"Alas, you judge us harshly." O'Connor looked mournful. "We wish merely to enquire the nature of the amenities on offer. And, of course, your usual tariff."

They looked marginally more agreeable then. "'Ow much you want to spend?"

"Show us the menu, Ma'am."

It came without frills, direct and brutal. "Toss you off for fi' bob. Ten bob for a naughty shortie in a taxi, once 'round Green Park. Sucky-suck's a quid a go. Or . . ." They eyed us calculatingly. "A fiver gets you all night in, an' anything you fancy."

"But no bleedin' breakfast," the second tart added, and laughed.

"Such delights . . ." O'Connor was sounding ecstatic, and I grew alarmed then: was he seriously considering . . . ?

The first tart ground ample hips beneath a skirt of unalluring tightness. "Well?"

O'Connor raised a finger. "One more telling question."

"Soddin' *questions!* Worse'n Bow Street nick . . ."

"Merely to enquire . . ." O'Connor smiled a sleepy cat smile.

"How you can provide us with more of a fun time than we're having already?" I breathed again; it *was* a spoof.

"Well, you can bugger off quick as you like if that's 'ow you feel." Their two faces were granite. I thought of the Gorgon Sisters, and began to giggle helplessly.

"Pair o' bleedin' poufters," the second tart accused. "That what you are, then? Bloody nancy-boys? Fancy a bit o' the brown, do you? Like your vice versa?" She sounded righteous and outraged.

"Go on, sling your 'ook," the first one said.

"Should I infer from that, dear ladies," O'Connor asked with unflagging courtesy. "That you'd rather we were elsewhere?"

"Bloody Yanks!" They lifted long-suffering eyes to an unresponsive sky.

*

Yet another cab stopped for us at Hyde Park Corner. O'Connor directed the driver to the Regent Palace Hotel.

We had agreed on the Regent Palace, a second-string hostelry off Piccadilly Circus. It suited me: I could not have faced Grosvenor House.

The cab driver took careful note of our well-oiled state, and outlined the ground rules. "Don't want you causin' no trouble in my vehicle."

We vowed that there would be none.

"An' no spewin' your guts up, neither!"

O'Connor sensed my bafflement. "The gentleman is concerned that we might puke over his pristine upholstery."

I called through the glass partition in honest enquiry, "is this one of those cabs where you can get a naughty shortie around Green Park for ten bobs?"

"We'll 'ave none o' that in 'ere, thank you," the driver told me stiffly.

We crawled along Piccadilly, ducking and diving amongst the big red busses with their windows netted over against bomb blast, and I thought anew of Heather . . . noticing the way that her face blurred in my now drunken memory. Being drunk enough for that to happen had to be a good thing.

*

Trying not to waken him, I asked O'Connor, "are you asleep?" "I might have been." He stirred on the other bed. "But for your damn-fool questions."

I said I was sorry. ". . . just thinking."

"A refreshing new experience for you, I'm sure . . . but must you do it out loud?" He sat up and stared at me. "Okay . . . I'll bite. Thinking about what?"

"Jeanne," I said.

Being with O'Connor in London while my head was filled with Heather, it followed that I would think also of the beautiful Wren officer. Here we were, though, celebrating something or other; Heather was not with us, and there had been no mention of Jeanne.

"So?" O'Connor enquired levelly. "What about her?"

"Wondering if she'll be putting in an appearance somewhere along the way?"

"Would it trouble you if she did?"

I thought of Azevedo then. "It would put me behind the eight ball where three's a crowd's concerned."

He said tersely, "forget about it."

"Is . . . anything wrong?"

"What should be wrong? No, nothing is, so relax."

"Sorry again. Also glad, let me say. I'd hate for anything to spoil it between you two."

"Nothing has, and nothing will." He was grinning again. "You incurable romantic, you."

"That's me," I said.

"All's well," O'Connor re-assured me. "It's just that Jeanne's far distant at the moment. Pursuing her nautical pursuits in Bonnie Scotland. This weekend, it's just us chickens, kid."

"As long as I know," I said.

"We're grown-up people, Jeanne and me," O'Connor offered

in explanation. "We have this understanding about no over-possessiveness or unseemly jealousies on either side. What we get up to away from each other is each other's affair, pure and simple . . ." He had lain back once more, and his voice was blurring on the brink of sleep. "Stick around awhiles with me, son, and you'll soon get the drift . . ." A drowsy chuckle emerged. "Some light dalliance to brighten our drab spinsterhood . . ."

After a little while he began, gently, to snore.

*

We ate dinner at the hotel: O'Connor's still-unstated plans appeared to be of a post-prandial nature.

He excused himself between dessert and coffee. "Time to make a call. Executive orders must be issued."

He was soon back and looking pleased with himself. "It's on, pard . . . we're hittin' them beaches."

"Any likelihood of you telling me what beaches?"

"Hold your horses." He wagged an admonitory finger. "This is to be your great big, fat surprise."

The hotel summoned the latest cab for us, and the doorman gave directions to Upper Berkeley Street.

"An address," O'Connor explained. "Sited at the outer limits of respectability. London West One by the skin of its teeth. You should know," he informed me. "That anybody who's anybody in this town covets a West One address. Nearby to this one, and just across the Edgware Road, it becomes West Two, which is most definitely the wrong side of the tracks."

"And, with all this," I supposed. "You're still not telling me what's about to happen at Upper Berkeley Street, London West One?"

"You know, you're right . . . I don't think I am." He leaned back then and appeared to go to sleep.

*

Even in the masking black-out, Upper Berkeley Street looked

seedy. Rows of terraced houses, flat-faced, three or four floors high, where furtive slivers of light betrayed carelessly-drawn blackout drapes.

I ventured, "looks like Charles Dickens' London."

"With some Jack the Ripper and Sherlock Holmes tossed in for heightened effect." O'Connor was paying off the cab. "So? What d'you think?"

"Not sure yet. Kind of creepy."

"It gets better as you go along."

"*What* does? Buzz? What the hell's going on?"

"Stand by one . . ." He shone a flashlight on a door number . . . 50. "You're about to find out." I followed the stabbing beam past 52 and 54. At 56 he said, "bingo." It looked as gloomy and unprepossessing as the others. There might be snob value attached to a West One address, but I could not see it. "Come on," I demanded. "What *is* this place? Some high-class whorehouse?"

He chuckled in the dark. "Would I lead my so-o-o-o virtuous pardner off'n the straight an' narrow?"

"I'd call it more than a possibility."

"What we have here . . ." He shone the light on the door again. "Is a li'l ol' palace o' delights." He knocked, and, soon, muffled sounds came from within. A woman's voice wanted to know, "who is it?"

"Al Capone," O'Connor called back softly. "An' I went an' brung Dillinger wid me."

The door swung open at once to reveal a dim passageway, a faint glimmer of light at its end, a waft of warmth that bore the dry mustiness of old buildings. The woman's form was outlined, the face unseen still, but there was laughter in the voice now. "O'Connor, you total *clown*."

He stooped to kiss her warmly. "How're you doin', Edie?"

"Smashing . . . now." She chided him in mocking tones, "although, as you'd say, long time no see."

"There's a war on, baby. Hasn't anyone mentioned it?"

"It's not any bloody war that keeps *you* away."

"I'm admitting nothing," O'Connor declared. "It's a bum rap."

"Come in," Edie invited. "And introduce your friend."

"He's no friend. He's an airplane driver."

The door closed and the passage light went on to reveal Edie fully, small and pretty, in her late twenties, I estimated, and blonde, the blonde looking genuine. She had a scrubbed, friendly and open face with a dusting of freckles across the nose. She looked tired in the way that people in England did look after a long, hard war. O'Connor drew her close, and made the introductions.

Edie offered her hand. "Welcome, Lieutenant."

"Denney," I said. "We'll have no ranks on a forty eight."

"That's much better." She had a big white smile. "Come through, then. We're ready." She wore a blouse, a tailored skirt and fluffy pink bedroom mules, and I wondered . . . ready for what? And . . . *we*? "Carole's dying to meet you."

At a loss, I repeated, "Carole?"

Edie gave O'Connor a look. "Don't tell me he hasn't said."

"Never a word. It's been his big secret."

She gave him a push. "You really are the limit, you know."

"I wanted it to be a nice surprise." O'Connor, looking uncharacteristically sheepish, offered me belated explanation. "Carole's just a great big bundle o'joy . . ." I recollected painfully then that he had said the same thing once about Gladys Gibbons.

"God! You make her sound like Two-Ton Tessie O'Shea, you clot!" Edie was laughing openly, and she was not at all 'B.B.C.' or 'Oxford' or 'posh'. She was open and natural, and I liked her at once, thinking . . . I can trust her. She promised me, "Carole's really lovely. Come and see for yourself."

*

Carole asked lightly, "so you're the famous pilot?"

"I fly the airplane." I held her hand for longer than the formal introduction required. "But I'll pass on famous."

"And modest as well." She smiled a good smile. Edie had not exaggerated: Carole *was* lovely, her figure breathtaking in a plain,

dark dress that flattered without obtrusiveness. She was older—
twenty five, I guessed, or more—and I felt the reflexive gaucheness
of the younger man before the more mature woman. Gaucheness,
though, was accompanied by an unmistakeable stab of sexual
desire. She told me, "blame your shifty friend O'Connor. Who
loudly sings your praises."

"Only when I'm drunk and incapable," O'Connor insisted.

She smiled at him very sweetly. "Duckie . . . when aren't you?"

Carole was as dark as Edie was fair, and the taller of the two.
With violet eyes under well-marked, unplucked brows. I hated
plucked brows. Her face was squarish, the chin firm, nose straight,
with delicate nostrils. Her full-lipped mouth smiled often, and
with warmth, the parted lips revealing white teeth that were a
little—and attractively—prominent. She stood before me
patiently and let me look at her. "Will I do?"

"Believe me . . . you'll *do*!"

Edie was a hairdresser, while Carole worked as a hostess at a
club in Chelsea.

"Hostess, my rosy red ass!" O'Connor turned to grin at her
with happy malice. "Go on, admit it. You're a high-class hooker.
A fifty pounds a night joy-girl."

"Carry on dreaming, O'Connor." Carole was unruffled by
the charge. "But you'll never, never know."

"That's a fact." He looked downcast. "I just don't have any luck."

"Oh, you miserable *pig*!" Edie took a swipe at him, but she
was laughing, and her eyes never left him. Watching them, I
thought of the conversation earlier in the hotel room: and did
the tolerance of the lovely Jeanne extend quite this far . . . ?

We made plans for the evening. We would hit, O'Connor
declared with firmness, "every pub, tavern, speakeasy and low
dive within a ten-mile radius."

Edie mused, "that ought to get us to Croydon."

"Uxbridge as well," Carole believed. "Not to mention
Leytonstone."

"Don't forget . . ." Edie snorted with fresh amusement.
"Cockfosters."

"Now there's a name," mused O'Connor. "To write home about."

"There's this smutty joke about Cockfosters," Edie told him.

"With a name like that, how could there not be?"

"The Max Miller one, you mean?" Carole wondered. Edie giggled again, and nodded.

O'Connor wanted to know, "who, or what, is Max Miller?"

"A famous comedian," Edie said.

"Can't be all that famous." He caressed her behind affectionately. "*I've* never heard of him."

"That's your bad luck, then." She pushed his hand away, coloring, and told me, "Max Miller's always getting had up for telling risqué jokes on the wireless."

"About Cockfosters?"

"That was one of his best," Carole said. "Or worst."

"Go on, Caro . . . you tell it," Edie begged. "You're much better than I am."

Carole lifted an expressive eyebrow. "I'd like to imagine a compliment lurking in there somewhere." She relented. "Oh, all right. Although, first, I should explain for our foreign guests . . ." She met my eye smilingly. "Cockfosters is the name of this north London suburb at the far end of the Piccadilly Line tube."

"Gotcha," O'Connor said. "So?"

"*So* . . . we're on a tube train in the rush hour, and it's jammed full, everybody standing, or else sitting on one another's laps . . ."

"I'm coming to like it more and more," O'Connor offered pensively. "Depending upon what kind of laps we have in mind . . ."

"Kindly shut up," Edie commanded.

"This rush hour train, then . . ." Carole glanced around in enquiry, but no one spoke. "Well, Max Miller's on it, and he's got a very pretty girl sitting on *his* lap. The train stops at a station, and she asks him, 'excuse me, is this Cockfosters?' And Max Miller tells her, 'no, Madam, it's *mine*'."

Edie hooted. "It slays me every time I hear it." She went on in wonderment, "he actually told that on the wireless, and they fined him twenty quid, and chucked him off for being offensive."

"Can't think why," O'Connor murmured. "I, for one, am not in the least offended." He turned to leer at Carole. "But then, maybe that's because our raconteuse is so ravishing."

"More likely because you're so rotten," Edie informed him distantly.

*

We never got to Cockfosters.

With no shortage of willing pubs within easy walking distance of Upper Berkeley Street, there was no need for that.

Edie, it was very clear, was more fond of O'Connor than could ever be good for her, although she hid it well for most of the time behind a smokescreen of banter.

We all got on, without awkwardness or tension between us. Those, sadly, came from an outside source when, in one of the pubs, a drunken naval officer tried to butt in, telling Carole, "come on, love . . . bugger these Yanks." He stood before us, red-faced with drink, and belligerent, unsteady on his feet as people nearby began to edge away. O'Connor and I waited and watched, saying nothing.

"Charlie . . . do stop being a silly arse," a voice called. "Come and sit down . . . behave yourself." The drunk was with two other officers seated at a nearby table.

One caught my eye, and shrugged apology.

"Balls to that . . ." Charlie went on staring at Carole. "What about a bit of loyalty to your own, then?"

"Look, sir," O'Connor began. "We're not looking for trouble . . ."

"No, shouldn't think so . . . that's the way with you lot, isn't it?" Charlie looked at him with open disdain. "You never are, not when it counts. So why not do what you usually do, and piss off, eh?"

"None o' that 'ere, thank you." A barman leaned forward.

"If you won't stop it, sir, 'ave to ask you to leave the premises." It was becoming dispiritingly familiar.

Carole suggested quietly to Charlie, "it might be better if you just went, please."

"Getting in the way, am I?" He watched her with disconsolate spaniel eyes, a nondescript young man in a creased uniform with a single wavy gold stripe on each sleeve.

"Yes, you are," Carole agreed. "Rather."

"Helping bloody Yanks spend their bloody money . . ." He looked O'Connor and me up and down. "Bloody musical comedy uniforms . . . medals for this, medals for that . . ." An elderly civilian said to him disapprovingly, "being a bit silly, old man."

"And *you* can piss off, too!" Charlie shrugged the civilian aside, and glared at O'Connor. "Bloody Purple Hearts if they cut themselves opening a tin of bloody Spam . . ." Everyone was listening, and O'Connor was looking embarrassed and angry.

"Right!" the barman snapped. "You've 'ad your las' warnin' . . ."

"You stupid old fart." Charlie's companions were at his side, the spokesman the one who had offered silent apology. "We'll have the dreaded Crushers here in half a shake, and you'll have us all in chokey."

They hemmed him in, guiding him back to the table, and the spokesman raised a thumb, smiling around. "No harm done."

Charlie went without resistance, telling them plaintively, "it's all right, really. I never meant to be a prat, and I wasn't after the skirt. It's just that I don't like bloody Yanks . . ." They seated him, bending over him, soothing him in his deep distress . . .

Carole gave a tight little laugh. "Thought for a sec I'd have to start swinging the old handbag."

I blurted then, "I felt sorry for him."

"I did notice." She touched my arm and smiled. "I thought it was sweet." She was standing close, speaking only to me. "I'm probably completely bonkers to admit this, but I quite like you, Denney P."

"I'm very glad you do." It was true. "And I'd like to return the compliment."

"I did wonder a bit . . . about that." Carole looked into my eyes. "Couldn't help noticing the way you'd gone . . . subdued?" I had been hoping that it would not show, the fresh attack of the blues that had crept up to dampen the high spirits of the evening. She asked, "is it me?"

"How could it be?" I shook my head at her.

"Well, you know . . . I'm me, not everybody's cup of tea." She shrugged amusement. "Sounds like a song, doesn't it?" She sketched out a tune, crooning breathily, "I'm ME . . . not EVERY-body's cup of TEA!"

"That's good," I said. Remembering Heather singing in the spring dawn. Of Broadway, and Manhattan babies . . .

"Don't worry, I can take a hint," Carole said dryly. "I shan't be auditioning for the Savoy Orpheans." No matter where you looked, I thought, there would always be another reminder . . .

Carole was saying quietly, "we can't expect things to work out just because we think they should. If you don't like me, Denney, all you have to do is say so . . ." Her mouth gave a wry twist. "I'll understand . . . shan't go all hurt and resentful, honestly."

"Carole, I mean this . . ." I faced her squarely, and there was no difficulty in doing that. "Honest to God, you're lovely. Just the way Edie promised you'd be, only more so."

"Thank you for that." She bobbed her head gravely.

"If I had one wish right now, it'd be that we'd met first."

"Before Heather?"

I was startled. "You know?"

"Our mutual chatty friend." Her eyes strayed to O'Connor who, oblivious of us, was gently stroking Edie's skirted thigh while the drinkers around them affected not to notice. Carole said, "it's partly why we're here . . . together like this. O'Connor said you'd been going through a bad patch."

"Something like that, yes."

"Edie and me, we're long-time mates, and we share the flat . . ."

Smiling wistfully, she watched her friend. "She's mad about O'Connor, of course. And accepts that it's not likely to work permanently." She turned back to me, and the violet eyes held mine. "I agreed to make up the numbers tonight. If that's what you'd prefer? Have some fun, but no complications?" She touched the wings above my tunic pocket with a fingertip. "It's your night out, after all."

"Thanks, Carole." I pressed her hand gratefully, and she held on to it.

"At the same time . . ." Her gaze was fixed on my wings now. "I'd sleep with you if you'd like me to?"

"We-e-ell . . ." Even after the extreme candor of Heather, this could still knock me back, *and* re-awaken the slumbering Puritan. O'Connor, supposedly rough-joking, had called Carole a hooker, and Carole had not denied it. She worked for her living at a night club under the euphemistic title of 'hostess', and what, exactly, *would* that entail? Could there be truth in O'Connor's bawdy charge? And, if so, then so what a sudden don't-give-a-damn resolve dictated then? I answered, as to-the-point as she, "I'd been hoping to hear something like that from the moment I saw you. Only . . ."

Her eyes came up to me again. "What is it?"

"Just that, the way things have been going of late, I'm not sure how I'd be."

"Would you be making love with me, or with Heather? Is that it?"

"I'm sorry." I confessed, "she *is* on my mind."

"If it would help at all to talk about it . . . ?" The suggestion was tentative.

But that was too much to expect of anyone. "We're meant to be having fun, right? And what do I do? Act like a God damned wet weekend, is what!"

"Fair enough." She pressed my hand again. "But if ever you want to, and doing it will make you feel better, then I'm here."

*

We hit several more pubs, and then, very late, drifted to a club for U.S. servicemen at Lancaster Gate. A place where the nights went on all through the night, and the bar stayed open to keep them company. There was canned music to dance and smooch to, and they kept the lights down low. A small corner of 42nd and 5th, State Street, or Hollywood and Vine, pre-packaged and shipped overseas.

I danced with Carole, and tried really hard not to think of times spent dancing with Heather, and was told by Carole that I danced well, and could smile at that, explaining that I had had a good teacher. And Carole had the tact not to pursue it . . .

Somewhere in the early hours I found the john, and the two G.I.s bickering monotonously in a corner.

"I *paid* you, God damn it! Right before we come out o' camp."

"An I'm sayin' you never did. You're holdin' out on me."

"Horse *shit*! You're dreamin', buddy. An' don't blame me if you can't keep tabs on your moolah . . ."

A drunk had passed out in an open cubicle, head sagging, snoring, a bottle forgotten on the floor beside him as someone else retched and gagged behind a closed door.

O'Connor, neat and dapper, was washing his hands. "How's she goin', son?"

"Pretty good," I answered. "And not so good."

He rinsed off and reached for the roller towel, saw the state it was in, and used his handkerchief. "You're not goin' sour on Carole?"

"No, not that." I unzipped, thinking drably . . . I'm going sour, all right.

The two G.I.s squabbled on. "That fi' pounds woulda made a world o' difference."

"An' I *paid* it you! Holy shit, how many times . . . ?"

" . . . the piece in the green dress been tellin' me it's okay by her. So, tell me, wise-ass, how do I get her in the sack without no money?"

"Smitty, for Jesus sakes, I'll lend ya the money! Whaddya need . . . five pounds? Ten? Don't matter . . . I'm loaded . . ."

"Sure you're loaded, you piker! With my dough . . ."

"Jesus H. *Christ!*"

The unseen man had stopped being sick. The drunk snored on. I rinsed my hands, and O'Connor offered me his handkerchief, saying dryly, "all part of life's rich tapestry." He looked into my face. "Can't get Heather out of your head, huh?"

"Everywhere I turn, there she is."

"You're on a heavy downer, kid."

"Tell me what I don't know." I returned his handkerchief. "What I need is a crying towel."

"What you need is a good, swift kick in the butt!"

Smitty, contrite now, was asking, "sure you can spare the ten-spot?"

"I'd give ya a lousy hunnert if it'd get ya off my back! Ask yourself . . . would I let a good buddy miss out on a great piece o' tail?"

A sergeant, white-faced and shaking, emerged from the cubicle, wiping his mouth on the back of his hand.

"Thing to remember," O'Connor confided. "Is, no matter how much you love them, and enjoy them, or have the hots for them, they're never worth gettin' depressed over."

"I know that," I muttered. "Now."

"So wise up, why not," he told me. "I mean no disrespect. They're pretty damn' good people, women . . . just kind o' screwed-up at times. But then, that's their way. Like with Jeanne," he went on. "If she ever pulled the plug on me, I'd hurt for sure, but I'd learn to live with it. I wouldn't sit around cryin' the blues. Nor you neither, not if you're smart. Especially when there's another sweet little honey just itchin' to habeas your fresh young corpus." He punched me playfully in the chest. "Time you started thinkin' again, son. And when you do, think on some good things like *that!*"

*

"Now," Carole suggested. "Let's talk, shall we?"

It was four in the morning. We had returned to the flat drunk and mellow, and, soon, Edie and O'Connor drifted away.

I tried to shrug it off, feeling uncomfortable. "What more is there to say? Same old story that you'll find in any tear-jerker magazine."

"Remember the friendly ear," Carole reminded me. "And trust me, I'm not a gossip . . . no kiss and tell. Not even with Edie who I share most of my secrets with. In case you were wondering?"

"Not a bit. No worries on that score."

"Well, then?" She cocked her head, smiling, and waited.

I told her some of it, keeping back what would have amounted to betrayals of confidence. Nothing of feyness, of magic spells, the unusual family background. And only the bare essentials of that other London weekend. Although Carole, I was certain, would find little difficulty in reading between those lines.

Once told, though, it seemed trivial and pathetic: guy meets girl and loses head. Girl offers encouragement. Guy gets what he hoped for, but wants more. Girl gets cold feet. Guy loses girl as well as head. All fall down. "It went slip-sliding away," I said, and offered fresh apology. "Not much of a saga."

"It's yours," Carole said. "And a sad one."

"Is that how you see it? Sad?"

"As you'd imagine, I meet lots of fellows at the club." She was looking pensive. "Some of them I'll go out with, and some . . . a few . . . will try to impress me by playing tough guy, all Jimmy Cagney and Clark Gable. And, if it makes them happy, and they don't overdo it, then I'll usually play along . . ." She looked at me, nodding slowly. "Then I meet someone who's not a bit like that . . . who's kind, and attentive, and has no need at all to play tough guy. And . . . who's sad."

I wondered edgily, "do you play along with that, too?"

"No. I listen, and I pay attention. And help if I can."

"You do help. A lot." I put from my mind the clear memory of saying the same words to Heather: *this* was different . . .

Carole and I lay on the carpet before the popping gas heater, and her hand slipped into mine. We did not speak for quite a while, and the hunger for her inside me grew stronger and more insistent. Her mouth, when I found it, was as soft and yielding, as generous as I had imagined it would be . . . and no less hungry.

She whispered, "what do you *want?*"

"I want *you!*"

"Then tell me exactly how you want me."

"Totally, completely. No intrusions, no memories . . . no inhibitions."

"The perfect answer . . ." Carole gave a low laugh. "And if she pokes her nose in, I swear I'll kill her."

"You do that," I said, and felt no remorse, no sense of betrayal.

"She's gone and missed the bloody boat," Carole stated with finality. "Which is her hard *luck.*"

*

Another grubby, sooty train on the same depressing stretch of track, same wires dipping and swooping between their poles, same succession of bleak stations with hunched, waiting people. I watched without seeing the mid-winter Essex countryside go crawling by. Thinking of Carole, remembering Carole's bed that she had shared with me. Inevitably—in the secret places of my mind where no one else entered—comparing.

She had slept at my side, as soft and relaxed as a cat, and sheer delight to lie there and watch her, until watching brought the hunger back, and I kissed her parted, slightly-pouting lips until she came awake, smiling. "Good morning." We kissed again, and she told me, "lovely way to start a day."

"We must do it more often."

"Tell me . . . did you stop to think before you said that?"

"If I had, I would still have said it."

She held me tightly for a moment. "You're gorgeous to wake up to."

"You, too."

She sat up, resting her chin on her knees. "I'd like it if you did want to see me again." I was given a sidelong glance. "If it doesn't work out with Heather?" I made no answer, and she went on, a little hurriedly, "you can have our number. You'll get Edie most evenings. I'm here more during the day."

"I'll remember."

"Look upon us . . . me . . . this, however you see it, as there if you feel the need." She made it sound casual, something of no great importance, to be accepted or declined at will. "Call it your port in a storm if you like."

"I'm grateful, Carole. For that, and everything."

"Although, if I never see my beautiful lieutenant again, then this *was* lovely."

"Why do you say that?"

"Because, the way you are now, I know I can't compete with Heather." There was a shadow in her eyes. "I can kill her . . . no trouble at all . . . but not compete."

"There was no Heather with you."

"That's lovely as well." She gave me a smiling wink. "A lovely, gallant fib." And, again, I could not answer. "But, any time, remember. Phone first to make sure, but it'll be all right. Meanwhile . . ." The smile grew into laughter, and the intimate moment was past. "You'll be able to tell your friends and your crew, and anyone else you can think of that you've met her at last."

"Met? Met who?"

"A particular type of bird that O'Connor's always wittering on about. The whore with a heart of gold . . ."

From somewhere, O'Connor was asking, "you still with me, bubber?"

"Sorry. Just remembering some things."

"Memorable gal, our Carole."

"Yeah. She is."

"How're you feeling now?"

"Pretty good."

"But Heather's still there, right? Riding your ass."

"I guess she is. But now, thanks to Carole . . ." I gave him a look. "And you, *and* your God damned sermons, it's getting so that I can almost handle it."

He looked pleased. "As long as you remember the olden golden rule . . . always plenty more fish in the sea. Carole's all the proof you need of that." He offered a confession. "That wise-ass crack I made about her bein' a society hooker . . . you can forget it. For the record, she's not, and never was. If it was troubling you?"

"It was . . . a little." I grinned my relief. "From the way you said it, and the way she took it."

"She always gives as good as she gets. Same time, she's no Virgin Mary, either. Carole's been around the block, and knows the ropes." O'Connor elaborated, "sometimes she'll date someone she's met at her club. And, again sometimes, if she happens to like the guy . . ."

"Like with me." Surprising to discover how much it could hurt, hearing that, even though Carole had made no secret of it. But she was on her own, getting along in the big, bad city. As a club hostess, such a possibility existed, and must be recognized . . .

"*Not* like you at all!" O'Connor eyed me irritably. "Jesus, you dumb cluck . . . *think* about it . . . were you a client at the club? Did we even go near her stupid club?"

"Well, no . . ."

"Well, no is right! On account of you and no one else, she took the night off, took her chances, sight unseen, and lost out on wages for that. Why? Because I sold her a hotshot bill of goods on you. Which, knucklehead . . ." O'Connor was scathing. "Happened to be true, and which she accepted with no way of knowing until the merchandise was delivered at the door. No obligation, no favors owed, and still she did it." With his mouth tight with disapproval of me, this was the other O'Connor, the pitiless prick of the long run-ins from I.P. to target. "And what do *you* do? You put her down . . . knock the product when it's freely offered, no strings."

I was crushed and ashamed. "I'm sorry. I didn't think . . ."

"Don't tell me that! Go tell Carole." I looked out, speechless, at bare fields and dead copses, at the dejected houses wheel-clicking past the window. Until, more gently, O'Connor asked, "will you be seeing her again?"

"She's invited me back . . ."

"That's not what I asked you." He shook his head, frowning. "Kid, I'm not tryin' to back you into a corner. But, come on, same time, why not level with the girl, huh? Either shit or get off the pot. Call her if you can. And if you can't, have the decency to give it to her straight."

I knew that he meant well, but he was beginning to get on my nerves: I wanted to suggest, unkindly, that he might do well to follow up his own advice with Edie. But all I said was, "as a matter of fact, we've already got an agreement on that."

He was not about to let me off the hook, not yet. "So? Don't leave her hangin' on some two-bit agreement. See it through."

"I will, soon," I promised. "It's just that . . ."

"Let me guess. You want to try and make it one more time with Heather?" I nodded wretchedly. "Then I hope you do. But my best advice to you," he ended in a chill voice. "Is don't hold your breath."

*

O'Connor and I returned to base sober, and only a little hung-over. Which was as well with a mission called for the following day.

In spite of the heavy weekend, I was restless and edgy, and impatient to fly. Someone had ordered it, so let's go. Get up there and try, once more, to survive. What, like everyone else, I hated, was having to sweat the dragging hours until take-off.

That evening, I sought solace in a dog-eared adventure from the base library: 'Biggles Flies East', with the hero and his side-kick Algy stuck in the desert somewhere. The moment of drama and pathos when Biggles believes Algy is killed. But the body recovered from the wrecked Sopwith is that of an unknown major with a neat blue hole in his forehead. Which would have taken some pretty nifty shooting, even at the reduced airspeeds of 1917. Horsing around, evading, doing violent aerobatics . . . then to put a round between someone's eyes . . . ?

The author, a Captain W.E. Johns, needed to fly awhile with us, I decided uncharitably. And see how it really was: how wild and indiscriminate bullets and cannon shells tore airplanes into flaming junk, men into raw hamburger. Limbs ripped off, like Le Maire at Antwerp. Men gutted, everything flopping out through their shredded clothing; the internal colors of them that were never intended to see the light of day . . . their blood in splashes and rivers and lakes . . .

I gave up on Biggles and his gentlemanly pursuit of war, my thoughts turning back with relief to the poky flat in the blacked-out street. There, with Carole, lithe and naked at my side, transparently honest and undemanding. And how, before that, it had been better than I had imagined, the slow and delicious act of removing her dress.

Now there was the open invitation to return; a straightforward phone call was all that it would take, no doubts or problems, no hair-washing, no emotional turmoil . . . no strings. The one problem being that the beautiful Carole could not divert me fully, not yet. She belonged for the time being—and maybe for eternity if tomorrow was to be the day—to that other world from which the impending mission excluded me.

*

Azevedo breezed into the Quonset, his plastered arm in its sling. "Hey . . . how was London?"

I looked at him steadily. "It was London."

He eased with difficulty out of his tunic and shirt. I saw how no one made a move to help him, and wondered—hoping—if people were wising up to Azevedo at last? He grinned across at me. "Great times, huh?"

"We made out," I said.

"I'll bet you *did*. Good-lookin' young stud like you . . . all them happy whores flockin' around." I said nothing, and he watched me, still with that tight grin. "Although, mind you, you don't need to hit the city to live it up."

The implication was crudely clear, and I wanted to crow at him that he was welcome because my weekend had been fantastic. To claim, however falsely, that there had been no thought of Heather from start to finish. I let it go: Azevedo could figure it out for himself.

He slid into his bunk, telling everyone with amusement, "big bad old mission tomorrow, fellas . . ." Men were staring at him in shock and disbelief: no one in his right mind would speak of that and break the inviolable taboo. But Azevedo would, and did so, aggravating his offense by demanding that we should, "keep the noise down. I'd hate for you to wake me up."

That could not be ignored, and I answered, "too bad you have to miss out, Tiger. Everyone else racking up missions . . . even your own crew." The others from 'Bomb Boogie', still derelict on the ground at Chiny, had been split up among different crews. Azevedo, fit to fly again, would have to await a fresh assignment. Gopher flying, I wondered, and the thought of it could make me smile as I told him, "so we'll just press on and finish our tours while you take it nice and easy, getting yourself in good shape for Tokyo." Others listening, were starting to grin and nod. "They tell me that old Pacific Theater's just one big thrill after another. Like you said, we don't need the big city for great times."

THIRTY

We sat shoulder to shoulder, tightly-packed, as Lieutenant
Colonel Friend issued his orders for the mission.

"It's another long one, men, with a night-stop in Belgium . . ."
Someone groaned, and he smiled primly. "What's your beef?
You've had it easy. It's time now to start earning your pay."

He faced a barrage of hostile eyes. Such talk might have been
borderline acceptable had Lieutenant Colonel Friend been riding
along with us.

He turned away, and his pointer touched the map deep inside
Germany. "Jena," he said. The muttering began then.

Jena, the site of one of Napoleon's big victories, lying well
beyond Frankfurt and Nuremberg, almost as far to the east as
Leipzig and Berlin. And, today, marching in the footsteps of the
French emperor, it was our turn, a foray into what, by our
reckoning, was strictly four-engine country. We had heard the
many scare stories of Jena and its complex of interlocking fighter
bases located dead center for the air defense of the Reich. Like
the hub of the web, with the black-crossed spiders sitting there,
waiting.

"Although, as we're aware with Kraut fighters," Lieutenant
Colonel Friend was saying unbelievably. "There's not so many to
trouble us now."

Behind me, someone hissed savagely, "since when was that
piece of shit *us*? An' if there's not so many, why are we friggin'
goin'?"

Jena . . . with that clutch of unfriendly airfields to hold the
remaining concentration of aircraft comprising the dregs (as the
High Command kept telling us) of the bled-white Luftwaffe
fighter arm. Now the R.A.F. and the Eighth Air Force wanted

439

those fields eliminated, and deemed it a task best suited to medium bombers.

"Once more . . ." Lieutenant Colonel Friend's fearless gaze drilled into us. "The Ninth has been picked for the task. And the Ninth delivers!"

It was kind of sad about Lieutenant Colonel Friend, an odd anachronism in this late stage of the European war. 1945, and things starting to wind up at last, yet he would persist in spouting the jingoistic catch-phrases of '41 and '42. When things *had* been tough all round, and there was a time and place for slogans like 'Can DO!' and 'Deliver the Goods'. But time had moved on and left Lieutenant Colonel Friend behind. While we, compelled to, moved on as well, grown old prematurely, grown out of knee-pants talk like 'Praise the Lord and Pass the Ammunition'.

We took off and flew, got shot at hatefully as we bombed, then a lesser number flew home to sit around and wait for the next one. Until the quota was filled, or luck ran out. We were bored shitless, and all too often bored to death. And at no time in any kind of mood for the antediluvian gung-ho of clip-winged Lieutenant Colonel Friend.

*

Jena qualified as a bad trip. Not as bad, maybe, as had been imagined, but a stinker for all that.

The pressure on our strike was eased somewhat, perhaps, by the diversionary mission sent a half hour earlier against Hanover with the intent of drawing off the defending fighters . . . or some of them.

Seven known airfields lay in the Jena area demanding our attention. So that, in spite of the Hanover attack, there remained plenty of them in wait for us. Plotting us on radar, laughing about the dumb Amis who imagined that they could pull such a feeble trick and get away with it.

An hour and ten minutes flying time from the base near Liège; two hundred and seventy air miles straight down a tight corridor paved wall-to-wall with flak. Until, somewhere deep inside ancient Thuringia, the guns stopped dead.

In immediate response to silence and clearing air, the adrenal glands flicked open, the blood starting to pound heavily at my temples as I scanned a cloudless blue and gold sky. Seeing, far above, the weaving vapor trails of the Little Friends. Thus far, though, nothing else.

The escorting pilots would also have noted the guns' silence, like the end of the Overture to Act One. They would be reacting, dumping their long-range fuel tanks, gearing up for the coming bar brawl.

'Way up there, the fighter jocks commanded wider fields of vision, and, soon, the command frequency grew raucous with their excited cries, exhortations, orders . . . the curt and irritable directions to "can the needless chatter!"

"Twenty-plus . . . two o'clock high!"

"Goin' for the bombers . . ."

" . . . Section Wichita . . . echelon left . . . GO!"

"One-Oh-Nines at one o'clock level . . ."

" . . . Got 'em in sight!"

"Let's go *nail* those mothers . . . !"

" . . . Whack 'em GOOD!"

"How about some radio DISCIPLINE here?"

"One-Nineties . . . twelve o'clock low!"

"Go *get* 'em, Tiger . . . !"

"Section Wichita . . . break right . . . GO!"

"Chuck! Watch your ass . . . One-Nineties up-sun!"

" . . . Son of a BITCH! See that baby BURN!"

"God DAMN it . . . how much telling do you people NEED?"

Up there so very high, the condensation trails tangling, a wild snarl of white knitting wool that petered out as the Little Friends came plummeting into warmer air to break up the ambush of hurtling gadflies meeting us head-on with their wings pouring fire. It was the situation we most feared: too many of them for the escorts to keep them all off us; they were getting through, scoring, wreaking their murderous havoc. And—a blessing of a kind—no time in which to ponder that as O'Connor comes to me, cold and clear on the intercom.

"Approaching the I.P. Hold her for me, kid . . . just so."

O'Connor calling the shots, mercifully diverting my mind from the horrors all around me.

*

At Jena the Group lost eleven Marauders, and eight of the fighters had gone down. We did not know for sure how hard the Germans were hit, but the claims were exuberantly high. Photo-reconnaissance revealed that the bombers had done extensive damage; runways, ramps and taxiways pitted, hangars smashed, a fuel storage area set ablaze. Aircraft were destroyed on the ground, many of these by the Mustangs and Thunderbolts going in low to strafe targets of opportunity. It looked and sounded good, but we did not fool ourselves too much: the beaver-active Germans would have their Jena airfields operational again before we had time to turn around. Unless—as was being hinted—we were to be sent back to dissuade them.

We cooled our heels at the Liège strip, and wondered anxiously if Jena was in the cards for the next day. The good weather was slated to hold: we were sitting under almost stationary high pressure, the best possible flying weather for both sides.

Jena cost the Squadron three B-26s out of the eleven.

'Sweet Maggie' (Donnelly, Petersham, Floyd, Ardello, Zeebricht, Purbright, Samuels) brought down by flak on the run-in to the target. Three 'chutes confirmed; no word yet of injuries or fatalities. Twenty seventh mission.

'Southern Comfort' with Galt, McInerney, Frobisher, Tenon and Scolley: one engine shot out already by the fighters, the other failing two miles short of touch-down at Liège. Galt, Scolley and McInerney killed. Mission Number unlucky thirteen.

'Bella Donna', flown by Andreas, with Hynes, Dickey,

Fogarty and Scaramella. Nailed by a 190 overhead Jena, the aircraft going vertically into the deck. Second mission.

'Big Apples', with thirty eight, went and came back without a chip out of her paint. No flak rounds came too close, and the fighters all appeared to be aiming elsewhere. We had flown as though cupped in protective hands, our new engine purring without a hitch. With all the evidence of the less-fortunate before us, how not to think of magic . . . and of Heather? I wanted to believe in her spell even now, that it was there, working for us. Remembering her laughter as she told me, "I'm good at putting them on, but not at taking them off."

Seeking for favorable omens, and finding one when the word was passed that the brass were so tickled with the results of the first Jena mission that they did not feel the need for a second.

Bringing 'Big Apples' in at Tiverell Lacey, I made one of my better landings, and O'Connor offered congratulations. "I think you're finally gettin' the hang of it."

*

Heather's note expressed the hope that I was well, and asked that I should telephone her whenever that might be convenient for me.

Struggling then to sort out jumbled feelings of confusion, astonishment, resentful irritation and, of . . . such unspeakable *relief.* Filled with a choking excitement that had me racing down to the overworked base payphone, there to stand and fume far down the line of other returned crews all eager to re-establish outside contacts.

Until it was my turn, and her phone rang on and on, and, disappointed and hurt, I was about to hang up when she was there, sounding as if she had been running.

"Oh, it *is* you . . . good. I hoped it would be." Explaining in a rush, "I was right down at the bottom of the garden . . . sorry. Mum's away for the day, and there's only me to answer . . ." She was laughing shakily. "The butler was getting at the cooking sherry, so we had to sack him."

I asked, "what were you doing in the garden?"

"Burning rubbish. Making a dreadful stink, and smoking out the neighbors. I'm a *sight*," she told me. "Old clothes, wellies, and smuts all over my face." I pictured her like that, and the picture looked good. She wondered then, small-voiced, "are you all right, Denney?"

"Not so bad. Why?"

"I thought you sounded . . . odd."

"We just got back from a hairy mission. Things like that can make you odd."

"I watched the landings. You were overhead today."

"It's all to do with the way the wind blows."

"Yes, I know. You've told me that."

"Must have forgotten." I said, "I'm a little tired."

"Sorry . . ."

"Why should you be sorry?" An uncharitable thought intruded . . . why *not*?

"I've been wondering lately if I smell, or something?" A playful note emerged. "The way you've been keeping your distance."

Maybe the famous perceptive powers were failing her? I said only, "it might be an idea to meet and talk."

"I want to see you, too . . ." She hesitated. "What should we talk about?"

Could she be kidding me? Knowing what weighed on my mind, yet still stringing me along? Or else—the preferred option—she was innocent and, once again, I had gone off half-cocked, reading the signs all wrong. Nothing would please me more than to have been mistaken about her, about the things witnessed in the pub, or to be compelled to grovel anew and beg forgiveness . . .

Still unsure, I replied, "oh, this and that. One or two recent developments."

"Sounds rather worrying." I waited, but she did not spell out her worries. "I wonder what these mysterious-sounding developments can be?" Her laughter seemed natural and unforced. "Shall we meet in our usual corner?"

Pretty cool, I thought. The apparently artless suggestion that we get together on the same old ground.

"Or, if you'd rather," Heather proposed. "You could come here."

"To the house?"

"Mum's away remember? In Town . . . she won't be back until the morning. We can have our intriguing talk undisturbed."

Margot Granger in London, and Heather would know all too well how willingly I would come to her under those circumstances. "That's the best offer I'm likely to get."

"I could make some supper."

I thought of the rationing. "Let me bring something . . ."

"Don't bother, it's all right. It'll be simple. Probably Welsh rabbit." The smile was in her voice, a hint of returning assurance. "Do you know what that is?"

"If it's what I'm thinking . . ."

"Grilled cheese on toast."

"What a relief." I laughed then. "At home, we call it grilled cheese on toast."

"How very prosaic of you," Heather said.

We agreed on eight o'clock. I would pick up some bottled beer at the pub.

"Meanwhile," Heather announced. "I'll just pop out and shoot a Welsh rabbit."

*

Bob Reeves sold me brown ale over the bar. "See the film star's not with us tonight."

I smiled. "You mean Azevedo?"

"That what 'e calls 'isself? What sort o' name's that, then?"

"Portuguese, I think. Or Brazilian."

"My word! You certainly get all sorts in Yankeeland."

"We're the world's melting pot," I told him. "Says so on the Statue of Liberty. Come one, come all."

He shook his head at me. "Never know when you young buggers are pullin' my pisser."

"That's what you call him, Bob? The film star?" I smirked. "That'll go down well on base."

"Well, 'e be'aves like one. Really fancies 'isself." He glanced around. "Usually 'ere by now, bangin' on the door sharp at six. 'Im an' 'is war wound."

"He got that from a burst tire."

"*Go* on. Way 'e tells it, you'd think 'e crossed the bloody Rhine single-'anded."

"He didn't even get off the ground. Although he has a way with words . . ." But I was being cheap and snide: Azevedo could not be faulted for the events of Chiny. Which did not prevent me from adding, "he stood on his nose in the mud."

"*Go* on," Bob Reeves said again.

I began tentatively, "the last time I was in here, remember?" He nodded. "Then my being away again . . . I wondered . . . ?"

"'As 'e been seein' 'er?"

"Yes."

"Now an' then," Bob Reeves admitted. "In the pub. Which is all I know about."

"Sure, Bob."

"Bloody cheek if you ask me, 'im bargin' in. Same time, though, there's not much ever 'appens. Not that you'd notice."

I said gratefully, "thanks for telling me."

"Well, you're all right, lad . . ." Some airmen came in to line the bar. "'Ang about while I serve this lot." He filled their orders and returned. "What I'm sayin' is, all they do is talk, see? Or '*e* talks. Buys 'er a shandy, then 'as a good old natter."

"He's renowned for the gab," I said, snide once more.

"An' all she does is sit there an' listen. Then she gets up an' goes. Home, I s'pose, although I never ask."

"Does he ever . . . ?"

"On her own," he insisted firmly. "She leaves him sat there.

Now . . ." He began to chuckle. "Does that make you feel better?"

"It makes me feel great."

"Better'n you was last time, then," he mused. "Proper down in the dumps *that* time."

"Not now, though," I said. "Not *now.*"

*

It was looking as though I had, indeed, misjudged Heather. She had done no more than meet Azevedo for a drink and a chat. She knew him, had his measure, and could stomach him. Bob Reeves had made it clear that she was keeping Azevedo in his place, having a drink with him, letting him sound off, and listening politely—always politely, I reminded myself with a grin—then leaving, always by herself.

All of which would be no more than the by-products of feminine contrariness, and when was a female *not* contrary? That, coupled with the need, as Heather would see it, to give my reins the occasional jerk, and keep me on my toes. That I could accept and tolerate: what was galling was the thought of her using Azevedo as an instrument for my correction.

I considered these and other possibilities during the walk to the house in Mill Lane, and was able to reach a conclusion that seemed satisfactory. Azevedo got to see her briefly during the times of my absence, was permitted to buy her a drink and engage her in conversation . . . or monologue, I amended with self-satisfied amusement. Until, satiated, she got up, thanked him *politely*, and walked out. While I, back from the wars, was met with letters of appeal and invitations home to eat Welsh rabbit!

THIRTY ONE

The cheese was more burned than grilled, and Heather was apologetic. "There are some things I do well. Cooking, I'm afraid, isn't one of them."

I helped her with the few dishes, said no to coffee, and poured more of the brown ale. We sat at opposite ends of the sofa, looking at each other until she said, "well?" It sounded like a challenge. She folded her hands in her lap. "You said you wanted to talk."

"Some things that need to be said." Walking here from the pub, the prospect had not seemed daunting; now, suddenly, it was. An almost palpable tension lay between us; the mood quite inopportune to an attempt at explanation and reconciliation.

I could see no way, then, but to come straight out with it. "I was in the pub one evening on my own . . . we didn't have a date." I would say nothing about telephoning, calling at the house to prowl like a thief in the night. "You were there . . . with Azevedo. So I left."

She answered calmly, "that seems a silly thing to have done."

"What else was there? You tell me."

"For a start, you could have tried being sensible." Her voice and manner were cool. "Come over and joined us. I would have been happy to see you."

"To see me butting in, you mean?" The earlier good feelings were receding, ousted roughly by fresh ire and bitterness. "It was obvious, from where I stood, that you weren't seeing much of anything but him."

"I went because he had invited me." She spoke as though that had been the most natural and logical thing to do.

"He did that . . . ?" I was incredulous and aghast. "And you *went?*"

"You saw me with him. Remember?"

"Heather, this is no damned joke!"

"That's odd," she retorted. "Because you're certainly making it sound like one."

Left with no effective riposte, I could only ask lamely, "did he phone you?"

"Of course. We're in the directory . . . it's not difficult to do." I heard no hint of regret or remorse.

"Jesus! While I get turned down for dates on whatever cockeyed pretext you can come up with! Thanks a lot, Heather."

"He simply asked me out for a drink, and promised to give me all the news . . . how you were, that sort of thing. So I accepted."

"Knowing the kind of creep he is, yet you still swallowed that line?" I exclaimed furiously, "you must be out of your everloving head!"

All thoughts of renewed understanding, of explanation and reconciliation, were lost over the side in that terrible, bitter and irretrievable moment. As Heather said very quietly, "thank you for that, Denney."

Heather, the child of two people who might have been too closely related, with all the biological risks attendant upon that, was not someone to whom such things could ever be said. Unless the desire was there to alienate her for all time. Now, sorry would not do. What I had blurted in crazy, unthinking fury, could never be forgiven or forgotten. There could only be the shame and despair that came—as Heather herself had accused once—'always too late'.

I offered miserably, "that was despicable."

"You recognize that." She watched me without expression. "But you said it."

"Yes, I did."

"If that's the way that people speak to one another in America . . ." She looked reflective. "I don't think I'd like being there very much."

"It was just a slip, a meaningless expression . . ." Like an utter moron, I tried to make a joke of it. "English-speaking . . . it probably came from here in the first place." Which made matters worse, and I burst out, "Heather, I'm so sorry."

"All because I dared to meet Terry Azevedo without your permission." Automatically, I registered the use of 'Terry', thinking it had got that far. "Because I presumed to use my own judgement and befriend someone you don't care for. I chose to think for myself instead of running with the herd."

"I'm hardly a herd . . ."

"You've told me how everyone dislikes him . . ."

"He *makes* people dislike him. He seems to get a kick out of it . . ."

She ignored my protest. "But that's a herd response, don't you see?" She was quiet, reasonable, explaining to me with great patience something which I should have grasped instinctively. "A feeling that you share, which places you in the herd. Whereas an outsider like me can feel more sympathetic."

I began, "you're no outsider . . ." And faltered as Margot Granger's warning echoed once more in my memory.

"You see, you're not sure, are you?" Heather knew at once what I was thinking. "You can't find the right, conforming answer. But I've known always that I don't fit in. One senses it everywhere, and the discomfort it causes for others." She laughed harshly. "It might be better if I were simply mad . . . out of my everloving head, as you put it so aptly. It would be easier then for everyone to grasp . . . like measles, or 'flu . . ."

"Heather . . ."

"But how do you cope with someone who defies precise definition, neither one thing nor the other?" She hurried on at once to answer her own question. "You don't, because that sort of thing is confusing and upsetting, and, really, you'd rather not know."

It was then that I knew that I was losing her for good, and that nothing I might do would prevent it now. Like a ship at dockside; she on deck as I stood below with only a frail paper streamer stretching from hand to hand, drawing taut.

"I have a fair idea of the things Mum will have said to you that day," she said. "She believes it's her fault, and Daddy's, because they married against the odds, and had me." She looked away, blinking back sudden tears. "The evening we met, I'm surprised you didn't notice then."

"At the dance?" But what had there been then that was out of the ordinary? It had been good, and fun: even the bad moments over the old jeep had been fun . . .

She looked back at me, composed once more, and dry-eyed. "Surely you remember when I walked in? How it was?"

That was something I would never forget: the shabby, beat up hangar with its hasty make-over. 'Dinah Might?' providing a backdrop for the band, an airplane long-since lost. The country girls flocking in with their brassy hair and thick red legs. And . . . Heather. The girl apart, special, different . . . but not in the way, surely, that she implied now? "You made the evening," I insisted. "For everyone."

"Did I?" The response was listless.

"You did for me."

"Then explain to me why people held back as they did, and left me standing there?" There was no accusation in the question, no evidence of self-pity. "Until your Major What's-his-Name came to the rescue." She added dryly, "probably much against his better judgement."

"Why should that have been?"

"Because with me," Heather replied matter-of-factly. "Others usually prefer not to make the first move."

"Aren't you being a little . . . unrealistic?" That was not the definitive word that I would have opted for.

"Or paranoiac?" She had gotten my true meaning at once. "No, Denney, this is real. A phenomenon that's no phenomenon at all." She was holding her almost-empty beer glass, swirling the dregs round and round in the bottom. "I've even made a sort of game of it, in the way that some people play word games."

"What game's that?"

"'Spot the Ones who are Put Off'," Heather answered at

once. As if that were a question she had faced before. "And don't know why they are, but whose hackles shoot up at the sight of me."

I protested without conviction, "come on, now . . ."

"It's so, really. I've known of it almost from the times of first awareness. And like attracts like . . . a searching for the rare kindred spirit. Two outsiders meeting. Terry Azevedo and me."

I found that a hateful comparison. "Guess I'm not too receptive to that."

"You were receptive to fey." Her eyes mocked me. "And we shouldn't forget the spells."

"But never to that cheap heel," I retorted hotly. "Azevedo *is* an outsider, and you and he have nothing in common."

"I have a colleague at work . . ." Heather swirled the glass, staring down into the small vortex of dark liquid. "One of the boffins. Who has what, probably, you'd call wacky ideas. About the life force, for instance. Which, he claims, is simple electricity. And how we're all nothing but receivers and transmitters, sending out signals all the time, and getting them back. I've seen the evidence of that with us . . ." She glanced at me quickly, then away. "You pick up things from me, and vice versa. What do you airmen call it? Loud and clear?"

"That's about it." I remained noncommittal, waiting for Heather to point out the precise direction this new line was taking.

"Tuned in to one another," she went on. "Whether it's one person or a whole crowd in a building . . . like the dance. Tune in and you'll get the signal, sometimes friendly and compatible, and sometimes not." She shrugged. "It just turns out that I'm one of the nots."

"So what you're saying is that, at the dance, people were picking up your signals warning them off?"

"Warned, or scared, one or the other." She accepted calmly these traits which she saw as peculiar to herself. "It wasn't any willful thinking of mine. All I'd done was come along, as I said, hoping that it might be fun . . . that I might meet someone nice.

Which, of course . . ." She smiled at me for a second. "I did. But I was playing my private game all the time. On the lookout for responses, and knowing just what to expect. I wasn't disappointed . . . it was evident at once that my signals were being picked up, and that no one knew what to make of them, or me. Again, as you might say, all dolled-up, but no takers." She finished simply, "I wasn't surprised."

"Sorry, but I can't buy any of this." I frowned in perplexity. "I still think you're making too much of it."

"Yet, haven't you ever wondered," Heather mused. "Why you could dance with me all evening with only a few half-hearted interruptions? All easily rebuffed."

"Now you're telling me . . ."

"That no one wanted to but you?" Her smile for me turned warm then, in the way that it been once, when things were good between us. "But you were lovely. Even if not a kindred spirit."

"A damned sight more kindred than Azevedo would ever know how to be!" I replied, freshly incensed.

"Yet I've felt no adverse reactions from him," Heather said levelly. "In the way that I have more than once . . . and be honest about this, Denney . . . with you. Angering you and *repelling* you."

Her choice of word was shockingly exact, and I wondered if she shared with me then the reflexive mind-pictures of that moment: the sunlit park, the monstrous killing machine growling overhead . . .

"Your look of undisguised distaste whenever I ask you about your missions," she reminded me. "Which has been as much over the asking as the topic. But, you see, that's something that's in me. I don't claim to understand it, and I can't change it. And the plain truth is that I don't really want to change."

"You know I'd never ask you to . . ."

She continued on as if I had not spoken. "Yet Terry never shies away, or looks as if he's being made to endure a bad smell. He doesn't get all stiff and righteous, or take fright when I walk into a room . . ." I thought with furious despair . . . to be compared with *him*, and found wanting? "He behaves well, and he's not unkind. All that's needed is to find a way through the bombast to the rather pleasant person underneath. And, as outsiders, we do find common ground."

"And that's the big attraction, is it?"

"I've said before . . ." A chill entered her voice. "There's no *attraction*."

I should have known to leave it there, and did not. "So what exactly *is* there?"

"What, I should inform you." The voice was pure ice now. "Is none of your bloody business!"

The ship edged a little further away from the dockside, the streamer stretching to its limits.

"That's it for us, then?"

Her reply was brutally direct. "I'd say it's been so for some time."

"Since London, of course." I was calm, telling myself, why fight it? "And Azevedo?"

"He won't be replacing you, if that's what you're thinking. I'm aware of his failings, and my own are quite enough to be getting on with. I've no wish to take on his."

"You wouldn't take me on, either."

She softened enough then to say haltingly, "I'm . . . I'm sorry about that, Denney."

It hit me then like a very, *very* belated flash just what it was with Heather. And it was a realization, full at last, and complete, beyond argument, that I *hated*.

So very late in the game, I had found my elusive and long-sought understanding of her as I said bitterly, "well, at least, he'll be a nice fresh source of war stories. And you the always-willing captive audience." She looked at me without seeming to comprehend. "Because that's what you *really* like, Heather, isn't it? All those cheap and painless thrills, and the poor dumb bastard you get your hooks into providing the source . . ." The belated nickel dropped down the slot, the lights lit up, and I did not spare her. "Like Tim, like me, like Azevedo now." I saw her flinch as the shot went home and, for the tiniest moment, I could almost pity Azevedo, one more happy, willing fly in Heather's web. It was a feeling that could not endure; Azevedo deserved all he got. "And it's not just the war stories, right. There are all those comings and goings as well. A Beaufort torpedo bomber, or a B-26 . . . every time one flies overhead there's that excitement and uncertainty. The big gamble . . . how will the dice roll *this* time? What card, good or bad, will turn up for you? That other game you get such a big kick out of . . . will he or won't he make it back?" I needled her savagely, and found, with some lingering shame, that I was enjoying doing that. "Kind of like Russian roulette, but perfectly safe for you. The trigger hits an empty chamber, and you're just fine, lapping up the thrill. Until the time comes when the chamber *isn't* empty. But, even then, *you're* still fine, aren't you? Because the other fool picks up the tab, and there's you with another war story, a real humdinger . . ."

I watched her, thinking, how could I have missed this when, all along, all the signs were there to be read? Other than because I had wanted to miss it . . .

"If that's what you want to believe," Heather said quietly. "Then please do."

"I should have seen it . . . damn it, I *did*." I put my thoughts into matching, contemptuous words. "But I didn't want to believe that . . . not of you."

"What was it that you should have seen?" She told me sharply, "*tell* me!"

"That you're hooked on war . . . you love the whole stinking, rotten business. Don't you know that?"

I made the same comparison with the one that had come to me in the park when the V-1 flew over, but aloud this time, comparing Heather with those in our number who would return from each mission to crow loudly of the pleasure that they drew from the danger and risk and destruction and slaughter. Pointing out to her, making it clear, how, as I saw her now, she belonged with them. Although, if anything, she was worse.

"They, at least, fly their missions and take their knocks, facing

up to the fact that it's them or the Germans, and no hard feelings."
She watched me in silence. "When you told me you were fey, I
looked it up, wanting an exact definition. And there was a part in
the dictionary that I disagreed with . . ." I waited for her to say
something, but she only shrugged. "It was about fey people having
premonitions of death, and I hated that, the thought of it applying
to you, and made up my mind that the dictionary was in error
on that one." I drew a long breath. "But I see now that I needn't
have worried. Because your premonitions are all to do with the
deaths of others. The risks *they* take excite you. And who can
tell," I speculated. "Maybe that's what puts them off you. They
sense it in you, and decide they'd rather not get too close in case
they get burned. Because you're like some beautiful ghoul who
loves to hang around men freshly back from missions, filled with
the horror and bitter juice of their experience, waiting to suck
out the juice."

She said in a low, controlled voice, "that sounds like a line
from some good, angry poetry."

Anger, unsuppressed, had served, I believed, to open my eyes
so that so many puzzling events of our shared past seemed to fall
into place. Like her antipathy to my time spent flying the Stinson
gopher plane. She would have viewed that as a handy sinecure
and not a stop-gap devised on the sour whim of Lieutenant
Colonel Delaney. A job like that, puttering around the local area
at ninety miles per hour, no risks, no one shooting at me, could
never have held Heather's interest.

"Now I've got two missions left to fly," I said. "After which,
if I survive, it's goodbye and scram. No longer the novice with a
whole tour before him who danced with you that night. And
who needs someone around who's no longer doing dangerous
and exciting things? When others are."

"Again, it's your right to think that," Heather murmured.

Relentless, I went on sniping at her. "But then, with perfect
timing, along comes Hotshot Azevedo with all those trips still
to fly. Lots of yarn-spinning during the long, intimate evenings,
and what yarns they'll be."

Still calm, she enquired, "have you much more that you want to say?"

There was very little more, but her mildness and reasonableness stung me into a final swipe at her. "You said once that you'd never send me a Dear John. But I'd have preferred one of those to *this* . . . finding out the way you really are. Something that I would never have wanted to know." She listened, not saying a word, as I wound up my long tirade. "What you should do, Heather, is look ahead. Ask yourself what happens if Azevedo doesn't make it. That's always possible . . . Jerry's still giving us a hard time. How will it be then? Will you cast more spells, and reel in some new fool? Who, like me, will hardly believe in his luck . . . that such a beauty could take a shine to him." And you are truly a beauty, I thought with sadness. Young and lovely and baffling and heartbreaking in my evergreen and ineradicable memories of you. I reminded her, "but the European war is almost over, remember, and there'll be no airplanes coming and going, no one calling on the phone. All the tall tales and cheap thrills . . . finito."

And I knew that my arguments were petulant and adolescent, lacking in any depth of thought. Because, with the war ended, and us gone, life would not stop then for Heather. There would be fresh chapters filled with incident to dim the memory of these passing times. They would lose their vividness and immediacy, fading, gathering dust.

Yet I remembered what I had written once to my mother at the time of the Invasion, telling her that in my future life there would never be an event to compare with that, and being a part of it. That memory made it seem possible that Heather might think along similar lines. For her, the war, and how it had affected her, then the proximity of the air base with its people and activities, could well be the high water mark of *her* life, and that, whatever the future held, nothing then would measure up to *this*. And in pointing out to her what would soon be history, perhaps I could wound as I felt that I had been wounded . . .

I watched her there in the firelight, loving her, hating her, as the ship drifted free at last on the tide, and the flimsy streamer tore apart and fluttered down. And all that was left to say was, "thank you for supper . . . for the Welsh rabbit."

Hearing her answer in polite apology, "I'm so sorry I burned it." She would be polite always. "And thank *you* for bringing the beer."

"That was the easy part."

"There's still some left." She wondered, "won't you take it with you?"

"Keep it . . ." I launched my final shaft. "Drink a toast to the next stage in your life."

THIRTY TWO

FLIGHT LOG.
DATE: 1/26/45.
AIRCRAFT TYPE: B-26C.
NO. or REG.: 43-2693.
PILOT-IN-COMMAND: Self.
SECOND PILOT: Nil.
CREW: O'Connor, Devine, Cohn, Patecki.
FLIGHT ROUTE: Eindhoven-Kassel-Eindhoven.
FLIGHT HOURS: 1.35.
HOURS VISUAL: 1.35.
HOURS INSTRUMENT: Nil.
HOURS NIGHT: Nil.
OBSERVATIONS: The penultimate mission!

We were to hit Kassel from the usual hastily-prepared forward airstrip, this one on the outskirts of Eindhoven. Everyone agreed, discussing it on the way over, that it would be pretty weird to fly from the place where, only six months earlier, the Germans then holding it had come very close to killing us.

Kassel was to be the target for no less than three Bomb Groups, all going for rail yards and trains, for factories, transports, barracks, or anything else, we were informed cheerfully, that might take our fancy. It was to be a turkey shoot. Flattening Kassel, the unfailingly-optimistic brass let it be known, would shorten the war by weeks.

"Ever take time to consider . . ." O'Connor regarded me with guileless eyes. "How long this-here unpleasantness might've got to be without us shortenin' it so much?"

Flip side of the coin, we were promised a world of flak, and best to watch out for fighters. Although the Little Friends would be there for us . . .

In the six-by, riding to the hardstand, he wondered mildly, "how you doin'?"

"Anyone I can. Why?"

"You'll pardon me for mentioning it, son, but, fact is, you haven't been exactly forthcomin' since our recent spree."

"Let's say I don't care to talk about it right now."

"Why not? It's no big deal." O'Connor looked pointedly around the truck's crammed interior. "No one in here gives a good God damn what you say. They all got troubles enough o' their own." He leaned closer. "Anyway, it's personal. When you got my young life, so full o' bright promise, nestlin' in your hands, then I can't afford havin' you go broody on me. Not when this is almost it . . . last but one."

"I've been awake thinking of just that for most of the night!" I said snappishly. "It's okay . . . my mind's on the job, so lay off me."

"Couldn't ask for more." He sprawled back on the jouncing bench seat.

I admitted, relenting, "I went to see Heather."

"Oh-*ho*! And may one have the temerity to enquire?"

"We'll call it over," I said. "Dead in the street."

"Then I'm sorry."

"Forget it. It was getting too complicated, anyway."

"I won't say the usual things. Like you're better off out of it, and plenty more where *she* came from, etcetera, etcetera."

"So why are you saying them?"

"Just a natural-born busybody, me." He eyed me thoughtfully. "As long as you can straighten up an' fly right."

"I'm on the ball, feeling no pain," I lied. "Trust me."

"Oh, I do, I *do*," O'Connor insisted. "I'm developin' that habit at long last."

*

O'Connor summed up Kassel with his usual insouciance. "As missions go . . . it went."

It had been average for unpleasantness, with heavy flak between Cologne and Dusseldorf, patchy thereafter; reasonably peaceful interludes alternating with others of nerve-shattering venom. Going in low through the steep wooded country of the Sauerland, hearing the hits called in; two damaged Marauders turning back, one burning, the remainder plodding on, three hundred aircraft with one shared notion converging on Kassel. On a clear, cold day with a thin overcast through which the sun shone down without color on a frozen-hard landscape. Where, from abeam Ludenscheid we could see clearly the vast smoke smudge lifting above the target still fifty miles distant.

When we got there, the defenses were well set-up, the surprise element long-lost; the Germans were hopping mad, and looking for payback. Flak soared, puffing bursts amongst the formations, and in tracer-gleaming arcs, as determined and wickedly accurate as anything known in the early days. The Germans faced the approaching end shooting from the hip. As at Cherbourg, Le Mans, Antwerp and Eindhoven, I was a mess, a loose collection of malfunctioning nerves, sweat and salivary glands, and rebelling bowels. Until the saving grace of O'Connor, dry and mocking on the intercom, "ten miles to target, brothers an' sisters. Eeny-meeny-miny-mo. Trouble findin' somethin' worthwhile left to hit."

He picked out something, and gave me an aiming point, the serrated roofs of an industrial plant that looked intact still. "Bomb doors open."

Riding her in, holding on tight as the flak crunched closer, big eighty eight-millimeter bursts rocking the wings, spent metal clatter against the fuselage. Sergeant Cohn, shrill and strained, reporting that splinters had punched clean through the after section.

I enquired the extent of damage, surprised by my own matter-of-factness: had they hit control cables or electrical leads, maybe a hydraulic line? Cohn coming back to report only holes in 'Big

Apples" thin skin. Like an afterthought, asking, "any holes in you?"

"Negative, Lieutenant."

"How's Mister Patecki back there?"

"Mister Patecki is A-okay," Mister Patecki advised.

Relief at the news made me irritable. "In which case, Cohn, shut the hell up about *holes*! I don't want to know about holes unless they're important . . . like big enough for you to fall out of!"

That said, and off my chest, I flew us through the smoke, and the airplane filled with the cloying reek of burning rubber, and O'Connor mused, "either a tire plant, or someone just blew up the last of the Wehrmacht's condom supplies . . ." And in the same breath, "bombs away!"

I shoved the throttles up to climbing power and burst out into cold, pearl-colored light, taking us to ten thousand for the homeward leg. Seeing, much higher, the vapor trails and silvery glints of the Little Friends. Weaving about with nothing to do but play tag. Not a single German fighter had bothered to show up for the party. Maybe that ugly mission to Jena *had* been worthwhile . . .

In forty minutes, I had the gear and flaps down for final approach, with the litany in my head keeping time with the engines' beat: 'thirty nine down . . . ONE to go!'

*

We were ordered to hold at Eindhoven.

Something big was in the wind, although no one was giving anything away yet. The wariness and the half-smiles, the avoidance of prolonged eye-contact from the senior hands, was all that we needed to tell us that Mission 40 would not be fun.

I faced it emptily, feeling very little. There was no pining now for England, no melodramatic imaginings of tears being shed for me back there should this last one prove to be . . . Nothing remained at Tiverell Lacey to tug at the heartstrings. I was, I worked hard to convince myself, just fine where I was, stuck, waiting, in another fuggy Quonset in the middle of flat, foggy Holland.

For two grim and empty days during which I tried to swallow my own make-believe. Until the last mission was called.

*

An unknown major conducted the briefing. He was gray-haired and leathery, and wore a command pilot's wings over medal ribbons from the old war. He would, he promised, be flying with us, and told us then where to. We were grateful in our concerted dismay because he did not try a snow job on us, explaining instead exactly how it would be, and why. What we were less happy about were the details.

Listening with the bitter belief growing that this was deliberate and malicious, worked out with the sole purpose of hitting us good and hard and finally on this last occasion when we must turn a propeller in anger. The major played it straight down the middle, and there was comfort of a kind in thinking of how he must hate what he did to us.

Sending us to God-awful Peenemunde.

An ugly name for an ugly place, an island up there on the cold Baltic coast. "It's said they're working on big new V-weapons," the major announced. "The word's out, although we don't know yet how true, they've got a rocket, the V-Three, that can hit the States . . ." He waited for the buzz to die down. "We can believe it, because those sons o' bitches will try anything once."

It was being seen in Washington and London as an attempt—as the failed Ardennes offensive had been—to make us re-think the declared policy of 'unconditional surrender'.

"They're looking to hit New York, Boston, Philly and D.C., and grab us where it hurts most." The major looked around, stone-faced. "And so, gentlemen, in a phrase, the upper echelons want it stopped."

The R.A.F. and the Eighth had struck hard at Peenemunde

already, flattening the place so badly that the Germans had been forced to set up a fresh test site out of our range in Poland. Now, though, the Russians had sent them packing back to where they came from, and Peenemunde was back in business.

Fresh tactics were being called-for; medium bombers in waves, at stepped levels from the treetops to five thousand feet, with the single aim of putting a final stop to the place. Nothing to it if you sat at a desk somewhere, far from where the action was. Scrawl your signature, pick up a phone, square your jaw, and say Peenemunde.

At other times, other briefings, there had been the feeling shared that this is where they get to kill us. Not so much the Germans as those at our backs who called themselves our friends. Who, as they turned thumbs-down, could still trot out the old spiel about ' . . . for the good of all'. Never knowing, or caring, what our feelings were; never knowing *us*. They, more than the honestly-angry Germans, were the ones out to get us.

In the past, even with the worst trips like Antwerp, Eindhoven or Jena, it had been possible, barely, to cling to a belief of two sides to the coin. Rough and dangerous, oh yes . . . but still in with a slight chance. Peenemunde—you knew it before you got started—was the *dead* cert. Last trip in every possible way.

*

The theory was that, in a few hours, the five remaining in 'Big Apples' would be all through with the war in Europe. For O'Connor, Andy Devine, Cohn, Patecki and me it should be game over, punch the clock and go home. Fly our tired warbird back to England, hand over to a luckless new crew, then endure the razzing doled out to the ones who had completed their tours, the happy seal set upon the fact of deliverance.

Peenemunde would change all that.

Because Peenemunde was the Germans' last card. They knew it, and we knew, and, sure as hell, they knew we knew it. The place where they could build, were *building*, rockets with which to bombard the United States. It sounded like a Flash Gordon fantasy . . . until you thought of what they had done already to London with their V-2s. For America they needed only bigger rockets, a greater fuel capacity. The hard work of development was done, complete and proven.

And our good friends in the back of beyond were worrying that, once more, the intractable Germans might alter the rules of play to suit themselves. To prevent that, we would fly today to Peenemunde. Even if it killed us.

*

A longish round trip of six hundred miles on a direct flight path via Munster, Osnabruck and Hanover, then on across the rolling Luneburger Heide. Past Wittemberg and the Muritzsee, above the wide open sweeps of Mecklenburg-Pomerania. Until we reached Pomeranian Bay. A considerable haul with most of it through unfriendly airspace. Although, as the gallows humorists pointed out, not as long as it might seem, with the strong likelihood of its being one-way!

Running through the pre-start drill, as commonplace now as tying my shoes or zipping my pants. Doing it as the others squeezed into their places, the airplane swaying under their shifting weight. A little time then for thinking, with only the one thing to think of . . . where we were going. The wish forming then to be turned into an automaton, a machine, pre-set to function, cold and uncaring, without thought. Like the V-1, swift and indifferent above the rooftops. The spark of current to start me off and make me fly, unknowing, to the selected destination, or to the point where I would coincide with the eighty eight-millimeter shell or the ambushing fighter. Where I would dissolve without pain or distress into a scattering of my component parts tumbling earthward, as accepting of that state as any other. How much to be preferred now that the protecting magic was there no longer to see me through.

Holding five thousand feet in our tight slot at the top of the stepladder of flights, an altitude much-favored by alert and superbly-trained flak gunners. Although, as yet, all is quiet, everywhere this spurious sense of peace. Nothing is happening although it is some time since we crossed into Germany. Flying ever farther along our straight-ruled, do-not-deviate line to Pomeranian Bay. Bielefeld and the Weser River lie behind us; we are on track for Hanover. And still no gun fires, no slender, black-crossed wing dips to challenge our claim of right to pass through this bright, cold sky.

Thinking with futile longing of how wonderful if it could be so all the way there and back again. But, of course, that cannot be: in the regions of the mind where reason and logic continue to rule I am not fooled any more than the waiting-to-pounce Germans are fooled. Peenemunde *will not* be easy, and that's an order. Anywhere else in these closing days of conflict, and okay, maybe. Not Peenemunde, though, not ever. Because we cannot allow Peenemunde to *be*.

Its defenders will know by now that we are coming; every ground observer and radar whiz-kid will be plotting our track to the last inch and finest degree. East-north-east out of Eindhoven, where the hell else could we be going?

Marauders, Mitchells, Bostons, some of the sleek new A-26 Invaders, the very latest technology coming on-stream, beautiful-looking airplanes, agile and fighter-swift. Soaring and roaring from deck level to a mile and more high, wave upon wave.

We have not fooled the Germans, and have not tried. Now, this emptiness stretching before us must be part of their deadly entrapment maneuver. Facing defeat, ruin and humiliation, those people down there retain their weird Teutonic sense of humor, playing the 'come into my parlor' game for all it is worth, milking it dry. Knowing that the game is being played, still we go, bomb-laden lambs to the slaughter. Fully aware that, any moment, a minute hence, or five, or twenty five, there it will be . . . big, bad surprise. Holding their cards close until the moment when they come and do it to us in their own special way, spectacular and final.

Until then, the land lies quiet under our wings, revealing no twitchy gunner or hothead Messerschmitt pilot with his death wish gripped in his teeth. Only a wide panorama of deceitful innocence that conceals The Game. Leading us onward, softly, softly, into the double whammy. The Kraut concept of high comedy.

And yet . . . ?

If they are waiting to spring the trap, it does seem that they are waiting a perilously long time.

Creeping on thunderous tiptoe into still and supine Germany, the checkpoints coming up with metronomic regularity, each picked out with ease in the chill light: the Aller River north of Celle, then Diesdorf, Uelzen, Salzwedel, Gardelegen, Havelberg, Stendal and Dannenberg . . . the towns and villages of Luneberg Heath go by, click, click, click. Pointing our way to the pewter glitter of the Elbe, at first far distant, then drawing in under the nose. Beyond the Elbe lies the worst and most Indian of Indian country. Where every Indian will be contemplating keenly his forthcoming tally of scalps.

Crossing the great waterway roughly on the centerline between Hamburg and Berlin, I am holding hard to my breath, and the tightness is winding up inside my chest, as bad as it has ever been. Like being strapped with iron bands.

Because, here, we are getting close. In still-peaceful skies unsullied by the smudges of bursting shells, where no opposing fighter cuts its track. One last hundred miles to go as we probe the Vorpommern high over Pritzwalk, Parchim and Neustralitz, with the Muritzsee off to one side. Plowing on to Waren and Neubrandenburg . . .

As O'Connor's voice crackles up from the nose, "target in sight." The tone grave, no leavening of wisecracks this time. Of us all, O'Connor still knows best. And there, dim in distance, the sea reflects the wide arch of the sky, with the darker rim of land clearly seen; the deep indentation of Pomeranian Bay, the lake-like Oderhaff with its slender umbilical channels binding it to the greater mass of the Baltic.

All eyes now fixed on the spot on the map that is the island of Peenemunde, which reveals what the map cannot, a spreading mushroom of smoke from where the installations lie. Rendered thus by the bombs of the first, low-level waves.

Minutes away now from our own turn to off-load, and still the trap has not closed. The realization, inconceivable until this moment, that we are being allowed to bomb! We have *bombed*, and caused immense damage. The last card in the German hand is smoldering before us, blackening around the edges . . .

Friedland slips by, then Altentreptow, Demmin and the Kummerower-see. Just ahead, the winding threads of the Trebel and the Tollense make their confluence with the Peene.

Forty miles to target.

There is a fifteen-knots wind on the tail, which spells headwinds on the homeward leg, and strange, indeed, to be alive still, actually considering what is beginning to look like the possibility of turning round and *going* home. Unless, of course, that is when the Germans choose to do it in some furious Götterdammerung act of spiteful, pointless revenge? Because even though they kill us all, they will gain not a thing now . . .

'Big Apples' is in the inbound flow over Anklam, with the stain of burning Peenemunde filling the windshield, when O'Connor warns of the I.P., ordering the heading he needs, warning me for the fortieth time to keep her steady *all* the way, or he will be forced to make his displeasure public.

The bomb doors grind open for the final time. Air thunders through the exposed belly as I fly us up to the smoke and on into it, countering the kicks and thuds of rising heat, smelling the thick acridity of scorched and devastated German industry. Until O'Connor hits the switch, and 'Big Apples', set free, soars in celebration. Once again—and from this moment nevermore— he returns control to me, and I wheel us around over Peenemunde on to the beautiful reciprocal heading for Eindhoven.

And the sky stays quiet.

THIRTY THREE

All through the flight back to England we went on discussing it, trying—and failing—to make sense of it. Numbed and bemused by what had to be the biggest anticlimax in our shared world of war. Happy, so happy, to be alive and safe; the long-elusive figure of '40' reached at last. Yet all of us sharing, and admitting to, a bizarre sense of . . . incompleteness, and actual disappointment. Until, shortly before landing, O'Connor summed up in a fashion the deeply-weird experience of Peenemunde, speaking the last words he was to utter on 'Big Apples" intercom system, "well, that's war for you."

*

Back at Tiverell Lacey to suffer the ritual of yells, Bronx cheers, whistles and catcalls, the cries of congratulation and rough-tongued badinage that were the lot of all newly-completed crews. Facing the bitter barrage of fire hoses, and poor Cohn, the eternal victim, being dunked by his fellow-sergeants in the steel emergency water tank, wailing futile protest as he went under the filthy half-frozen water. No one, though, caring to take his chances with Patecki, who smiled unpleasantly and crooked his huge axeman's hands, vowing " . . . to take a half-dozen o' you dumb pricks along with me."

Even as I submitted to the icy hosing, and made the expected responses to the chaffing of those less fortunate, I could not find the way to enter fully into the mood of celebration. Able to think only, broodingly, of Heather.

We should have been meeting to rejoice together over the completed tour, over what, now could have been our virtually-assured future. Instead, chilled and dripping, I trudged to the Quonset with O'Connor and Andy Devine, agreeing that, yes, after we had showered and shaved and changed, we would get together at the Officers' Club and tie on a whing-ding. Going along readily with that because there was nothing better, now, to do.

O'Connor, sensing my mood, advising me to, "stick with it, Denney. Only a little longer. Tomorrow, next day, they'll cut our orders, an' we'll scram outta here." He smiled, his brows wig-wagging encouragement. "Stateside, kid . . . the big new ballgame. Season's beginnin'."

*

It did not work out like that.

We were handed a seventy two-hour stand-down, and we had our drunken party. I put away too much, and, in the process, grew maudlin, expressing what I viewed as an urgent need to call Heather. Just to tell her, I explained to the others, that we were finished and going home, and how I wanted to tell her goodbye before I left, and to part as friends, and wish her well, and hope that she would always be happy with . . . *whoever*. As that person could not be me. Over the beer-sopping table, above the nightly racket of the Officers' Club, I pondered my options aloud: I would go to the house and ring on the bell; I would meet her at the Sunday Roast for one last polite chat . . . always *polite*.

It took considerable effort and persuasion by O'Connor and Andy Devine before I could be headed off from doing those foolish and pointless things.

*

My crew had split up, its members gone, their places assigned on a C-54 bound for Boston Logan via Iceland. Home for them, but not for me.

It felt like bereavement, or having a limb taken off. After ten months of a very special closeness, of an interdependence honed fine by daily use and careful cherishing. Until, with the scrawl of someone's casual pen, it was all undone.

While no word came for me, not the desired orders sending me home, or a posting to another base, another job. For my erstwhile fellows, the moving finger had writ, and moved on. Giving me the finger as it went by.

Loyal to the finish, the others commiserated, offering their uncertain assurances: it had to be a hitch somewhere in the system, more dumb-shit luck. Trying to conceal from me their relief that this was not happening to them. That same feeling that had shamed us all when someone else took the flak or the cannon shells. Each insisting strenuously, convincing himself, that my orders *would* come through soon, any time now: it had to be some dope of a shipping clerk sitting with his head in his ass. They sought ways to cheer me, and, pettishly, I wished that they would not, but, instead, shut up and fly away as they were meant to do. Like a disappointed child, I chose to wallow, beyond consoling, in my unhappiness.

With great tact, O'Connor steered the talk in less-painful directions, telling of how he had pulled strings to get his flight home deferred; he would be taking a furlough with Jeanne in Scotland. "No more screwin' around, not now that we're home an' dry." He gave me a wink. "An' you can take that how you will." He said then, "I'll do the right thing this time, if she'll have me."

"*Marry* Jeanne?"

"Sounds okay to me . . ." But he would not meet my eye. "We'll talk it through. I want to marry her, but the final decision has to be hers. The goods on offer aren't bad, just a little shop-soiled. She'll want to take that into account."

I had to ask, "and Edie?"

"I was waitin' for that one." His expression was rueful. "You're right, kid," O'Connor acknowledged. "Where she's concerned, I've been every possible kind of shit." I would have sworn before judge and jury that his regret was genuine. "An' after readin' the

Riot Act to you over Carole, as well. I don't need tellin'. An', seems like, I'm goin' to go right on bein' a shit." He looked at me then in appeal. "Only, seeing as how you're goin' to be here a while longer . . ."

"What is it, Buzz? Want me to talk to her?"

He bent his head. "If you could see your way clear? Although," he added quickly. "No pressure on you."

"I guess I could." Conscience dictated that I should refuse, that this was something he must face up to on his own. Conscience got the brush-off because I owed much to O'Connor, certainly *that* much. My bombardier, right or wrong, I thought, and promised, "I'll call her."

"It's a bullshit excuse, yet I should let you know, in my own cockeyed way I've always leveled with Edie."

"I know. Carole said as much."

He was nodding slowly. "It's just that now . . . and I'm not proud of this . . . I don't have the heart, or the balls, or whatever it takes . . . know what I'm saying, son?"

"Loud and clear," I said. "Now tell me what needs to be said."

"That I'm *honestly* sorry. And that I'm a dickhead." He held my gaze now. "What else is there? It's not as if she doesn't know that already."

He gave me a telephone number in Scotland where I could contact him. In case, as he put it, there was anything at all I might need . . .

Bombardier, navigator and two remaining gunners; they left on the following morning, and, in their going, were reduced to another brief footnote in the dusty official history of the Ninth United States Army Air Force.

*

Lieutenant Colonel Delaney informed me, "we're sending you on to the aircraft pool at Warrington."

"But, Colonel . . ." I stared at him in shocked disbelief. "I'm due to go home."

"The Army says Warrington." He watched me without expression; no evidence there of triumph, regret, apology . . . nothing.

God damned *Warrington!* The big central depot from which delivery flights were made to the bomber squadrons and fighter wings spread across England and the Continent. But I was time-expired, missions completed, signed, sealed and delivered, and these bastards could not do this to me! It had to be a trick, a low-down, flagrant conspiracy against me, and *why*, for *what?* I wanted to weep at the injustice of it, and to pound on desks and raise Cain, and then . . .

And *then*, a possibility presented itself. Because, from Warrington, selected aircraft were flown back to the States, through Scotland, Iceland, Greenland and Labrador, and on to Maine. For such flights experienced pilots were needed.

I would get to fly over the Big Pond, which would be something to shoot off my face about later, carefully-casual, "oh yes, I just flew a B-Twenty Six across the Atlantic." Me and Lindbergh and Alcock and Brown; and how fine *that* would look in my log book!

"Would that be to take a ferry flight home, Colonel?"

"I see nothing in your orders about it. Only that you're to go. Once there, what happens to you is in the lap of the gods."

I said, "yes, sir." Worried, but still hoping.

"Ask about that when you check in," Lieutenant Colonel Delaney advised me, and smiled without discernible warmth from behind his desk. "One way or another, they'll fix it for you. And if it's any consolation, Lieutenant, you're not alone in getting the short end. I was due home in December, in time for Christmas. I, too, appear to be lost in the shuffle."

*

It had been spelled out: the Army need not send me home at once. It could no longer—for the time being, at least—make me fly missions. There was nothing, however, to prevent it from employing me in some other capacity of its choosing. I was, after all, *in* the Army.

At Warrington, I discovered that there was no immediate prospect of a trans-Atlantic flight. I was there for 'non-operational flying duties'.

I registered formal protest with a sympathetic-seeming major named Boothroyd. "I've *finished* my tour."

"So you have. But then, this isn't a tour." He pointed out in an irritatingly friendly manner, "if you hadn't finished, you wouldn't be here, right?"

"But I don't *want* to be here!"

"That's what they all tell me. Do you honestly imagine that you're the only one getting shafted? If so, think again." His smile was regretful and confiding. "There's a dozen in the same boat, time-expired jocks like yourself."

I did not give a hoot for them or anyone else. I declared without logic, "but my crew's already gone."

"Indeed they have . . ." He remained patient with me. "But then, it's pilots we need here. Not bombardiers, navigators or gunners. Pilots fresh in from the States go to the bomber and fighter outfits. We're not permitted to borrow those guys, so we must make up the numbers with fellows like you. It's the luck of the draw. We got you while others, quite literally, flew the coop."

"You're telling me it was a lousy *draw*, Major?" In that way I had been picked before to fly as a courier. But that was not the same . . .

"Pretty well," Major Boothroyd conceded.

"Jesus Christ!"

"It's too bad, but it has to be so." His voice chilled perceptibly as he reminded me, "the Army decides, and will so decide until the day you muster out, and can turn round and tell the Army where to shove it." His point of military discipline made, the friendly smile was allowed back. "I know . . . it's a hell of a disappointment. You've bust your balls in the E.T.O., but there's a need to be filled, and someone must fill it." I made no reply, what would have been the use? "It's not so bad here, really. Nice easy flying, perfectly safe, and not a great deal of it. Simple deliveries to the various squadrons. You're a Baker Twenty Six man, so you'll fly 'Twenty Sixes."

A rota system was worked; your name came up, you were assigned an airplane, and flew it to where it was wanted. That done, you came back on the train. Few, if any, questions would be asked, should a pilot, on the return leg, choose to treat himself to an unscheduled night-stop at some hospitable watering-hole along his way.

I was assured that I would not be overworked. A considerable percentage of all delivery flights were undertaken by the British Air Transport Auxiliary, civilian pilots in uniform who seemed able to fly on demand, and at a moment's notice, anything from an open cockpit basic trainer to a four-engined bomber. The A.T.A. numbers were limited, however: they could not meet all demands.

"Which is where you fellows enter the picture," Major Boothroyd explained. It seemed to me quite a come-down after forty combat missions to wind up flying second-string to a bunch of civilians! "And be assured that this is *not* a sign of official disfavor."

"No, sir?"

"One of those things," Major Boothroyd insisted. "As I've explained, some didn't get picked . . . you did. Even so, it's not as bad as it may seem . . ." He must be compelled to hand out this spiel frequently, I concluded. Few arriving at the place for the first time would enthuse over Warrington. "And you won't be here for long," he offered. "Try to see it as a brief hold-up on the road home." That comment reminded me of then Technical Corporal Flaherty's one-time description of the town of Millinocket in Maine: 'a piss-stop on the road to Hell'. I could smile then, imagining his graphic description of Warrington.

I asked, "any idea how long, Major?"

"Few weeks, a month maybe? Until some other lucky stiff gets to take your place." Major Boothroyd smiled disarmingly. "Other men are finishing-up all the time, so there's plenty of choice. Bite the bullet," he advised. "You could even get to like it here." I wanted to suggest that he take no bets on that. "In this man's Army, there are worse places than Warrington." Which would mean that such places must be quite spectacularly awful. Sounding playful then, he wondered, "now, what would you say to a little something to ease your pain, huh?"

"Major . . . ?" I debated silently the possibility that he might produce a bottle, and pour me a stiff consoling drink.

"Get yourself a set of bars from someplace." He was beaming now. "And put them up right away, *Captain* Pilgrim. No delay expected."

I goggled back at him. "Since when?"

"Came through on the hot wire this morning. Congratulations . . ." He offered me his hand. "Sorry to hold out on you until now, but it seemed opportune . . . the ability to come up with a little sweetener. Something to help see you through a bad patch?"

*

I hated what was being done to me, but a captaincy, at least, could make it seem marginally more palatable. With that went also the small comfort to be drawn from the vague assurance that my time at Warrington need not be long.

Fourteen of us comprised the pilot contingent, a motley gathering of less-than-delighted fighter, bomber and transport jockeys. We displayed to the world our disillusionment and group rebelliousness by pursuing a willfully unruly and untidy existence, rising late, missing out on shaving and haircuts, sitting around in yesterday's rumpled clothing as we bitched and griped, wrote letters, read the tattered, weeks-old funny-papers from home, or played poker and pool. And, once in a while, got off our slothful behinds to go and fly something somewhere.

The latter event was very occasional. We were woefully under-employed, and this served merely to aggravate our rumbling discontent: most trips were taken by the A.T.A. pilots in their dark airline-style uniforms, while we hardened veterans sat around, kitted-up for a call that came seldom.

For days I flew nothing, spending my time reading the handling notes for the many aircraft types that passed through the Warrington pool. Or watching, sour-faced, the flights coming and going, listening to the A.T.A. hotshots, all haw-hawing British cheery, who eyed us—we came to believe—with amused pity.

Warrington could have been more tolerable, perhaps, had there been something there to play around with, to fly simply for the hell of it: a Piper L-4, or a Stinson. With fond nostalgia I recalled the once-disdained L-5 at Tiverell Lacey, and could have hugged it, and kissed its chipped little wooden propeller.

Our lukewarm explorations of the Warrington area revealed it to be unalterably bleak, and lacking in any kind of cheer, stuck there on its grim isthmus of land between gray, smoky Liverpool and gray, rainy Manchester. In rolling country besmirched by the smoke and soot of heavy industry: detesting the region, we dubbed it with scorn 'England's Ruhr'. A landscape wherein resided pale, unsmiling people who spoke a type of English that was as incomprehensible to us as the German of the Ruhr would have been.

The few excursions we made in 'borrowed' jeeps disclosed little anywhere in the way of improvement, traveling to Liverpool and Stockport and Manchester, the latter city bearing no resemblance that we could observe to its namesake in New Hampshire. We passed through St. Helen's, and saw Wigan— where there was a traditional joke about a pier which, like the local patois, we did not get at all.

All of us had been led to believe that Blackpool was a kind of homespun Atlantic City, a northern English rival to Malibu, Palm Beach or Key West. The reality into which we stumbled one day was shrieking winds coming in off the Irish Sea, and rain that sheeted horizontally across Blackpool's answer to The Boardwalk, named, bafflingly, the Golden Mile.

Our unified response to Warrington and its environs was one of unremitting despair and loathing; it was to be expected that the place, and its undeservedly-maligned citizenry should respond in kind to a carping crew of foreign malcontents, the whole developing into a depressing downward spiral. Warrington was like waiting and waiting in an ugly, cramped room for a train that never came.

*

After ten days some flying came my way: quick delivery hops to bases in Norfolk and Cambridgeshire. Where, from one, I ferried back an ancient and battle-scarred B-model Marauder, a sad dog of an airplane with beat-up engines, one of which failed judderingly in the final twenty minutes of the flight. Tour-expired or not, I decided sweatily as I carried out another shaky single-engine approach, *some* bastard was still trying to kill me.

A more interesting trip was offered then, to a former Luftwaffe base near Trier, close to the Luxembourg border. It would be my first landing inside Germany.

This initial close contact with the ground-level realities of the war-shattered Third Reich was a profoundly shocking and sobering one. Trier was only one small fragment of the entire catastrophe, the sad, wind-chilled desolation of which ran on for hundreds of miles, from Rhine to Oder, from the Alps to the Baltic.

After handing over the new B-26 and completing the paperwork, I was to wait there for a place on a C-47 flight back to England. With time to burn, I wrapped up warmly, and took a walk out over the cratered runways and taxi strips to the graveyard where the forsaken German aircraft lay. Returning the salutes of tommy gun toting M.P.s standing guard over threadbare P.O.W.s employed on airfield repair work.

A cruel, cutting wind promised more snow from a steel sky, and went mourning through the airplane carcasses.

A Junkers 87 dive bomber stood on its nose in the steep-descent attitude in which, once, it had stormed down upon its targets. I clambered on to the spatted landing gear, and over the 'inverted gull' wings, feeling the wreck sway slightly under my moving weight. In the cockpit, the strange German flight and engine instruments were all in place; the throttle, and the levers for mixture and propeller controls, for flaps and dive brakes. The stick with its gun and bomb-release buttons; the guidance and warning placards hand-painted in spiky Gothic script. The cockpit, left open to the scouring elements, retained an alien, acid odor that was quite unlike the distinctive scents of American and British aircraft. A German smell, an *enemy* smell . . .

Walking on from there to meet at last, and touch, our most feared opponent. A Focke-Wulf 190, still and silent, harmless now, with splinter gouges in wings and fuselage. The Butcher Bird, standing tall and incorrigibly arrogant on its long-legged landing gear, with flat tires and missing canopy, the cockpit half-filled with dry, drifted snow. And what if *this* had been the one that almost fixed us for ever at Eindhoven. As much might have been as not.

The Focke-Wulf bore its fading jagdgeschwader emblem, the pilot's rank chevron, and his personal motif, a jaunty, grinning Mickey Mouse. It seemed sad now, and ironic, that they could hate us so murderously, yet keep a place in their hearts for the creations of Walt Disney.

There were, also, under the cockpit rim, eighteen stenciled white stars that spoke of victories over American planes, picked out perhaps by some Luftwaffe equivalent of buck Sergeant Flaherty. The vanished pilot, dead, or in a glum P.O.W. cage, or even simply called quits and gone quietly home, had been an ace.

Impossible, facing the brutal evidence of the painted stars, not to think once more of men and aircraft long gone: 'Millinocket Joy-Girl', 'Roman's Ruin', 'Sweet Maggie', 'Abbie 'n' Slats', 'Dinah Might?', 'Rebel Yell' . . . and so many, many more.

Neat white stars to represent exploding fireballs and blazing engines, and the last long dive into the receiving earth. A star for an oil slick, an empty life vest, afloat on the sea. For smoke rising a thousand feet above the spot where a wheels-up landing went fatally wrong . . .

I shivered among the ghosts of both sides, and turned away to hurry back to the crew room and the stale coffee and raggedy magazines to be found there. Back to the *living*.

*

Flying those trips all alone, there was ample time for thinking, time which I would spend, inevitably, thinking of Heather.

It was over, and yet she was there with me still as I cruised tamely, far removed from danger, doing nothing that would ever hold her strange interest. The same question persisting, unanswerable . . . what was it that I had done—or, again, not done—to turn her from me?

I was still certain that I had got it right about her in the end, that she craved endlessly the excitement of war from a remove, the stimulating company of those who participated flat out and full time in the events of war, people for ever larger than life. And I was not like that, and no one knew it better than me, and war, and combat missions flown, and medals to show for them, could not alter the fact. I was the son of a good and successful attorney; I had attended better-than-average schools and an Ivy League university. With the war ended, should fortune continue to smile upon me, I would fly passenger airplanes. Or, if not, follow the route mapped out for me by my mother, becoming a Manhattan corporate lawyer just like dear old Dad. Where was, or could be, the glamor in any of that?

In the rackety solitude of a crewless B-26, I could figure every angle, and the result would come down against me always. Nothing done or said . . . not done or not said . . . just *me*. Heather had sensed that, and elected to cut her losses. Because that was the way Heather was with her questionable genes, unpredictable, unfathomable . . . *fey*.

Although, precisely what had made her so: was it Tim's death, or the mental imbalance of her father, or those events revealed to me by Margot Granger which had led to Heather's being?

There had been none of the imbecility or monstrousness

foretold by the 'doom merchants', no fettered horror in a turret room, nor final and terrible resolution such as that depicted in 'King's Row'. But was what had resulted from that union in the outer guise of beauty, wit, poise and intelligence worse, perhaps, than those other things might have been?

*

The C-47 dropped me off at Croydon, after which there were taxis and trains, and a summoned jeep to complete my journey to Warrington. Where a week went by in idleness and crushing boredom, relieved only by grumbling and trying—without much success—to be nice to the busy-bee A.T.A. pilots. Until Major Boothroyd sent for me.

"Another trip for you and, with it, some good news." He was at his most genial, and I waited, reflexively mistrustful of his 'good news'. "You'll be back Stateside in about ten days." He put on a what-do-you-think-of-that look.

"Thank you, Major." I waited for more.

"That trans-Atlantic hop you spoke of the day you arrived? Well, seems you're getting it."

That got my attention. "Sir?"

"The old beast you brought back from Cambridge . . . the one that tried to lie down and die on you, remember?" I nodded. "They're getting her ready to fly home. Apparently she's a warbird with a big reputation, and is to be preserved for posterity. Probably outside a gas station in some Midwest hick town," he added, smiling. "And you're nominated to take her across with a co-pilot and a navigator who knows how to use a sextant."

"My-y-y!" I breathed. And, deep inside, turned a rapturous cartwheel.

"Seems only fair," Major Boothroyd was saying. "She gave you that sweat ride . . . we should try to make up for it."

I was suitably humbled. "Thank you very much."

"Destination Dayton, Ohio." He grew waggish. "Reckon you can find it okay?"

"You head west from here, don't you?" I laughed aloud. "And there's always that navigator."

"Now . . ." He leaned back comfortably in his chair. "There's the matter of the other chore. A last little service?"

"Anything to help out, Major."

"*Well* now . . ." He grinned at me with good-natured malice. "Isn't it just wonderful what a little good news can do for an attitude?"

I could feel my face reddening. "Sorry . . ."

"Forget about it. I have. As this up-and-coming joyride should demonstrate."

"Major?"

"Your chance to play conquering hero, the old alumnus made good," Major Boothroyd said. "Want you to take a brand-new Twenty Six over to Tiverell Lacey for me. Can do?"

*

FLIGHT LOG.
DATE: 3/7/45.
AIRCRAFT TYPE: B-26E.
NO. or REG.: 44-11706.
PILOT-IN-COMMAND: Self.
SECOND PILOT: Nil.
CREW: Nil.
FLIGHT ROUTE: Warrington-Tiverell Lacey.
FLIGHT HOURS: 0.50.
HOURS VISUAL: 0.50.
HOURS INSTRUMENT: Nil.
HOURS NIGHT: Nil.
OBSERVATIONS: The 41st Mission, and no milk-run!

Major Boothroyd would, of course, be seeing it as his special little treat, assigning me a factory-fresh Marauder to fly on a clear, cold day in early spring. Less than an hour point to point. Going down to chew the fat with all the old buddies, batting the breeze, telling lies, bragging about my forthcoming flight across the Pond. Never imagining in his boundless generosity of spirit that I might hate the very thought of going there. No less than I had hated going to Le Mans and Eindhoven and Peenemunde.

The control tower gave me a long straight-in approach on runway zero-nine of enduring memory. Which spared me the pain of having to fly in over the research station where, in mid-morning, she would be at work.

I taxied in, climbed down, and went to the ops shack to hand over the papers and obtain the receipt for Warrington. To where, with Major Boothroyd's blessing, I need not hurry back.

"Spitting distance from London." He had smirked knowingly. "Give yourself a night on the town . . ." Which had been my intention anyway.

It was a small blessing to find only a few familiar faces still at Tiverell Lacey. Things had changed in the month since my departure, but Sergeant Tallichet, our former crew chief was there to bring me up to the mark.

"Still workin' on the old bird, sir." I saw him eyeing my bright new captain's bars. "She's goin' strong with a new crew."

"Where is she?" The hardstands were full, the Squadron apparently on stand-down, but no sign of 'Big Apples'; taxying along the line of parked machines, I had felt an anticipatory dread . . .

"Would you believe . . ." Sergeant Tallichet was laughing. "God damn' courier ship . . . *again!*"

He gave me all the news: the new hands were doing okay with six missions racked up; a crew of five with an older captain on a second tour handling the flying, the bombardier a greenhorn second looie. Those roles had been reversed. They gave Sergeant Tallichet little grief. "Decided they'd keep the old name as is . . . figured maybe it was lucky." Providence still ruled the roost. "Not th' same around here no more," he admitted. "War's nigh on over . . . place goin' to the dogs." He sounded disapproving. "Every swingin' dick's busy shittin' serious bricks over Japan, an' not takin' no interest no more."

Lieutenant Colonels Delaney and Friend were back in the

States, and the C.O. would rotate soon. Captain Azevedo had completed twenty three missions, and won a D.F.C. at Nuremberg.

"Kraut fighters shot the bejesus out o' them. Navigator an' tail gunner mashed . . . a real mess." Sergeant Tallichet recited the events with somber relish. "Come back with one engine out, an' one almost. Damn' airplane looked like a sieve . . . I still can't make out what kept 'er up." He was shaking his head in reflective wonderment. "A bullshit artist from way back, but the sonofabitch can fly."

And how much must Heather have enjoyed hearing of that, and Azevedo's all-the-trimmings recounting of it. It beat the pants off anything that I had been able to offer. Another very good move by Azevedo. Who had the board to himself now.

*

I was given a jeep and driver to take me to the Colchester train station. We rode down the familiar lane toward the village, and I was trying to count off in my head the number of times I had traveled that way before, the good times and the bad. At my request, the driver agreed to a detour through the center of the village; I explained about places and people I needed to see.

He waited for me outside the Sunday Roast. I offered in apology, "just a few minutes with an old friend."

"Captain . . . it's your ride." He yawned and produced a greasy copy of the Saturday Evening Post.

Neither Heather nor Azevedo, I found with relief, were there. Bob Reeves shook my hand and poured me a pint on the house. "Thought you was long gone, lad." He peered at my rank insignia. "Come up in the world, 'ave we?"

"It was to shut me up," I explained. "I was griping too much." I told him of Warrington, and about going home.

"All the better, I should think, for 'aving to wait a bit for it," he observed. I enquired—my true reason for coming—about Heather, and he pulled no punches: she was seeing Azevedo on a regular basis, and it had ceased to be a matter of a drink, a talk, and goodbye. Azevedo was where I had been and, tormenting myself, I pictured them together before Colchester's Roman walls, and dining at Banxted. Did they go biking through the lanes and . . . visit London? Had it been Heather's gratuitous magic which brought Azevedo home from Nuremberg in an airborne sieve with two dead crewmen on board . . . ?

Bob Reeves spread his hands in a gesture of resignation. "You know how these things are." And yes, I knew. How they are, I thought, and how they had been.

And what, I wondered then, would the shrewd and perceptive Margot Granger make of Azevedo? Would she be dismayed, aghast, wanting to put a stop to it, to 'lower the boom'? Or, as seemed likely, to remain mute and leave her daughter to pursue her own course, trusting in—hoping for—Heather's innate common sense. I imagined him being asked to tea, and regaled with Victoria sponge cake and stories of instability, shellshock and neurasthenia, of married cousins, and the beautiful child who had tweaked the noses of the doom merchants, but who was no less monstrous for that . . .

Bob Reeves wished me a safe journey, and told me that he would welcome me back to his pub at any time, war or peace. I finished my pint with prickling eyes, and left, knowing already that I would not return. Like the destroyed airfield at Trier, there were too many restless and unsatisfied ghosts, my own among them.

I should have known, right there and then, to call it quits. Instead, I told the bored driver, "like you to wheel me round the village a little."

"Sir . . . ain't you worried about your train?"

"There are plenty more trains, so I never worry about them."

He concealed irritation. "If the Captain would kindly state where he wants to go?"

I smiled, remembering how, in the past, I had adopted a similar tone with then Major Delaney. Getting nowhere for my pains, as the driver would get nowhere now. "Just humor me, and drive. I may see someone I know." We went through the village to the well-known corner. "Take it slow down here," I directed.

We eased past the house, silent and empty-seeming behind its high hedge, revealing no secrets. No chimney smoke rose, no figure moved about the conservatory: I checked my watch, and Heather would be at the labs still. Beyond the house and garden the line of boundary poplars stood bare and motionless: the dark beds that I remembered as bright with July's flowers, turned over, awaiting the spring's coming warmth. As dead-seeming as the relationship, and maybe, just maybe, that *was* for the best? Had Heather appeared suddenly, or Margot, what would there have been left to say?

I told the driver, "let's go."

We were on the Colchester road, passing the gaunt council houses where Gladys Gibbons lived, when the driver ventured, "reckon we never seen that someone you was lookin' for."

"No," I agreed. "But it was fun trying."

POST-MISSION . . .

All it *had* been, though, was an empty exercise in self-indulgence which left me more saddened, more alone, than ever. Once, challenged by Heather, I had denied loneliness airily: I was a loner, but never lonely, oh, no. So easy to claim that in the moments when one was not alone. In Heather's company, loneliness did not apply, and I could boast to her of my preferred solitary state, and my ability, unfailingly, to handle it. Now, Heather had called my bluff by bestowing on me that condition that I professed to prefer. I was, once more, a loner, and it was proving to be painfully difficult to handle. Loners, I was discovering the hard way, really could get lonely.

From that line of thinking it was a short—and, to me—logical step to remembering Carole, and Carole's words. 'A port in a storm' she had called it then, the casual tone conflicting with the unasked question in her grave violet eyes. Now, lonely and feeling distinctly sorry for myself, it could be very soothing to ponder the port in a storm, the friendly offer of comfort and female companionship which seemed so necessary at that moment. That was what was called-for, a quiet and welcoming place in which to hole up for a while until things looked better. And ignore the whisper of conscience about the self-serving misuse of people and their feelings and affections.

Hide *that* load of guilt behind the convenient excuse of an obligation to be fulfilled; my promise to the shamefaced O'Connor that I would call around and try to square things with Edie: a valid reason—as it could appear then—for turning up, hangdog and forlorn, at the door in Upper Berkeley Street, West One.

Carole had made the offer, although, in my return to her,

even as I aired my phony reasons, would she discern my real one for coming, and what I sought from her, and despise me for that? Or, mindful of a promise, simply play along as she did with the occasional would-be tough guy, without protest, concealing what she felt? I *liked* Carole, and she gave point and purpose to my planned London stop-over; a goal . . . a port in a storm. Until, refreshed and restored, I could move callously on, knowing that my return was most unlikely.

Aware of all this, and in spite of it, still I would go back to the little flat in the dingy street, and think only of the moment, letting future events there, if there were to be any, slot into place of their own accord . . .

The driver ground his brakes in front of Colchester station. "Anything else you'll be needin', Captain?"

I shook my head. "Can't think of a thing."

The London telephone number was safe in my billfold. I should be able to find a payphone without the driver's assistance. And then proceed, once more, to do the wrong thing. I was getting to be something of a dab hand at doing the wrong thing.